see you. He, Halder, and Beck are waiting. Which do you prefer, death or a job interview?"

Heydrich's response was to safe his pistol and finish dressing. He hoped he'd be given time to shave as well. Always best to look sharp for an interview. He could show them where they needed him. He didn't exactly expect them to trust him, but if Nebe had gotten him over THAT hurdle the rest was doable. Reinhardt Heydrich was a man who prided himself on landing on his feet.

[earlier]
1923 hours
23 June 1940
airfield, occupied Belgium

Albert Kesselring, commander of Second Air Fleet, was a man to grasp opportunities out of events other people saw as career disasters. He had a dead Hitler on his hands and a planeload of hysterical flunkies. He ordered his adjutant to round up a dozen reliable men. The ex-Führer's body was put on ice, literally, in a meat freezer. The flunkies were herded into a supply bunker, locked in, and, for the moment, ignored. The base was sealed. No people in or out. No exceptions. No comm traffic beyond routine acknowledgement of receipt of messages. He himself took off with his best multiengine pilot for a flight to Berlin. This was the sort of news one delivered in person.

0422 hours,
24 June 1940,
Central Berlin – Gestapo/SS HQ

Walter Schellenberg was back at his office and working late in the early morning hours. An alert assistant on the night shift had called him in. Something big was up. Gestapo Müller had pulled key people out of the building for an unspecified "major operation". Calls around to Schellenberg's usual informants in the bureaucracy had produced chaotic responses. There appeared to be a second Blood Purge in progress, but no one had details beyond wild rumors about the Führer's death, Göring, and the Army. Sadly, the situation seemed to be clarifying. The Army had surrounded the entire block. There was a tank outside with a thrown track covering the main entrance. It was making a lot of noise. So was its machine gun, which was killing anyone trying to exit the building. Was the Army staging a coup? Himmler was unreachable. The Führer was coming back from Paris. Heydrich was missing but police callbox messages seemed to suggest a gun battle around his house a few minutes earlier. Schellenberg kept dialing, hoping to find someone in authority.

0515 hours
24 June 1940
Army HQ, Berlin

Heydrich was smiling by the time he reached the conference room. All his surmises had been confirmed. The outer offices had army majors issuing clear instructions to secure this or that location. The "plan" was mostly improvisation, but this sort of competent staff work was an old Prussian specialty. The inner offices had senior colonels and generals of the Army and Air Force. They were huddled in little circles whispering while casting furtive glances at each other and shocked glances on seeing him in full SS uniform. It was just as he thought. The top people were clueless. They did need him. They just didn't know it yet.

The conference room had Army Generals Beck and Halder, Chancellor-Designate Göring, and Gestapo Müller. Trust Müller to land on his feet. He'd been anti-Nazi until the day of the takeover and then had turned coat without a moment's look back. He was also Heydrich's subordinate. Time to remind him of that. Heydrich ignored the three, senior people and dealt with Müller first. Heydrich had used the drive over to write out some fast notes. "Here's a list. Try to get these out of HQ alive. We'll need them later. Now off you go and see if you can keep the Army from blowing up the card files. We'll need them also. The next two weeks are going to be chaotic. The official story is a Second Blood Purge. Himmler and the rest assassinated the Führer. We are cleaning house. Tell your informers we are paying for information on the lesser members of the plot."

Müller stood there blinking. He was unsure whose orders to take. The two army generals were turning red in the face, about to explode. Göring had looked uncomfortable and apprehensive. Now he looked confident. He was catching where Heydrich was leading. He drew up to his full height and in a command voice barked, "You've been given an order by a superior officer. Execute it at once!" Göring then turned and offered his hand to Heydrich. Escorted him to a chair and loudly directed a hovering minion to get his "friend" coffee and brandy.

Heydrich waited for his coffee. Neither general was quite able to get beyond sputtering and glaring, so he saw that he would have to open the discussion. Amateurs. "Gentlemen, I am aware that I may leave this meeting feet first; therefore, dispense with the threats. You don't trust me." Heydrich shrugged. "I don't care. You need me. You haven't even answered the key questions. From the look of you, they haven't occurred to you." Now he was met with two blank faces and a smile from Göring. "Precisely what is happening here? So far, what I see is a half-assed opportunistic coup by you as representative of the old elites. The Führer's dead. The Party is not especially popular. What, you'll bring back the Kaiser with a regency council?" He saw a half-sheepish look from Halder and a belligerent one from Beck. Right again. "Won't work. Would have in '32, '33... maybe '34. Hindenburg was as popular as Hitler. Also the nation was seven years younger. Nazis were in many ways a youth movement. A lot of our supporters were too young to matter. Hindenburg's dead. A new generation has come of age. A mostly Nazi one. You have the colonels. We have the corporals and lieutenants. The twenty-somethings. Adolph Hitler saved them from the Depression. Restored Germany's honor. Defeated France in 60 days. Victory without an endless, blood-drenched war. He's a demigod. Your only chance is to take power in his name." He paused to see if ANY of this was sinking in. He had Göring. Halder was more than halfway there. Beck was going to be the problem.

"General Beck, how do you propose to govern without a coalition with the Nazis?"

Beck was livid. "We will give orders and they will be obeyed. The best people are all with us."

Heydrich repressed the urge to laugh at the old fool. He didn't bother to hide his smile. "Yes, they mostly are. Military. Industry. The bureaucracy. Middle-aged and older people of experience and wisdom. Same was true in Petrograd in 1918. Remind me how that turned out for your lot." He let the shock sink in with Beck before continuing. "Shoot me. You have a pistol. I presume you were trained in its use. Shoot five thousand more like me. Now tell me how you get the young, ambitious ones to follow your orders? Remember your choice in 1933? Us or the reds. Choice hasn't changed. Those are the only two groups with mass appeal. The Party as an institution may be unpopular right now—lot of petty tyrannies by the Gauleiters and Kreisleiters. The Movement is popular and just acquired a dead deity. We need your expertise. You need our ability to mobilize the masses. Göring here is a good front man for our union. He's a Kaiser-era officer. A war hero. Married originally into the aristocracy. Knows how to attend your parties and show proper manners. Yet he's an old Party comrade. Marched at the Feldherrnhalle. Nazi Speaker of the Reichstag. Built a Nazi Air Force. He's the link pin. However, he's not a nuts-and-bolts bureaucrat. You need someone to assemble a new Nazi cabinet...."

Beck started to explode. Halder cut in over him. "How much of the cabinet?" Halder was sensing the outlines and was ready to bargain.

"All of it. This is theater. The news photo should have a cabinet in Party uniform. You'll get your power at the next level down. Secretaries of State, ministry chancellors, undersecretaries. It's your general staff system. The top man has titles and you appoint a few competent professionals to do the actual work. We've got to show the mid-level Party people that their career paths are still there. That's part of why a Blood Purge. If we shoot every Gauleiter and Minister, the new Führer and I get to appoint new ones who will be properly grateful for their elevation. We need jobs for people who don't have vons in their name, who don't have degrees from the best universities."

Göring suddenly was showing signs of life. "Shoot ALL the Gauleiters and Ministers?"

"Oh, save a few protégées. But each one you save is one less promotion to give out. Now where you need me is Göring won't do the scut work. He'll be the public face. Make speeches, attend functions, do all the ceremonial. But day-to-day you need a Stalin. That's me. Someone who knows the mid-levels of the Movement. Someone who will handle the administrative and personnel details. For example, have any of you thought how you are going to stage the Führer's funeral?" He saw three blank looks. Typical. "That is what will cement your initial hold on power. We need a stage production more elaborate than the Nürnberg rallies. Where's Speer? Someone get him for me. We've got to clean up Berlin for the lying in state, the parade, the mausoleum construction. We'll need something bigger and grander than

Lenin's tomb in Moscow. You've killed off Goebbels. Good. I'll need Leni Riefenstahl to help organize this."

He had them. They saw how little they understood. Göring showed he was following by asking the obvious question, "Stalin, you say. So, you expect to overthrow us one by one like he did?" Heydrich outright laughed. He HAD them. "They let him. Paid no attention while they plotted against each other. Are you three THAT stupid? No. You'll stay allied and watch me like a hawk. That's fine. My place is the next echelon down from the three of you. Me. Todt. Speer. Riefenstahl. Müller. Göring, you created the Gestapo. Have them follow me night and day. I don't mind. I pride myself on landing on my feet. I was Himmler's minion. Now I'm yours."

The meeting went on toward midday, but the essential workings of the new regime were already in operation.

Chapter 2

0800 hours
24 June 1940
Frankfurt on Oder

Klaus Steiner was hiding his teenage angst by following orders. A leader in his HJ unit had woken his entire house to get him up, in uniform, and moving. Something big was happening and he had been "mobilized". Klaus was a gawky 17-year-old. He'd "joined" the HJ because trying to opt out got you noticed, got you in trouble. His parents' attitude was keep your head down and do what you were told. Klaus was quite in agreement but for different reasons. Coping with his growing body and changing voice was more than he could handle. Actually asserting himself in front of others was beyond the possible. All he wanted to do was avoid being noticed, avoid having to explain or justify anything. Standing in ranks or following simple orders was just fine with him. And now, here he was, on a commandeered municipal bus with a scrum of HJ, Party members, SA, and the odd SS trooper, headed for Berlin. Headed to do what, no one was quite sure. Someone at Party HQ had gotten a cryptic call from someone supposedly on Reichsmarschall Göring's staff to turn out people for a "major operation" in Berlin. Operation to do what? Why? Apparently, people didn't ask questions anymore. The local Party leader had requisitioned every bus he could find and off they were going. Klaus was content to let the important people make sense out of it.

0915 hours
24 June 1940
Kesselring's HQ airfield, occupied Belgium

Albert Speer had been moping. The Führer was dead. Hitler was his patron and without his support he was just another young architect without prospects. He was locked in a supply shed awaiting some unknown but probably nasty fate. The Führer's medical staff had been pulled out a bit less than an hour ago (the shed had poor lighting, so he was not exactly sure he had read the time on his watch correctly). Some forty minutes later, there had been the sound of machinegun fire. Now suddenly the door was banged open, and a tall, blonde, immaculately dressed SS officer was calling his name. The daylight hitting the half-dark hut was near-blinding. Everyone else in the shed edged away from him as if he had suddenly shown plague symptoms. Speer fought to show a bit of personal courage (which he was not feeling) and walked toward the SS officer. The officer compared his face to a printed page. Yes, he was himself. He was then asked if he had a briefcase or other personal luggage. He pointed and an SS sergeant fetched the portfolio. Then one large SS man grabbed each of his arms and he was hauled onto a transport plane whose engines were already running. Speer plopped himself down, letting his face show his fears and doubts. No one offered a word of explanation but he was provided a flask of coffee laced with brandy. So, this is what being a prisoner of the state was like?

1410 hours
24 June 1940
Air Ministry, Berlin

Walter Schellenberg was confused. SS HQ had surrendered a little after midday to Gestapo Müller and his men. Müller's men had cleared the building floor by floor. Most had been put on buses and led away. A smaller group had been taken up to the top floor canteen and left there under guard. A few had been shot out of hand. There were no interrogations. Apparently, there were lists. Lists prepared by whom? Schellenberg himself had been escorted personally by Müller into Müller's own Mercedes limousine. Müller remained behind but four trusted Gestapo men had driven with Schellenberg through the streets of Berlin. The streets seemed quite normal. There were Army or plainclothes guards on a few more buildings than usual, but no sign of what they were guarding against. Now he was being quick-marched down the corridors of the Air Ministry. His SS uniform was attracting attention and muttered gossip from the military and civilian officials they encountered. The offices seemed quite busy, but again nothing extraordinary.

All this changed at the far end of the corridor. Suddenly, he was in a sea of Party, SA, and SS uniforms with HJ and BDM running errands in frantic haste. Yet, none of these Movement people looked frightened or under guard. Perhaps this wasn't quite an Army coup, after all.

The Reich Without Hitler: The Falcons of Malta

His confusion became worse when he was marched into the
big corner office and saw his nominal boss, Heydrich, behind a big
desk barking into a phone. Something about funeral arrangements
and a parade. Schellenberg was content to wait his turn. While
he did so, someone brought him a good cup of coffee and a small
pastry. Schellenberg wasn't sure if it was proper to eat in front of a
superior in such a situation, but Heydrich made hand motions that
seemed to indicate yes, so he did.

The call took a good ten minutes, after which Heydrich had the
room cleared before addressing him. "Simple question. Do you
want to live or die?" Schellenberg thought the question absurd
but gave the obvious answer. Heydrich was in one of his didactic
moods. "Fine. I am going to say something to you. You will repeat
it back to me. Then we will discuss it. Two plus two equals five."
Schellenberg gave the required reply. Heydrich seemed pleased.
"Good. I am about to tell you things. Things that may contradict
facts as you know them, that may contradict logic, that may be
insane. Keep telling yourself two plus two equals five. Reality
is what the Movement needs reality to be. You must never
contradict this reality to anyone, even to yourself when sleeping.
The sentence is death. I need your brain and initiative, but some
things are beyond debate and discussion. Nod if you wish to live."

Schellenberg nodded. He was prepared to be insane and
alive. Heydrich resumed his lecture, "Our Führer is dead. He was
poisoned by his SS doctors on orders from Himmler, Bormann,
Goebbels, and Hess. There may be other involved in the plot.
I think every Gauleiter and Minister was in on it. Our new
Chancellor, Party Leader, and Führer, Air Marshal Göring, has not
yet decided who the guilty are. A few thousand other conspirators
will be unmasked. You will assist me in preparing a list."

Schellenberg tried to keep his face blank. He failed. His
jaw dropped. He may have drooled slightly so great was his
shock. "Two plus two is now four until I tell you otherwise. It
really doesn't matter who gets axed. We need enough dead to
have promotions to hand out and not so many as to break the
Movement. Surely, you've encountered enough dead wood since
we came to power. Think of it as a housecleaning. It's a mix of
theater and politics. Oh, and now two plus two is five again. Our
Führer's body will be conveyed to Berlin tomorrow. There will be a
grand funeral, a loyalty parade, a public viewing line, a spectacle.
That will be Speer and Riefenstahl. I need you to see to another

matter. It would be useful if our beloved Führer left a widow. Locate that mistress. Tell her she married the Führer last week. Arrange the necessary documents. You and Speer were witnesses. Tell her she will get a nice pension and living allowance. Also, it would be useful if she were carrying the Führer's heir. Arrange to have her inseminated from proper Aryans of approximately the right body type, hair, and such."

Heydrich stopped, as Schellenberg's eyes were almost bugging out of his head. Heydrich knew Schellenberg was neither squeamish nor stupid. He saw that he would have to explain. It annoyed him to waste the time but he needed this done properly and he simply didn't trust anyone else for this delicate task. "Things are in flux between the Army and the Movement. Frankly, our dead Führer is far more popular right now than either the Party or the SS. Too many stupidities since 1933. A widow and, if possible, an heir are a focus of popular devotion. If the silly woman objects or seems difficult, just shoot her. Shoot her sister if you liquidate the mistress. It is vital that none of this leaks. Then interview the stenographers. If you find one willing, she's the widow. If not, liquidate them all and try the servants or other staff. Worst case, just find someone who was vaguely in his service. You'll need a couple of good forgers. The camps are full of them. Promise them pardons and then liquidate them personally once the documents are finished to your satisfaction. It's not as if anyone will ever contest them. Contest them to whom? To us? Oh, yes, and draw up the papers giving yourself a promotion to Oberführer and making you my #2. I'm now head of the SS and Deputy Head of the Party." Heydrich smiled to himself. He doubted anyone would notice his promoting himself in this chaos.

Schellenberg lacked the words to cope. He came to rigid attention, saluted, did an about-face and exited. He grabbed two BDM as runners, commandeered a desk with a phone and got to work. Two plus two could be five hundred for all he cared. He was alive. He had clear instructions. He had a title and some power. And yes, he could think of dozens of people he would enjoy seeing dead. Most he would enjoy killing himself.

Chapter 3

1440 hours
24 June 1940
Lehrter-Bahnhof, Berlin

Gunter Strauss was sure he'd made the right decision. An old drinking buddy from the Feldherrnhalle days had gotten word to him that a second Blood Purge was in progress. In addition, a big operation was on in Berlin. Movement people from all over Germany were being mobilized to take part. Gunter had a low Party number from back in the early twenties. He'd drifted out of the Movement for a few years when he'd been overseas, but had been a staunch street fighter in the march to power in the early 30s. Even in his years in Manhattan, he'd kept up his Party dues, had kept involved with the small New York chapter of the Movement. And still found himself out in the cold again in '34 when the Blood Purge had decapitated the SA. Strauss had learned to be an intelligence officer in the Baltic during the postwar chaos. Had kept him and his Free Corps company alive. Didn't help this time. Hitler turning on the SA had been a closely held secret until the day it happened. No time for Gunter to switch sides opportunistically. The best he had done for himself was to use his contacts to get a job as a postal employee. Even that had worked against him. He'd tried to reenlist when war broke out. Somehow, postal-sorting on the night shift had been deemed necessary war work and he'd been refused. As if. It was the SA junior officer rank in his file. The Army didn't want ex-SA officers and the SS didn't want ex-SA anything.

Thus, he made the most of this second chance. He had rounded up every connection he could bully or cajole and marched them to the train station. He'd expected to have to bluff his way onto a train to Berlin from Solingen. Turned out not to be necessary. This mobilization was huge and the station was a mad house as mobilized people appeared. The SS major on the platform just took his name, rank, and number of men and assigned them to a railway carriage. Gunter was on a roll. His luck had changed. Whatever this operation was, he was part of it. Now all that remained was to make the most of the opportunity.

1455 hours
24 June 1940
Air Ministry, Berlin

A very nervous Speer was standing before Supreme SS Leader
Heydrich. Speer was terrified but also curious how this promotion
had taken place. Heydrich had just finished giving Speer an absurd
account of the Führer's death. Speer in turn had signed a formal
statement attesting to the lies. He was frightened enough to have
gladly signed a statement that the sun rose in the south and flew
in circles in the sky.

Heydrich was now outlining his task. Millions of people were
being mobilized into Berlin. It was Speer's task with Riefenstahl
to organize a grander spectacle than a Nürnberg rally. The
Führer's body was being conveyed back to Berlin tomorrow. Its
progress to the mortuary and then a grand lying in state must
be accomplished as a perfect spectacle and filmed for mass
distribution. Berlin must be decorated for this, including a mass
loyalty march by the Movement people to show their allegiance to
the new Führer, Air Marshal Göring. Speer was to liaison with the
Air Ministry for a giant flyby. There would be a grander torchlight
parade than the one in 1933. Speer should consider himself an SS
colonel under the direct orders of Heydrich and his new deputy
Schellenberg.

The final instruction was the killer. Speer had thirty minutes
to prepare the preliminary drawings for a grand monumental
tomb for the Führer. Something grander than both Lenin's tomb in
Moscow and the Egyptian pyramids. Classic but Germanic.

Before Speer could sputter the impossibility of this,
Schellenberg had his arm and was guiding him out of the office.
Walking him to a smaller office past a covey of BDM flunkies.
Schellenberg sat him down and smiled. "Relax. The Boss can be a
tad overwhelming. He's dealing with too many things on too many
levels at once. That's why he has me...and you. You do want to be
with the winning side, don't you? You're either with us or one of
the plotters... and you don't look suicidal."

Speer huddled in the chair Schellenberg had placed him in,
near-hyperventilating. The walls were closing in and he couldn't
breathe and...CRACK. Schellenberg slapped him hard across the
face. "Control yourself. I haven't got all day. You are potentially
useful, but scarcely irreplaceable. It doesn't matter if what you

draw is physically capable of being built. It's a pretty picture as part of the show. Nothing real is going to happen until the war is safely over and we need public works to employ people. No one will question you 'revising the initial concept' then. Right now we need a drawing to print in the newspapers and then a plot of land to rope off as the preliminary building site. This is stagecraft, same as Nürnberg. Speaking of which, I'll also need to know by the end of the day how many searchlights you'll need for the pillars of ice lighting-effects you did so well at the rallies."

Speer got control of himself. Pain overcame fear. He asked for clean paper and a good technical pen. He let his imagination soar and started to draw. He just told himself he was doing a drawing for a Wagnerian opera set. If they wanted fantasy buildings, he would design what Wotan would have felt was a pyramid.

Chapter 4

1205 hours British Double Summer Time
24 June 1940
London, UK

Kim Philby was late for his meeting with his handler. Late and worried. All he had was office gossip from SIS, but it would raise a huge reaction from Moscow. A reaction that would demand details he didn't know if he could get. An old Cambridge friend had passed him word that Germany was all in a tizzy with huge numbers, perhaps millions, of people being shuttled to Berlin for "something big". This had come in via some signals chaps at Betchley Park. Moscow always wanted granular details, preferably with documents. Philby didn't have them. He didn't even begin to know how he would get them. But the zinger was that a second rumor had kicked back from Abwehr contacts. Hitler was supposedly dead. Philby was wracking his brains trying to find a set of old chums who could get him posted to this signals group.

2400 hours
24 June, 1940
Berlin, Chancellery balcony

The torchlight and banner parade with marching bands had been going on for hours and still had hours to go. New groups kept joining the end of the line at the jump-off point. Göring had taken the salutes with Beck, Halder, and Heydrich by his side. Göring was amazed that Heydrich had pulled off something this big this fast. Having a million men and boys chant your name had proved to be intoxicating.

Beck's response was closer to apoplectic. He kept alternately sputtering and threatening to shoot Heydrich if this farce wasn't stopped. Halder was taking it in more thoughtfully. Heydrich in turn was quite sarcastic back to Beck. Kept asking him if he understood yet. This was what the Movement brought to the table. As the noise of the massed marchers singing and chanting was deafening, Halder pulled the threesome inside, leaving Göring to the public duties he seemed to relish.

Halder had great respect for Beck, but was starting to see

his own role as peacemaker between the two halves of this new coalition. "Think, sir. The man has delivered. There's no political space left for a serious opposition. It's the same choice you made in the early 30s when you sided with the Nazis."

Beck took a minute to compose himself. He was a logical man as well as an opinionated elder statesman. He had used the Nazis initially. He was then appalled to see them use him and disregard his advice, the advice of his class, of the better sort of people. Was this really a second chance for a union of equals? "Heydrich, what is your game here? The truth for once, please."

Heydrich had not expected the old man to begin to see reason this soon, but he was prepared. He prided himself on always being prepared. "Let's start with our new Chancellor and Führer. The crowd loves him and he loves the adoration. So far, very much like the man before him. Except, unlike Hitler, our Göring does not have a policy agenda to push past us all. A certain amount of personal luxury, a certain indulgence of his personal lifestyle, and he will gladly let the rest of us do the actual work of governing. He hates the day-to-day drudgery. As long as he has power on the big decisions, he'll let your lot and our lot actually rule Europe. Which we can do better united than feuding. Your lot lost the Great War and allowed Weimar to implode. Ours proved better at taking power than managing it after 1934. Hitler took insane gambles, plus luck was with him. The trick now is to bank our winnings and stop taking big risks. We need peace with Britain. We need no expensive defeats. We need to watch our backs with the Bolsheviks. Anyone disagree?"

Halder thought he saw where this was going. "We don't invade England?"

Heydrich shook his head. "High risk, low chance of success. We have no navy left after Norway. They have one of the world's great fleets. Next to us, they have the best air force in the world right now. What does it do to our prestige as the new rulers if the initial landings fail? Or are a marginal success with massive casualties? Then the story is how we are unworthy heirs of the demi-god Hitler. Bank our winnings. Fight the British in the South. You are the main arms bearers of the state. Leave enough divisions in the West to keep the French down and the British on their island. Don't worry about constabulary garrisons. We'll create a new Party Militia for that. Something for the million down there to do. It gets rid of the huge host of Party organization men we gave jobs to during the last decade. It was necessary in the beginning. Now it's a lead weight on our economy. Let them be police and bureaucrats across Europe. Take your big armies and move them east. Occupy Romania and Hungary. Set up a front to keep our so-called allies in Moscow honest. Then let's demobilize forty or so divisions. You've got a bunch of badly armed reserve formations. Put them back in the civilian economy. We hold a victory parade for each before it goes back into the reserves. Göring loves parades. He enjoys the glad-handing and ceremonial."

Halder was not sure he was following. "But the war isn't over. What do we do about the British and the Soviets?"

Beck had a different problem. "Why Hungary? Why Romania?" He feared some new ideological crusade just when he was hoping for sanity from Heydrich.

Heyrdich had the answer ready. "Oil. Do either of you really trust Stalin?" He paused for the two generals to shake their heads. "Well, beyond what he sells us and ignoring his endless delivery delays, that means Ploiesti. Getting to that oil means Hungary. Railroads and the Danube for barges. Plus Hungary has some oil. Nothing like Romania but we need every drop we can get until we take Iraq and bring that production home. The idiot Magyars have territorial claims on every neighbor including us. Stalin has claims we validated on Romania. So, we take both countries. With their cooperation, if possible. By force, if necessary. That prevents the locals destroying the oil fields or blocking shipment. That prevents Stalin preempting. Without Romanian oil, we are not a modern power until we take Iraq. And that's part of why the southern campaign. Beyond driving the British out of the war, we must have plentiful petroleum to be a modern power with planes, tanks, and trucks."

He now turned back to answer Halder's question.

"Soviets first. You start on two warplans. First is for a defensive war if Stalin attacks. He might. He never expected France to fall in six weeks. Should be pissed as all hell. Second is if we decide to attack after the British pack it in. Took us three years to beat the Czar, so plan on a three- to five-year war to get beyond the Urals. No need to assign probabilities. It's all hypothetical now."

Beck could not contain himself. "Why hypothetical? What about the British?" Beck had served on the Western Front in the Great War. He respected the British as opponents.

"We attack them through the Mediterranean using the

Italians. I'll need some equipment and two of your divisions. Third Mountain, the ones from Narvik with Dietel. He managed an insane situation well. Seventh Panzer. Rommel was Hitler's pet. He's insubordinate but a natural storm officer. Also, Rundstedt's ex-chief of staff, Manstein. He seems to have an operational brain, or so my contacts at OKW tell me. I'll bulk this up with the parachute forces, the Waffen SS, and the better pieces of this Party Militia. Add in Kesselring's Second Air Fleet. Nominally we are supporting our brave Italian allies. Any defeats don't have a lot of German dead, so it's just the inept Latins. Any victories, we play up how well our men did. Italy can keep the land won until we reach Iraq. We keep that. Oil. Gets us out from under Stalin's thumb. Keitel and Jodl can manage this. Gives them something to do and avoids pissing contests on which HQ controls what."

Beck and Halder were not liking some parts of this. "How big is this new southern army going to be?"

"Weak air-transported corps for Malta. The paratroops, glider units, and the mountain division. It's light, therefore, air transport is possible. Mechanized Corps for Libya. It's all we can supply through the Libyan ports. We bring in a second corps after we take Egypt, as we'll have a better port with Alexandria. Probably the light corps from Malta with captured British trucks and a few tanks. This cannot grow out of hand, if that is what you are worrying about. Supply."

Halder was dubious. "Who did your planning?"

"Half a dozen staff officers you trained who transferred to the Air Force and Waffen SS. Took them three hours today. It's a map exercise. We can switch forces from West to South orders of magnitude better than the British can. More so as we can switch them back just as fast. British have to prioritize defending their island. Gives us a window to jump through with both feet and fangs out. Yes, it means working with the Italians, which will not be fun. Probably going to have to threaten to bomb Rome to make them comply. But what I want is to drive Britain out of the war by colonial defeats while we rule Europe for our benefit. Soviet policy we leave to the future and Stalin's actions. On no account do we provoke the US into entering the war. That's what lost us the Great War. Drove the Russians out and pushed the Americans in at the same time. What we need is a decade or two to remake Europe in our own image. Can you sell this in outline to your technocrats and officers?"

Halder leaned over to buzz into Beck's ear. Beck made a face as if swallowing something rotten and then nodded. "Yes, but why this emphasis on a Party Militia?"

"Jobs. This huge parallel bureaucracy is strangling us. I cannot dismantle it unless I have new posts to hand out to enough people. We need a modern, efficient state. We've won a round in the game of world dominance. There will be a second round. We are stronger than the US or the Soviets if we unite Europe. We cannot remain this divided at home and unite what we now hold. You people came up with the idea of Middle Europe before WW1. Well, we now hold an expanded version. Spain, Sweden, Switzerland, Finland, Yugoslavia, Bulgaria, Turkey will drift into our orbit. Perhaps Greece and Portugal as well. " Heydrich caught two looks on Finland. "Yes, we promised it to Stalin. That was then. This is now. The Finns are Aryans. There will be another round of negotiations in due course. He'll want things. Perhaps Persia. We get Finland back. Or we don't and evacuate the Finns. Same as I'll try to get the Balts out of him. The land is gone but maybe we can save the people. Good Lutherans mostly. Germanizable. You should appoint a staff section to start prepping for those Soviet talks. Probably a major conference at Brest later this summer."

Halder took a few moments to compose himself. "How did you work through all this so fast?"

"Outline was easy. Things I saw get screwed up these past seven years. No clear lines of authority. Conflicting bureaucracies. Tremendous waste. I never expected to have the power to fix it, but it was a mental exercise. I keep my brain alert playing 'what if'. Wasn't the 'what if' I expected. What I expected was Himmler liquidating me. You solved THAT problem for me. You people have technical skills. In addition, you are more socially acceptable to the ruling classes of our new European satellites than we are. We can do mass mobilization, see to the Home Front. We can also train more of our young ones to be technocrats. Careers open to talent regardless of birth. At heart, we are all German nationalists, no?"

Beck had another issue to raise, "What about the Jews?"

"You don't like them any better than we do. You're just more squeamish. Fine. Rome gave Europe the Jews, the gypsies, the flood of black-robed priests. Italy is now our ally. Thus, we return the gift. Let Italy ship them to Egypt, to Africa. We take the Germanized part-Jews and park them working for us in Iraq. It will be racial chaos out there anyway. Our late Führer welcomed emigration, or at least said so enough times for us to hide behind. We kill some, some die of starvation or disease, and the rest vanish. We pronounce Aryan Europe Jew-free."

"Not Palestine?"

"That's an Italian decision. Why should we care either way? We'll keep an enclave around the port of Haifa and the oil pipeline back to Kirkuk, but what do we care about Jerusalem or Bethlehem? Let Il Duce and the Pope argue about each meter of that cursed ground. More colonial territory per se just means more race mixing. Why take land that does not serve the Reich? Let the Italians handle it. They are racially inferior anyway."

The discussion went on until dawn with stenographers called to take memos. The committee of four was turning into a committee of three.

0200 Moscow Time
the Kremlin, Moscow
25 June 1940

Lavrentiy Beria worked at keeping a calm demeanor as he entered his limousine to be driven back to his office. He didn't know for a fact whether his driver and bodyguards were reporting on him back to Stalin, but had to presume someone was. The Boss always had multiple sources of information.

It had been a BAD session with the Boss. Soviet Embassy in Berlin had reported a major change in government, but had no details as there was as yet no official announcement. The Boss expected answers and, so far, there weren't any. His best agent, the Party official Bormann, was dead. Murdered in the coup. This had been confirmed by several sources, including his handler. His next best, the Gestapo chief Müller, had made himself unavailable. Understandable in a fluid situation, but the Boss was not an understanding man. Beria did not allow himself to sweat but inside he was frightened. There were always subordinates eager to advance over someone's dead body and, having made it to the top of the NKVD's ladder, it would be his body.

The deeper nets simply didn't report quickly. They were even slower being re-tasked as that required the agents arranging transfers to new departments. That left one informant who had reported in. Some supply major in the Air Ministry, sending what amounted to office gossip. What was worse, the report came out via Switzerland through a GRU network. A network the Interior Ministry thankfully had penetrated. He could report to the Boss that the military and the SS were running Germany. That a new Party Militia was being created for unspecified purposes. That major military formations were to be shifted east. That Hungary and Romania were to be occupied. That some major operation was in work with the Italians. The Boss wanted details and documents. Time to filch this Air Force officer from GRU. Time to get someone into this new Führer Göring's entourage. The man had an actress for a second wife. There was an agent who was an actress....

Chapter 5

0700 hours
26 June 1940
Berlin

Klaus Steiner was exhilarated, exhausted and confused all at once. It had been two of the most wonderful, horrible, and confusing sort of days of his young life. It had started with getting essentially abandoned and lost in the vast crowds pouring into Berlin from everyplace within a day by bus or train within Greater Germany.

Klaus had never been in a big city. It was huge and loud and smelled strange and...and one second he was still in sight of his HJ troop and the next he wasn't. This frightened him despite his being anything but alone. He was buffeted up and down streets he didn't know by masses of people, some moving purposefully in groups, many just gawking as he was. Yet, before he could fully panic, up strode this large SA officer , a little under two meters tall and built like a weightlifter with a thick neck, barrel chest, and huge muscled arms and legs. He was blonde and blue-eyed, with a harsh gaze. He seemed to have stepped off a Movement recruiting poster. This giant was leading a ragtag band ranging from boys a year or two younger than Klaus to clearly middle-aged folks. He himself appeared to be in his late thirties.

Klaus flinched back from the gaze , which attracted the troll's attention. "Boy, who are you with?" As Klaus tried to stammer a reply, with words coming out in disjointed order and his voice breaking twice, the ogre's hand grabbed his collar. "Never mind. You're with me now. Consider yourself recruited. There's work to do."

Work there had been. Searchlights to manhandle into place. Posters to put up. Signs directing people to different processing centers to emplace. Their officer kept finding them new jobs, food, drink. He even found them a banner. Some geezer was waving an old Freikorps banner on a street corner while bellowing out some slogan in a Baltic accent Klaus could barely understand. His officer had come to attention before the man, saluted in the old style and chattered away in that dialect. Something about having served up in the Baltic States at the end of WW1 or maybe immediately after. Klaus caught a few place names—Riga, Courland, Latvia, Estonia—but really couldn't follow much of the rest. The dialect was too strange to him. He could follow the officer's normal Rhenish speech, but not this. However, the old man had given them the banner, and now it was his unit's flag. Klaus had even gotten to carry it in the big parade.

The parade had come later and been the high point of Klaus's young life. A million or more men and boys marching, stamping, singing, shouting. Waving torches and banners. And above them all on the balcony their new Führer Marshal Göring roaring salutes and greetings back. Even with loudspeakers no one could hear a word the great man said. It didn't matter. The street itself shook with the marchers' stamping feet and upraised voices. It was still one Reich united in victory. Klaus felt himself part of something vast and grand and beyond the common everyday world. It was as if God had come down to Earth or the crowd had ascended to heaven. Klaus lacked the words to describe it, but it was beyond anything he had thought possible. Nothing in his 17 years prepared him for this.

And now here he was signing up for the new Party Militia, the Nibelungen Legion. Klaus did not recall making a decision or even being asked his opinion. Over the course of the preparations and the march, most of the older guys who had already been with his officer, who he now knew to be Lieutenant Strauss, had vanished in dribs and drabs, being replaced by more young strays like himself. As one of the early "recruits", Klaus had found himself bumped to Corporal. The Lieutenant had simply marched the "unit" off the end of the march to the nearest Nibelungen Legion recruiting post. Klaus had even helped keep the boys in line as one by one the Lieutenant told them they were signing up to avenge the original Führer, Adolph Hitler. Klaus was the tail end of the line. He could have drifted off. He could have said no. A few boys did. They were screamed at, but, if they persisted, they were sent on their way.

Instead, Klaus had meekly signed up, answering all the questions on his HJ experience. He had never made a decision. He had simply let it happen. He had to laugh at one part. The clerk had misheard him on glider experience. He'd been up in them twice, but was now listed in his brand new paybook as a glider pilot. As if. The Lieutenant had gotten every recruit to sign a preprinted card to his parents saying he was now a soldier in

The Reich Without Hitler: The Falcons of Malta

the new NL's. A new word for a new world. His hastily printed armband said NL. His new stripes were held on with a safety pin. Corporal Steiner got his "men" back into a shambling version of a line and followed his officer off to someplace. Hopefully, someplace where they could get a meal and a nap. The two constant needs of a soldier. Klaus was learning fast.

> 1300 hours
> 27 June 1940
> Air Ministry, Berlin

The official reception for Il Duce and the Italian King with the new Führer Göring and Generals Beck and Halder was being held at the Reich Chancellery. It would be formal and endless with nothing of substance done over the course of an afternoon and evening. The real meeting was at the Air Ministry. Four specific Italians had been requested—Crown Prince Umberto, Count Ciano (foreign minister and Il Duce's son-in-law), Giovanni Messe (army general and motorized troop specialist), and Italo Balbo (air force general, Fascist Party senior official, and governor general of Libya). The Italians were uncertain of what to expect and equally uncertain of why the four of them had been chosen , yet the new German government had requested them and refused all additions or substitutions.

Heydrich was chairing the meeting on the German side. He had Schellenberg, Kesselring, and two army generals (von Paulus and Keitel) with him. On the wall were two maps: a blowup of the Malta archipelago and a more general map of the East Basin of the Mediterranean. The room was stifling hot, even with fans and open windows. Aides seated the Italians and saw to refreshments. The Italians were sensible enough to let the Germans open discussion, but Heydrich waited until the refreshments had been finished and the dishes cleared. He clearly wanted privacy for what was to follow.

Once it was just the nine principals in the room, plus two interpreter/secretaries of junior officer rank, he began. "Thank you for coming to see us. We are going to brief you on our joint war plan for the next six months." He paused, waiting for a reaction.

The Crown Prince was no one's fool. "I gather we are being told, not asked." The tone was neither antagonistic nor subservient. The two Fascists were angry and not hiding it well. The Prince prided himself on being a realist.

Heydrich smiled. He had expected typical Latin histrionics. It was nice to be dealing with another adult. "In private, yes. In public, no. You, Prince Umberto, will officially be joint commander. Italy will have more than its proper share of the glory via our united propaganda. You will also get the bulk of the new territories, so the propaganda will seem real to your people and the world. Essentially, we are cooperatively going to drive Britain from the war by destroying the portion of their empire within our reach. The first target is Malta. We will start rotating air units under Kesselring here to Sicily within a week. The invasion will take place the first week of August. We go in with airborne and glider forces. Do you have any?"

The four Italians were uncertain. After a brief conversation, they said maybe a few weak battalions. Kesselring replied that they had three weeks to get him exact numbers, as it was better that they be included so the operation seemed joint. Balbo asked what about the Italian Air Force. Kesselring said they were welcome to participate if Balbo could organize them, but Germany would send more than enough planes to overwhelm one silly island with a few airfields and almost no fighters. Balbo started to loudly defend his service, only to be silenced by the Prince who motioned for the Germans to continue.

Heydrich explained that von Paulus was to be the Prince's liaison officer. Seeing the Prince's sardonic smile, he explained further. "No, really. Marshal Kesselring will in fact command the Malta operation. Von Paulus is your liaison, your conduit to Berlin, to Kesselring, to whoever among us you need to contact. The British only have a few brigades on the islands. Beyond AAA and some coast defense guns, they have no heavy weapons. We are talking a close quarters infantry fight. Between the original para and gliders and air transportable follow-up, we will simply flood them out. They are stubborn fighters, but their commanders are quite old-fashioned. It will be bloody for a few days, but once your fleet follows up by landing still more troops, they will fold. They simply have no counter to dawn-to-dusk air attacks."

He shrugged. "Their navy may, of course, sortie. That may cost you a few ships. Empire isn't cheap. We take the island. You keep it. All we want is the use of an air base. You can even keep the Italian flag over it. With Malta gone, we ferry a German mechanized corps to Libya. General von Manstein will command. You'll meet him somewhat later. You will assemble what mobile Italian troops you have in a companion corps under General Messe here. These two corps plus the air fleet defeat the British in the Western Desert and take Egypt. Shouldn't take more than two months total. You keep Egypt, including Suez. All we need is Alexandria and we'll give that back after we take Haifa in Palestine. There will be a pause in Egypt while supply is reestablished and the air fleet is staged forward, then it's on to Palestine. The two mobile corps go there, still under your nominal command. The unmotorized Italian forces you now have in Libya can occupy Egypt and then proceed south into the Sudan to link up with your forces in East Africa. We get Haifa and a zone around the pipeline to Iraq. We will expand the corps to a small army and take that place with the oil. You get Palestine, Transjordan, and Cyprus. If the British still haven't surrendered, we can discuss further advances into Africa. You'll keep the bulk of that but we hope the British will see reason after losing Egypt and their oil. Questions?"

The Prince looked around to the other three Italians, making sure no fool was going to speak instead of him. He used those seconds to compose himself. "First, you tell us we must obey, then you offer us an excellent deal as if we had bargained. Why?"

Heydrich gave him back a level gaze. "Our nations fought each other in the Great War. No love lost between our peoples. The alliance was personal between the two leaders, one of whom is now deceased. Yet here we are. Our choice is to use you or defeat you. We could crush you, but you are more useful as a happy ally of the second rank. You wanted glory. You wanted an empire. Yet you are bankrupt with inferior military forces. Your war against the French was an absurd failure. It suits our interests to take these places from the British, but we have no need for them ourselves. A big colonial empire runs up against our racial theories. It also takes major forces to occupy them. Your troops are good enough for occupation duty. Everyone wins. Now there are a few other little points. First, your Alpine Corps. Find a commander for it. We're sending it to Hungary. Before Stalin gets big eyes we're occupying Hungary and Romania. We've promised him part of Romania, but he expected us to get bogged down in France. We won fast and cheap. May panic him to do something fast and stupid. Second, next month we will be sending a delegation of technocrats to review your industry, especially arms. You are making inferior weapons. It's wasteful. We'll be giving you better plans of German technology. Essentially, we'll be establishing an industrial cartel. Makes cooperative warfare easier. Finally, your original Roman Empire dumped some undesirables on Europe. Jews, Roma, Catholic clergy. Over the next few years we will be returning most of them to you. Populate Africa with them. Shoot them. Whatever. Your choice, but we will send them and you won't block it."

"And if Britain does not choose to make peace? Surely you must invade."

"If we had such a plan, surely we wouldn't tell you. Between yourselves and the Papacy, too many leaks. We don't care if this plan leaks. We have interior lines and can switch south faster than the British can redeploy. That's just geography. Same way we won't tell you our ultimate intentions on the Soviets. This is an alliance of convenience, not a marriage of equals. Just do understand that sabotaging the war plan will have real costs. Milan, Turin, and Rome will always be within range of our bombers. You had your chance to join the West and stop us. Those days are gone. Ended when Paris fell."

The Prince silenced his other three merely by a glare, then turned with a bland face to Heydrich and asked if there was some joint communiqué for him to sign? On being told no, he politely asked if there was any other business. When again told no, he motioned his people up, shook hands all around, and left. Heydrich told von Paulus to go with them to see to their stay in Berlin. Once the six had left the room, he told his interpreter to do the same. That left Schellenberg and the remaining two military men. Kesselring spoke first, "Don't believe the implied promise of cooperation. I'm asking for enough additional German troops to safeguard my air bases. Only way to keep them honest."

Heydrich shrugged. He believed in letting good subordinates run their operations. All he cared about were results. Nothing ever went as smoothly as the opening meeting seemed to promise. Before he could formulate a reply, an aide came bustling in. The Soviets had begun an invasion of Romania. They were demanding not just Bessarabia, which had been promised, but the Siret River Valley as well. Never a dull moment.

Chapter 6

1800 hours
26 June 1940
Heydrich's temporary office at the Air Ministry,
Wilhelmstrasse, Berlin

Obergrupenführer Paul Hausser arrived for his appointment the standard fifteen minutes early, the military's version of on time. He was amazed that instead of being asked to wait he was immediately ushered into Heydrich's office. The new Reichsführer SS greeted him warmly, as did his new deputy, Oberführer Schellenberg. That these two would land on their feet amazed Hausser not in the slightest. Their promotions did. He mentally shrugged, presuming they had promoted themselves. Opportunists always prospered in such times.

He was curious what these two headquarters operators wanted from a combat soldier such as himself , more so as the two kept the talk to pleasantries and generalities until after a very elaborate coffee service had been prepared. Then, as soon as the servants exited, Schellenberg unfurled a map of North Afrika running from eastern Libya to Sinai. So, it was to be a military brief, but by these two? What did they know of war?

Heydrich was adept at reading people. "You fought for the Kaiser, whose knowledge of war was limited to fantasy saber charges at the end of maneuvers. You loyally served the Reichswehr, which did the bidding of Catholic lawyers and Socialist orators simply because they won elections. You served industrialists and landholders with the Stalhelm. You served a crank who was also a bankrupt, failed, Bavarian chicken farmer, my late, unlamented predecessor, Himmler. Now you serve a committee of four while being under my command. Is it really any different? Grand strategy is made at levels above yours. The Waffen SS was a hobby horse of Himmler's. He's dead. But for my patronage, it dies with him. Do you wish a career or not?"

"At what price?"

"A certain mental flexibility. The direct military part is simple. For now, the Waffen SS will be reduced to one division. Yours. It's been re-designated as a Panzer Grenadier division..."

"What on earth is that?"

"An experimental type, like when you were with Kempf's

division in Poland."

"What does this strange type look like?" Hausser had visions of the absurdities people who knew nothing of modern war could create. He was also getting frustrated at the knowing smiles from the two glorified police clerks.

"It means anything the three of us say, it does. For a start, it's your division with your missing regiment back. You get the artillery regiment from Eicke's division. In addition, a few other this-and-thats from him. Pioneers, anti-tank, anti-aircraft. You get the guns from the Police division, but we'll have to find you new men from the SA and NL to man them."

Hausser shook his head. A single division with three artillery regiments. The proportions were all wrong. He waited to see what else was coming. Heydrich went on. "Also, each of your nine-line battalions will get an armored company. Now, in a perfect universe these would all be new upgunned MK.IV's. We don't live in a perfect universe. It will be nine companies of whatever we can find, including captured French vehicles. Tanks, tankettes, assault guns...". Heydrich put up a hand before Hausser could interrupt. "Yes, a maintenance nightmare. Hence, you will also get a depot and repair brigade. Another mixed collection of service types manning it. Some of your technical types may even wear naval uniforms, as a lot of the battlefleet is no longer considered critical to the war effort. Part of that flexibility is having an enlarged unit where your men may have half a dozen different service uniforms, which makes for some limits on higher forms of discipline and the like. You'll have SS, SA, NL, Navy, Air Force, Hungarians. At a later date, probably Dutch, Norse, Balts, and a bunch of other things."

Hausser had to interrupt. "What disciplinary authority will I have?"

"Total on an administrative level, and that includes prior written approval for drumhead courts-martial or shooting people out of hand."

"That extreme?"

"Yes. Just don't abuse it. However, for routine courts-martial as opposed to field punishment, you must kick them back to their respective services. Similarly, you won't have promotion authority for Navy and Air Force, although you will have authority to authorize their transfer with their consent to the NL, where you will have total authority on promotions up to the level of Major General. NL is dispensing with the SS and SA rank names. Going back to the old system."

"Three artillery regiments is still too much."

Heydrich's smile got even wider. "I'm not done. After getting the nine companies of armored vehicles, each of your three regiments will then get a battalion of three companies of armored vehicles and one of motorized or mechanized infantry. After that, you will then get a full panzer regiment of four battalions of armor on the three and one model plus one of armored infantry in French-made half-tracks on the one and three. There will be other add-ons. In essence, you will have a panzer corps by the time of the final push into Iraq."

"Then why call it a division?"

"Politics. I promised the Army that only one SS division would go to war this time. Therefore, your command is a division. I always keep my promises. To the letter." The other two officers laughed, so Hausser joined them. This was proving interesting.

Heydrich paused while Schellenberg poured more coffee. "One division, but you won't be the only SS divisional commander. Brigadeführer Steiner will command another experimental unit designated the Afrika Division. Another of these panzer grenadier divisions, only his will be called 'light', so that its total lack of resemblance to yours won't arouse comment. He gets an oversized brigade of Frenchmen claimed to be German borderers returned to us now that the frontier has moved again. And whatever bits and pieces don't fit in your division. Nominally, his division is NL. In fact, it will be an amalgam of services." Catching Hausser's look of confusion, he continued, "This is Roehm's Second Revolution. The NL will provide a home to the SA and Party types that were promised good jobs in the '30s during the march to power. They will be scattered over Europe as gendarmes and petty officials. Right now they are a parallel bureaucracy clogging up the efficient running of our state. Scattered over Europe they provide three things. The first is the populist revolution the Movement promised and then never delivered. The second is a nucleus for the Germanization of much of Europe over a period of a few generations. Forget the biological racism the Movement once taught. That's a pretty set of slogans for the masses. The real history has been cultural Germanization. The real Drang Nach Osten involved Easterners—Slavs, Balts, Magyars, whatever—moving to town or the castle keep. They would take German names and, over a few generations, German culture and language. So, your eight NL in some Polish or Belgian town recruit a few dozen local helpers. Over time the helpers all learn to speak German, wear German uniforms, marry into the German people. By the time your grandson becomes a general, there are more Germans in Europe than Russians and Frenchmen combined."

"What about the ones who won't Germanize?"

Schellenberg made a pistol with his hand and went "Bang!"

Heydrich replied, "Read the definitions on Class Five Volksdeutsche. Germanizable elements. That means whatever we wish it to. Thus, the NL uniforms are for the new Germans. The SA uniforms are for their sons. Their grandsons can join the SS, as can Aryans such as Norse and Dutch now. The British and Romans used versions of this. The Americans have made patriots out of anything that isn't too black. The Kaiser even made good German soldiers out of blacks. Fought quite well in East Africa and Cameroun. I plan on getting those veterans back when the peace comes."

"Blacks in Germany?" Hausser was appalled.

"As colonial troops in Iraq. And Congo if the war lasts that long. The Race Laws don't apply out of Europe. Be sure your troops know that. Once they cross the Mediterranean, they can screw anything with a pulse. It's what soldiers always do in the field, anyway. The ones who want to keep their dusky damsels will just have to put in for colonial duty. Most won't want to keep them. But we'll gather the women and their brats for Iraq. A half-German caste will be useful. The British use such a caste in India. Hell, we accept as Germans the bastards the Allied occupation troops left behind in the Rhineland." Heydrich paused as he saw Hausser's raised brows. "Yes, we liquidated the ones who appeared black, but did anyone look twice at the towhead whose absent father was a Yank or Brit or Frenchman? Armies have been marching across our lands back to Julius Caesar. And fucking our girls and leaving by-blows behind. It's the way of the world. Anyway, the third thing this does is provide a counterweight to the generals. They will seamlessly link themselves to their fellow aristocrats in the new Europa. We will link ourselves to the ambitious working class and lower bourgeoisie. Part of Germanizing is Party membership. As Deputy Head of the Party, I will see to the organization being quite flexible on this. We shot most of the old Gauleiters. The new ones are mostly our new Führer Göring's cronies. Content to enjoy their new higher salaries while diddling their stenographers. Their administrative staffs are my people. Subsequently, your wounded veterans who are invalided out can be sure of careers. A good word from you or your staff and places will be found. The new purpose of the Waffen SS is a training school for ambitious young Aryans."

"How so?"

"NL and SA will mostly only have ranks up to major. The general staff and more senior ranks will mostly be Waffen SS. You will have the means to get higher careers for good performers who pass through your command."

"What about the other two divisions and the LAH?"

"LAH first. They return to being HQ guards. Back to Berlin, increased in size, and put under the new Führer's personal command. Beyond their showpiece function at the Chancellery and his residences, they will be a coup protection force along with the Air Force. What just happened won't be allowed a second time." Heydrich paused to see if Hausser was wise enough to read between those lines. The tight smile on Hausser's face showed he already knew the obvious, that what ruled Germany now was a successful coup hiding behind a propaganda façade. Heydrich decided his conclusion had been reaffirmed. Hausser was bright enough to be part of his new visions for the SS. Heydrich planned on a Waffen SS as his coup protection. A Waffen SS whose brilliant war record will get the best volunteers, as befits an elite force. "LAH had a decent war record. Dietrich is loyal. He will have to personally bond with the new Führer, but that shouldn't be too difficult. The Police division did nothing of merit in the French war. Then again, they are just cops doing reserve duty. Fine. Cops they are and cops they shall be. We are downgrading the division to a field security force. You will get the artillery and any serious weapons. They will be permanently posted to Paris. It's the most important capital we hold. Occupying it will be police work and fits what they know. Eicke's merry band of thugs were a failure in combat...."

Hausser felt he had to set the record straight. "Not totally their fault. The anti-tank guns were useless."

"Yes, they were. Others had similar problems, but did not come apart as badly. They also didn't murder several hundred British prisoners for mere convenience." Hausser winced. He had hoped that mess had been safely buried. His opinion of how thorough Heydrich's staff work was went up a few notches. "You don't do that with civilized troops. I expect you to see to that in your campaign. I want proper treatment for British prisoners, even the wogs and colored. Make sure. Make examples if you have to. The purpose of the campaign is to end this silly war with Britain on terms favorable to ourselves. Destroying the British Empire beyond the Middle East is not in our interests, as we are in no position to pick up the pieces. Why should we shed blood so Japan and the US get stronger? Restrict the British so they have no heavy bombers on their island and let them hide behind the Channel."

Heydrich shook his head wearily. Hausser presumed this meant he was repeating an old argument he was tired of. Hausser marked that for future thought. "Anyway, Eicke is a thug and a butcher. The lunatic part was spite and SS politics. We send him and his boys to Warsaw where we will rule with a heavy hand. Most Poles will never accept us as their overlords. They are as crazy in their nationalism as the Irish. So, Poland gets the iron hand and Eicke is the man for it. You'll get papers letting you cream his division for any men your staff deem interesting. They did have some frontline service. Some of them may make useful thugs instead of cowardly ones. But none from the unit with the massacre. We want to avoid a repeat. Any questions so far?"

Hausser asked the obvious question. "Why me? I'm not one of your cronies and this is a plumb assignment."

"Because what I value most is competence. Loyalty, of course, but competence first. You are the best we have. The southern campaign is my idea. I want the Waffen SS to shine. Forget the propaganda. When the four rulers review the progress of this theater of war, who will do better than you leading an SS field force?" Hausser's smile said he already knew THAT. "You did well in the Reichswehr, but you will do better under me. All the army can offer you is your old seniority back. I'm the one who can keep raising you higher. Command, promotion, fame—tell me that those coins don't buy loyalty in a military hierarchy? Do you prefer being a junior Army general to being the commander of a rising independent service? Tell me now and I'll write you your transfer order back to the Army and give Steiner your command."

Hausser put a hand up. "Oh, I'll take the bargain, and deliver my part."

"Just remember that your division reflects on my personal prestige. Forget propaganda headlines. I need senior army generals to look at the daily situations reports and see you as an elite general leading an elite division. You are a professional officer. You have the best troops and will have more than your share of the best equipment. From Egypt through to Iraq I expect yours to be the best division in our new Afrika Korps. I can then bring you back to Europe to create first an enlarged panzer corps and then a panzer army on your model. A mechanized storm army of Europe's best storm troops."

Heydrich put out his hand to shake and seal the new partnership.

Chapter 7

1700 hours
27 June
Chancellery, Berlin

The four members of the ruling German junta had yet to formalize functions as opposed to titles. Indeed, Beck even lacked a title beyond his rank as a retired senior general. It didn't matter. They ruled and were accepted as rulers. The first order of business was dealing with the Soviet ambassador. The fool had wasted the last twenty minutes alternately blustering, being evasive, and pleading lack of instructions. Göring had had enough. "Simple question—are we at war? Yes or no?"

The Soviet ambassador simply refused to give a direct answer. Heydrich cut off the new evasions. "Fine. You know nothing. We are putting you on a plane and sending you home. Would the Chancellor be kind enough to instruct some staff officer to see this fool to the airport, prep a passenger plane, and ferry him to Moscow?" He turned to the Soviet, "You will get to call your embassy from the airport. We suggest they telegraph Moscow immediately and without code that you are coming. Be a shame if your fighters shot you down on the way home. Crawl to your master and bring back these words. It's a simple question really. Does he want war right now or not? He's broken the old agreement. It's dead. His doing. We are willing to discuss a new one, but the power relationships have changed. We suggest a conference at Brest. It's our common border; everyone should feel safe. But it's up to him. We'd prefer peace but are prepared to fight. If I thought you were a man instead of a whipped cur, I'd have you ask him if two more Romanian provinces were worth this rupture. Instead, I'll have our embassy in Moscow raise the issue through channels." Heydrich looked around the table to see if any of his associates had anything to add. No one did.

Beck waited till the Soviet was out of the room before turning on Heydrich with a different matter. "Since when do you give movement orders to army units? That is our function."

Heydrich offered a placating smile. "It was an emergency and part of the agreed plan. You'd already given us Rommel. He was on his way back. We had him detour through the mountain jäger school and put a rump battalion together. One of my staff people found a few NL units that rate parachute or glider from some prior HJ training. This bulked up the battalion. They are already in the air to Ploiesti. We cannot risk losing the place. We cannot even risk it being sabotaged the way it was in 1916. Therefore, we need a force with a German flag to assert our claim. OKH was copied on all the orders, so you never actually lost command authority."

Before Heydrich could go further, Halder cut in over him. "Yes, you did sketch this out and yes, this is an emergency, but we will NOT let you make a habit of it. Now what's this about the Balts?"

Göring chose this moment to assert himself. "Officially we are just sending the Navy to speed the departure of the Baltic Germans per our agreement with Stalin. All we are changing is accepting as German anyone who claims to be one, regardless of what language they claim it in. Keeping those people if we could was in the original plan. Opening the frontier to 'refugees' fits right in. So does having the Foreign Office inform the three governments that we will take all their people, their military as formed units, et cetera. Just good staff work. Pity the Navy is not being cooperative. We've got two admirals outside who want to argue their orders."

Beck and Halder had no love for the Navy. Accordingly, it was a united front that saw to Admirals Raeder and Doenitz next. Raeder wanted to argue the entire strategy of a move south and evacuation of the Baltic states. His warships were too valuable to be used as mere transports with no proper plan for what to do if the Soviets chose war. Sending the entire U-boat fleet to Taranto was impossible and would ruin the war against England and besides....

He never got any further. Göring exploded. "I am Chancellor and Führer. You are the head of the least significant service. You are dismissed from your command. I will give you a chance to redeem yourself as commander of the torpedo boat squadron we are sending south. Admiral Doenitz, if you argue, you'll be commanding a naval infantry brigade in Sicily. Germany is a land and air power, not a world-spanning sea empire. Adjust to your proper status or be relieved." Doenitz's face flared and then broke. He saluted stone-faced and then left the room dragging a sputtering Raeder with him. Göring enjoyed the feeling of power from being in charge. He was also happy that Heydrich had spared him the scut work of assigning ships to ports and all the other grubby details. Göring had always wondered how that fool Himmler had accomplished so much. He was now seeing who had done the real work. The idea of keeping and using Heydrich now seemed brilliant. He was going to have to send Nebe a case of good champagne as a thank you. Then a better idea came to him. Better to couple it with a promotion and assignment to directly head the new Chancellery Guard. A paramilitary force reporting directly to the new Führer and doing his will. Who better to keep Heydrich in his place?

The four had no sooner settled themselves than they heard screaming and cursing out in the antechamber. That must be the Hungarian ambassador and his number two. A phone call to Budapest to inform the Hungarian government of certain realities had produced nothing beyond a tiresome recitation of territorial claims and assertions of sovereignty. Time to set matters straight. Gestapo men dragged in the two Hungarians, who were shouting about diplomatic immunity, sovereignty, insults to national honor. Fools. Göring walked over to the older one, who he presumed was senior. He grabbed the man by the shirt collar, forced his head upright and blew his brains out with his sidearm. Brains and blood drenched the other one, the floor, and blew back on Göring himself. Göring didn't care. He was playing a part. "Take this fool into the other room. Get his government back on the phone. They have one hour to sign whatever we put in front of him or we bomb Budapest flat. We will be sending two generals, one each from the Army and the police. They will have total authority over all of Hungary, civil and military. Those are our terms. Total subordination or total war. If it's war, we will kill every Magyar down to infants. Enough of rearguing borders and history. The new Europe has one capital: Berlin. It has one sovereign: me. If they want a few counties in Slovakia or Transylvania, let them earn it." Thus the fate of Hungary.

Beck was livid at this sort of gangster behavior. He planned to have words with Halder later. If they were joint rulers, limits would have to be placed on Göring's ego. Beck then caught himself. The only way to do that was an alliance with Heydrich. The exact behavior Heydrich had warned them against, that had led to Stalin's sole power in Moscow. The politics of national leadership by committee were proving more complex than a mere colonel general had thought.

The Reich Without Hitler: The Falcons of Malta

Beck proposed General Günther von Kluge for the Army. Göring decided he could dispense with Gestapo Müller, as he wished to reassert his own control over that force. Nebe could do this better with the old boss out of the way. That left the Romanian ambassador, who nearly fell over himself agreeing to everything. A German commander of Romanian forces? Certainly. A German garrison? Please, yes, and as quickly as possible. A German force already in the air towards Ploiesti? Just give the ambassador a phone to make arrangements. Food aid for the refugees fleeing Stalin? Romania was eternally grateful. It was obvious who was going to be the favored child between Hungary and Romania.

Chapter 8

2200 hours
27 June 1940
Ploiesti, Romania

Gunter Strauss was amused. The silly boy says he once was in a glider. The clerk checks the box for glider pilot. Another clerk makes his entire company glider troops. Company. He laughed quietly to himself. More like a platoon, but he was bumped to Captain and told more recruits would be forwarded to him. Whoever this General Rommel was had looked his lot over on the runway. Had shrugged, smiled, and said welcome to the ersatz storm jäger battalion. Better find the boy some glider manuals to study. This Rommel seemed one likely to rise. Best to show he was useful. Reminded Gunter of the storm officers he had served under as a kid at Riga in '17 and France in '18. The taking of Riga and the Michael offensive had been Gunter's introduction to serious soldiering after enlisting underage in 1917. He'd learned about storm officers by serving under them. Rommel had no staff stripe on his trousers. Just a single combat decoration, the highest. A Blue Max wearer. The ones like that spend men like water, but the survivors got promotions. Gunter had gotten bumped to sergeant after two such battles had hollowed out his battalion.

0830 hours
28 June, 1940
Romanian oil fields

Erwin Rommel was bored. He had "occupied" the facilities. Occupied? He had been feted with champagne by the local Romanian dignitaries, offered a key to the city, and a horde of the locals threw flowers at his men as they marched in from the airport. The men appreciated the wine bottles, and kisses more. However, all dawn had brought was more rounds of joyous welcome. No one was threatening the oil fields. The Soviets were elsewhere. They were the threat. Time to do something about that. He had one of the jäger instructors round up vehicles for his men. This NL Captain Strauss could hold the airport and oil facilities until reinforcement arrived.

The Reich Without Hitler: The Falcons of Malta

The roundup of vehicles had produced both volunteer drivers and a hastily formed company of Iron Guards who insisted on accompanying him. Also, a dozen Romanian officers who volunteered as guides and liaison officers. Good thing that. He spoke not a word of the language. The only words he sort of remembered from fighting there in 1916 were variants of "I surrender." They had done a lot of that. Hopefully, they would do better this time under German command, but he doubted it.

0915 hours
28 June 1940
Villa Reale, Monza near Milan, Italy

The two Italian negotiating parties had avoided discussing anything until they were safely back on Italian soil. They correctly feared German eavesdropping. Milan was closer by air than Rome. The King had insisted on meeting everyone at once to emphasize his prominence. He was upset that the Prince and General Balbo had added another general, Tellera, without asking permission. The King was more upset that his son had been treated as the most important Italian by the Germans. Il Duce was mostly upset that with Hitler gone, and Göring clearly forgetting the debts he owed for help after the failed Beer Hall Putsch, his power in regards to the German connection was fast waning. He was aware of the actual power imbalance, but Hitler had shown outsized respect based on past favors. This seemed now to be at an end.

The Prince tried to ease his father's fears and temper. "Father that's not precisely what happened. You and Il Duce met with their top three people, equals to equals. Beyond ceremonial, did anything of substance get discussed?" When both shook their heads, the Prince went on. "Reichsführer Heydrich was making a point. He is the only one of the four rulers who cares about Italy one way or the other. It would have been a blow to both of your prestige to meet with him directly. More so to be given what amounted to orders from a superior at such a meeting. Instead, he arranged to work with the second level in Italy. Preserves appearances, which will matter a great deal for the prestige of the realm, dynasty, and regime. He offered a choice—secondary ally or conquered territory. Do either of you really want war with Germany?" Again, the two seniors shook their heads. "Then we take their war plan on their terms and acquire an empire instead of losing what we have."

The two co-rulers were faced with an impossible choice. The way to assert dominance was a hopeless war. The King spoke before Il Duce could. "So, you are the ones dealing with the Germans. You are still subordinate."

Balbo answered before the Prince could. "Of course. To the degree any of us have any choices, the King of Italy and the Italians and Il Duce of the Italians will make them. Except right now we have a choice between glorious victories and ruin. You have both wisely made the choice of victory, but that means that effectively we follow the German plan and German orders. Yet, so far, this had been to our advantage. General von Paulus out there has been exactly as advertised. We asked for the Vickers tankettes the Belgians had. He got a yes in under two hours. There's a problem with shipping. The rail system is being pushed beyond capacity. That's what General Tellara is here for. The German delegation is coming next week. They are creating continent-wide cartels for rails, production, and similar. He's the best technical person we have to make sure Italy's interests are seen to."

Il Duce was NOT liking Balbo's elevation, but lacked a ready weapon to use to stop it. They had been old rivals within the Fascist Party. Mussolini had thought he had sidelined Balbo by packing him off as Governor General in Libya. Now the Germans had resurrected his career and expanded his power. "Can the Germans really deliver what they are promising?"

Now it was the Prince's turn to answer for Balbo. "The two of you should plan on how you will make your triumphal entry into Cairo. Six months at the most and we have it. Didn't even have to bargain the Germans for it. They don't want it. Their silly racial theories again. One last thing: I don't want to step above my place but someone with full authority must make clear to our industrialists and bureaucrats that the usual silly games and delaying tactics won't work this time. The Germans will expect us to shoot people who obstruct , whole families in serious cases without consideration of personal and family influence and connections. Senator Agnelli must be advised, and Commercial Director Doctor Valletta from Fiat, as they will be the first to test the boundaries. It's good that Count Ciano's father is no more amongst the living. The Germans are quite humorless in this. They are willing to preserve our prestige and autonomy in public only as long as they get what they want when they want it." The King and Il Duce dismissed the rest as they pondered this. It was a demand they could neither safely delegate nor safely ignore. Yet both found it distasteful, more so as it might well take making numerous examples before the lessons were learned.

0940 hours
28 June 1940
Ploiesti Airfield

Klaus Steiner had been promoted again. He smiled at the thought that his officer had unknowingly given him a birthday present. Here he was at 18 an officer and with his first taste of foreign travel. He was now a Lieutenant in charge of two dozen local German lads who had heard there were German forces and arrived with their families to seek protection. The local Romanians were spooked by the Soviets and in the mood for a pogrom. Rommel had somewhat quieted things by taking the worst Iron Guard fanatics off with him. His newly minted captain had rounded up some hunting rifles and shotguns to arm this platoon. Steiner's job had been to sit at the airport and direct reinforcements to the oil fields. He had a few preprinted maps and two trucks. What he expected was some real officer arriving and telling him what to do. What he got was six planeloads of experts and technicians, none of them armed, and none very sure what on earth they were doing in Romania. They had been rousted out of bed by the Gestapo and many arrived in their nightclothes. As a result, he had half a dozen of his "men" shuttling them to his Captain. In the meantime, the planes were being refueled. It seemed a shame to send them back empty when there were German refugees here that he had no idea how to protect anyway. Best to send them back and let some competent adult deal with things.

1200 hours
28 June 1940
Oil Fields, Romania

Captain Gunter Strauss had promoted himself to Major. He was quite sure he had no authority to do so; however, he was equally sure it was necessary. Steiner was sending him this stream of experts. They all needed food and housing. Most needed clothes and incidentals as well. He hadn't seen a fuckup this bad since the worst days with the Iron Division in Latvia. Experts don't listen to captains. They will sometimes pay attention to majors. Besides, small groups of minority nationalities were turning up led by old Austro-Hungarian and White Russian captains and majors, decked out with medals on their twenty years out-of-date uniforms. They were hoping for protection and offering their services. Germans, Magyars, White Russians, even some Jews, of all things. All arriving with cars or horse carts, possessions and families in tow. They would take orders from a major, so Major he was.

This was feeling more and more like Livonia. His shattered storm battalion had been near-destroyed by the end of Michael. His commander had pulled a few strings to get them posted to Livonia for the rebuild and somehow managed to keep them there. In the chaos of war's end, Gunter had become a lieutenant and second-in-command of a company. Gunter had developed into an intelligence specialist. He had a flair for languages on a street or pidgin level. He also had the ability to know when to befriend, when to intimidate, when to do trades. He found the unit recruits, supplies, vehicles. He cultivated locals for information. He learned to do quick recon on a motorcycle, turning half-ass maps into real stores of terrain knowledge. In a chaotic war of shifting alliances—of reds, whites, multiple flavors of multiple local nationalists, German units of varying loyalties— he'd learned the game of war. His men didn't get surprised. His local guides didn't sell them out. His local recruits weren't double agents who slit throats during night sentry. Indeed, making a new larger unit out of volunteers of multiple nationalities with questionable credentials and dubious motives was second nature to him. So was working with non-Germans.

One of the recently arrived experts had thrown a fit at the chaos and insisted on calling Berlin. Far from being angry, Strauss had agreed. Then laughed when the proper ministry in Berlin had refused a collect call from somewhere in the Balkans. Before the overseas connection was lost, Strauss had pulled his invented rank on the bewildered Berlin operator and gotten a connection to SS HQ. They had taken the call because it came from a field officer. Strauss had then almost swallowed his teeth when the call was forwarded directly to Reichsführer Heydrich and Oberführer Schellenberg, who had been in conference on the situation in the southeast.

Strauss decided to just brazen it through. He admitted inventing the rank. He said honestly that he was unsure who the NL reported to, so he had presumed SS. He described the situation and Rommel's actions in clear simple sentences. He ended the conversation a lieutenant colonel with rank tabs and a new paybook to follow by air within a day. He was told to recruit whoever was available, even Yids. Get some sort of guard posted on the facilities and hold them pending reinforcement. The funniest part was when he was asked for his Party number. THAT impressed his two new bosses. Turned out he had a lower number than either of them.

Lieutenant Colonel Gunter Strauss got off the phone a happy man. He had salvaged a career. Trick now was to not lose what he had. Time to organize this shambles before Berlin got bad reports and sent a real officer to replace him.

Chapter 9

1200 hours
28 June 1940
SS HQ Berlin

As the phone call ended, Schellenberg looked at his boss Reichsführer Heydrich. He wasn't sure he had heard what he had clearly heard. Heydrich understood the unasked implied question as if a telepathic link existed between them. "Yes. Why not let him recruit any useful Jews? This is the NL, not the SS. Just mark him for transfer to North Africa. If he can sort out this mess until we fix the Hungarian debacle, he's worth the promotion. The Jews and whatever undesirables he picks up just go with him. You list the families as support troops. After we untangle the mess Müller and von Kluge have made of Hungary, you will assign some good Aryan protégée of yours to the new oil fields' guard division. Let us just hope that those two clowns and Rommel between them don't lose us the war this week."

1220 hours
28 June 1940
SS HQ Berlin

General Erich von Manstein had been waiting in the anteroom of Reichsführer-SS Heydrich's office for nearly two hours now. Aides had made clear this was no discourtesy, but rather a chaotic situation to the southeast. He had been given good coffee, a small snack, and two hovering aides to keep him occupied. Well-groomed, pleasant young junior SS officers. Educated men, but unable or unwilling to tell him why the Army had exiled him to the SS with no word of explanation beyond some vague mention of a campaign in the South. He knew he was in poor repute with General Halder and OKH over his alterations to the Western Campaign plan, where he had used a courtesy meeting with the dead Führer to advance his concepts over the heads of his superiors. He had been right, but being right and being promoted were seldom the same thing in the Army.

He had been in worse repute with the SS under Himmler. He had fought them on excluding part-Jews from military service.

The Reich Without Hitler: The Falcons of Malta

Why refuse men who had volunteered to serve? Yes, it was
partially self-serving. Two of his nephews were of mixed blood
and they were good lads, loyal Germans. Indeed, the SS claimed
doubts on his Aryan heritage. Shrug. On the eastern borderlands
there was always a Slav, Balt, or Jew buried in a family tree if you
looked far enough back. Consequently, one looked at culture, at
language, at a record of service, not some great-grandmother or,
more often, her alleged lover. If every rumor of irregular liaisons
was an incurable defect, what of the stories on Hitler's parentage?
Or Heydrich's?

He was pleased when the Reichsführer finally found the time
to see him. He came in, noted some Oberführer in attendance,
came to attention, saluted, and presented his orders. He was
directed to be seated by the Oberführer. Heydrich read the
orders and handed them back. "So, you are aware you are under
my orders?" Manstein nodded. That was what the orders said.
Heydrich laughed. "That simplifies things. It's what OKH agreed
to, but word and action sometime don't match. Welcome to the
team. You are now commander of the Afrika Korps, the German
component of the Italo-German Panzer Army." Heydrich and
Schellenberg then gave an outline of the campaign.

Manstein politely let them finish and then said, "Let me
recapitulate. I have a good Army Panzer division. Did excellent
work in the last campaign. You are replacing many of the vehicles
with no training time for familiarization. The commander is
an insubordinate bad boy who is also one of your favorites
who I essentially can neither relieve nor control. I have some
experimental SS mobile division with a good commander and
a made-up table of organization with even less real training on
their new equipment, stray manpower from half a dozen services,
and no new tactics manual on how all this new equipment is to
function as a formation. My third division is an even more abstract
combination of a French brigade of uncertain quality, again with
zero unit training, plus odd elements you will assign over the
course of the campaign. The divisional commander is a jumped-
up battalion officer who had a few weeks' line experience running
a motorized regiment. My supposed force multipliers are a few
battalions of anti-aircraft guns used in an anti-tank role whose
supposed effectiveness is based on one battle in France, which has
more conflicting contradictory accounts than Christ's crucifixion.
Oh, yes, and bottomless air support from two generals who

outrank me. My nominal army commander is an Italian aristocrat with no particular military skills who will probably delegate the actual work to unknown other officers. I am to rely on an Italian mobile corps whose commander owes his reputation to doing good work running a motorized brigade against poorly armed African savages. Their tankettes are a joke. Except against the Austrians in 1918, they haven't won a battle since Rome fell to the Germans hordes in the Fifth Century. Oh, and just to make life interesting, Rommel must cart around some battlegroup of no military utility because you will want them to be a garrison and police force in Iraq, if we ever get that far. I am to defeat two of the best regular divisions of professionals the British possess, plus a division of Australians, a Commonwealth nationality who were shock troops in the Kaiser's War. I am to do this quickly and brilliantly at a location they have been preparing for over a year to defend. I attack at any agreed date regardless of how many of my men have arrived and have under a month to defeat both this elite British corps and the equivalent of a second one of garrison troops. Have I left anything out?"

Heydrich chuckled. "No, that about covers it. I think it will be an easy victory. You can, of course, refuse the assignment. You'll be returned to OKH, who undoubtedly will find some minor garrison command to bury you in. General Halder will never let you live down proving him wrong against France. I really don't care if there's a Jew buried somewhere in your family tree, or a Pole or a monkey. I care that you were right about attacking in the Ardennes and had the moral courage to commit career suicide to win us a victory. Now that Himmler is out of the way, I'm also prepared to concede you were right on the part-Jews. I'll give you legal authority to return them all to service under your command, starting with those two nephews of yours. We've already established precedent that the NL recruits any blood lines, even Yids. You will have paperwork authorizing promotions at your discretion up to the rank of colonel. As we are doing amalgamated units, the NL rank covers wherever you assign them. Also, the game is to get into contact with the British and bomb the hell out of them. You defend if they attack you. You pursue if they shatter or are forced into rapid retreat. But this is operationally offensive and tactically defensive. Flat open desert and the flat river deltas like Holland. The key is flat. The British will have nowhere to hide from your firepower during daylight. Night time, you fort up. Let them wear themselves out doing night attacks. Come the dawn your bombers are back. Accomplish what I want through Iraq and there's a colonel general's rank for you, plus I'll throw in purchase money for a proper estate for a family seat."

Manstein's iron façade broke into a thin, bitter smile. He was being given an impossible assignment but rewards to match. "Can I choose my own staff?"

"I can promise anyone you need through the rank of colonel. For higher grades you will have to show a family or service connection. And before you ask how I can guarantee the rank, it's simple really. Our new Führer has the authority to force the Army to act. If he refuses or they contest this, I'll just give you the rank myself with NL tabs. Same pay and pension after all."

For this price, Manstein was prepared to turn mercenary and join Heydrich's legions. Hausser had been a good army man before doing so and seemed to have prospered.

1340 hours
28 June 1940
Remains of the control tower, Budapest airport, Hungary

Gestapo Müller morbidly laughed at his current situation. He had flown in at dawn with Army General von Kluge, a battalion of Mountain Infantry, and two companies of NL that had been swept up from a sports stadium where they had been sleeping. The Mountain troops had arrived from Munich. Everyone else had come from Berlin. They had been met by a delegation of senior Hungarian officers and a fleet of limousines waiting to take them to meet with Hungary's leadership on Castle Hill. Müller had argued for holding in place, for having the Hungarians come to them. Von Kluge had called him an old woman. Had taken the word of honor of three aristocratic Magyar officers who said security measures weren't needed. Had gone off with only an aide de camp...and promptly been taken prisoner.

Müller had instead received a large delegation from the Arrow Cross Party, a set of extreme rightists out of favor with both the Horthy regime and the local Nazis. These Magyars warned of treachery and said they were the only Hungarians Müller could rely on. Instinct made him agree and they had brought in a few thousand armed militants...just in time for the Horthyites to demand his surrender. He had gotten off a radio message to

Berlin before an artillery barrage had taken out the radio. Now he was hunkered in the ruins of three buildings awaiting rescue. He wished he had a way to contact Moscow, but that would have to wait until things settled down and his new handler made contact.

1350 hours
28 June 1940
Airspace over Budapest

Air Force General Alfred Keller was too senior to be leading a mixed force of bombers and second-line Me 110 fighters, but this entire operation was a kludge of the first order. Hungary surrenders, then reverses itself, then wants to negotiate. His orders were to support Müller. Müller, when last heard from, was at the airport. There seemed to be some sort of combat there, but it didn't look like much. However, unless the SS General found a radio, there was little to be done. Therefore, Keller and his planes were doing slow circles over the center of Budapest waiting for someone to make up their minds what to do next. The last message from Berlin was confusing. The two Army generals reported fighting at the rail junctions to Austria and Slovakia and advised caution. Göring wanted him to level Budapest. Keller was not quite sure who was actually in command of Germany at the moment. He was also not sure if Göring having a temper tantrum was the equivalent of a proper order.

Then matters clarified. There had been a few Hungarian fighters up. They maintained distance and were clearly observing. Keller instructed his people to do the same. However, there were occasional German transport flights through the mess, shuttling people back and forth to Romania. One of the Hungarian pilots took exception to this. Fired warning shots at a transport on the return leg. The transport pilot was pleading over the air that he was carrying civilian refugees—German women and kids. The Hungarian's next warning shot clipped the Tante Ju's tail and down it went.

Before Keller could do anything, his fighter pilots had gone into action. They blew half a dozen of the obsolete Hungarian biplanes out of the sky before the rest fled. Keller felt his decision was made for him. He radioed his bombers to follow him and began his bombing run on Castle Hill. Heading home, he told his fighters to strafe every road. If Hungary wanted war, Germany would give it to them.

Chapter 10

1620 hours
28 June 1940
Ploiesti airport, Romania

Lieutenant by the grace of whimsy, Klaus Steiner still had trouble thinking of himself as an officer. He was 18, barely. His voice kept breaking. He'd been an unknown rear rank HJ a week ago and a newly minted corporal two days ago. His rank insignia was borrowed from a former White Russian officer and he had no idea what rank it supposedly showed. He was commanding by now eighty-odd people older than himself, several with war medals and officer tabs to prove they knew things he didn't.

He had a single garbled phone call from his lieutenant-turned-captain who somehow was now a lieutenant colonel. Berlin wanted him to recruit anyone he could find. It was sounding more and more like his bus ride to Berlin. The big guys in the big offices gave vague orders and people like he and Strauss just made it up as they went along. Yet now his quite-delayed lunch was being interrupted by what sounded like a riot up by the airport gate.

Klaus had no idea how officers did things, so he just ran shouting orders to everyone he saw to follow him. He was still amazed that they obeyed. When he reached the gate, he found a mob of over a hundred Romanians surrounding two horse carts with refugees. An old grandfather type was on the ground being stomped to death. Three girls were screaming as men tore their clothes off. A middle-aged man had a noose around his neck and the mob was punching him, jeering, trying to find a tree to hang him from.

Four of his had their rifles leveled, but were hesitating. Klaus decided that officers make decisions and acted on them. He ran up to his four and shouted, "One volley over their heads. Then aim at the crowd. You fire on my command. Aim! Fire!"

It worked. He had the crowd's TOTAL attention. He motioned for one of his guys who spoke the language to go with him and walked into the crowd with his pistol drawn. He'd never fired it, but he had fired a pistol on a range. How different could it be? "Who is in charge here? Stand forward and report before I shoot you all!" Klaus hoped that sounded like what a proper officer would say.

Three Romanians in weird uniforms came bustling up. His translator said these were Iron Guardists. They were protesting. These were Magyars, the common enemy of Germany and Romania. If the German officer wanted first crack at the girls, sure. Anything his excellency wanted.

Klaus had never been called "his excellency" before. Indeed, he had never had an adult show him deference of ANY sort before. It was intoxicating. Drawing himself up to his full height of 1.6 meters, he barked at them the way a teacher would have barked at Klaus a week ago. "They are enemies in Hungary. Here, they are recruits for the NL. I have personal orders from Reichsführer-SS Heydrich. The Jews, the Magyars, the Germans, the White Russians are to be brought here. They have been conscripted for German service. See to it at once!"

By now a proper Romanian officer had arrived. He actually spoke German, which obviated the need for the translator. He also took one look at Klaus and laughed. "Little boy, who made you an officer? Your mother? Those tabs are from a Ukrainian nationalist major. That army died before you were born." Putting the full weight of adult scorn into his voice. "Run along and let real men handle business. Have your balls even dropped yet? You have direct orders from Berlin? Not likely, child." He laughed again sarcastically.

Klaus could have argued. Klaus could have explained that actually they were his superior's orders, a relay from the Reichsführer. Klaus was tired and hungry. He thought of an easier way to handle the problem, a more adult way. He raised his pistol, watched the Romanian's eyes get huge, and blew a hole in his head. He was aiming between the eyes, but the man turned and partially ducked, so instead he just blew the top of his skull off. The body collapsed, kicking. Klaus took his time with the second shot. That one killed the man. He could smell the bowels and bladder void. He pulled the man's tunic off before it could get fouled.

He had his translator repeat his orders in proper Romanian. Told the assembled Romanians that they had just volunteered to join Rommel at the front and fight the Soviets. He detailed a former Austrian captain and three men to march this mob back to town, commandeer buses and drive to the sound of the guns. Klaus remembered that line from a historical movie. The captain knew the Romanian language, and enough of his new command knew the words in the original German that a ragged column of twos was formed. Shepherded by the captain and three armed German guards, the column left behind the stiffening body and moved briskly down the road back toward town.

He had his remaining men throw the body off the road into the surrounding field. He found jackets of some sort for the three half-naked girls. They were kissing his hand babbling thanks. One was thanking him in German. He hadn't a clue to what the other two were speaking, but the meaning was obvious.

He pulled the German speaker to her feet. She got a frightened look, expecting him to claim the traditional reward. Instead he surprised her. He didn't look down the remains of her blouse. He looked directly at her, making eye contact, and asked if she knew how to sew. She was shocked but nodded yes. He tossed her the Romanian tunic and then his own. Told her to pull off the Romanian rank tabs and put them on his tunic. He hadn't a clue as to what rank he had given himself, but at least it was from a current army. Decided he would keep the Ukrainian tabs as a souvenir. The girl was confused and somewhat in shock. Her mother came running up and took charge of her. The mother also spoke German. He asked what the Romanian rank tabs were. When told first lieutenant, Klaus laughed. Close enough for now. He got his new recruits back into his airport. He found the concept that he had an airport almost as funny as being an officer. He supposed at some point he would have to think about the fact that he'd just killed a man, but wasn't war about killing? Right now, he was mostly focused on getting back to his by now-cold lunch.

2100 hours
28 June 1940
Airport [or remains thereof], Budapest, Hungary

Gestapo Müller now had a radio. It had been airdropped less than an hour ago. It hadn't much range, but he was in contact with planes overhead who could relay messages. He also had a shaky ceasefire around the airport. Two Hungarian officers had advanced under a white flag with a German diplomat. They had wanted to arrange a truce for the entire country or, failing that, the entire city. Müller had pleaded lack of communications. They had offered a telephone connection to Berlin, but he had refused it as it was not secure from Hungarian eavesdropping. He felt he could defend this answer in Berlin and that Moscow would be pleased at the chaos he was causing. As is, fires were raging out of control on Castle Hill and in scattered other areas around the city.

He had accepted a truce for the airport and two kilometers in a circle from the remains of the control tower. It was now nearly wall-to-wall with refugees from the city, including most of the non-diplomatic foreigners. Only two embassies had come to the airport. The rest had fled—to the countryside, to Belgrade, to Bratislava...it varied and frankly didn't interest Müller very much. The Italian and Vatican ambassadors were essentially taking charge of the mess, which was fine by Müller. One less headache.

So far, the Luftwaffe had honored the zone, but to be sure the Italians had arranged for fire barrels to be lit in a circle clearly marking it for when darkness fully fell. Everyone was hungry and ashes were raining down from the city fires, but one night of fasting wasn't likely to kill anyone. He was hoping by tomorrow Moscow would arrange a new handler and he could get proper instructions. He was not used to being an active asset instead of an intelligence source.

2348 hours
28 June 1940
Foreign Ministry, Rome

The nightshift officer normally looked at his position as a dead-end sinecure. Even in the modern world of 1940, with radio, teletype, telegram, phone, and such, the ministry tended to keep a five-day week with gentleman's hours. So, the wartime staffing of the nights, weekends, and such was mostly quiet time. One read, chatted, or dealt with a bit of routine correspondence. He had been dealing with a silly case of an Italo-American whose passport had been seized by his father. The boy was in Naples and thus, in father's eyes, should do his military service. The boy was in his twenties, a legal adult, and saw matters differently. So did the US embassy, which—while not yet issuing a new passport—was claiming him provisionally as a citizen. It was the sort of bureaucratic mess that normally occupied this shift. Much paper was generated, little was actually decided, and even less of it truly mattered in the larger picture.

Except he now had the ambassador to Hungary on an open phone line through Yugoslavia needing to talk to the Foreign Minister, Count Ciano. Something about Hungary needing Italian mediation for a war they had blundered into with Germany. Which left a major decision to be made. Does one wake such an exalted figure as the Count at this absurd hour? Either choice could be career death.

0310 hours
29 June 1940
7 kilometers into Hungary along the rail line from Vienna

General Guderian had been in command here since late last night. Command? He laughed to himself. More like herding cats. He'd been flown back from France yesterday and given this assignment by phone from OKH. Generals Halder and Beck had been on the line, thus it was clearly a valid order. The problem was, command of what? He'd been promised a panzer division formed out of the various school troops from the mobile forces. However, the two generals were quite vague on when these units would arrive and in what condition. He was told he would get his own staff from his panzer group, but again no exact answer as to when, much less whether it would include the communications battalion that went with it. Guderian had originally been a signals officer and knew the value of that branch.

But what did he command? A frontier guard company. Two self-mobilized battalions of Austrian SA. Two platoons of traffic police from Vienna. Random companies of this new NL Militia. Some Oberführer Schellenberg from Heydrich's office had kept finding bits and pieces. Had found him a few staff officers stolen from the SS and Luftwaffe who had actually had proper Reichswehr staff training. Some AAA batteries had presented themselves. All OKH had managed to find was a temporary company of random men in transit who had been in the main Vienna rail station, with orders taking them from various random places to other equally random ones. The officer in command was from the supply services and normally ran a school for military cooks. Guderian hadn't seen chaos like this since the Iron Division. His bits and pieces fought well enough when he could manhandle them into position, but lacked both heavy weapons and any ability to maneuver.

The Reich Without Hitler: The Falcons of Malta

Luckily, the Hungarians were both poorly equipped and abysmally led. They were a mix of frontier guards and self-mobilized volunteers. They had made one tentative push at the frontier guard company. When repulsed, they had let themselves get slowly forced back by quite small threats to their flank. This was less warfare than some lurching dance. The big problem was that they were sabotaging the rail line as they retreated. This would limit Guderian's advance as the trains were his only source of supply, and even that was dependent on this Schellenberg. OKH was doing everything by the book, which would take days to get in place. Just then, he heard vehicle sounds. He sent a junior to investigate and was told his first mobile troops had arrived. Three truckloads of troops, each from a different base. Each told the same story of chaos moving out and vehicles being left on the sides of successive roads from technical problems. This was looking as bad as the motor march into Vienna in 1938.

0350 hours
29 June 1940
Ploiesti oil fields, Romania

Lieutenant Colonel Strauss had finally taken a short nap just after midnight. He knew he needed more sleep, but the story of what his kid Lieutenant Steiner had done was bothering him. The boy had definitely handled the situation, yet it was clear he needed at least a bit of adult supervision. Better to drive over and have breakfast with him. Hold his hand, pat him on the back, and make clear what was to be done. He had found a decent touring car and the road wasn't bad.

0700 hours
29 June 1940
Ploiesti airfield, Romania

Greta Levi was a most frightened young lady. It was never easy being a Jew in Romania. However, the last few days had been terrifying. First, the Soviets invade. Naturally, the local Romanians blame everything on the Jews. All Jews were Bolsheviks as far as the Romanians were concerned, and thus responsible for anything the Soviets did.

Greta had been visiting her mother's sister's family near the oil fields. The summer trip was in lieu of a more expensive present to celebrate her 18th birthday. Her uncle-by-marriage did something with the metal for the pipes on the refinery or something like that. Whatever. He had to live there. He'd been an officer with the Hungarians in the Great War, which was another reason for the Romanians to hate him. Hence, the Soviets invade, the Nazis land at the airport, and her uncle loads the family into a truck his business had and drives everyone out to the airport to join the Nazis. Jews running to Nazis for protection. Her uncle says they will need whatever he and his firm do to keep the oil running. As if Nazis care about such things.

Yet, so far, it hadn't been too bad. Her uncle had been taken on to do his work. She and her aunt had been assigned to the food tent. These military types in their different uniforms or arm bands all made her nervous. Then there was that horrid incident at the gate yesterday. Three girls almost gang-raped. That could have been her. She was completely at the mercy of men with guns who all hated Jews.

The only one with a kind word to say about Jews had been this Lieutenant Steiner. He said Lieutenant, but she saw captains and majors take his orders. It was confusing but maybe he was superior because he was a real German. Greta knew only a small bit of German and what she knew was the local German dialect, not "real German". He mostly pointed to what he wanted. He smiled when he did, which made Greta feel a little safer, a little more welcome in this strange new world.

Only now, here was Steiner walking into the cook tent with this superior officer the size of a troll from a children's story. A troll in a fully Nazi uniform. A troll who would hurt her, rape her, kill her...Greta was melting down...she started shaking her head as her little German fled out her ears. She would not understand what he wanted and she would die and she started crying as he spoke, saying in Yiddish. "Please don't hurt me. I've forgotten my German. Please don't...."

And the ogre's hand reached out for hers, caught it, and asked, "Girl, what is the matter?"

Greta was in shock. He had asked in Yiddish. In Yiddish. Strange pronunciation, but Yiddish. There were no Jewish Nazis but he spoke Yiddish.

He also knew how to read faces. "No, girl, I'm quite Aryan. Half a dozen years in New York. I know street Yiddish. Same for Italian,

Polish, and Norwegian. Know a few dozen words in maybe ten more tongues. That city's the tower of Babel. Think of little ethnic villages three or four streets long plopped end to end from here to Bucharest."

Greta had stopped sobbing. The ogre seemed almost pleasant for all his huge size, massive muscles, and terrifying uniform. It turned out that the evil he wished was breakfast for two. Meat, potatoes, bread, eggs, and coffee. He and the Lieutenant would be in the main building so, when it was ready, walk it over and find a helper if it was more than she could carry. He had then assigned the lieutenant a task. He was to teach her five German words a day and she was to teach him the same five words in Yiddish. Something about how some big-shot Nazi wanted them recruiting Jews, so it was best the lieutenant learn the language.

0750 hours
29 June 1940
Bessarabia, formerly Romanian and transitioning back to Soviet control

Erwin Rommel was in his element. His rump battalion was, by now, a short division. He had his Germans, Iron Guards, Romanian regulars, Romanian volunteers, White Russians, Bulgars, Tatars, Magyars, local Germans, even a short company of some Zionist youth group called Betar. The Soviets had proven to be slow, chaotic, and shambolic. They seemed incapable of doing anything except pushing down roads until they met resistance and then attacking. The only competent ones had been some mobile units from the NKVD. So, what happened was a series of skirmishes, as Rommel kept extracting as many refugees as he could from the Soviet advance. OKH was supposed to have sent a real general to command the Romanian front, but it seemed this was being held up by the mess in Hungary. Right now, he was letting an NKVD battalion advance a few hundred meters deeper into the trap he had set. He was using the Iron Guards as bait. They were undisciplined, but fanatics. Thankfully, Lieutenant Steiner had sent him another company of them. Still better, he had sent four decent cadres who were some sort of part-Germans. He left the new company as the bait and shifted the cadres to running the Zionists. Crazy people, those Yids. Used girls as fighters right along with the boys. Jews always had strange ideas.

Enough of daydreaming... the NKVD were off their trucks and committed. Time to hit them in the flank and rear. Time to finish them off. The Zionists were slamming into the Russian rear right on schedule. He wondered where he could recruit more of them. They actually obeyed orders and knew how to read a watch.

0900 hours Moscow Time
29 June 1940
Kremlin, Moscow

Normally, getting the Boss up early was NOT a good idea, but Beria had a report that simply wouldn't keep. The actress had reported in. Not only had she gotten into Frau Göring's confidences, which was amazing in such a short time span, but the husband was using both women as his advisers on major state policy. Turned out the man didn't trust his colleagues. That he needed constant advice on how to maintain his position, which was mostly accidental—the generals' revolt had needed a Nazi figurehead. This Heydrich turned almost being liquidated into a position on their Politburo. Now Göring was worried that this deputy would eat him alive, but also believed that without the deputy the generals would do the same. The actress didn't have documents, but had a good memory for dialog; claimed it's necessary for her art. Hence, the handler spent three hours getting a complete rundown on every plan and decision made since the coup. That document was coming out by courier, but would need a few days to reach Moscow. The key points arrived by coded telegram.

The Germans won't fight for the three Baltic States or the three Romanian provinces but will fight if pushed further. Will try to trade for Finland. The offer of a conference in Poland is sincere. The skirmishes with this General Rommel in Romania are just an attempt to get people out. People. Not to retain the land.

Further, the Soviet advance in the south has been a disaster. Rommel has reported that other than the NKVD units, the advance had broken down without even making much contact. His boys were fighting hard. He had German backup to his ministry's reports on the disaster. The Kiev and Odessa Military Districts had failed at staff work, supply, command, control, and common sense. The army was nothing but bunglers.

The last part would be the trickiest. The actress had a request.

The Reich Without Hitler: The Falcons of Malta

Wanted her brother sent to Berlin. Said she had talked Göring into using him as a personal assistant on Soviet matters. A personal assistant had access to documents. Having the brother in the Soviet Union was a guarantee of the sister's continuing loyalty. If the two defected, it could be Beria's head as their advocate. And yet...and yet the gains from having an agent at Göring's side was huge.

> 1130 hours
> 29 June 1940
> Air Ministry, Berlin

Logically, the meeting should have been at the Chancellery. For whatever reason, Göring had insisted on his old suite of offices here. The agenda was the Hungarian mess. The Italians had contacted Berlin. Hungarians were trying to use them to broker a truce. The Italians were willing, if and ONLY if Berlin deemed this useful. They were claiming close former relations with the Horthy regime that might make this possible. It was an assertion of Italian competence and power after a German fuckup of epic proportions.

Right now, the German "government" was proving why you don't create committees with even numbers of members. Göring wanted to just keep bombing Budapest flat. The two army generals mostly wanted the problem to go away. They were keen to take the Italian offer as long as a few token Hungarians were surrendered to them—vengeance for the death of their fellow general, Günther von Kluge and his aide.

Heydrich was refusing to cast a vote. Said whatever he did, he would be seen a week from now as "playing Stalin"—playing the factions of leadership off against each other to advance himself. Kept saying that the important things were getting control of Hungary's oil, transport links, and communications. He kept stressing Romania and the twin bluffs Rommel and his man Strauss were running down there. No one else knew who Strauss was, but all somewhat accepted that the SS had taken over the oil fields. For the good of Germany, of course.

Göring finally agreed to letting Heydrich make whatever deal he could with the Italians. The two generals were content to let Göring think he'd "won" the debate because he would keep bombing until a deal was concluded.

1300 hours
29 June 1940
Villa Savoia (aka Villa Ada - Savoia), Rome, Italy

Count Ciano was just finishing his presentation to the King and Il Duce. Heydrich had said yes, but attached terms and conditions. If the Hungarians agreed, he wanted an Italian division shipped straight to Budapest by rail via Yugoslavia. Claimed he would get Yugoslav agreement. Hinted this would be by threatening to switch the bombers from Budapest to Belgrade. He also wanted an Italian general along to take command of the Hungarian army. He needed a dozen Hungarian officers to hang for the treachery to von Kluge. These had to be Magyars of good birth. No pawning off Jewish or Slovak reservists. Horthy and his circle would be exiled to Sardinia or Sicily or someplace out of the way. He would let Italy choose the new government from those circles with Italian connections. However, he was reserving the ministries controlling posts and telegraph, railroads, natural resources, roads, the Danube, and the police for some White Guard faction, Arrow Cross, that had rallied to the Germans in the airport fighting. All Arrow Cross members and all local Germans were to be released from custody to this SS Police General Müller at the airport as a sign of good faith. Finally, he couldn't call off the air strikes until there was a firm deal and at least some armed Italians in Budapest, so time was of the essence. Ciano advised proceeding, but awaited the decision. It took an hour of discussion to arrive at yes.

Chapter 11

1030 hours
30 June 1940
HQ Sicherheitsdienst in Prinz-Albrecht-Palais, Berlin

Workmen were scattered throughout the building to repair the damaged caused by putting down the "coup" and rooting out Himmler. Repair work had progressed enough that Reinhard Heydrich, head of the SS and Deputy Leader of the Party, could return to his old office. Heydrich thought about taking over his old boss's office, but decided keep his own. One of the first things on the agenda for today was a meeting with Julius Dorpmüller, the transport minister and General Manager of the Deutsche Reichsbahn (German Railroad). Professor Dorpmüller had kept both of his posts after the Second Blood Purge for the simple reason he was highly competent. He had been a railroad engineer since 1898. The good doctor had requested the meeting to discuss the latest crises caused by the flood of Balt refugees and the need to move them.

At the appointed hour, Prof. Dorpmüller and Richard Wagner, the chief engineer of the Reichsbahn, were escorted into Heydrich's office. Heydrich stood up from his desk as the pair was brought in and he pointed to chairs in front of his desk. "Gentlemen, welcome. Now what is so important that the head of national railway company and its chief engineer need to talk to me?"

"Reichsführer-SS, it is simple. The railroads are being taxed too hard by all the demands made on them. At the same time, we are attempting to return home forty divisions for demobilization. Now the army is having us move a large force to the Hungarian border." Prof. Dorpmüller wasn't a man given to histrionics, or to tolerate it among his subordinates; still, he really wanted to scream right now. "We will get these required tasks done...."

"I detect a BUT about to be inserted, Professor Dorpmüller." Heydrich interjected.

Dorpmüller nodded as he continued, "BUT, for how long I cannot guarantee. We are meeting these demands by delaying scheduled maintenance to keep engines in operation, having the crews stand eighteen- and twenty-four-hour shifts. This has costs in the short and long term. Men and machines get worn down, Reichsführer-SS. I have figures…."

Before Dorpmüller could reach for his attaché case to pull out the binder, Heydrich waved him off. "Professor, I do not presume to instruct experts in their art, and your figures no doubt prove exactly what you say they do. Now, what is the simple version of the story they tell?"

"You were a teen during the Great War I believe, Reichsführer-SS, so you were no doubt aware of the hardship and economic problems in general terms."

Heydrich nodded, "No one escaped the economic problems."

"One of those problems that occurred was during the winter of 1917, when the rail net simply collapsed from overwork and three years' worth of delayed repairs. Think of it as the bills coming due for the prior emergency overuse."

Searching through his memories for a moment brought understanding, "Ah, I recall there was a coal shortage that winter."

"Exactly. Shortages of everything that winter, as supplies could not be delivered because men and machines broke down from overuse and not enough replacements."

Heydrich could see where the man was going with this. "Very well, how do we deal with the issue, and no, we cannot scale back requirements. If anything, demands are going to increase over time, not decrease."

Dorpmüller managed not to sigh at the second part of the response he received. "We need more men, more engines, more…."

"I get the idea, Professor. More resources can be provided, but I suspect not to the degree you are looking for. So, let us dispense with the haggling. What can be done to alleviate this lack of resources? What short cuts can be taken?"

At last, Dorpmüller gave a motion to Wagner to join the conversation. "Reichsführer-SS, you said before that demands would no doubt increase over time. Could you give us some idea as to the time scale we are discussing? I had hope that peace would soon return."

For several moments Heydrich paused to consider what he would say and then made a snap decision. "What I am about to say are state secrets and if you even think of them outside of this room, you and your families will come to very painful ends. It is possible that we maybe at war with the Soviets in the future and the war with the British will not end any time soon. As long as the fighting is just with the British, the fighting will not be in Europe and, therefore, you will not have to move millions of men about once you are done with this redeployment. If the Soviets attack...I assume you can fill in the rest."

The two railway men looked at one another.

Wagner frowned, "I take it we shouldn't hope for any war with the Soviets to be over as quickly as the fighting with the Poles and French proved."

"Assume for creating your plans, three to five years."

The engineer was lost in thought for a bit and only a cough from Heydrich got his attention. "Sorry...In that case, the ideas we are considering will not be adequate. You are talking another Great War, then. That could break the nation. In which case, normal considerations of things like short-term cost and longevity of locomotives and rolling stock simply do not matter. From our experience in the Great War, and the merger of various state railways into the Reichsbahn in 1920, we started producing a set of standardized steam engines from 1925 on. We could attempt to streamline production by trying to simplify the designs to make them easier to produce and use fewer raw key materials— like copper, which will no doubt become unavailable. Remove any parts or finishing not absolutely essential for operation. This will play hell with fuel efficiency and part life, but such would be acceptable in a national emergency to produce these Kriegslokomotive."

"War locomotives." A thought occurred to Heydrich, "Explain more about the standardized locomotive engines?"

Wagner, being an engineer and—like most of the breed—more than happy to discuss nuts and bolt details, started a detailed and highly technical review of the advantages of the standardized locomotives. Dorpmüller could see that Wagner was in danger of falling down a rabbit hole and jumped back in to give a simpler version, "Reduced numbers of designs and, between designs, have interchangeable parts where possible. This speeds production and maintenance along with reduced costs."

Heydrich made some notes at this point. "What else, gentlemen?"

Before the Great War, Dorpmüller had traveled through Russia a great deal and so had some idea as to their standards of operation. "The army has ignored railroad construction and repair units. They have been getting by for the moment because of the short campaigns, borrowing from us and our looting of railroads in the occupied territories. Also, from the army's point of view, everything east of Brest is a different rail gauge, so we have to change trains or rebuild the railroads. That's not going to work and the army will need more construction and repair units. Even if we don't rebuild the lines, they are going to need a great deal of work. Russian quality is low."

Hearing the part about looting occupied territories received another note and, of course, one for the construction units. "I would say we have a plan then, gentlemen. Work on your simplified locomotive engine designs and send me your requirements and I will have them addressed. You mentioned looting of the occupied territories; have a report on that prepared for me. One last thing: who suggested that you talk to me?"

The head of the Reichsbahn looked up in surprise, "I thought you knew. General Georg Thomas sent us to see you."

"The head of the Army's Economic and Armament Office?"

"That is the one."

Heydrich stood, signaling an end to the meeting. Once the two railroad men left his office, Heydrich looked down at his notes.

STANDARDIZED DESIGNS
WAR AUSTERITY DESIGNS
INTEGRATION OCCUPIED TERRITORIES
LOGISTICAL PROBLEMS WITH FIGHTING SOVIETS

Then, picking up his phone, Heydrich spoke to his chief aide, "Set up a meeting with General Georg Thomas of the General Staff at once."

0700 hours
30 June 1940
Military Headquarters complexes of OKH and OKW, at Zossen, 20 miles south of Berlin

Two Mercedes sedans pulled up to the gates of the military complex. The gate guards did a double take on seeing the black uniforms with silver trim within, but of course waved them through since they had the correct passes. Then, as soon as the cars went in, the lieutenant on duty called his superior officer.

The Reich Without Hitler: The Falcons of Malta

There was no love lost between the Heer and the SS, and with Heydrich himself here, the top men would want to know.

The complex was large, with multiple other internal checkpoints. Heydrich could tell that their passage was being delayed. No doubt his visit had ruffled some feathers. This amused Heydrich to no end. Then, when they reached their destination, the most ruffled rooster was waiting there. Generaloberst Ludwig Beck.

As Heydrich and his personal security detail exited the cars, they were met by a red-faced Beck and an entire platoon of guard troops. "What are you doing here, Heydrich?" The general sputtered at the head of the SS. He did not regard unannounced visits as permissible.

Seeing the man unbalanced so told Heydrich that he had the edge. Angry people were stupid people and made mistakes. Never let your passions control you. It is no wonder that a quack doctor managed to kill Hitler by accident versus all of the years of Beck's petty schemes that had nothing to show for it. Well, not exactly nothing. Beck was back in government and one of the four heads that ran Germany now. In a voice of sweet reason, Heydrich answered, "I have a meeting scheduled with General Georg Thomas."

This caught Beck off guard. His eyes narrowed and for the first time he started to think. It was just Heydrich, his aide, six overt bodyguards, and the drivers. While the six bodyguards glared back at the Army troops like the good little Dobermans they were, they weren't a threat. Grasping for answers, Beck barked at Heydrich, "What business do you have with the head of the Economic and Armament Office for the Army?"

Heydrich couldn't help but smirk. The idiot Beck was half a step behind and wasn't considering the long-term implications of Germany's situation. The war wasn't over and the Soviets were a growing threat. "I told you before that you, Halder, and Göring need me. To handle the endless details that our new Führer simply can't be bothered with between his rounds of diplomatic parties and glad-handing of the economic and social elites. The war isn't over, my dear Generaloberst."

"Which I warned you about back at the beginning, before you declined to directly attack England."

Typical, oh, so typical, all focused on the short term, Heydrich thought. "Could you have guaranteed a success as cheap as

France? A success at all? We really cannot get at their island. Now, of course, they lack the strength to reinvade the nations we conquered in Western Europe. Protracted stalemate. However, the British can hope for the Americans to enter the war...or Stalin. The Americans are rearming like mad and have immense industrial capacities. We have already had clashes with Stalin in Romania. Rommel's playing his bluff brilliantly, but it's still a state of possible war. The British played this game once before versus another power that wished to control Europe, Napoleon Bonaparte. At one point his empire was the same size as our own but, in the end, he spent his last days rotting on a rocky island in the south Atlantic as a permanent guest of the British. Also, Churchill is a romantic and he won't be swayed by pure economics or correlation of military force. We are going to have to push the British past the breaking point while preparing in case our "friend" Stalin tries something. Hence my meeting with General Thomas. The economy needs to put on a proper footing to continue the war." Heydrich smiled, "You are, of course, welcome to join us, Generaloberst, as we talk about weapons production and the economy."

Beck glared daggers at Heydrich, "Remember your place, Heydrich," He hissed, deliberately not using his title as a petty insult. "No movement of Army troops! All such orders go through us, AND...."

At last tired of the game, Heydrich interrupted, "AND keep you and General Halder informed what is decided, my dear Generaloberst."

In a huff, Beck stormed off and Heydrich went on to his meeting with Thomas.

"I received your invitation, General." Heydrich said to the Army staff officer.

Thomas put up a confused look, but it was a front. Heydrich was used to dealing with better liars. "I don't know what you mean, Reichsführer-SS...."

"Of course, your sending of Minister Dorpmüller had nothing to do with getting my attention. It was subtle, to avoid attracting attention of your superiors, to make it look like I reached out to you, rather than the other way. So, we can dispense with the game. Your smokescreen functioned perfectly. Beck and Halder think I came to see you."

The Reich Without Hitler: The Falcons of Malta

The army general made a motion. These were uncertain times and caution was necessary in the Third Reich, especially for army generals. "There are things that need to be done, Reichsführer-SS...."

"I quite agree. The little chat I had with Minister Dorpmüller was most illuminative and steps are going to be taken to deal with the railway congestion caused by our various movements in the East, moving refugees from the Baltic states and troops into Hungary and Romania, and so on. What else needs to be done?"

Thomas pointed at the various charts and calendars hanging on his office walls. "War Production is a mess...."

"One of the few weaknesses of our late Führer. He loved to meddle in the details, but was too prone to listening to the last man to talk to him. Hence conflicting and contradictory priorities. One of the reasons that Reichsminister Todt was made Minister for Armaments and Ammunition."

There was a slight movement on the face of Thomas at hearing Todt's name. It was as Heydrich suspected. General Thomas was hoping to replace Todt as head of the war economy for Germany. His SS file made clear that he was greatly upset when first the four-year plan was created back in 1936 to try to get the German economy ready for war, and then when Todt was made Minister for Armaments and Ammunition once it was clear that Göring and his cronies weren't up to the task. Both times, Hitler had chosen Party associates rather than a technocrat like General Thomas to manage things. Of course, as was so typical in the Third Reich, Göring had kept his title, resulting in parallel authority and, as head of the Luftwaffe, he still had control over Air Force production. As did Admiral Raeder over Navy production before he was sacked by the new leadership. In essence, Todt had at best control over Army production and that was imperfect. Thomas here was looking to jump in.

"I am sorry to disappoint you, General, but you aren't going to be replacing Reichsminister Todt. Our new Führer still considers the Luftwaffe his private fiefdom and he isn't going to accept an army general running the economy. Of course, as Führer he won't have as much time for his personal toy, and no doubt Luftwaffe Chief of Staff Hans Jeschonnek is all the happier for it and can get down to the business of running the Luftwaffe on a day-to-day basis. Todt, as a civilian, has to stay."

Thomas frowned as he looked away.

Into the silence, Heydrich made some tsking noises, "I am disappointed, General. I thought you were concerned with getting things done rather than mere titles. In any organization, it is the people just below the top that make the actual decisions, the technical specialists." Then, pausing for effect, "Such as yourself."

"What do you mean?"

"We both agree that the economy is a mess, so it needs to get cleaned up. Also, we have a new empire to administer. All of Europe, whether we occupy it or not, must be brought into the fold, so to speak. Even if we bring the British to terms, they can always cut us off again in the future from world trade. No need for a blockade. The City of London is still key for much of the world economy and the majority of the world's shipping still flies the British Red Ensign. Hitler was right. We need to be able to stand without imports. With the current situation, that means all of Europe is our economy, not just the Reich itself." Heydrich looked at the General to be sure Thomas was with him. He received a nod to go on. "Todt and Speer are going to have a great deal of more work to do and they will need helpers, technical specialists. Vice Admiral Werner Fuchs, the head of the Navy construction office, General Ernst Udet as Director-General of Luftwaffe Equipment, and General der Infantry Georg Thomas, head of the army Economic and Armament Office."

"So, if I go along with this, I get promoted and will be one of three officers to help Todt reshape Europe's economy?"

"If you can show me that you can do it. Consider this a job interview."

Thomas was nothing if not adaptable, "Fine, first bit of advice is ditch Udet as one of the three. He was a fine fighter pilot, but he has no technical skills and is at best a mediocre administrator. The hash he has created of the Ju-88 bomber program alone should be enough to get him disqualified."

Heydrich made a note to look into the Ju-88. "No objections to Fuchs? Oh, and just to simplify matters, the Navy's priority on production now rates behind the railroads, industry, and food. What on earth do we need a battlefleet for?"

The snort from Thomas told Heydrich that Göring's little show where Raeder and the Navy were gelded was getting around.

"If not Udet, do you have a suggestion instead?"

Thomas answered at once, "That is easy. General der Flieger Wolfram von Richthofen. He has an engineering degree and was in the Luftwaffe technical branch before working with Udet drove him crazy and he demanded a field command to get away. I believe he commands Fliegerkorps VIII, currently. In case you want more information on the Ju-88 fiasco, ask Richthofen. It was his recommendations on it that Udet pissed all over and the result was the overweight cow the Luftwaffe got in the end."

Heydrich made sure his aide was taking careful notes. Pausing to raise an eyebrow at Thomas, Heydrich just looked at the man. The question was obvious.

"How does an Army officer know about these problems? I made it my business to know about them. As you said, I wanted Todt's job. Besides, the stories have been making the rounds. The idiot dive-bomber requirement added thousands of kilograms to the aircraft's weight and, therefore, costs."

Satisfied with the answer, Heydrich moved onto other things, "Now, Dr. Dorpmüller mentioned standardization about trains. What about with weapons? What about with the panzers?"

Thomas shook his head. Heydrich was an intelligent man and had been a military officer, naval lieutenant, before getting drummed out by Raeder, but he was a junior officer. Such people tended to think on weapons over logistics. "Not panzers, trucks. Yes, there are problems with panzer production, with too many types and no commonality of parts."

Heydrich had prepared himself and looked into the armor-production situation, "The Panzerkampfwagen II, III, IV, and the Czech 38(t) are being all produced right now...."

"One hundred and fifty."

"Excuse me?"

Pleased to have the upper hand for once, Thomas smiled. "The number of types of trucks we are building right now. One hundred and fifty. This doesn't count all of the trucks we seized in Poland and from the West. If you think it's bad for the number of tanks and the four you listed, don't count the sub-types like the StuG and the like. No. One hundred and fifty different types of trucks are a bigger problem, plus twenty types of infantry weapons, over two dozen artillery pieces not counting flak and antitank weapons. All of these need to be rationalized, but logistics is the key, especially if we end up fighting the Soviets. General Halder has ordered a study on that, I am sure you know."

Heydrich give a motion that said whatever spin Halder put on it he had something to do with it.

"The distances in the Soviet Union are vast and their transport infrastructure is primitive...."

"Dorpmüller warned me on the railway problems and the need for more railroad construction and repair units."

The two continued to talk for some time on the state of the German war economy. The need for rationalization and standardization of production. Integration of Europe's economy fully into German and, of course, the need for oil, oh, yes, oil to fuel it. Hence the movement of troops to Romania and the continued emphasis on the Synthetic Fuel Program.

When finished, Heydrich merely said, "You are hired and I want a full report on all of this and more."

Thomas had one last point to raise. "We are using depot maintenance between campaigns. This will be impossible in North Africa and more so in the depths of Russia. We need to start forming field repair depot units, including proper recovery vehicles. I'm going to have to raid the Navy and Luftwaffe a bit to get proper technical officers with the right mix of engineering and administrative backgrounds."

Heydrich thought about this one for a minute. "Won't work. I can get you the people. However, you control neither postings nor promotions in the Heer. Halder and Beck won't allow it and one cannot blame them. What I can do is the following. I'll get you the people on secondment from their existing services. If they want promotions, they will be transferred to the Waffen SS where I can control both promotion and posting. As long as you have command authority, do you care what uniform the people wear?"

Thomas outright laughed at this. Asked if he could use this back door on promotion for some of his own protégées. Each man regarded this as a most successful meeting.

0730 hours
1 July 1940
Heydrich's Office, SS HQ, Berlin

One of the least glamorous aspects of bureaucracy is how tedious much of it was. Having to grind out the day with meeting after meeting to cover the small, medium, and large details. Which is what made me so valuable to the New Order, Heydrich thought. Göring was far from a stupid man, but he lacked discipline and focus. Generaloberst Halder was an excellent staff officer, but specialized as a soldier. Which left the role for someone to grind through these meetings, make the connections, and then get things in motion.

Meeting two railroad executives led to a meeting with a staff officer, and that in turn led to this meeting with Albert Speer and his boss, Fritz Todt. Of course, Heydrich had known Todt for years. The man had joined the Party back in 1922 and had been the late Führer's pet engineer. Responsible for overseeing the construction of the Autobahn as Inspector General for German Roadways, in March 1940 he was made Reich Minister for Armaments and Munitions to attempt to bring some order to the chaos that was the German War Economy.

Despite his competence, Todt had been uneasy in the days since the Second Blood Purge. He had kept his titles and power, but many others had not, others who were now dead or in camps waiting to learn their fate. It still was amazing that Heydrich had not only survived the Second Blood Purge, but prospered. The rumors of how this elevation had occurred, combined with Heydrich's role as head of the SS and other security services, caused more than a little apprehension when the request for a meeting arrived to "discuss certain questions of the war economy."

When escorted into Heydrich's office at HQ of the Sicherheitsdienst, Todt couldn't help but notice the workmen patching the bullet holes in the walls or the one building section where artillery had been used to crush the last of Himmler's holdouts. The later wing of the building would take a bit of time to rebuild, the engineer in Todt thought. Those 105mm howitzer shells tend to make a mess of things. The aide announced the two, "Reich Minister Todt and SS-Standartenführer Speer."

Heydrich looked up from the various memos on his desk. Many things demanded his attention, so he opened with, "Gentlemen, thank you for coming, SIT."

Speer and Todt recognized a command voice and both did as they were bid. Todt was a combat veteran of the Great War, and was tired of this feeling of doom that was hanging over him. Despite Göring's assurance's, Todt was frankly waiting for the other shoe to drop, "If you are going to have us killed, please get it over with. I am sick of waiting for some of your goons to show up and put two bullets in the back of my head."

Hearing what Todt had cast into the face of Heydrich, Speer

did a double take at his boss, then felt a need to be very still in his seat to avoid getting Heydrich's attention.

At first, Heydrich blinked, and then laughed, "My dear Reich Minister, I don't have people shot that are useful. Enemies of the state, the inconvenient, and the incompetent, I have THOSE people shot. If you are worried about being shot, I suggest you strive to be useful. Besides, I like a brave man."

Speer held his breath waiting for what Todt would say. He didn't have long. The latter looked Heydrich over and then said, "Just trying to avoid an argument. So, if we aren't to be shot, then what are we doing here?"

"Attempting to be useful and keep the state running. Please read." The head of the SS handed over a copy of a memo to Speer and Todt.

While the two read, Heydrich hit the intercom. "Refreshments for myself and my guests."

A voice crackled from the speaker, "At once, Reichführer-SS."

A servant brought in a tray of snacks and a pot of tea. Heydrich helped himself while the two finished reading. At last, Todt spoke, "I see that you have been talking to General Thomas and Professor Dorpmüller. The lack of standardization, conflicting orders, and parallel projects is why the economy is such a mess. That and frankly more than a few people would rather weave a fantasy instead of giving an honest report."

At the last statement, Heydrich turned grim. "Names."

"Excuse me?"

"Names, Minister Todt, names. You said that you are aware of people giving false reports. Such is a crime against the state and, therefore, treason. Give me the names of the five worst offenders and by the end of the day, they will be custody; by the end of the week they will have very public trials, and the week after that they will be very, very DEAD. As I said before, I don't shoot those being useful, but those on that other list of traits? Yes, I will have those killed."

Todt looked over Heydrich, trying to decide if it was bluster or not, and then said, "Some of these are long-standing Party officials, some are associates of Hitler...."

"The late Führer was many things—a great man, among them, now a demigod to the masses—but he is also dead and he can't protect his cronies and the Reich can no longer afford their incompetence."

Without another word, Todt wrote five names on the back of the memo and handed it back to Heydrich. The latter looked over the names and circled one, "I recognize him as a toady of our new Führer. We will deal with him, but it will take a little more effort. Come up with another, please."

Todt replaced the removed name with another. Heydrich then copied the names onto some of his letterhead. Into the intercom again, "Send in Oberführer Schellenberg."

The three waited in silence, Todt watching the show put on by Heydrich and Speer just glad his name wasn't one of the five. Then Schellenberg came into the room and snapped a salute to Heydrich, "Heil Göring!"

Heydrich returned the salute and handed over the sheet with the names, "I want these five arrested, publicly. Charges are corruption and high treason. Conduct the usual interrogations. Also, arrest their families."

"I will see to it, Reichführer-SS."

Once the SS man had left, Heydrich raised an eyebrow at Todt.

"I didn't think you were serious," The other man returned.

"Obviously. Hence the need for this little show. Sweep out the dead wood, and if any of Göring's toadies from the Four Year Plan get in the way, let me know and I will see what can be done to sideline them. Now what can be done to improve the situation?"

Todt again laughed, "Oh, there is a great deal that we can do, it appears, to streamline production. There are 151 different types of trucks, 150 types of motorcycles, over two dozen types of artillery, a grab-bag of small arms, four different tank chassis being built...."

With it clear that Todt had a plan, Heydrich waved him off, "Good. You know what to do and I will not delay you further. Keep me informed and get it done. However, you two and Minister Dorpmüller have a little travel coming up. You are off to Milan in a few days. Schellenberg and some Army general will go with you. OKH hasn't picked one yet. Time to coordinate with our Italian friends. Figure that will take three days, then off to Zurich for a day and from where to Paris for two days and then a final day in Brussels. It's all one European economy now. Time to get everyone working on the same production plans. Except for the Italians, this will mostly be a meet-and-greet. Expect the other three nationalities to be unprepared to make commitments, so you arrange meetings in Berlin later this month. Just remember that as the main war is in the south now, Italy gets priority on what you decide they need to prosecute this war. National chauvinism that conflicts with this will merit summary execution of the guilty and their families. Make sure this is known, but nothing in writing." Heydrich was amused to see Speer blanch and confirmed in his good opinion of Todt to see that he was not fazed.

With that, Todt and Speer stood up, with Todt and Heydrich shaking hands. Leaving the room, the two were ambushed by Schellenberg who wanted a memorandum prepared. Todt looked blankly. Schellenberg was to the point, "Write out what you think was just decided. I will get it typed up and on the Reichsführer's desk. He may make amendments, but you'll have a signed copy in a day or two. Less room for misunderstanding that way. Human memory is fallible and selective. Paper isn't."

Todt and Speer were shocked, but delighted. Hitler had been phobic about bureaucracy. Too much business had been done verbally and what paper trail there was tended to be edited by Bormann for bureaucratic advantage. They were even more shocked two days later when the meeting memo arrived back to them with carbon copies for the other three leaders at the bottom. Germany was being run in a new way.

1900 hours
2 July 1940
Outskirts of Budapest, Hungary

Italian Corps General Federico Ferrari-Orsi was glad the ceremonial part of the transfer of authority was finally over. Under the supervision of the Italian ambassador and the Papal Nuncio, he had taken the surrender of Admiral Horthy, the Hungarian government, each of their armed services, and the city of Budapest in the person of the mayor. Each of the dignitaries had used the occasion for a speech justifying their actions over the prior week and reciting yet again every Hungarian complaint at the injustices of history and fate back to the initial Ottoman invasion half a millennium ago. The day was hot and the air still bore the smells of a bombed-out city: a mix of ash, rotting flesh, and industrial wastes.

It was now Ferrari-Orsi in command of the Hungarian armed forces. He had under five thousand Italians from his former command, the 1st Celere Division Savoia. They had been rushed onto trains without full unit complements, without heavy weapons, without their horses or vehicles. Indeed, what he had for transport was a random collection of Hungarian trucks and autos repainted in Italian colors. The rest of his division, its horses, and equipment were due within the week with two more Italian divisions to follow at a more moderate pace and as complete units under proper administrative procedures. The amazing part wasn't the chaos of the move, but the relative efficiency of handling such an absurd order. You simply do not order a division to march to the railroad station and board a train with no prior warning. There hadn't even been time to load provisions. Instead, the food concessions at the railroad station were pillaged for everything to be found and the Yugoslavs of all people had provided more at several brief stops while transiting their nation. What strings had been pulled to force neutral but quite unfriendly Yugoslavia to allow armed Italians to transit its rail net was a question Ferrari-Orsi would love to have answered for him.

His German military opposite number, General Guderian, had proven easy to deal with. The man had orders to guard very specific sites, mostly having to do with transportation and oil production. Beyond that, he left Ferrari-Orsi with half a dozen Italian-speaking Austrian field officers as liaisons. The basic bargain was leave the Germans alone and they would return the compliment.

The same could not be said for this SS General Müller and his insane Hungarian cohorts from Arrow Cross. Ferrari-Orsi was evacuating the senior Horthyites as per the truce agreements. Each train from Italy went back crammed with refugees. The problem was that Müller was letting his Hungarians run wild. They were trying to run a nationwide pogrom against the Jews and a witch hunt against their Horthyite enemies. They apparently had two decades of scores to settle on officials down to the level of local postmasters and village clerks. These twin actions were producing a cascade of new refugees seeking Italian protection. It was also provoking clashes with the Hungarian army and police who were nominally now under Ferrari-Orsi's command. Ferrari-Orsi had tried discussing this with Müller, but the German had insisted he only answered to Berlin. Hopefully Rome was actually reading his missives and would contact their opposite numbers in Berlin to resolve this.

Chapter 12

1100 hours
3 July 1940
Heydrich's office, Berlin

The newly promoted SS Sturmbannführer stood at rigid attention before Reichsführer-SS Heydrich's desk. As a protégé of Kaltenbrunner, he has been expecting career death under the new regime. Yet for some reason his expertise as a Jewish and Zionist expert was now suddenly needed. Heydrich wanted a report on what Betar was and whether the newly expanded Reich had any of them.

Eichmann knew that the Betar movement had been active in Poland, but hadn't a clue as to whether it had retained any organizational coherence after almost a year of German occupation. He was also at a loss as to what answer would please this new boss. Schellenberg was in attendance and saw Eichmann's predicament. "Sturmbannführer, the days of Himmler are past. Our new Reichsführer-SS wants facts, wants truth. No truthful answer is wrong. In reverse, ideological soundness won't save you if your facts are wrong."

Eichmann breathed a visible sigh of relief. He gave a brief factual report on Revisionist Zionism, its Betar youth movement, and the paramilitary training it gave. He expanded on this to mention that the Marxists, the Labor Zionists, had a larger youth movement. It had less paramilitary training but also access to greater resources if their American cousins were allowed to send money.

Heydrich cut him off before he could go further. Eichmann was now the head of the Zionist Youth Office. He was to organize these people and prepare them for shipment. Start with the Baltic Jewish refugee wave. Create a new camp around the Krakow airport near Nowa Huta. The location had been on the SS office list for locations to form ghettos. This was to be a resettlement camp. Call it Palestine #1 to show the American cousins of these Jews that, as good Zionists, they should pay for their relative's upkeep pending their return to their true homeland. The Marxists were to be used for labor, starting with building the new camp. When that was done, find something useful for them to do. A liaison from

The Reich Without Hitler: The Falcons of Malta

Deputy Administrator of the Four Year Plan and Standartenführer Speer would find some industrial firm who could use their labor until transport was available to ship them to Italy. Use the Betar as guards for the Marxists and continue their military training. They were to be conscripted into the NL and as requisitioned sent as replacements to Battlegroup Strauss in Libya. Members of Betar had performed well in Romania for General Rommel and Lieutenant Colonel Strauss, so they were to be sent more of them. Also, prepare housing at the camp for the families of the Betar conscripts who would at a later date be moved overseas to link up with their young folk. The youngsters were tagged to be German colonial troops in a new colony in conquered territory, starting with the Palestinian city of Haifa. Tell the Marxists they were going to Palestine, but under Italian rule.

Eichmann left the meeting elated as to his career, but ideologically confused. He had helped force Jews to emigrate from Austria and had negotiated with Zionists in the Middle East, but it had all been contradictory make-believe, like so much of Nazi ideology. Now he had clear orders. Who to find, what to do with them, who to report to. Eichmann decided if he could make this function properly he had a future organizing camps and workshops. He had come a long way from career death. Now that he had Heydrich's attention, he resolved to keep it. His Betar would be so well-trained that maybe there would be another promotion in it for him. What was confusing was the lack of any clear anti-Semitism. Why was the SS treating Jews as if they were human? Eichmann thought about it for a bit on the way home, but in the end decided that the answer was above his pay grade. The Jews would leave Europe and higher leadership wanted it done this way. A wise bureaucrat followed orders. Eichmann would follow his.

1100 hours
5 July 1940
Ploiesti airport, Romania

The twin ceasefires were holding in Romania and Hungary. General Rommel was back at the airport, having turned his rump division over to a new commander, a protégé of the new German viceroy in Romania, General von Reichnau. Rommel had kept most of his original jägers and been gifted back the Jews and others, such as Tatars, that the new man found inconvenient.

Now Rommel and his subordinate Strauss, who he had left as a captain but had somehow turned into a lieutenant colonel, were doing a handover of the oil fields to Heydrich's man, Standartenführer Otto Ohlendorf. Ohlendorf wanted the Germans, but not the other nationalities. The issue was what to do with them. Ohlendorf knew Heydrich had authorized the recruitments but found the situation awkward and distasteful. Strauss saw his new career imploding, but Rommel solved the problem. Told Strauss to just consider his force a battle group attached to his 7th Panzer Division.

So, Strauss was trying to do a head count. Rommel wanted the battle group split in two. He wanted the 'glider troops and parachutists' split off to join his jägers. Rommel has somehow talked this combined force into being part of an airborne attack on Malta. Strauss laughed to himself. Steiner was no more a glider pilot than he was King of Siam. However, lieutenant colonels don't say no to generals. He promoted the boy to first lieutenant and sent him around to find every HJ who claimed they had ever been up in the air.

The tricky part was organizing pay books for the women and older children. He had verbal permission for this from Schellenberg. Verbal was better than nothing. As is, his unit would look like something out of the 17th century, with a pack of camp followers.

The most "delicate" part was the Jews. He was doing those papers himself. Any name that looked Jewish he was just changing, starting with his favorite little cook. Greta Levi was now Greta Schwabe. He listed her as part of his personal headquarters. She was an abysmal cook, but a pleasant person. Besides, she seemed sweet on Steiner, and Strauss regarded the boy as his good luck charm.

1200 hours
5 July 1940
Ploiesti airport, Romania

Greta Schwabe/Levi had decided life was confusing. She'd been enlisted in the NL as a headquarters cook. Greta had no illusions as to her culinary skills, yet the two Nazi officers had rejected attempts by other more experienced ladies to take over cooking for the two excellencies. They sent for her when they needed food. They chatted with her in a friendly manner. Greta hadn't a clue as to why. She was a perky 18, but scarcely a beauty. Besides, she hadn't had a real change of clothes or bath since she had become a cook. Everything was rush, make do, and then collapse when one had a chance.

The truly absurd part was that her family and the other Jews had decided she was to be the mistress of this Lieutenant Steiner. He had her sit and do language lessons. They went for walks together while he checked on sentries and such. He was a pleasant young man, but had yet to even try to hold her hand, much less kiss her. Yet her aunt and uncle had been quite direct. Her virginity was not to be an obstacle. Give the man what he wanted and preserve his protection, lest he find a more willing partner. Greta was willing, but how did one rape a superior officer? He simply never made a move. She had flirted as hard as she knew how, but...nothing. He just seemed to like talking with her. Maybe on the train ride to Italy she would have better luck. Hopefully, if she got things started, he'd take it over, as she was less than certain she knew exactly what to do even after quite detailed instructions from her aunt.

Chapter 13

1750 hours
5 July 1940
Military airport, Oran, Algeria

General Jean Joseph Marie Gabriel de Lattre de Tassigny had seen the smoke from the still-burning harbor facilities when he had flown in yesterday. The treacherous British had attacked a French fleet at anchor on the flimsiest of excuses. France had been pushed into this war by the British, who had then run away at Dunkirk to hide on their wet little island. Now he was here in Algeria to plot France's revenge.

An open declaration of war would lose France her colonies. Therefore, France would use Gallic cunning and British obsession with legalisms. The Foreign Legion had a number of Germans. The French forces had a larger number of Alsatians, Lorainners, Burgundians, and such who had been Frenchmen two months ago, but were now from departments the Germans had separated from the occupied zone to treat as recovered German lands. The boundaries of this all were somewhat opaque, but this would now work for the benefit of France.

Assembled before him were a hundred officers who had volunteered to revenge themselves on the British. De Lattre began his main presentation after outlining these geographic facts. "You will surrender your livrets militaire. We will issue new ones based on new places of birth and residence. Nominally you are citizens of the Reich being returned to your proper Fatherland." He saw a few dubious faces. "Do not worry. A special department in the Marshal's private offices will keep track of who you really are. Service will still count for retirement. You will keep your ranks unless the Germans promote you, in which case it will be as if you attained the promotion in our French service, because whatever the legal fictions you will be serving France, even if in German uniform. Those of you with worries about how your families might feel are free to use names of convenience. I will be using 'François Kellermann' as he was an Alsatian. You will then go out and recruit more patriots. The idea is to form a motorized brigade. If the men ask what the unit will be called, tell them 'The sons of Oran', for we will avenge ourselves on Perfidous Albion. Who is ready to teach these English a lesson they will NEVER FORGET!" The answering roar was deafening.

Chapter 14

1900 hours
5 July 1940
SS HQ, Berlin

Oberführer Schellenberg made it part of his duties that all communications regarding this new NL Lieutenant Colonel Strauss and his unit clear his desk before other processing. This man Strauss had captured Heydrich's fancy. Anything that interested his boss was something Schellenberg wanted to be up-to-date on. So here, sitting on his desk, was a notice that Strauss had given a field promotion to First Lieutenant Klaus Steiner for exceptional service in defense of the airport against a Romanian mob of some kind. Reading between the lines, the young man had been left on his own while Rommel went off gallivanting and Strauss wisely focused his own attentions on securing the oil facilities, which were of far greater importance. The boy had avoided disaster and acquitted himself well in some skirmish.

Schellenberg paused to sip some of his coffee. He savored the taste and aroma. It was a first-class Turkish blend. At his rank, one could still find coffee in Berlin. Britain's blockade was never airtight on luxuries. The NL was Heydrich's idea. Here was a success story. If this Steiner had repulsed Soviet Partisans instead of some mob, there was a propaganda story here. Schellenberg rewrote it so Steiner killed the Red Commissar in single combat. He approved the promotion, adding an Iron Cross Second Class. He still knew people at the Propaganda Ministry. They could interview the boy's parents, obtain from the family a picture of him in his HJ uniform, and make it a big story for a day. He prepared an eyes-only memo he would hand to the Boss, showing how the situation had been "improved". Heydrich's star was rising and Schellenberg meant to rise with it.

2100 hours,
6 July 1940
Gare du Nord RR Station, Paris, France

Former Prime Minister Pierre Laval and Naval Minister and Admiral Jean Darlan headed the large group of dignitaries waiting for the incoming train. As French military were barred from Paris by the armistice terms, it was a police band and honor guard that awaited the first trainload of returning prisoners. It was only twelve-hundred men, but it was a start. Twelve hundred older prisoners, reservists with NCO or officer ranks, were being released by the Nazis as a token of appreciation for the use of the two Tunisian ports and other still-to-be-defined favors short of war. This new SS chief Heydrich had proven to be a sensible fellow. France wanted her men back. Heydrich was willing to return them in slow stages as France adjusted herself to its new role in German Europa. Both Laval and Darlan were prepared to accept that France had little choice in its future alignment. The British had run away to hide on their island. They had treacherously stolen French ships and attacked others. Certain conclusions followed. Best to make the most of what could be done. Realism was the key. General and former junior minister De Gaulle (leader of the so-called "Free French") was in London assuring France a place on the British side if things turned out otherwise.

0600 hours
7 July 1940
Railway siding somewhere in Hungary

As the train shuttled off onto yet another siding, First Lieutenant Klaus Steiner was pondering the workings of fate. His promotion was now official, endorsed by the Head of the SS and his chief deputy. He had also acquired a "glider company" as a command. It was some Jewish Militia called Betar that had fought with Rommel against the Bolsheviks. Their German cadre from that fight had stayed behind in Romania. He now commanded over a hundred men...and girls. The Militia took both sexes as fighters. Weird. Strauss had promised him more glider pilots before they went into action. HJ had others and they would be ordered to volunteer for NL. Others. That was a laugh. He'd been a hundred meters up in the air twice for a few seconds until the glider essentially landed itself. This was not what it took to land a nine-seat military model cut loose thousands of meters in the sky. Strauss was aware of this, but promised the manuals would catch up with him before they went into action.

Meanwhile, he had a bigger problem. Strauss had assigned him Greta as a translator/personal assistant. She spoke Romanian and Yiddish and was teaching him a bit of both. The problem was that Strauss had made a joking reference to this giving him more time with his girlfriend. Girlfriend? Klaus had never had one of those before. He sort of knew those things happened, but the social dynamics had been beyond him. He hadn't been tall enough, old enough, athletic enough, anything enough. The BDM girls preferred other, more charismatic boys. Greta seemed to be a few years older than he was. What did she need a gawky 18-year-old for? Yet she seemed very friendly, very eager to please.

Klaus knew the boy was supposed to take the initiative in such things. Fine. He was an officer. He could take initiative. He'd shot that Romanian, but he'd seen war movies. He had something to guide him. Here she was, snuggled up to him on this interminable train ride. They had been alternately talking and dozing while their train got sidelined for various intervals on every side track between Bucharest and Austria. Right now she was cuddled across his lap. It felt good. It had also given him an erection. Fortunately, her body hid this. However, she was only half-asleep and her movements back and forth as she kept rearranging herself were both pleasuring and paining him. What to do? If he didn't stop her, he wouldn't be able to contain himself and everyone would see the wet spot on his trousers. But to move her, he would have to touch her, to wake her, and then she would see what she was touching through the cloth of his pants...and Klaus would die of embarrassment. Besides, this felt much better than when he did it himself. The scent of her hair was in his nose and it was... stimulating...that was a good word. It was stimulating.

Greta was wondering what more she had to do to show the boy she was interested, was willing. Boys usually pleaded with you to touch it. Well, she was touching enough. She could feel it under her, responding to her movements. Should she just continue until he "finished?" Would that be "enough?" She had had a few sort-of boyfriends, even a couple of fumbling encounters with that thing in their pants. She was still a virgin, but she had the basics of what got rubbed 'til it got wet. What more was she supposed to do in a car full of people? Pull the officer's pants off in public? As is, she was getting knowing looks from a few of the Betar girls in the crowded railway car and more than a few smirks from the guys.

As the train jerked to a stop, there was suddenly a loud noise. Three men in funny uniforms had loudly bounded into the car with drawn guns. They were screaming "Jews out!" in German and Yiddish. Greta jerked her head up and out the window she could see three men hanging from the station's light pillars. They were quite dead, swaying in the breeze. Two had yellow, six-pointed stars pinned to their chests with knives. Greta screamed Klaus's name and jerked herself upright.

Greta's scream was matched by Klaus's as he couldn't contain himself anymore and came with the biggest rush of his young life. He also turned beet-red at doing this in front of everyone. He needed a distraction. He jerked himself fully to his feet and screamed back, "These are NL troops. Who the fuck are you to tell a German officer what to do?"

The Hungarians were taken aback by a boy with wet pants screaming at them. Obviously a Jew who had pissed himself from fear. They snarled and turned to point their guns at him...and Klaus fired first. Half his unit joined in. They had been traveling with their weapons. Their volley put the three Hungarians down. Half a dozen Betar then used knives to complete the process. The Betar then spilled out of the train onto the platform, shooting every Hungarian in a uniform they saw.

Gunter Strauss had been getting some well-deserved sleep two train cars in front of Klaus's when he heard the shooting. He was down on the platform in under a minute, bellowing "Cease fire!" alternately in German, Yiddish, and Magyar. His newly learned Magyar was ungrammatical but got the point across. It took him under two minutes to find a surviving Hungarian gendarme sergeant who explained what had happened and what the Arrow Cross idiots had been doing. They had rounded up Jews, Horthyites, and anyone who struck their fancy. They were looting whatever they chose, as well as torturing and hanging random prisoners at whim, plus the usual rapes and beatings. Their makeshift prison camp was half a kilometer up the road.

That was all Strauss needed to hear. He left Steiner and his Betar to secure train and station while he marched two other companies up the road to the camp. The guards fled ahead of him. Less than an hour later, he had his thousand or so new recruits back on the train. It was amazingly overpacked, but no one cared. He also had two counties' worth of loot from the camp as his new unit treasury. If he was going to command a unit that looked like a mercenary band from the Thirty Years War, it was time to adopt those mores. He also snagged his lieutenant a fresh pair of pants. When he handed them to him, Klaus turned so red and stammered so badly that it was almost pathetically funny. Like a toddler caught with his hand in the cookie jar. The girl had more sense. She just took him by the hand and led him into the train station's water closet to help get him changed.

The train sat on the siding for four more hours. The gendarme had food and beverages brought from town. The locals were glad to be rid of the White Guardists. They asked if his excellency could leave a garrison to maintain order. One of the Magyars from the oil fields volunteered to take command and 60 of his men volunteered with their families. Strauss left them with NL arm bands. Told them to wire Berlin for a new unit ID. The ex-Honvéd major found being a German officer quite a nice idea in these chaotic times. Turned out he spoke enough German that he might understand Schellenberg's return telegram.

1400 hours
8 July 1940
A railway siding somewhere in Austria

Lieutenant Klaus Steiner had been shocked to be pulled off the train by a team from the Ministry of Propaganda. At first, he thought he was being put under arrest for killing that Romanian. He'd been lucky that his stammer and voice breaking kept his excuses from coming out coherently before Strauss had shut him up. So now he was a hero who had killed some Soviet Commissar while saving a strategic facility from Red Partisans. Strauss did all the talking while pinning an Iron Cross 2nd Class on him. Had kept talking long enough for him to figure out that this was all some silliness about earning the first Iron Cross in the brief history of the NL.

He had been even more frightened when the cameraman had noticed Greta and half-shoved her into a few pictures with him. Strauss had passed her off as the hero's romantic conquest, a good Volksdeutsche from Wallachia. Klaus was now frightened that someone would check the story and arrest him for violating the Race Laws. This whole thing with girls was a most difficult part of growing up—delightful, exasperating, and terrifying all at once. He'd been safer as a rear ranker in the HJ, but those days were in the past. Hopefully he would be long gone before everyone realized what a fraud he was.

      1640 hours
      9 July 1940
      Off Calabria in the Mediterranean Sea

      The British Admiral Cunningham had been prepared for the Italian air attack. He was quite surprised to also be hit by two dozen German Ju-87 Stukas. The Stukas did little real damage. Three near-misses on the aircraft carrier Eagle had knocked in some side plates, but the ship maintained trim, even if at a reduced speed. What was important was that the "most secret" intelligence was confirmed. The Germans were coming south. Malta was doomed.

      0900 hours
      10 July 1940
      SS HQ, Berlin

      Heydrich read the propaganda article and ruefully shook his head. Schellenberg stood at quite rigid attention before him. At least he'd had the sense to bring the problem to his attention instead of burying it and praying like most fools would. Heydrich left him sweating for five minutes while he disposed of some routine paperwork. He could smell the fear on his subordinate, but the body remained at attention with the eyes locked forward. Okay, enough of toying with him. He was a useful tool and this was just bad luck. "So, our hero is violating the Race Laws?" He saw Schellenberg nod, but keep silent. "Those forgers you had doing the work-up on the new Frau Hitler. Have you disposed of them yet?" Again, a clear nod and again, no words. "Find a few more. Set up a documents shop at Ravensbrück. Separate compound adjacent to the women's camp. This time we don't liquidate them. They get good food, whiskey, access to female prisoners, all the reasonable comforts as long as their work is satisfactory. Aryanize the girl. The same with any relatives Strauss has along and as many more as he thinks necessary to keep this under wraps. No written record of my ordering this. You send one of your little protégés to him for the list. Send a photographer with him to take pictures so proper files can be set up. Send two of the smart ones. This same protégé carries the finalized documents back himself and makes sure each new Aryan knows what the penalty is if this leaks. I want this done seamlessly.

"Now, for the commandant of this new print shop, I want a blind-obedience type. Someone who will follow orders and never think about them. Make clear that any of the documents from this shop being sold or used in corruption means his head. He can have easy living, avoid real war service, and avail himself of the camp women, but he runs a tight shop. He's dealing with criminals. They will try to find a way to sell documents or use them to free themselves. He is to monitor everything. Especially watch the use of paper and ink. Assign him two NCOs who understand administration. We'll want every sheet of paper accounted for. If this is going to be a permanent shop, I'm sure you and I will find many uses for it." He watched Schellenberg visibly relax with his inclusion. "I value you as a subordinate. I prize your initiative. However, what I especially value is that you didn't hide this. We can fix most things, but the first time you leave a hidden land mine for me to step on, we will have a much less pleasant discussion. DISMISSED!" The air in the office imploded as Schellenberg vanished as if by magic.

Chapter 15

1000 hours
10 July 1940
Stendal, Germany, Garrison of 7th Flieger-Division

It was an unusual situation. Generalleutnant Richard Putzier, the acting commander of the 7th Flieger-Division, had requested a personal meeting with General Hans Jeschonnek. Asking to meet the Chief of Staff for the Luftwaffe was a strange request by a mere acting division commander. However, since the 7th Flieger-Division was scheduled to have a key role in the Malta operation, Jeschonnek had agreed and decided to come to Stendal. Anything concerned with Malta was a priority. It was a matter of Führer Göring's prestige. Besides, he liked getting out of Berlin, seeing what was going on with active units. The bureaucracy could choke a man without some contact with real units fighting real war.

As Jeschonnek's convoy arrived at the base, there was a beehive of activity as hundreds of soldiers were training. A company of fit, young men was out on a run. Another company was holding a large canvas tarp as a Fallschirmjäger climbed up a set of stairs and then jumped out a door frame; this was in preparation for parachute training. Jeschonnek noticed that many of the men seemed quite young, almost as if they were fresh recruits. The units also looked less than crisp, as if they were still doing initial workups. After pausing a bit to look around, Jeschonnek and his escort made their way to Putzier's office.

A brief exchange of pleasantries followed in the garrison building. Putzier proceeded to start with the standard apology for requesting to meet with Jeschonnek outside of the chains of command, "General, thank you for traveling from Berlin. It would have been no trouble for me to...."

"Don't worry, General. I need to see what real soldiers look like from time to time. Now let's get to business. You wanted to talk about the reich Malta operation, I believe." Jeschonnek then paused to look at the other two officers in the room and raised an eyebrow. He clearly had been expecting a private meeting with Putzier.

"Let me introduce General Major Sturm, commander of the Second Fallschirm-Jäger-Regiment, and Oberst Heidrich, commander of the Third Fallschirm-Jäger-Regiment." The two officers came to attention and then shook the general's hand when offered.

Jeschonnek had met Sturm previously, but this Oberst Heidrich was new to him.

Not wanting to waste time, Putzier handed Jeschonnek a sheet of paper with three signatures on it. Jeschonnek quickly read the document and, despite over 35 years of military service, he was actually taken back. It was a formal protest in writing, signed by not only Putzier but also both of the other officers present, against the Malta operation. He could only think of a few occasions where a commander had done such thing in response to orders if, for no other reason, by making the protest in writing it was impossible to later change course. "You have my attention." Senior officers committing career suicide was a sobering experience to witness. "General, in this document, you cite insufficient time to make good your losses from Fall Gelb and Unternehmen Weserübung. I want hear more. For example, why isn't the commander of First Fallschirm-Jäger-Regiment also here?"

Relieved and hoping for this response, Putzier let out a sigh of relief. He had halfway expected a screaming response from the General. "General Bräuer is in the hospital recovering from his wounds and I was unwilling to put Major Walther, the acting Regiment commander, on the spot by asking him to sign also."

Jeschonnek needed no more explanation. Most commanders in his position would be outraged at receiving such a memo. To say the least, they might make the careers of all involved very unpleasant. No need to wreck the career of a mid-grade officer. All this reflected very well on the honor of these three men as German officers. They had chosen duty over their personal advancement in the finest traditions of the Prussian officer corps back to the days of the Great Elector. "Very well, continue."

"As the document outlines, by the conclusion of fighting in France, the division was in very poor shape. It only had five battalions to start, six counting Hauptmann Koch's Sturmabteilung and overall casualties were over 50%. The first battalion of the 2nd Regiment was effectively destroyed in Holland. To conduct operations in Holland after the Norwegian losses, we had to make use of trainees, putting them into ersatz companies and one of those also suffered heavily in Holland. Which, of course, did nothing good to the training program and since then we have been ordered to not only make good our losses, but also expand.

The Reich Without Hitler: The Falcons of Malta

Hence, we established a Third Fallschirm-Jäger-Regiment, added a third Battalion to the Second Regiment, and, remember, that the first Battalion of the Second is nearly starting over from scratch. To achieve this, we raided the other battalions for cadre and they were depleted to begin with. In some ways, what is worse is the losses of the transports, as over 500 Ju-52s were damaged and destroyed. It is my understanding that 52s too damaged to fly are being repaired at a Fokker facility outside Amsterdam and they are overwhelmed with the amount of work. Production is only 30 or so a month, and to get numbers they raided the training establishments just like we did the jump school here. September is the absolute soonest we should attempt a major operation, but even then the Division wouldn't be the same quality as we started in the spring. You will have lumps of half-trained men who need workups from squad through Regiment for a further three or four months." Putzier stopped, waiting to see what the response would be. This meeting would probably end his career, but he would be damned if he sent the men to destruction and did nothing to stop it. His honor as a German officer demanded nothing less.

Jeschonnek was nonplussed. This was not good at all. Göring had been going on and on about how HIS Luftwaffe would have a key role in Heydrich's mad scheme to blitz the Mediterranean. The new Führer would be less than pleased to hear that the Fallschirmjäger were taking themselves out of the opening operation, the conquest of Malta. What if Heydrich went forward without the Fallschirmjäger? Heydrich was treating the Italians as a real military force instead of the joke they had proven to be in Spain and against the French. He was sending in some absurd force of Rommel's, including a commando of NL that had defeated Soviet partisans out by the oil fields. The combined storm battalion was to be landed using barely trained Hitlerjugend to be glider pilots. Heydrich was totally committed to this strategy. By all reports, the British on Malta were terribly weak, so it might just work, even without 7th Division. And, if it did work, it would make dealing with Göring and Heydrich even worse. Or, what if the attack failed? A lot of irreplaceable cadres would get killed in a failed attempt and that would weigh very heavily on his soul and that was it, wasn't it? If this was to work at all, the Fallschirmjäger have to go despite the risks. "General, I believe everything that you say. However, we have to move forward. And since you lack confidence in the operation, I will not ask you or these other officers to take part. It will be treated it as a lateral move and not as a question of discipline." He then took the letter and tore it up. "There will be nothing in the files to show your action. I presume you have personal copies on such a matter of honor. Keep them, but in your private papers. Feel free to show them should there be a Court of Inquiry afterward." Jeschonnek was making it clear that, in the event of a disaster, he was prepared to fall on his sword. It was his decision and he would bear the blame alone.

Putzier and the other commanders looked at one another with expressions from relief to disappointment. Clearly, they were hoping that the appeal would work but they were glad they were not being drummed out of the service. Then Putzier nodded, "Very well, sir, but who will replace us?"

"That is a good question. Who is the most senior officer now?"

"That would be Oberst Ramcke, Hermann-Bernhard Ramcke. He is on the division staff and new to the division, but his service record has been excellent. I assume you want to talk to him?"

"Yes. Call him in now. And be sure to tell him ALL your misgivings." Jeschonnek also planned to tell this Ramcke that he was ordered not to add his name to this missive. He would call in a stenographer and dictate such an order in writing to Ramcke. Ramcke was to take this command and execute these orders regardless of misgivings as a matter of his honor as an officer. All blame would be on the commander giving him such an order. As in the time of Fredrick the Great, a direct order in writing fully placed all blame and guilt.

1400 hours
10 July 1940
Chancellery, Berlin

Herman Göring was surprised to see a joint appointment with Heydrich and Nebe on his daily schedule. He had been feeling out Nebe about his Chancellery Guard idea. Nebe had seemed interested in the promotion. Now here he was showing up with Heydrich, who was the slated loser in this bureaucratic reshuffle.

Göring's temperament was not improved when Heydrich requested the room be cleared, as this was private business at the highest level. The man was forgetting his place. Heydrich blandly ignored his ill temper and had a memo on his desk as soon as the room was cleared of toadies and flunkies.

"Nebe and I took the liberty of refining your idea for the Guard."

Göring was now angry. "Refining? I am Chancellor and Führer!"

"And I am not a toady like Bormann who will flatter errors to keep my place. Hear me out and then you can always reject my proposal. It won't work your way. Not in the ways you need it to." Heydrich paused as he now had Göring's attention as well as his distemper. "You gave Nebe the entire Gestapo. That drowns him in administrative trivia. He'd be managing a force that will stretch from East Africa to the Arctic. Ninety-nine percent of which doesn't matter to you in terms of what you need, which is regime and personal protection. So, we let Nebe form a new force. He will have full authority to pull people from the existing security agencies and to dump back the ones who displease him. Your force will have double pay; thus,there is an incentive to please. His job is you, your household, Berlin, your other residences, for protection. His security brief is to watch me, the generals, the senior Party people, the cabinet. The two hundred people who would be needed for a coup against you. A certain amount of seditious talk from the generals is a given. Nebe's job is to make sure it stays at the officer's club and doesn't go operational. From the Party people, it is easy to just shoot any fool who says the wrong things. Me you watch day and night for the rest of my life. As long as I'm loyal, you have two competing security services who will protect you and watch each other. Anything you don't like so far?"

Göring stared down Heydrich for a full minute. He used the time to reflect on this odd, hyperactive, maniacal, single-minded man in front of him. It was amazing Himmler hadn't liquidated him. The man was indispensable, uncontrollable, and infuriating all at once. The Stalin comparison of Heydrich on himself did not do the man justice. Göring saw in Heydrich some malign genie from an Arabian Nights tale. Or perhaps a guardian angel. Or, even worse, perhaps a creature who was both.

Göring covered his shock by asking Nebe for his views. Nebe replied, "Recall, I was the one who advocated for Reichsführer Heydrich. He and I are not friends, but I know his competences and knew you needed them. You agreed. It seemed obvious for he and I to work out how to best protect you from the generals..." Nebe paused to smile and cough. "And, of course, from Heydrich himself."

Before Göring could mentally regroup, Heydrich took out a big binder and handed it to Göring. Seeing the dubious look on the new Führer's face, he passed across a one-page executive summary memo. "To free up our friend Nebe to do his work, I've written up a proposal for him to draw his administrative services from the Air Ministry. Payroll, purchasing, personnel records, everything. They are already set up. They are staffed by your loyalists. Frees Nebe up for operational work. Now, we've added a few other features. The LAH and General Dietrich were traditional guards of the Chancellery and of the Führer's residence in Bavaria. Then they went off to war. Time to bring them back. Let him grow the regiment to a small division. Then add an Air Force ground division of similar size, a Herman Göring division. The two divisions are your coup protection force. Stationed around Berlin and on direct report to you. In an emergency, you can use them at the front, but then you form a replacement division for each out of recruits. If Nebe gets reports of a coup and you agree with his judgment, your power is safe."

Göring took a few minutes to digest all this. Heydrich had worked up something Göring could never have thought up on his own. It seemed to have no defects for him. Heydrich was not his friend. The obvious question occurred. "Why are you doing all this? You're not my man. Different clique from the Old Days. Why aren't you empire-building? Because the generals will shoot you if they overthrow me?"

"Partly it's that. Mostly it's because I don't want your job. I detest the glad-handing and ceremonial. You revel in it. You detest the day-to-day grind and I excel at that. We make natural allies far more than Himmler and I did. You lack a set of lunatic ideological ideas to push regardless of efficacy. Himmler near-drowned us in crank notions on everything from runic magic to nutrition. You let me focus on making the machine of state work better. I'm nationalist enough to want us to win this war and selfish enough to want to be powerful in the peace that will follow. As long as I do well, why would you replace me? If I do well and you tire of me, perhaps you will let me retire quietly instead of executing me. However, I do have a few small requests. Not quid pro quo. You are the Boss. But I want to step on some toes." Göring motioned him to go on. "Personnel and bureaucratic moves. I want to clear the dead wood out of the Four Year Plan. Yes, I know many are your 'friends'. Let them keep their salaries but I want the authority to assign them to your Chancellery staff. You can find other jobs for them with proper titles. All the Plan now does is fight with the Arms Ministry and Army procurement office. I want to subordinate it to a committee with Minister Todt, Standartenführer Speer, and the three service procurement offices. You will keep the title of head of the plan. That's a matter of your prestige. Standartenführer Speer becomes deputy head and does the work. I also want General Thomas and his entire office moved from OKH over to OKW. Generals Kietel and Jodl won't fight what I have to do. I can work with General Thomas. I'll need you to force a one grade promotion through for him. You have the legal authority. Generals Halder and Beck will throw fits, but it is a prerogative of the Führer."

Göring could see he was saving the most difficult for last. "What's the bitter pill?"

"General Udet. He's hopeless. I want to flip him with General Richthofen. General Udet is in love with dive bombers. Let him command them against Malta. General Richthofen is a trained engineer. He will fit in with Minister Todt, General Thomas, and the rest of the committee. Our war economy is a mess. It needs complete revamping. Failures will hurt your prestige."

Göring glowered at Heydrich a moment longer before uttering a small curse in a low voice and signing the summary memo. He told Heydrich to leave but motioned Nebe to stay. "Okay. He's out the room. Do I shoot him or back him?"

Nebe expected the question and had the answer ready. "Back him, but do have me watch him. I already have been. He's working sixteen- to eighteen-hour days, to the point where there is strain in his marriage. Just keep remembering that, to him, the Movement was never about anything more than career. When the Navy threw him out he needed work. Himmler was hiring. There were family connections to Himmler's circle, but beyond that he could have as easily taken a job with an insurance company. He really did expect Himmler to liquidate him."

Göring put a hand up to stop Nebe for a few seconds. An image was crossing his mind of Heydrich as a demonic genie remaking that insurance company into a juggernaut that conquered the financial world. A smile crossed his lips, although the image was as much horrifying as morbidly funny. Göring took a deep breath, composed himself, and then motioned Nebe to continue.

"I would say have your wife befriend his, but I doubt they would get along. Frau Heydrich is too plain for yours. However, I would suggest you make a social effort with General Dietrich and a few others. The two loyal divisions should have officers loyal to you. You should get some loyalists back into the economic structure, but you need competent ones. I'd start with General Richthofen. Fly him back here and give him his promotion yourself. I'll call Heydrich and tell him to hold off, to leave the handover to you personally. You take General Richthofen to someplace nice in Berlin. Toast him as your greatest engineer. Make it clear to him that he is your personal representative on this committee. Not just the Air Force's man, yours. Have him send you private memos." Nebe saw the worried look on Göring's face. "Hire three youngsters to read them and prepare a two-paragraph summary. The Movement and the Air Force are full of ambitious twenty-five year-olds. You don't sabotage Heydrich, but you do remind him you are watching. See to General Udet yourself. Stress that you value his loyalty, but need him in a combat role. That he's wasted as a bureaucrat. It all comes down to building a personal clique. I don't need one. I'm quite at the limits of my ambitions. I can watch Heydrich in certain ways. General Richthofen can watch in another way. Piece by piece, you build a loyalist web."

The conversation ran down into five minutes of small talk after which Führer Göring dismissed General Nebe. He ruefully thought that this business of being top man was a lot of stress. He would have to review this all with his wife. Coming out of the film industry she seemed to understand this endless scheming quite well. He thought he'd also invite her new friend, Olga, who had proven very helpful as well. She was a relative of Chekhov and a White Russian refugee. They seemed to understand conspiracies as easily as a fish understood water. Amazing woman. He was glad his wife had taken up with her.

1500 hours
12 July 1940
Chancellery, Berlin

Herman Göring had decided that one of the privileges of being Führer was no longer having to work mornings. Accordingly, he would try to limit office hours to the afternoon from now on, leaving his evenings for entertainment and ceremonial. Those were the parts of the job he liked best anyway. He had Heydrich, Nebe, and, soon enough, Richthofen for the boring bureaucratic drivel. Therefore, when Nebe requested an appointment, Göring's staff had put him in for after lunch. A two- to three-hour working day did not allow a lot of appointments, but Nebe was always priority.

Göring was somewhat worried when Nebe insisted the meeting be totally private. Was there a coup being prepared? A plot? Instead, it turned out Nebe wanted to talk about the problem Göring had been hoping would go away: Müller in Budapest. "He's a disaster. It's obvious to everyone. A disaster you chose on your own Chancellor. Therefore, it reflects on you. Should I arrange an 'accident'?"

Göring began to sweat. He didn't like any of his choices. Removing Müller meant admitting error. Leaving him in place advertised poor judgment. Killing him could not be done secretly. If Müller walked in front of a truck or choked on a fish bone, everyone would presume it was an assassination. After passing Hitler's death off as intentional, conspiracy thinking was running wild. Germany hadn't gotten as paranoid as Stalin's Russia, but....

Nebe saw that his boss had no ready answers. Good. Then perhaps he would accept Nebe's "solution". "Call Müller back for 'consultations'. Let him sweat for a few weeks in Berlin. Then call him in and you and I will berate him. When he grovels and apologizes sufficiently, you give him a lateral transfer. Move him to the General Government. Governor General Frank is a disaster, at least as big a one as Müller, and somewhat corrupt. You arrest Frank, try him for corruption and incompetence, and execute him. You give Müller a second chance, but have his subordinates do weekly reports to me as your security head. Odds are we can find some good reason to kill him later. Each subordinate will want his job. In the meantime, send Gruppenführer Kaltenbrunner to Budapest from Vienna. He and Heydrich hate each other, so he will be happy being a direct report to you." Nebe paused while his Boss took this all in.

Göring signed the expected memo. He was happy to let Nebe clean this mess up. His wife and Olga had been arguing for leaving Müller alone lest acknowledging the error reflect poorly on his prestige as Leader. This sort of sidestepped that. Besides, it was one less unpleasantness to think about. Now he could go off and do his first pair of victory parades. Parades, a banquet, speeches, drinking, and high-spirited comradery. He'd take Olga as part of the official family. She would show up well in the newsreels.

1730 hours
12 July 1940
Chancellery, Berlin

Newly minted Generalmajor Hermann-Bernhard "Gerhard" Ramcke exited from his appointment with the new Führer Göring a confused and somewhat angry man. He was happy for the promotion, of course. More so that he had been deemed worthy of the promotion being directly at Göring's hand. Indeed, he felt it was a quite deserved reward for exemplary service. But the national leader, and head of his own service, had shown zero interest in his attempt to report on the difficulties of assembling a force for this Malta operation. He was still reviewing in his mind what more he could have done to get the leader's attention when he heard a voice call his name. He looked up to see an SS Oberführer he didn't know. The man was immaculately dressed. Some sort of rear-area hero who had never heard a live round go past his ear.

"General Ramcke. Allow me to introduce myself. Oberführer Schellenberg, chief assistant to Reichführer-SS Heydrich. He instructed me to bring you to him once you were done with the appointment with our Führer."

Ramcke was now disgusted instead of angry and confused. More stupid rear-area conspiracies and politics that prevented anything useful from getting done. Oh, well. No way to avoid this. Better get it over with.

Thirty minutes later he was seated in an office in the still-being-reconstructed SS Headquarters. Workmen were banging away and there was dust everywhere. Heydrich had been polite, but wanted to discuss the Operation. What sort of divided command was this?

Heydrich read his face easily. "It's a division of responsibilities. Our new Führer does the ceremonial. My office does the actual work. Now would you please tell me why you believe the plan is impossible so I can either get you more resources or see to changing the plan?"

Ramcke was taken aback. "You are chief of staff to the

Führer?"

Heydrich gave a low chuckle. "Closer to Grand Vizier or Deputy Chancellor. The actual staff work will be OKW. Generals Keitel and Jodl are good enough for routine staff work as long as given clear instructions. Our Führer finds such bureaucratic work to be a bother, so my office does all of that. Now before you tell me there is no chance to get your 7th Division in fighting shape by August or even Christmas, I already know that. It doesn't matter anyway. After the losses from Norway and Holland, we don't have enough Ju-52s for a full division drop. Given these constraints, what can you put together in two weeks?"

Ramcke took a minute to gather his thoughts. All his excuses and justifications were gone. At last he was dealing with a realist. But the Air Force did not trust the SS. "You know the casualties we took in Holland?" Heydrich nodded. Ramcke went on. "If I wreck the training establishment, I can cobble together a weak brigade. That's it. Four battalions with limited cohesion because I will have no time to run them through exercises. They will be lumps of men. Good men. Well-trained, individually, but not accustomed to working together. And that's before the chaos of scattering on a drop onto an island, I presume at night?"

"Daylight is better? Presume the RAF will have no fighters, but the AAA will still be there. Kesselring does not believe he can destroy the guns by bombing alone. I think he's right."

"Daylight. Moonlight. Magic light. No light. One excuse for a brigade against two British. They are good troops on the defense."

"There will be an Italian parachute brigade. I'm told they are elite," Heydrich paused to let a wry smile play across his face. "For whatever elite means to Italians. Not the world's greatest warriors, but they will drop with you. There will be a good German mountain division waiting to land as soon as you get an airstrip. A second Italian one to follow. Again, supposedly elite for whatever elite means to those people. Plus, a seaborne invasion with another division and a few elite battalions of Marines. Italian again. The big deal will be the Air Force. Hundreds of bombers at your beck and call. Total air superiority."

"All my boys have to do is take an airfield? Then the mountain troops fight the battle?" Heydrich nodded. "And how well-defended are these airfields?"

"Based on air recon, they have no combat troops at all. I'm sure the base personnel have weapons and some sketchy training,

but essentially you are making a rear-area raid. The British
were not impressed with your operations in Holland. They have
over a thousand of yours that they evacuated from Holland as
prisoners. They think the panzers won Holland. Subsequently, the
British have deployed to beat off the landings from the sea while
defending their harbor so they can do a second Dunkirk."

Ramcke began to smile. For the first time this absurdity began
to make sense. "So, we can drop at dawn?" When Heydrich didn't
contradict this, he went on. "Take an airfield, hold a few hours,
and the first mountain regiment is down. This is something that
might work. Why didn't anyone spell it out this way?"

"Because, sadly, I must wait until those officially responsible
fail before involving myself. Office politics. Every nation has this.
Now you have a day to think this over. If the first week of August is
impossible, I must know what is possible. Oberführer Schellenberg
will see to finding you an office, some staff assistance, and a billet
for tonight. I'll put you on the calendar for lunch tomorrow here
at my desk. It will be quite informal. Just the three of us. I need a
workable plan with realistic deadlines. Fast is good, but victory is
better. Can you live with those parameters or should I find another
officer for this operation?"

Ramcke's pride would not let him decline this "honor". This
operation might kill him. It might also get him a star on his rank
tabs. He was already past 50 years old. A chance for advancement
this good simply did not come along that often in a career. He had
to see if he could find a way to make this clusterfuck work.

Chapter 16

0800 hours
13 July 1940
Governor General's place, Tripoli, Libya

Italo Balbo and his confidential assistant, ex- Royal Carabiniers Lt. Col. Ivo Levi, took early morning coffee with the French General, who was pretending his name was François Kellermann. They were well aware of who he really was, but if the French chose to play silly games, the Italians were prepared to humor them. This "Kellermann" had arrived late last night with the first battalion of what the French were calling the Demi-brigade de Legion "Grande Bourgogne". Again, the two Italians were aware of what the Sons of Oran were, but went along with the charade. The façade had allowed for Italian use of the ports of Tunis and Bizerte, as well as French railroads in Tunisia. The logistics of deploying major new formations to Libya were difficult enough that every little bit helped. Marshal Balbo would have preferred to have been given the field command, but understood the politics of Prince Umberto getting that role.

It was a fairly easy meeting, as such things went. All told, the French proposed to send some eight-thousand combat troops, plus a service and repair depot. Balbo proposed basing them near Tobruk for the moment. The Germans had decreed that this brigade was to be part of something called the Afrika Division under SS General Steiner. Except that neither Steiner nor any of the German part of this division had yet arrived. Indeed, no one was quite aware when they would do so. General "Kellermann" proposed that in the interim he serve under the Italian XXIst Corps and General Messe. Both parties took this meeting as the first step in the long, slow process of forging a Latin Entente within the new German Europa. The old colonial rivalries seemed childish compared with the new threat of a super-powerful Germany.

0850 hours
13 July 1940
Minister of War's Office, Bendler Block, Berlin

General Beck had finally decided on a title for himself. He

was now the Minister of War. As was usual in the morning, he held a conference with General Halder in his capacity as head of OKH. Also, as was usual, Halder had over an hour of time wasted listening to Beck's whining about what the Nazis gangsters had done this time. The latest "outrage" was the failure of the new commander in Romania to return some of the Jäger school cadres Rommel had poached. Beck had instructed the staff to issue a clear order to that effect. Instead, the new commander, General Reichnau, had called Chancellor Göring to plead to be allowed to keep these 'key personnel'-. Göring had countermanded Beck's order. Rommel had of course vanished with the rest of these cadres. Doubtlessly somewhere in the south, but OKW was proving unhelpful in locating him, much less initiating return of the desired cadres. A proper branch school had been gutted by Rommel and Heydrich to meet some transient crisis. Beck felt this was both very irregular and a slight on the Army's powers. Guderian had sensibly returned the school troops from the Austro-Hungarian border once the crisis was past.

Halder was beginning to get bored with having his time wasted. "Sir, are you proposing a new coup? A civil war in the midst of a war with the British and with no guarantee that a Soviet war won't break out this summer?"

Confronted with reality, Beck caught his breath, shook his head no, and forced himself to calm down. "Of course not. But what did the last coup really accomplish? Göring blows with the wind almost as badly as Hitler did. Heydrich is just maddening. Have you seen the latest revisions to our weapons programs?"

Halder had. Was in fact quite pleased with them. Simplification of production to fewer types was a giant plus to logistics and administration. The new higher production had yet to actually happen, but his staff officers had done plant tours and everything Heydrich and his minions claimed had been proven true by visual inspection by officers he trusted. "Sir, you saw the million men marching in Berlin. The young ones among them, the HJs, are our next few conscription classes. If we move against the Party, do they stand with us or with Heydrich?"

Beck made a face like a man swallowing pickle brine. "With them." He then paused to consider something. "That was not a mistake you just made, a slip of the tongue. You meant it when you said Heydrich. The bastard did it. Walked into a room condemned to death and emerged as a de facto ruler. Göring's a cipher."

Halder continued his campaign to educate his senior colleague. "Not exactly. Göring still is the senior...when he exerts himself. Which isn't often. Nebe is the prime mover for him and whose man Nebe is remains an open question. It was Nebe who rescued Heydrich after all." The two generals spent minutes drinking their coffee in silence, pondering the situation. They were disliking all the answers.

> 0930 hours
> 13 July 1940
> A railway siding in Italy somewhere north of Bologna

Even this early in the morning it was already extremely warm and horridly humid in the Po Valley in high summer. The absence of a breeze just completed the discomfort. Gunter Strauss was watching the SS team creating new temporary documents for his clan of Aryanized Jews. He was also pondering what it meant to have the Reichsführer's attention to this degree. Patrons on that level were a route to an ascendant career...as long as one kept producing results. And his biggest "result" was the hero of the hour, the callow boy Lieutenant Steiner. The lad truly was his good luck charm. Oberführer Schellenberg's man was a blond Standartenführer. Immaculate tailored uniform, trim physique, obvious university education in his choice of words. The Movement was full of degree-holders who had been without jobs from the early 30's Depression years. Himmler had gobbled these up in their thousands. The minion beat Strauss in education. Strauss had the advantage in a MUCH lower Party number. Still, best to cultivate this headquarters' functionary. Friends in Berlin helped one's career.

All it had taken was a good bottle of Hungarian wine to get a more detailed briefing from the man while the list of those to be Aryanized was being compiled by what Strauss was coming to think of as his "Elders of Zion". Greta's aunt and uncle, a few ex-officers, and two senior technicians from the oil fields were the de facto spokespeople for these Hebrews. It made dealing with them easier.

The Standartenführer had spelled it all out for them. They were for colonial service. A few for Malta because Heydrich wanted the new hero's name associated with that operation. Then through Libya to Egypt and beyond there through Palestine to Iraq. Strauss was tagged to be a big man running the new oil fields they would take from the British. Said it would be a permanent posting. Life among the lesser breeds of humans, but more rank, plus a chance to modestly feather one's nest if one were discrete about it. Also, the Race Laws would not apply out there, so take a harem for all it mattered. All Berlin cared about were results. Just repeat what he had done in Ploiesti. Make the oil flow out of the ground and from there back to some port city called Haifa.

When the minion had gone off to start the paperwork, Strauss had taken time to have a cigarette and review the situation. He had the start of a brilliant career. The young hero was a key piece of this, so Strauss mentally decided he would personally go to Malta with Steiner's company. He was a combat veteran and could help keep the boy out of trouble...or write a suitably heroic ending for him should fate decide to take Klaus's life. If Berlin could believe that tripe they had written about a Soviet partisan attack, they were clueless enough to swallow almost anything.

Of course, Fräulein Greta was now a part of this heroic tale, the Brunhilde to the new Siegfried. If they were to be lovers...time to arrange that part, too. He had her provisional papers done first, then told her to find Klaus and report to him.

Klaus Steiner had been sitting on a bench half-dozing in the oppressive heat when Greta came to fetch him. He had come along easily enough. Strauss was the Boss, and sending Greta to fetch him was far from unusual. However, he was not prepared to report on the history of his sexual activities with Greta in such clinical detail, more so as beyond the wonderful and embarrassing time on the Hungarian railroad siding it had mostly amounted to kisses, brief caresses, and a few hurried applications of her hand. He started to stammer. His voice broke repeatedly. His face turned crimson with ears turning beet red. If he could have found a hole to crawl into, he would gladly have let the earth swallow him. He had never been this humiliated in his young life, and it got worse as Strauss kept laughing and rolling his eyes.

Strauss was having more comical fun than he would have watching a vaudeville show, but he didn't want to break the boy's spirit. He saw a sergeant, a Magyar, taking six men off on a work detail. He called the noncom over and told him to clear the railroad car behind him. His detail was then to guard it until the Lieutenant was finished with a special project inside. The sergeant laughed heartily, slapped Klaus on the back, and saw to it. In a minute he reported the car "ready for action", followed by more laughter.

Greta could see that Klaus was paralyzed by embarrassment. As she had with his wet pants several days before, she just took his hand as one would a child's and led him up the steps and into the car. It had bench seats. Even with the windows open, it was hot and muggy enough to be a sauna. Klaus was stammering madly, trying to explain something. What on Earth was there to explain? This time she had no one to get in the way. She put a finger over his lips, a silencing gesture that he seemed to understand. Unlike the last time in a rail car, there was no audience, so she could just pull the officer's pants off. She undid his belt while stroking his face. With precious little help from him, she pushed him onto a seat while getting his pants and underwear off and down to his ankles. The young man at least was capable of getting an erection on his own. She used her mouth to get it wet, then wet her fingers in his mouth to use to at least moisten herself. From the shock on his face and the glazed look of his eyes, he was going to be no help in this. But she'd had instruction from her aunt...and besides even idiots and animals managed this. She mounted him and proceeded to fuck his brains out.

By the second time, he was cooperating. By the fourth, he was even doing his share of the work. The sweat poured off both of them, but it was fun, exciting even. After the seventh time some two hours later, it was clear the boy's energies were too spent for an eighth try. They helped each other dress in a playful, exhausted fashion. It wasn't a perfect job, but it would do. She then steered him off the train.

He was following her, guided now by her arm around his waist. He had an idiot's grin, with the largest smile she had seen beyond an illustration of the Cheshire Cat in her Alice book. He could barely coordinate himself to walk. She was sore in several places and none too steady herself. However, her look was one of serene triumph. Apparently, their antics had attracted a small audience. There were cheers, whistles, ribald comments, and some interesting suggestions. Greta thought a few were unlikely to be physically possible, but she looked forward to experimenting.

Klaus responded to all this by more blushing, but the idiot grin never left his face. He mumbled a few thank yous without his voice breaking or stuttering.

Greta just did a small curtsy in the direction of the Lieutenant Colonel, then took her man's hand to guide him to the railway station water closet to wash them both off. She felt she had more than done her job. She was a young lady who had found her place in life. Officer's mistress and headquarters cook.

Chapter 17

1540 hours
13 July 1940
Governor General's Palace/ Palazzo del Governatore, Tripoli,
Libya

Italo Balbo was quite unprepared for an unscheduled drop-in from Prince Umberto. No prior appointment, no entourage, just a cryptic phone message that the Prince wanted a private meeting to discuss the coming campaign. A message from the airport after the Prince's unscheduled flight was already in Libya. Most strange and potentially dangerous. It smelled like a plot. Balbo had quickly cleared his calendar and was waiting. The Prince seemed clearly ill at ease. It took half an hour of pleasantries for him to get to the point. "General von Paulus has been after me about the last naval battle. Admiral Weichold even more so. The Germans are quite unimpressed. Their naval attachés and liaison officers basically see our fleet as having run away and done a poor job even of that. They also are quite caustic about the lack of coordination between the fleet and the air force. They want changes, and they see the two of us as the ones to make them."

"We lack the power."

"Not the way they see it. We are their chosen Italians; therefore, their power is ours. I've talked them out of sending a few divisions to Rome as 'help' but, essentially, they want you in charge, a new government, and massive command changes without regard to seniority and patronage. They want competent people they have vetted in charge. They want Italy to run a competent war effort. They want an end to fantasies like Italy fighting a parallel war. Our glory will be the new empire and the victories that created it but these will be joint battles conducted jointly, if nominally, for propaganda purposes, under our supreme command. If we are to be the number two power in Europe, they want it to have a functional government run by professionals, not some grand opera pretense such as our pathetic invasion of Albania last fall or our miserable failure of an Alpine campaign a few weeks ago."

"I am in basic agreement. Italy needs major changes to be as great as we wish, as great as the current situation requires. But we cannot just shoot Benito and the King, your father. That would mean civil war."

"So I've told them, and their Hungarian debacle makes a good example of where heavy-handed German pigheadedness can lead. They are willing to let us do it our way. I need you to fly to Rome with me. Officially you are going to finalize plans to move thousands more trucks here. The French have given us nearly unrestricted use of Tunis and Bizerte, plus their railroad in Tunisia. Romania and the Soviets are supplying oil. Malta will be gone in less than a month. You will be motorizing all your good troops here, plus bringing in more tanks. While you are in Rome, you and I will make a courtesy call on Director General of the National Police Bocchini. He is the missing piece to get the Grand Council to force a change. Mussolini stays as Premier. Purely titular. You become Vice-Premier and head of the Party. You and I will create a new list of ministers and commanders for Bocchini to vet both for us and to reassure his German connections. I ask you to agree to this as a patriot."

"And your father?"

"One step at a time. I'm not acting for personal ambition. What I do will be for the good of Italy, of its people, of the dynasty, of our national institutions, for our glorious future. Indeed, I will be acting for the personal good of my father, however little he may choose to see it. For right now he stays as King. I will become Lieutenant General of the Realm with command of the armed forces. The justification will be to avoid my father having to take German orders on military appointments out of seniority. I shall bear the shame of this capitulation. When the moment of national danger is past, he can even send me off to East Africa for a time as 'punishment'. However, first things first. The new cabinet will vote as we wish, as the Germans require. You will help make known that when the time comes I am prepared to be the designated scapegoat. Their reputations with throne, nation, and Party will stay spotless."

"The King will never permit this."

"Explaining how poor his choices are is a family duty I do not relish. However, as was explained to us in Berlin, our options are quite limited. Do we wish to reduce Rome and Milan to burning wrecks like Budapest?" The Prince put up a hand to cut off the obvious rejoinders. "I don't question the bravery of your Air Force. I question the quality of their planes. Do we wish a Caporetto in the air? It's only a temporary measure, anyway. In a year or year and a half, this war will be over and he can have his full powers back. Indeed, the decree naming me will just be for the duration of hostilities."

"If you are sure this is necessary, I will, of course, as a patriot comply. What happens here in Libya?"

"Appoint whoever you want as your deputy here and keep the title yourself. You and I have to make this war work and the war will be waged from here. It was absurd for Italy to have entered this war, but here we are. We have mounted the tiger. We had best learn to ride it lest it devour us."

2200 hours 13 July Eastern Time
0400 hours 14 July CET
A small back-of-the-building room at the Willard Hotel, Washington DC

Harry Hopkins was getting tired of this third-rate spy movie idiocy from his Soviet contact. "This is the last meeting like this. If you want me to keep supplying information, you make an appointment during business hours at my office."

His Soviet handler knew this was a difficult agent to run. Hopkins was, in effect, Deputy President of the United States. He also had the absurd belief that what he was doing was just political dialog and not espionage. "I will be noticed by Mr. Hoover and his FBI."

Hopkins was normally an affable and somewhat diffident man. It fit both his initial profession of social worker and his current role as number two to FDR. Franklin did not like other people to hog attention. Roosevelt was the only star of his political road show. "You think Hoover's people haven't tailed me here? Haven't figured out what room I am in and who I'm seeing? That's why I insisted my contact be a woman. Better he think that than brand me a queer. The man is obsessive on that topic, probably because he's one himself." Hopkins gave a bitter laugh. Hoover's surrounding himself with tall, well-built, young men was a running White House joke. "Just do it the way I told you. Join some do-gooder organization. Each time you come, ask me for a small favor for them. Someone who needs a job, a public works project they believe in, maybe someone who needs a prison sentence commuted. I must meet with a hundred people who badger me for small things every month. The President is hopeless at detail work and, with Farley clearly out of favor, it all increasingly flows to me. Hoover opens a file, verifies your organizational contact, and it ends there. It will just seem to him as if I am showing favoritism to a former lover."

The argument on competing techniques wasted forty minutes and half a pot of coffee before the key data was passed along. The Nazis had asked for a new Hoover Relief Agency to feed the Jews and Poles. Churchill was refusing to consider allowing the blockade to be breached, but the President needed those votes for November. Could shipment across the Soviet Union be arranged if the British proved difficult?

Hopkins left the meeting still convinced he was not really a spy. The Soviet regime was odious in many ways, but at heart they were fellow progressives. With the world at war, with fascism and reaction on the march, the forces of progress must stand united. Besides, many US Communists had been allies of his on other reformist projects, especially rights for the oppressed Negroes, so he just humored their sectarianism.

0500 hours British Double Summer Time
14 July 1940
A seedy hotel room in Westminster, London

Kim Philby had failed to get posted to that secret signals unit. He was now explaining to his Soviet handler that this had proven to be a good thing. He'd been put on an emergency committee tasked with exploring what a break with the US would do to Britain's war efforts. Churchill was livid at the proposed new Hoover Agency breaking the blockade. Was trying to persuade his cabinet colleagues to risk shooting incidents with the US if necessary. The cabinet was disagreeing. They were also fighting Churchill on sending reinforcements to Egypt. Felt the need was greater in the Home Islands. Churchill was fighting the Med Fleet commander, Cunningham. Cunningham wanted to pull everyone possible off Malta. Claimed it couldn't be defended. Cabinet agreed, but Churchill could not be brought around. Kept growling variations of "No more retreats".

Philby wanted direction from Moscow on which way he should steer this committee. His handler promised to try to obtain a response, but Moscow moved at its own pace. They shared a morbid laugh over that. They shared a second one over the fact that, for all the fears, London had not yet been bombed. The air war seemed limited to the Channel and the southern ports.

Chapter 18

0700 hours
14 July 1940
Hauptumsiedlungslager für Juden Rakowitz / Palestine
#1 Jewish Resettlement Center, near Krakow in the General
Government

The ground-breaking for the new camp had gone quite well.
As Eichmann had feared, the Polish Betar organization had been
well and truly trashed from German occupation. However, the
Lithuanian and Latvian branches had come out in the refugee
tsunami as fully formed entities. The tentative peace had released
the populations of all three Baltic states to the Reich. Over 90%
of them had come. A simple directive moving the Jews toward
this camp had produced over fifty thousand of them with more
arriving daily. Meanwhile, another edict through the various
branches of the SS to forward Jewish professionals with their
families had produced architects, construction foremen, army
officers, police, and virtually anything else Eichmann could use. It
had also produced enough literate, clerically trained Jews for an
improvised camp administration. People were living in tents and
an amazing assortment of emergency housing. They were building
their camp while helping with guard duties at other German
installations in the vicinity.
   Eichmann had received a memorandum of praise from
Schellenberg, with a CC to the Reichsführer-SS. His career was
progressing excellently. So why did he feel dirty and demeaned?

0830 hours
14 July 1940
Cluj / Klausenburg, Transylvania , Romania [formerly Hungary]

Israel Levi had an essentially tragic view of life. It had not been
easy being a Jew in Hungary when he was growing up. Jews did
well in the capital of Budapest, not so much in the provincial city
he'd been raised in. However, four years in the trenches fighting
Serbs, Russians, Romanians, and Italians had been worse still. He
felt himself blessed by God to have survived this, and physically
relatively whole. He had lost the tip of a finger and had a shoulder

wound that hurt when the weather changed.

Getting handed from Hungary to Romania was another tragedy. Hungarian discrimination and the odd beating was better than Romanian beatings and the odd pogrom. His marriage to his wife Ruth had been similarly tragic. She was a decent woman and a good mother. She had no control on her mouth or temper. Neighbors joked that, if left alone, she would quarrel with her own shadow. This was bad enough among their fellow Jews, but could be a disaster with Gentiles. So far, he had been able to shield her from the worst life could do. He could never get her to see what he did as shielding as opposed to weakness.

Now their daughter Greta had vanished. He had taken a brief train trip and asked around. Depending on who you asked, she had been kidnapped by the Nazis, had joined them, or been shot out at the airport. Israel had judged it wise not to press further. His Ruth had screamed and sulked at that answer, damning him for a useless coward and threatening to go herself.

He had been saved from that disaster by a new, worse one. Romanian police, local German boys with an armband saying NL, and a Nazi officer had arrived. The officer knew no Yiddish but Israel knew enough German. The entire family had been arrested. Pack two bags each and be ready to be moved in thirty minutes. Israel had accepted the inevitable. These were men with guns. Deported was better than beaten and dead. One child lost was a tragedy, but there was no reason to condemn the rest to death.

Ruth had chosen to argue. Go where? How could she pack without knowing? Bring food? What would happen to their things left behind? What about her husband's job? Their savings at the bank? Israel could see the officer visibly losing patience. He tried shouting down his wife. That never worked. For the first time in their marriage he hit her. Three strong blows, back and forth across the face. It should have gotten her attention, let her see this was not the time to antagonize someone who wouldn't do what she wished. Perhaps if he had beaten her earlier in their marriage, had accustomed her to accepting that sometimes a husband was right...she reacted by going into a frenzy, her voice rising as she shouted him down, tried to shout the officer down and...Israel saw the officer's patience exhausted. He had just enough time to put his hand over his youngest child's eyes and begin the proper prayer before the shooting started....

Chapter 19

1100 hours
14 July 1940
The apartment of the Director General of the National Police's mistress, Rome, Italy

Director General of the National Police Bocchini had asked no questions when an aide to the Prince had called from Rome's Lictor airport to set up this meeting. That in itself was strange. He met the two men, the Prince and Air Marshal Balbo, at the apartment's door, and ushered them in as if this were the most normal thing in the world, for them to request such an out-of-the-way, off-the-books encounter. He let the Prince repeat his speech, and then smiled. "I told my SS friends you would arrive at the correct conclusions. Do you need me to confront your father with you, to explain the seriousness of the situation?"

The Prince declined the offer. His father would understand the situation quite clearly. The King was cold and formal, reserved in his human relations and politically reactionary. A quite difficult, distant personality, made more so by his social rank, age, and upbringing. That said, King Victor Emanuel III was a very knowledgeable person, better informed than the Chief of the Government, Mussolini, about every important governmental issue. His Majesty had, in addition, a larger and deeper culture and practical understanding of international and military matters, with a much more realistic and sober attitude, devoid of the ideological blindness and self-convincing coarseness of Il Duce. The strict self-control imposed by their Prussian-style military instructors on every young male member of House Savoy was the exact opposite to the unbridled, slipshod, and rhetorical naked ambition of Il Duce's. Mussolini was an orator, journalist, and conspirator, but lacked the temperament of a ruler. Umberto didn't need help getting his father to comprehend the situation. The difficulty would be getting the King to emotionally accept that the Germans had found the son more worthy than the father. It was the insult, coupled with the threat to the dynastic order. His father was more likely to be stubborn if there were other people in the room. The conversation would be difficult enough.

Balbo was curious how Bocchini knew all of this? "Because

The Reich Without Hitler: The Falcons of Malta

I have daily phone calls with important colleagues at SS HQ, so I know that they are sincere in not wishing Italy to be a puppet they have to rule directly. Reichsführer-SS Heydrich has made this crystal clear. If you both can do your parts, rely on me to make sure Berlin understands your difficulties and the limits of how much you can accomplish and how quickly. My office gives me the information to make me sadly aware of how poorly we have been governed." Left unsaid was how much or little of this had been passed onward to Berlin.

Balbo pressed the issue. "But we are not their friends. It was a personal relationship between a dead man and a man about to be retired in place as a titular ruler, but without power or hope for resurrection. How do they see things?"

"The phrase Heydrich keeps using to his key SS subordinates is that Germany should quote, bank their winnings, unquote. He sees Germany as the equivalent of a man who imprudently bet his life savings at the roulette table and, by pure chance, suddenly has a huge pile of chips in front of him. In his eyes, you cease playing. Cash in the chips, go home, and buy government bonds. France is crushed. The Soviets are at least nominally their allies. By the time this campaign is over, Britain will have lost a valuable piece of its Empire and all financial control over the continent of Europe. That leaves Italy. He proposes to choke Italy like a cat fed too much cream. He'll gift us with a huge empire, just what we asked for. An empire that will take us a generation to digest and will permanently estrange us from Britain, the empire's former owner. By the time France regains enough independence to ally with us against him, he plans on making Germany so powerful it will be suicide." The Police Head paused to make a discrete, if somewhat sadly, obvious point. "Leaving aside, of course, the many historic difficulties between ourselves and the French, as well as their inherent inability to accept Italy as an equal."

"What about the Soviets? Does Italy have no say in this, as well?"

"Heydrich sees this as up to them. If they are sensible, why go to war? If they are not sensible, a stronger Italy makes a good partner in the destruction of the Soviets. His estimate is it will take a five-year campaign for the new Europe to cross the Urals and destroy Stalin. Even that might not in his opinion destroy Bolshevism in Asia. And yes, I keep saying Heydrich. The new Führer Göring seems content to concern himself with the ceremonial functions of office. The Army generals and their allies among the old elites are doing a reprise of the early Thirties. They seem concerned purely with their social and caste prerogatives. They have let Heydrich create a parallel supreme headquarters, OKW, for our new joint campaign. They essentially allowed Heydrich to steal the Army procurement bureaucracy. They show zero interest in the continent-wide cartels he is creating. They have let him take over the diplomacy with the new French government at Vichy and with ourselves. The foreign ministry should be a natural strongpoint of the old elites the generals represent, yet they allow its influence to be gutted. Essentially, of the four co-rulers, only Heydrich involves himself in the day-to-day operation of the government. The other three have a vote on major policy, but leave him to implement it. The generals have shown so little interest that even their natural allies among the technocrats are gravitating to Heydrich. Therefore, I have a permanent liaison in his office and, after your reorganization of the cabinet, I will have an SS liaison here at my headquarters." He stopped to see the somewhat frightened looks from his co-conspirators. "Be of good cheer. Heydrich let me choose who it would be. This is liaison, not a superior to me. If you are wise, you will let me find another von Paulus so you can each have one. This national cooperation is tricky. Best to have someone who knows the right phone numbers...has the right relationships."

Balbo asked the obvious question. "Why Germans here and not Italians there?"

"Because we never offered them. We have the usual diplomats, attachés and liaison staff, but no one with direct practical relations and access to the key people. To Heydrich, Todt, General Thomas, Speer, Richthofen...I can get you a list of who has real power and over what. Each should have an Italian you two personally trust directly as part of their headquarters family. Von Paulus's links are to OKW, so we are covered there already. Have I your permission to do so? Our old military command was too hidebound to do this. Il Duce was too obsessed with this idiocy of a Parallel War, and of his own special relationship with the late Führer, a beast now safely removed from life. Oh, and a gift from Reichsführer-SS Heydrich for your talk with your father. If your father will see to these things Heydrich wishes, Germany will do its best to get the British to return any private funds the throne had banked or invested in London. This will be made as part of their reparations at the peace conference."

The Prince gasped and then smiled. This would be a powerful card to trade to his father.

> 1200 hours
> 14 July
> Railway switching yard, Bologna, Italy

Back when plans were firming up in Ploiesti, Gunter had sent a few telegrams off to some old chums offering them jobs. He had given Oberführer Schellenberg as the mail drop to reply through. The two who had said yes were waiting for him as his train pulled in. Both had their old SA uniforms on, only with new rank tabs making them majors in the NL.

Gimpy-legged Gregor Voss was leaning on his cane with his "nephew" Hans by his side. Gregor was in his early forties with an artificial foot, a bad leg, and a scrawny body. Four years at the front and then the Iron Division afterward. He'd lost the foot in the "liberation" of the Ruhr from the Reds in 1920. Hans was a big boy of 25 with the mind of a 12-year-old. His father had died in the war. His mother had abandoned him during the hard days of the Depression. Gregor had taken him in, knowing him as a well-meaning, if slow-witted, soul who should not be left to wander the streets. While Gregor had worked with Gunter at the Post Office, Hans had run packages for a local grocery. There was no cash pay, but they did feed him after a fashion. Apparently, he didn't need much food as he had grown tall and strong, with straw-blond hair and childlike blue eyes. They each had a cloth carry bag with their few possessions.

Adolph Wrede was another veteran of the trenches, Freikorps, and SA, who landed up in the Post Office. He was a short, well-muscled man in his mid-forties, his brown hair starting to gray and his brown eyes hard and sharp. Beside him was the source of much of his troubles in life, Wanda the Polack. She was a tad more than half his age and was built for endurance not beauty. Her body showed the musculature of a woman who had done heavy labor since her early teens. Beside her were her six brats. The oldest was in his early teens, the youngest still a toddler. The two youngest were Adolph's, but the brood came with Wanda as a package deal. He was deeply hooked on this foul-mouthed neighbor of his. Their possessions were on a dolly. Gunter didn't have to ask. He'd helped the two of them move a few times. Where Wanda went, the equipment for her still went. The "vodka" she brewed could double as paint remover. It was cheap and potent. She always found a way to pay off enough cops to stay in business, at least in the ends of town that would rent to the nominally German brat of a Polish veteran from then-Russian Lodz who had fought four years for the Kaiser and then had gone to work the mines of the Ruhr. Wanda's parents had turned her out at 12 as incorrigible with regards to men and whiskey. She'd been thrown into the gutter, but never stayed there. The woman was a born hustler and a willing worker, even when drunk.

Wanda had also scrounged up an urn of what passed for ersatz coffee in Italy. Whatever it was, it was brown and warm with a lot of some kind of sugar. Just Wanda being Wanda. He gave her a hug and gathered the three adults in to explain things. Adolph did the talking. Wanted to know how Gunter was now in with big-shot SS officers?

"I'll tell you the whole story when we get further south. Remember that Berlin rally you turned me down on? Said I was crazy, that old SA guys like us couldn't reverse what the Blood Purge did to us? Well, I'm a lieutenant colonel now. You are both majors. Do right by me, and when I'm a general, you'll be colonels with big houses."

Wanda started to laugh. "You seem to have landed on your feet for sure. Some SS Standartenführer shows up once we telegraphed, yes, and made magic with the paperwork. He even gave me papers to get my 'headquarters kitchen equipment' onto the railroad and through Italian customs. So, where's this hush-hush thing we're off to?"

Just like Wanda to get to the meat of the problem. "I'm going to some island called Malta with a few of my boys. Some Brit asses we've got to kick. You two are taking the rest of my battlegroup to some Italian port called Taranto. I'll give you a list of how many trainloads, but essentially you get a space to camp out, get our people assembled, and wait on shipping. I've got some other officers we picked up along the way. Hungarians, Jews…"

Gregor interrupted, "Yids? And us…with the SS?"

"Approved by the Reichsführer himself. Indeed, on his express orders. There's a colony being grabbed out in some half-desert wog-land southeast of here. Got lots of oil. I babysat an oil field in Romania for a few days, so I'm an instant expert on oil fields." Gunter paused to wipe the sweat from his face. It was oppressively hot, plus the usual chaos of a rail yard. Dozens of nasty competing odors, plus coal ash descending from the skies as the locomotives belched the bad war-time coal back out. "Anyway, this is the NL, not the SS or SA. Our unit of the NL is tagged for colonial service. Like in the Kaiserwar, where we put uniforms on all those blacks. What leaves Europe with us doesn't come back. Now, I've got these different old-time captains and majors to run things internally. However, the German military, much less the Italians, aren't going to take some guy who can speak two hundred words of bad German seriously as an officer. That's where you two come in. One of them tells you when there is a problem. You and he march off through the offices to get it fixed. He knows what needs fixing and you are the real German to prove this whole thing is on the level. If you hit real problems, you just telegraph Berlin. Our superiors there can work magic. Good pay, good prospects, and, yes, you can bring the families along. Most of my troops have done so. Berlin knows and approves, hence there is nothing you have to hide. Oh, and our other protector is an army general named Rommel. Blue Max-wearer. We are part of his guys, 7th Panzer Division. You are the main party of battlegroup Strauss. You are going by ship to Libya, and then wherever they tell you until we take Egypt."

The two guys stood there blinking. How the fuck did their old buddy Gunter pull this off? Majors! Wanda just started yelling at Hans and her oldest son Adam to get the equipment loaded onto the train. Wanda knew a good deal when she saw one. A big military port and chaos. She'd have the still up in a day and be peddling vodka to thirsty boys.

1400 hours
14 July 1940
Railyards, Bologna, Italy

They were stuck going nowhere yet again. Her Lieutenant was off with the Lieutenant Colonel picking up a freight shipment for the company. Greta had found a pile of timbers to sit on. There was the hint of a breeze here for some reason, so it was a better place to sweat a bit less. Her life had changed radically these past few days and she was taking a timeout to reflect on all of it.

Many of the other women were bustling about with various

chores for the unit or their families. Everyone knew better than to assign work to her. She was the Lieutenant's. Only he or the Lieutenant Colonel gave her tasks.

A month ago, being sent for the summer to stay with her aunt was an adventure far from home. Now she was in her second new country, or was it her third? She was less than sure if Austria was a separate country or part of Germany or still part of Hungary. She knew there had been several changes since her father was her age, but none of that had seemed important for a teenage girl to learn. She was going to send a card to her parents when they arrived wherever they were going. Klaus had promised her and the young man seemed good at keeping promises. Greta found him strange but quite pleasant. It wasn't at all like her aunt or the rest of the elders thought. She wasn't a slave, a concubine. She sort of understood that he could have treated her poorly, that he had all the power. Instead he was kind with her, gentle. He really seemed to want her to like him. Very strange and it all needed thought. Life was proving to be nothing like what her parents had prepared her for. She was thankful she had her aunt to guide her instead of her mother. Her mother got loud and angry when the world failed to work the way she, Ruth Levi, had decided it should. Her aunt seemed better at accepting how paradoxical things were. Much more like her father, which was funny as she was her Mom's sibling.

These half-houghts were interrupted by a group of Betar girls approaching her. This somewhat startled Greta. The Betar folks, male and female, treated Greta with respect. She was their commander's woman. Respect, but also a definite social distance. They all somewhat knew each other. They were all part of the same youth movement. They were veterans, or so they told everyone who would listen. They had fought with the mighty General Rommel. They were Jewish warriors, like the Maccabees or the Zealots. Yet, here they were. The leader, a willowy girl in her mid-twenties with midnight-black hair and dark eyes, approached still closer. "Miss Greta. Would you like to learn to use a gun?"

Greta was startled. "A gun? I'm the officer's mistress and the cook. What do I know from guns?"

"Aren't you going to Malta with us? We are supposed to drop from the sky in gliders. There will be British there. The same as what oppress us in Palestine. We will fight them as part of our road to our homeland. We must redeem our land with battle."

Greta's family had been vaguely Zionist the same way they were vaguely socialist. Zionist because Romania had been a bad place to be a Jew. Socialist because no one else would have the Jews. They really hadn't been much of anything. Her father wasn't a joiner because he saw all such organizing as futile and dangerous. Her mother...her mother would fight with anyone about anything. She wouldn't join anything and, anyway, no one would have her. But that was then. This new Aryan Greta was in the NL, and apparently that meant being in Betar. Greta knew the word, but not the whole history and ideology of what made Betar's Revisionist Zionism different than any other flavor. She was having enough trouble figuring out how she could be an Aryanized ex-Jew in a military that was part of the SS, except it sort of wasn't. Even stranger, important SS generals knew her name, had specifically approved of her. This was a lot for an unworldly 18-year-old to take in. "Will It be useful for me with Klaus?"

The leader, whose name proved to be Naiomi, assured her it would be. Modern men wanted women who could fight beside them, not little painted dolls who fainted, like from their parent's generation. Greta wasn't at all sure, but it would pass the time. They found a bunch of discarded crates and oil cans. Set them up as targets next to a sand pile. The girls then began teaching her a bit of pistol and rifle. Once the Betar girls discovered that she didn't see herself as some princess because she had an officer, they became quite friendly. They were amused to discover that Greta had been a virgin before all this. They gave her instructions on sex as well. A lot of things her aunt either didn't know or didn't think Greta could cope with. Some Greta thought she lacked the gymnastic abilities for but, even if it didn't work, trying them should amuse Klaus. He could not seem to get enough sex. The girls told her boys were like that.

The noise of the shooting in a railyard quickly attracted Italian attention. The freight yard staff called the 6th Railway Legion, whose Militia members were charged with protecting this facility. A large patrol was sent immediately. They quickly located the source of the problem—some of the Germans passing through. They had strict orders to avoid any incidents with these people, but they couldn't just permit such shooting to continue. The problem was compounded as they didn't speak much German and it turned out neither did these so-called Germans. The initial impasse gave time for one of the Magyars to amble over to see what was going on. He turned out to have in civilian life been a commercial traveler who knew a bit of Italian, enough for communication of a sort to occur.

While it was being sorted out, other members of Strauss's battlegroup arrived with bottles of wine and various types of sausage and edibles, looking to join what sounded from a distance like a party to liven up the boring wait in the railyards. As those were passed around, the Militiamen decided that a bit of shooting under their supervision would not be a problem. They had to prove they were better shots than mere girls. Pretty girls willing to flirt. The honor of Italian manhood was at stake. It turned into quite the party. A bit later, a small patrol of Royal Carabiniers arrived to find the festivities in full swing, with a Roma band from the prisoners liberated in Hungary providing music for dancing. This gave time for a Militia officer and one of Strauss's to both arrive, placing limits on the shooting, if not on the convivial eating, drinking, and laughter. More Italians arrived with bread and other Italian specialties to show that hospitality flowed both ways. Both officers decided a small party was a better way to pass the time than an altercation that neither chain of command would welcome.

Eventually Klaus returned and the noise and laughter led him to Greta the Aryan gunslinger. The freight had been their uniforms. They had been "gifted" with two freight car loads of WW1 French blue uniforms. These had apparently sat in a warehouse since 1919 and smelled to high heaven of various preservative chemicals. A wash area was being constructed of old oil barrels to boil the clothes clean. The girls got the hint that this was work they would have to take part in. Greta had a different idea. Told them to clean out one of the passenger cars from their train and guard it. She then led Klaus off to try a few of the new sexual possibilities. Some worked. Some didn't. Either way they got a few hours of strenuous exercise and found new muscle groups to work to soreness. Teen spirit at work.

1900 hours
14 July 1940
Royal Palace, Rome, Italy

Prince Umberto hoped never to have to go through another encounter as unpleasant as this meeting with his father had been.

He had expected his father to be difficult. He had not expected endless vituperation of his own sexuality, or his wife's. What mattered such petty things when the fate of the nation was at stake? He had been a good son and prince. He had not hurled back the truth, that the Germans were prepared to sanction the King's murder if that was the price of getting their own way.

Still, he had the decree. He was Lieutenant General of the Realm until the conclusion of peace with the British Empire. The Grand Council would meet tomorrow morning to complete matters.

Chapter 20

0100 hours
15 July 1940
The largest beer garden in Bonn, Germany

Herman Göring was having a wonderful time. The victory parade had been excellent. The crowds were wild with joy to see their men back from the war and ready to be demobilized. His speech congratulating them on their fine war record had been quite well-received. His comparison of a six-week campaign to four years of slaughter in the last war had provoked roars of approval. No one wanted another Great War. Hitler's victory was becoming in the public mind a joint victory of both Führers, old and new.

The luncheon afterward had been a success as well. The notables of the town, the senior military men from both the town and the division, and the Party leaders from the Gau, had all been feasted at the best hotel ballroom in town to conquered French delicacies and champagne. The proper toasts were made and the proper speeches ensued. Göring could easily fulfill these functions. His actress-second wife simply treated it as another script to learn. A few hours of fake joy and rigid formalities.

The night party was another story. It was a less formal affair. Free beer and wine, an open buffet of simple, hearty German food. It was for the junior officers, the decorated enlisted men, gold Party badge-holders, activists from the Kreis levels of the Movement, HJ leaders, and anyone else who could talk their way past the quite lenient guards.

At what had supposedly been Nebe's suggestion, Göring had brought along a squad of photographers. His wife had arranged for Olga and a bevy of starlets from the Berlin film industry to join the party. There was little formal speech-making. Mostly it was endless people coming up to shake his hand, make a few minutes of small talk, and have their picture taken with him or one of the starlets. Göring was winning personal loyalties. A small squad of note-takers were at his side, as many of these men had small requests. A license to be expedited for some business. A brother to get early demobilization for the holidays. Little things, but like a king in medieval times, the favors from the throne would be remembered and praised by each lucky recipient to friends, work mates, and family. The more Göring thought about it, the more he became convinced that this was Heydrich's idea, using Nebe as a conduit. Heydrich...the man was a mystery surrounded by an enigma. Still, better on his side than opposing him.

> 0240 hours
> 15 July 1940
> Railway siding northeast of Florence, Italy

Gunter Strauss had been wondering how to convert the bulkier loot he had acquired in Hungary into more manageable form. Now opportunity had presented itself. There was a German truck convoy pulled off to the side of the road adjacent to the railway siding. Support units from the new Afrika Korps moving south by road because of the absence of enough railway cars to send everyone by rail had produced strays all over Italy. The German military police, the chain dogs, would gather these up into ad hoc convoys and shepherd them south towards the embarkation ports. Strauss wandered over to this convoy. The senior officer proved to be a reserve lieutenant, a middle-aged veteran of the Kaiserwar. Turned out he and Strauss had served in a few of the same places, if not with the exact same units. Besides Strauss was a field officer. In the end, half a dozen bottles of wine passed over to the lieutenant and cargoes were rearranged, freeing up a truck for a "special mission". Strauss signed a receipt for the truck, which covered the lieutenant adequately.

A quick work party loaded the various liberated items into the truck, which Strauss would drive to Naples, the designated port for this vehicle. He also loaded six Magyars—tough, young guys who knew enough not to gossip too much. Besides, none of them spoke Italian, so who in Italy could they tell? He put Gregor in charge of the train. Adolph's judgment was often suspect, more so when in proximity to Wanda. Gregor was to take the people through to wherever they were headed, then forward Steiner on to Sicily. He handed Steiner his orders and repeated what the boy was to do. When he arrived at the station, find the first German officer he saw, present his orders, and get directed to proper transport. He doubted the boy could screw up something this simple, but if he did, so be it. The priority was converting the art works, antiques, and other items into folding money, gold, or jewels. A condotierre must see to finances first.

0650 hours
15 July 1940
Freight yards, Florence, Italy

The young people had been slowly gathering since dusk. The story had been passed from family to family—the Race Law of 1938 was being set aside. Young Italians tagged as racial Jews would be allowed to show their patriotism, to rehabilitate themselves in the eyes of their nation. The initial story had been for Revisionist Zionists with some training in military activities and sound Fascist idealism. The story had morphed in the telling as it bounced from family to family, street to street. Those that defied their parents and reached the railway station were from a variety of political backgrounds. In addition to other flavors of Zionists, they included Republicans, Socialists, and just plain oddballs. Some were not even racial Jews, but had Jewish friends or neighbors. The one fragment that remained constant regardless of storytelling was that a company of Romanian Betar volunteers was passing through. Volunteers that brave, young people could run off to, bypassing such silliness as formal mobilization, recruit barracks...they could be adventurers like the ones who had marched with Garibaldi.

Young Oriana might just be the oddest ball of all. She was mostly there because she was told she couldn't be. She was too young. She was politically oppositional. She was physically too little. Oriana did not cope with authority well. Telling her she couldn't do something was, in many ways, the fastest way to get her to insist. She had snuck away from home without even a change of clothes. She ignored the older volunteers repeatedly trying to send her home. When they chased her around the station, she just hid and then crept back near them. Now she was following the pack to the train with the Germans they would be joining.

A few of the volunteers spoke German. That got them sent to Steiner's Betar company. A few more of the volunteers spoke Yiddish. Most of Steiner's people spoke Yiddish, although of a different dialect. Lieutenant Steiner accepted that the volunteers were now his until their own officer appeared. Just who that officer was or where he would be appearing was not something Steiner was focused on. Beyond more sex with Greta, his sole concern was not disappointing Strauss. However, he didn't have to worry about Sicily until the train arrived someplace. By an hour later, when the train left the freight yards, these new Italians were part of the established order. They had also learned they were going to Malta.

0700 hours
15 July 1940
Stendal Germany, Garrison of 7th Flieger-Division

Major General Gerhard Ramcke returned from Berlin elated at his career prospects. He had met with the highest levels of German command. He had been shown a road to promotion and favor. He had been allowed to amend the original insane plan to something that might just work...if the intelligence were correct. However, a potentially intractable problem remained. He had to sell this to his field grade officers, who by now had been made aware through the usual gossip networks that every other senior officer in the division had requested transfer to avoid what promised to experienced parachute officers to be a worse debacle than Holland. Ramcke was not an experienced parachute officer. Indeed, he had yet to take that course. He was a relative stranger to most of these gentlemen. This would prove to be an interesting professional challenge.

His new adjutant had the field-grade officers assembled for a morning presentation. They did not seem a happy lot. Ramcke put his best professional face on. He stressed that this new plan had been approved at the highest levels. The division was to be split into a four-battalion storm brigade and a cadre division that would, over time, be rebuilt to full strength. The brigade would take an airfield in a daring dawn parachute descent...and before he could get the rest of this out, a major interrupted to ask how a general with no parachute training proposed to land. Was this brigade to include one glider as the general's personal chariot? The meeting had descended from there into chaos and acrimony. None of the officers here trusted higher command's glib intelligence assessments. None had any faith in him as a leader of men. This was an elite unit and Ramcke was a lateral transfer with an undistinguished career. Ramcke could feel his collar tightening, his temper rising. He was reduced to screaming sessions as, one by one, officers came up and handed him a written request for transfer.

When those with written requests were done, others were waiting with verbal requests. These probably had been waiting to see if the mutiny would happen. Indeed, captains and lieutenants, alerted to what was happening by their superiors, began queuing up. He lost his temper with one lieutenant, damning him as a coward and ordering him to withdraw the request. The young lieutenant, a veteran of the Rotterdam drop recently returned from convalescent leave, remained rigidly at attention and simply said, "Please give me that order in writing, sir. As a German officer, I will obey orders. However, after Holland, I will not lead men on another suicide mission. Bust me down to private and I'll gladly make the drop. Unlike you, I actually know how to jump out of an airplane with a parachute. That doesn't frighten me. Death or wounds don't frighten me. Losing all but two of my platoon in the first ten minutes of an operation that stood no chance...is something I will not willingly do again. You, sir, know nothing of airborne operations. Officers that supposedly did know accepted a plan that was a disaster against the half-trained Dutch. You expect me to believe the British, professional soldiers of a great power, are leaving an airfield unguarded?" The young man laughed bitterly and held out his hand. "I'm waiting for that written order or the demotion, sir. Have you the moral courage to do either?" When Ramcke stood there paralyzed, the lieutenant laughed even more mordantly, did a perfect salute, an about-face, and marched out of the room as if on dress parade.

The remaining officers went no better. At last, Ramcke was alone in the room. Even his adjutant had deserted him...and the adjutant returned with tea and a biscuit. Ramcke sagged on seeing this. He barely knew the boy lieutenant's name. He had been gifted with this Lieutenant Alois Schmidt on his Berlin visit. He was well-spoken and seemed to have some education. Now this Schmidt guided his commander into a chair, made him sip some tea, and at least nibble the biscuit. Caffeine and blood sugar. The universal cures. Ramcke had his head in his hands. He was ruined. When he reported this disaster to Berlin, he would be relieved. What a sad, demeaning end to a lifetime of service and....

"Sir. It's not that bad."

"Not that bad?" The puppy was clueless. "How do I form a

brigade without officers?"

"Sir. I escaped from the Air Ministry to be your adjutant. It's overfilled with young lieutenants and captains eager for something more vigorous to do than hold doors for generals and get tea for colonels, than moving dossiers on office supply inventories from one desk to another." Ramcke had the sense to flush, seeing as this servant's current function was just what Schmidt had performed. Schmidt saw recognition dawn and smiled back at his superior. "Let me call back and I'll get as many young, fit, junior officers as you need. So they don't know how to jump out of airplanes. Some will die or cripple themselves when they drop untrained over Malta. I'll tell them the risks. I know dozens myself. People I worked beside. Good lads. Bored out of their minds. It won't be the first time a captain commanded a battalion, or a lieutenant a company. Besides, after Malta you may choose to promote many of them into the proper rank for their functions."

Ramcke stopped and thought. Maybe not perfect, but not anything that needed to be reported to Berlin either. He knew an old comrade in the Air Ministry personnel office who could grease the transfers if he mentioned Heydrich's name. He could hide the officers' rebellion here by detailing all of them to the cadre division he was leaving behind. After Malta...was after Malta. Either he'd be dead and it wouldn't matter, or victorious...and it wouldn't matter. His command presence returned. "I will make a phone call to Berlin to set up this process, Captain Schmidt. You will be returning to Berlin tomorrow as deputy commander of the Ramcke Brigade. Part of your tasks will be to locate a new adjutant for me, one who will live up to the high standard you have set."

Young Captain Schmidt gave a crisp salute, executed an about-face himself, and set off to pack. He planned on being Major Schmidt after Malta. He did not consider dying as his superior had. He was a healthy twenty and, therefore, immortal.

1400 hours
15 July 1940
Villa Savoia, Rome, Italy

The actual meeting of the Grand Council had taken less than half an hour. The united front of the King, Prince/Lieutenant General, Governor General Balbo, and a small cadre of German friends from the various military and police services had made the situation crystal clear even before the meeting was formally called to order. The new cabinet was voted in. The two parliamentary chambers would ratify it to be official, but that was a mere formality, as all assembled here were aware.

The Duce was packed off for a month's well-deserved rest at the Villa Melzi d'Eril in Bellagio. The Royal Carabinieri escort was done with all proper pomp and ceremony. It would not be obvious to casual observers that these were also de facto jailors. It was not officially exile. Mussolini retained all his titles and glory. It was his power of which he had been stripped, but only the ruling elite was aware of this. The EIAR news release spoke of easing the strains on the great man to preserve him for Italy's future, and of adding the Lieutenant General and Vice-Premier to take administrative burdens.

Balbo was in the front of the meeting hall, letting each new minister and secretary kiss the ring as it were. They all knew him, but were now in the process of beginning to firm up their relationship with him as ruler, as boss. The Prince was off to the side, in a different corner from his angry, aloof father. An SS officer approached him, introduced himself as Gruppenführer Karl Wolff. The Prince took the greeting coldly and formally, asking if Wolff was to be his new "minder".

"Only if you wish it to be that way. Hopefully you are not as pigheaded and short-sighted as the Horthyites. Even they repented in a day."

"Then why are you assigned to me?"

"To avoid a Budapest here. Making a bureaucratic super-Europa needs personal relationships. Needs face-to-face associations, not diktats from Berlin. Hungary was as much bad timing as anything else. Our new regime was quite unsteady in its working structures. Two weeks later, it would all have been better handled. The Reichsführer would have been given a directive and carried it out with better personnel than General von Kluge and SS General Müller. We would probably have enlisted your good offices. The Vatican's as well."

The Prince took a few minutes to consider this. "So, the offer to try to get my father's money back was sincere?"

"Certainly. The binational committee on peace proposals will be formed after the fall of Egypt. The idea will be for our two ambassadors in Switzerland or Portugal to make it known to their

British counterpart that this is a cabinet war for limited objectives, not a war to the death of nations. Churchill does not have the confidence of the bulk of his parliamentary colleagues. In time, if the elites of the major British political parties can be made aware that we are offering sensible terms, we expect him to be voted out. Then a peace conference in Lisbon or Geneva."

"Britain will never truly accept a German-dominated Europe."

"We'll settle for an armed truce. Our only non-negotiable demand will be no heavy bombers in the British Isles. An easy enough demand to verify. A few hundred German and Italian officers given free access to airfields to report on runway lengths and construction. No need to see inside hangers if the runways are short enough and not rated for weights above specific ground pressures. Runway inspections and some overflight rights by photo reconnaissance planes. The general public would not see our officers often enough to feel national outrage."

"Bank your winnings?"

"For us, yes, once we have Iraq. Ask yourself this. Three weeks ago, staring at national bankruptcy and your joke of an Alpine campaign, did you wish more war? An ill-timed war that pissed away much of your merchant marine, of your father's wealth, that seemed likely to lose you your African Empire? Now we offer you an expanded empire and probably your merchant ships and money back, or at least most of them. Merchant ships and overseas trade that Italy badly needs. You lost over a third of your merchant tonnage—a nation that depends on sea transport for 84% of its pre-war imports." Wolff paused as if trying to visualize a prior set of briefing notes. "If I remember correctly my briefing by the Reichsführer's staff, you lack the rail capacity to do without this even if there were enough Alpine tunnels to handle the added traffic. Having gotten your ships and money back, why would you willingly risk your winnings? Berlin chooses peace and consolidation in the manner of Bismarck after the French War. If the British or Soviets want a new war, we'll deal with that, but that's their choice. One of the marks of a statesman is knowing when to quit gambling your nation's future."

The Prince looked this pompous fool over. He'd be doing a lot of business with this Wolff, so best not to put him in his place. "Beyond the ships, how do we get the British to trade with us, to allow our goods to pass their fleets onto the oceans of the world? Our major trade partners were in the Americas and the Balkans.

We will need British permission to reach the first, and yours to reach the second."

The pretentious ass of an SS general surprised the Prince. He stopped, took the comment in, and advised the Prince to start assembling the proper experts for this joint committee, as no one in Berlin had considered that this would have been one of Italy's needs. The Berlin minder seemed to actually care what the Prince wished, what Italy needed. Perhaps he really was a facilitator and not a minder after all.

The Prince was left with food for thought as General Wolff began to circulate around the room, introducing himself to the new rulers of Germany's Italian ally.

Chapter 21

1600 hours
16 July 1940
Seaside road, Naples, Italy

Joey Bats was bored. He'd come to Italy with his father in early May. Having finished mourning for his dead wife, his father had returned to Naples to meet with several of his dead wife's nieces and cousins and find a replacement. As a property-owning prosperous man in his early fifties with multiple successful businesses in fabled New York, many families were quite willing to discuss marrying their daughters to a man twice or more their age. Everything was being done with proper decorum and chaperoning, which made this a slow process. Dad got to feel he was a big man and some girl of twenty would acquire American prosperity.

Dad had pushed Joey to accompany him. Said it was time for him to find a wife. As if. Joey had his own reasons for saying yes. It was a good time for him to be absent from New York. He'd been warned that a grand jury subpoena was coming for him as a "material witness", that it would be wise if he relocated for a while. Joey wasn't a serious wise guy. Neither was his father. During Prohibition, his father had provided trucks with drivers for various bootleggers. Joey was a mechanic. He'd dropped out of school at ten. He fixed trucks, cars, appliances. There wasn't any sort of mechanical device he hadn't learned to master. If it involved eye-hand coordination, tools, and machines, he was a wonder. This had led to him being recommended to a particular crew out of Brownsville who wanted very fast, reliable cars. Fast, reliable cars that could be chopped expediently after one use. Joey and the boss at the auto wrecker he worked at knew what these guys did. No one wanted to know details. The Brownsville Boys had another name in the papers—Murder Incorporated. These were not people it was wise to annoy. Besides, they were very good customers and paid premium prices in cash.

Only this prosecutor, Dewey, had been hammering on the Boys for years now. That attack eventually had reached Joey's employer, who had sold the wrecker yard/chop shop and advised everyone to leave town for a year or two 'til things blew over. Joey had been planning on trying his luck in LA, where he had a few cousins. Then his Mom had died suddenly after a brief illness. Sad, but at least it hadn't been painful. His father had suggested a paid vacation to the old country. Joey had shrugged and gone along. Was supposed to be a few months, after which he'd catch a boat to LA.

Then came this stupid war and Dad had gotten patriotic. Wanted Joey to "do his military service". Joey had zero interest in joining the Italian army. Italy was the Old Man's country. Joey regarded himself as American. In the ensuing family dispute, Dad had stolen his passport and cut him off financially. Shrug. Joey had prudently brought his own bankroll with him. US dollars in big bills could be swapped for lire at quite interesting rates if you knew the right people. Through a cousin, Joey had gotten to know some of the right people. Had found a flop, some part-time work souping up auto engines. He wasn't hurting. But the US consulate in Naples was stalling on getting him a new passport. The excuse was "clarifying" Joey's draft status in Italy. What was there to clarify? He was American-born. A friend had airmailed him a copy of his baptismal certificate, plus a few sworn statements of folks who knew him. Maybe it was a stall until that grand jury paper caught up with him. Meantime, he was hanging out at this café off the harbor road between jobs. The coffee was good but it was getting boring. Went on much longer and he'd just buy a street passport. Problem was that Joey wasn't sure what passed for quality with those. A fellow could get in a bottomless pit of trouble if that went bad. So, he waited. And got bored. Joey got bored easily. Life in New York did not include boredom. There was always places to go, people to meet, things to do. Times Square ran all night, as did a bunch of even less savory places.

He'd spent half an hour watching a broken-down German truck a few tens of meters up the road. Colors said German, field gray. Shape said Ford, possibly British. The officer seemed willing to get his hands dirty, but he also seemed clueless. He'd done the basic checks and gotten nowhere. Joey decided this might be interesting....

Gunter was beside himself. The truck had died before he could begin trying to find a shop to fence his stuff. Sooner or later, a dead truck would attract official attention. Attention he didn't want and attention Berlin would not be pleased with. He was in the process of cursing a blue streak in several languages when this

135

local crossed the road and walked up. Guy looked in his twenties. Dressed a bit better than a workman, but not up to the standards of a professional or a shopkeeper. The hands showed the sort of ground-in dirt and grease that said mechanic. This could be the answers to his prayers.

Guy said hello in bad German. Gunter took his hand. Guy introduced himself as Joey. Joey? Now Gunter placed the accent. "You from New York?"

Joey switched to English. "Joey Bats." At Gunter's uncomprehending look, "Giuseppi Battaglia. That's what the baptismal says. Joey Bats is what the street knows me as, but I also answer to 'Brooklyn'. Mind if I give this truck a look?" Not waiting for a reply, Joey dove under the hood and started doing things. Gunter could hear noises, minor curses in all three languages, and a bit of banging around as Joey started requesting tools. Twenty minutes later, the engine was again making functional noises. Barely. "It's running. For now. I give it under an hour 'til it stops for good. You need three parts and a bit of work. Where's your depot?"

Gunter thought fast and asked in English, "If I paid cash can YOU make this happen?"

Joey gave a laugh and hopped into the cab. Ten minutes later, the truck was in a lot next to a garage where Joey had done some work. Two hours later, the needed parts had been located and the truck was purring like it was almost new. In the interim, the two men had fenced a bit. Which neighborhoods did each know? A few names were dropped. A few knowing smiles were exchanged. They turned out to have had bosses who knew each other. Gunter had also driven trucks for bootleggers, had done muscle work, had run in circles similar to Joey's. This had led to a further discussion of whether perhaps this Brooklyn fellow might know a shop who dealt in antiques and art objects. Joey had sent a passing friend of a third cousin who returned with two gentlemen experienced in the acquisition of goods of doubtful provenance. When told that this German officer was willing to sign a bill of sale and provide the details of his military ID as proof should the Italian police make enquiries, prices were revised quite a bit upward. All in all, it was a profitable day's work for all concerned.

Joey was pleasantly surprised to see that this Gunter guy had given up a 5% finder's fee beyond his mechanic's charge. Naples was starting to seriously bore him. Fuck the old man and fuck Italy.

A good way not to be there for the Italian Army to decide they owned him was to just leave. Joey became Joe from Brooklyn, a good Volksdeutsche volunteering for the NL. Joey left a few lire with a buddy to see about forwarding his mail. Gunter provided the military postal address for the unit. The buddy said he could find the main German depot at the port to send any mail from the US Embassy onwards. Joining up with this Gunter guy seemed more like joining a New York street crew than actually joining an army. No boring stuff about a recruit barracks or saluting or any of that jive. Joey just sent for his carryall bag and tool kit. New things to fix and new places to go. A guy who could find a way to steal a truckload of swag in the middle of a war wouldn't be boring and Joey hated being bored.

2100 hours British Double Summer Time
16 July 1940
House of Commons visitor's gallery, Westminster, London, England

Ivan Maisky, Soviet Ambassador to Britain, had failed to get a meeting with Prime Minister Churchill. He had settled for one of his parliamentary secretaries. His orders from Moscow were quite clear. This information was to go directly to the top of the British government, but there was to be no paper trail. Strictly verbal. Maisky's contacts with the British ruling circles were well known. Moscow counted on them. The message was simple. The next German attack was to be on Malta. The attack was to be the first week of August. It was to be from the air and sea. The Italian fleet would be compelled to come out and fight. The attack force was four reinforced divisions and would include a new German air fleet. A divebombing expert was being sent from Berlin. There would also be a German naval contingent. Maisky's hardest task was to refuse to explain either how Moscow had gotten this information or why they wanted the British to have it. It helped that he had no clue as to either answer. He could also see he was less than fully believed. He chose not to include that part in his report to Moscow. Too many diplomats had already been liquidated.

0200 Moscow Time
17 July 1940

The Reich Without Hitler: The Falcons of Malta

The Kremlin, Moscow

The report was so good that Beria had almost been afraid to present it to the Boss. The actress proved to have a near-photographic memory for conversation, which she saw as dialog. She was also extremely good at providing mood to go with the words. The problem was that this Führer Göring proved almost phobic about actually doing his job, so what she had was endless social detail of his encounters with the mostly modest folks Göring spent his time with at the post-parade parties, plus his complaints on how much his ministers and minions wasted his time with details. The brother's report confirmed this. He had arrived by plane from Stockholm and been on Göring's staff before the day ended. Except instead of getting documents to photograph or otherwise steal, he discovered he would be creating those documents himself. Göring gave him five minutes of generalities and then made him his representative on the committee that was preparing Germany's position for the peace conference. The committee had two other members. One was a staff general whose sole purpose of existence seemed to be to reject out of hand everything that Heydrich's man proposed. Heydrich's man kept advocating an armed peace; accordingly, the generals seemed to want war, or perhaps they just hated Heydrich. The brother would need more time, but for now expect the Germans to arrive unprepared.

0240 hours
17 July 1940
Main railway yards, Napoli-Sperone Smistamento, Naples, Italy

Afterward, Gunter would plead exhaustion and distraction. He had clearly left Gregor in charge. He had avoided dealing with the chaos whirlwind that was Wanda. Adolph could never control her. Most days nothing could.

Wanda had added up the situation and decided she wasn't leaving the Steiner situation to anyone else. She had been handed the opportunity of a lifetime. For some absurd reason this callow, silly boy Steiner was a key to her future prosperity; therefore, she simply took charge of him.

Wanda had always been facile with languages on a street level. The gutter neighborhoods she had lived in had always been multinational Towers of Babel. Within a day she had picked up a hundred words of ungrammatical street Italian from Steiner's newbies. They had told her that Naples was the proper place for Steiner to transfer to Sicily. It was a big city and had a big train station, so she had detailed her man Adolph to hand-walk Steiner's combined company to a proper German transport officer. She had even stolen enough NL armbands for the Italians to void their civilian clothing. Adolph wasn't a smooth talker, but he was a major and he did have two magic names to throw around: Heydrich and Schellenberg. Wanda had the wisdom of the streets. Few junior bureaucrats wanted to involve the big boys in the big offices.

She kicked the boy awake, got his "troops" moving and then "improved" the situation. She had Adam and Hans with her. As Oriana joined the moving line, the boys grabbed her. When she fought, she got the back of Wanda's hand. The blow half-knocked the small girl out. Coming back to her senses, she found herself neatly tied up on Wanda's train carriage. Oriana started to howl and got Wanda's fist in her face. The child had the sense to shut up. Oriana reminded Wanda of a younger Wanda. Just what Steiner didn't need. Wanda morbidly laughed to herself, thinking of how much trouble she could have caused a combat unit in the chaos of battle. Oriana needed street-schooling, and Wanda appointed herself the girl's tutor.

0500 hours
17 July 1940
German Army Vehicle Park, military port of Naples, Italy

Gunter had treated his guys to a night of celebration. Joey had known a club. They had a good meal, lots to drink, and a small bevy of young tarts for dessert. Needless to say, no one got any real sleep, but everyone enjoyed the party. Returning the vehicle had proved interesting. It was clearly German military property. With a bit of pushing he had gotten the duty officer to accept that his smelly old French blue clothes could be an NL uniform. The story of how Gunter had come by the truck was stickier. It was outside normal practice and there was no accompanying paperwork. The captain on duty was an aged reservist who insisted on involving his superior by phone. Which meant waking the man, who was not amused at being awakened to hear a stupid story about a field officer from another branch whose "crime" was returning a truck without proper papers instead of the usual crime of demanding a truck with no papers at all. More time was lost while the awakened major berated the captain and then apologized to Gunter for his idiot subordinate. It was a German truck. Gunter was a German officer. If anyone had any problem later with why this truck had arrived in this place in the custody of this officer, there were procedures to involve the various chains of command. However, the big daily problem was vehicle convoys arriving short of vehicles because of alleged breakdowns. Command was going crazy trying to locate these. Now one had reappeared on its own. How and why could be left for historians to untangle.

Gunter's Magyars had sensibly used the time to doze off at the side, ignoring the noise and chaos. Joey was nowhere to be seen. One of the Magyars knew a bit more German and was able to point Gunter in the right direction. At one hundred meters, Gunter could see a crowd of enlisted types gathered around a truck. They were watching something. At ten meters, it became obvious that the something was Joey, assisted by two German Army mechanics, doing a rebuild on the truck's engine while Joey called out a running commentary on what was wrong with it and how you check. Gunter stopped, joined the audience, and twenty minutes later joined the applause when the formerly dead truck started to purr. He then retrieved Joey and extracted him before the resident staff found more trucks needing his miracles. This young man was a keeper.

Chapter 22

0900 hours
17 July 1940
Heydrich's private office, Berlin

As the new chief of the Chancellor's Guardians, Nebe felt somewhat strange requesting a meeting with Reichsführer Heydrich. Nebe knew he was supposed to be guarding Göring against Heydrich. Now he needed Heydrich's help to protect Göring from himself. Heydrich cleared his calendar with no questions and met him in private without Schellenberg. Nebe felt more and more awkward as he outlined Göring's guileless and probably brainless use of an almost certain Soviet agent. Heydrich heard him in silence and then passed across a dossier. Nebe opened it. He found his suspicions confirmed, including the name of young Lev's probable handler. What was even more explosive was the name of the handler of Lev's sister, an agent even more firmly placed in the Führer's intimate circle. Nebe did not shock easily. One did not rise high in the SS or the German police under Hitler while maintaining a delicate conscience. "You knew?"

"Suspected, and took proper precautions. Finding watchers in Berlin is easy. We are badly overstaffed. It just gave some lesser minions something to do. What do you propose to do about it?"

Nebe took a minute to compose himself, sipping tea and thinking furiously. He had expected several possibilities, but not this. "Why? You could use this to destroy the spy and advance yourself with Göring."

"That advances the cause of the generals, not ours or his. Accept our new Führer for who and what he is. He's an excellent head of state, but must be shielded from the burdens of government as much as possible. We save the two spies for when our Führer chooses to assert himself and do something disastrous. This is a card that can only be played once. In the meantime, spies we know of are of use. We feed them both what we want Moscow to hear. I've been doing so at these worthless committee meetings. My man is parading production totals we hope to hit in two or three years as if they were happening by this Christmas. He is also making clear that the SS and the Party desire a peace on reasonable terms with the Soviets. All the bellicosity is from the Army's man. This will all be reported to Stalin. We are his unwitting friends and advancing our interests serves his."

Nebe sipped more tea, engaged in more thought. Heydrich was content to let him wait. "Are we now conspiring against the Führer?"

"No. We conspire to help him behind his back. Isn't that what royal servants do? Make the Boss look good despite him. One of the faults of the prior regime was that the people at that level—Bormann, Himmler, Goebbels—all were so busy maneuvering for their own power and projects that they brought out the worst in our late leader. We must do the opposite. We all seek Germany' victory and the Movement's popularity, no?"

Nebe accepted this. He understood that in doing so he accepted that his greater loyalty was now to an abstract of Germany than to Göring, and that this made him in part Heydrich's creature. But as a patriot what else could he do?

1000 hours
17 July 1940
SS HQ, Berlin

Schellenberg finished reading the report from Romania . He would reduce it to a three-sentence summary for his ever-busy boss. He also knew how to read between the lines. The SS Hauptsturmführer had simply lost patience and liquidated the family. Mentally, Schellenberg shrugged. It was a suboptimal outcome, but quite within parameters. The original idea was to end queries on the missing daughter by arrest and deportation. The family would just tag onto Strauss's wandering gang of misfits at some point. The mother did not appear to be the type to be quietly Aryanized and vanished. Public liquidation would end interest in a missing daughter. The remaining task was to pull all record that the family had existed. No chance they would get every piece of paper. Romania was sloppy. Hungary, the former national home of this clan, was in chaos. The records handover for Hungary's lost lands had been spotty at best. However, if enough records were seized, the trail would be quite hard to track. "Perfect" is often the enemy of "good enough". Easy to send a memo to Budapest, Bucharest, and Vienna, which he added at the last second in case some of the father's war records had migrated from one War Ministry to the other. A thorough records search for this man, Israel Levi, and all relatives. Levi identified by street address, profession, names of parents, and military service identification. The Hauptsturmführer had sent a large packet of family records gathered from the house. This Levi had been meticulous on such, but then bookkeepers tended to be.

And so the wheels continued to turn, to erase that there had ever been a person once known as Greta Levi.

1100 hours
17 July 1940
War Ministry, Bendler Block, *Tiergarten district of* Berlin

General Paul Hausser found the summons most peculiar. He was invited to appear at this meeting for "orientation", but the invitation was verbal, with an instruction to wear his old Reichswehr uniform instead of his current SS one. He had alerted Heydrich's office and been advised by Schellenberg that it was best that he complied. The tone implied that his SS superiors were aware of this, and that he had passed a loyalty test by calling.

The colonel who made the invitation had arranged for Hausser to be chauffeured to the Ministry and then guided Hausser in through a side service entrance up to the Minister's office. Hausser recognized a few faces as he was walked toward the inner sanctum, but everyone made a great show of not noticing him. Interesting.

What was even more interesting was that neither Minister Beck nor General Halder showed any interest in being given a precis of Hausser's coming campaign or of the reorganization of his division into this new panzer-grenadier format. Instead the talk was of Heydrich, and what was being done with the other two Waffen SS divisions. Almost as if these senior officers did not believe the reports their colonels had sent them.

"It's simple really. I have a real division and will do real fighting. The police will be civilized police in Paris and Eicke's boys will be the thugs they are in Poland. Is any of this a problem to the Army?"

Halder did the talking for the two seniors. "It's confusing. Why isn't Heydrich fighting to have more divisions instead of fewer?"

Hausser took a few seconds to compose his words. This was a most peculiar discussion. Surely these gentlemen knew he was scarcely in the inner circle around Heydrich like Schellenberg.

The Reich Without Hitler: The Falcons of Malta

"There isn't room in Africa for loads of divisions. Logistics. Mine is the best of the three. General Josef Dietrich might contest that, but his lot are the dress parade guards. They are also only a regiment, although I know there are plans for their expansion. LAH has a ceremonial function they can return to. By restricting the service to one elite division, Reichsführer Heydrich builds the Waffen SS's prestige...and his own, of course."

"We have heard reports about the Death's Head division and the murders of British prisoners...."

"Sadly true. They are thugs. Another reason to bury them in Poland where no one cares." Hausser hoped the LAH's similar misdeeds stayed buried. "I have firm instructions to fight a gentleman's war against the British. Even coloreds are to be treated as befit civilized soldiers. Indeed, I have been given the power to execute out-of-hand for violations. The orders are to make no provocations. Just honest war. All proper forms to be observed as if this were the time of Frederick the Great."

"And when you reach Palestine. What of the Jews?"

Hauser again paused. The Waffen SS didn't handle Jewish policy per se. Besides, the officer corps had never been particularly friendly to "those people". "That's an Italian problem. Look at this from the SS's point of view. We started out with under a million Jews. We killed a few thousand and chased many of the rest out. Then we took Austria and the Czech lands and got back to where we started from. We chased another chunk out before the war, then we took Poland...and got stuck with three million more." Hausser could see the looks of distaste on Beck's face. Absurd. The man supported the Nazi rise to power and only turned against them when Hitler risked war over the Czechs, a war Beck expected Germany would lose. "Yes, the SS killed a few tens of thousands in the first months of occupation. That was a mix of Himmler and the border Gauleiters." These two already knew this, so why the question? There had been nasty words between the Army and the SS over those pogroms. Somehow the Army ignored its own massacres of imaginary Polish partisans. Partisans! Poorly trained Red Army troops had shot anything that moved. "Germany also picked up another million or so more Jews between Hungary and Romania. Himmler was a bumbler. A fanatic on the Jewish Question, but surprisingly squeamish in practice. Heydrich is the reverse. He wants a Jew-free space for us, but is completely agnostic on how we get there. Mass murder is messy. He's gotten this new Hoover Commission to take over feeding them. A few will starve on the transition and more than a few will die of disease in the ghettos we will push them into. But the project is to use them as a labor reserve until the rail capacity opens up to move them to Italy. Probably the Hungarians ones first, as Italy is taking the lead there. But, give it a few years, and our half of Europe will be Jew-free, without us getting our hands that dirty or upsetting the gentlemen of the officer corps. He's worked around the scruples of our caste and class. He's even allowing Manstein to recruit the halflings." Hausser paused to give the two a withering look. "There's a new officer tasked to the Jewish Question. Name of Eichmann. I forget his rank or the exact title. Do you want me to arrange a briefing?"

"We heard of him. In addition, that he's recruited some Jewish paramilitaries." This time Beck was doing the talking and clearly disgusted with the whole topic.

"That was your General Rommel in Romania. It worked well. Heydrich is a good technocrat. There's no way to apply the Race Laws in Iraq. So why not Jews, halflings, Tatars, Magyars, and whatever locals prove useful? The more of them we can use, the fewer good Aryans dilute their seed in colonial garrisons."

"Yes. It's all very logical and efficient, and..."

"And very unlike Hitler or Himmler. Heydrich is different. He doesn't need the dramatics of the early Nazis. To him, the Movement is a bureaucracy to master, not a cult they helped nurture. Over time, the clueless fanatics will be eased out of power. His dream is a Germanic superpower on the order of the Soviet Union or the British Empire."

Halder spent a minute thinking how to phrase this. "You were one of us once, a regular general in a civilized army. He's a cashiered junior naval officer. Can we really ever be comfortable with him?"

Hausser had to fight to control his temper. These men and the caste they represented had pushed him out in 1932 and never asked for him back. They had been content to let him make the rest of his career among the paramilitaries. Now he was suddenly a brother officer? How convenient for these swine. Hausser had never been a true Nazi, but there were times like this when he quite sympathized with the Movement's class prejudices against the old elites. "He was cashiered over a romantic entanglement. Scarcely the first junior officer to promise marriage to one girl and then marry another. Scarcely the last. He's been relatively faithful to that wife ever since. He's a man, and I'm sure there might have been the stray other women, but no scandal...and the SS gossips like any other service. His only vice seems to be overwork. Had Admiral Raeder been less of a martinet, he'd still be a naval officer...and you would be dealing with Chancellor Göring's ineptitude without someone below him to actually do the work. Perhaps not the ideal son-in-law, but we've had worse as generals. Shall we discuss von Blomberg's choice of wives?" Both seniors winced, recalling the scandal of the War Minister and the tart. "In terms of the Movement, Reichsführer-SS Heydrich is the best you will find. Unless you wish a civil war you will probably lose, I'd suggest making your peace with him." And with this, General Hausser got up and took his leave. This meeting had done much to help convince him he had chosen the right side.

Chapter 22

1130 hours
17 July 1940
German Army transit office, Napoli-Sperone Smistamento
Railway Station, Naples, Italy

Gunter had mentally prepared himself every way he could think of for appearing without papers. He had never considered this possibility.

"Oh, that unit. Your Lieutenant Steiner just passed through. You barely missed him." The captain paused to glance up at a station board. "His train left less than three minutes ago. Next transport to Sicily won't be until tomorrow, a bit before dawn. Wait five minutes and I'll get proper transit orders typed up for you. Meantime, another part of your unit is back in the freight yards. Major Wrede went off for a drink, but he should return in a few to get the revised movement orders. I don't know who told you to be shipped to Taranto. Wrong port. Your lot is for Bari with the rest of 7th Panzer. No one can find division HQ. The commander seems to have vanished...."

"He's off to Malta. I'm supposed to meet him there. We have a battlegroup taking part in that operation. Personal orders of Reichsführer-SS. How do I spell your name for my report to him?"

It was amazing what name-dropping can do with bureaucrats. A lieutenant colonel who sends reports direct to Berlin was worth finding real coffee for. That in turn allowed enough time for Major Adolph to return.

"How come you are here instead of Gregor?" Before the words were out of his mouth, Gunter answered his own question. "Wanda! Why do I bother putting one of you two in charge? That Polish witch pays no attention."

"She got your boy Steiner off on time and kept back the silly child who had snuck in with them. Everything's fine. Steiner even had me get a note back home posted from Greta. Just mailed it."

1800 hours
17 July 1940
War Ministry, Bendler Block, *Tiergarten district of* Berlin

The Reich Without Hitler: The Falcons of Malta

Minister of War by self-appointment, Colonel General Beck was still angry over the meeting with SS General Hausser. How could a proper Reichswehr officer who had reached the rank of general have so changed his loyalties? Beck was completely incapable of seeing that a forcibly retired man of 51 would have needed employment. Beck was neither evil nor stupid. He was, however, a man of narrow views linked totally to his caste and profession. He simply found the Nazis distasteful. He put out of his mind his pro-Nazi stands of the early 30s, when they had seemed a useful tool against the Communists.

Nominally Beck was only Minister of War, not Army Commander. However, General Brauchitsch had been informally put out to pasture on "extended medical leave", allowing Beck to take those duties as well. Sitting on Beck's desk was a memo from the Army transport office about the request to move the 3rd Mountain Division from Norway to Sicily. The transport office was pleading difficulties and suggesting that 1st Mountain, then on occupation duty in France, be substituted. Beck was well aware that Heydrich had chosen the division to get its commander, General Dietel. Beck was tired of treating a cashiered naval lieutenant as a professional equal. He approved the substitution and CC'd OKW, but neither Chancellor Göring nor Reichsführer-SS Heydrich. Neither deserved to have any command authority over operational matters. So there. Even grown men—even senior generals—could act like children when it came to petty spite.

0800 hours
18 July 1940
RN HQ, dockside, Alexandria, Egypt

Admiral Andrew Cunningham had had better days than yesterday. Churchill's emissary, Harold Macmillan, had been obdurate. There would be no further evacuation from Malta, civilian or military. The Empire could not afford more retreats. It would ruin Britain's morale and her diplomatic position with the other powers. Such was London's view and that was that.

Easy to say in London, looking at a world map. It didn't change the facts. The Axis had massed over one thousand aircraft to assault Malta daily. The RAF and RN between them had never mustered as many as twenty fighters to oppose them, and most of those were obsolete biplanes. Malta was losing fighters faster than both services could scrape up reinforcements. The Empire didn't have a thousand spare planes to send to Malta. The Empire didn't have enough planes anywhere outside the Home Islands. Didn't matter. If you magicked up the planes, Malta had no place to put them. Feeding planes into the Malta inferno was just a sure way of making sure the same problem would be repeated when it was Egypt's turn. Egypt was obviously next after Malta. Every battalion, every AAA battery, every air squadron sent to Malta was being sent on a death ride, a fool's errand. Egypt and Suez were the keys. If those were at risk, his fleet could be lost along with the only army the Empire had to protect everything from Uganda to the Persian Gulf.

Cunningham had considered resigning. That was a coward's way out. He had a better plan. It would be the end of his career, but his duties to his service and the Empire came first.

Chapter 24

1200 hours
19 July 1940
Garrison of 7th Flieger-Division, Stendal, Germany,

Captain Alois Schmidt was entertained to be confronted by the same belligerent parachute lieutenant he had last seen giving his general hell. Schmidt had been amused by the mutiny. Now he was waiting for the mutineer to begin facing the results of his "success".

The lieutenant saluted and requested a moment of the captain's time. Schmidt nodded and gestured to the chair opposite him. The lieutenant preferred to remain standing in a position of near parade rest. "You have requisitioned my entire platoon for this new brigade. I'm not about to leave them to die while I hide back at base. I request permission to be assigned with them."

Schmidt laughed. It was not a pleasant laugh. "Oh, you wish to retain your command? Might even have a duty to your men? I'm not some general hung up on honor and caste loyalties. Why should I take you?"

"Because I'm damned good. Because I know these men and I'll get the most out of them."

"And because your mutiny didn't wreck the operation. No way it could have. This one was decreed at the highest levels. Why do you think I cashed in all my favor points to get posted as General Ramcke's adjutant? The Air Ministry is one giant gossip factory for junior officers and the young fräuleins from the steno pool. This southern campaign is the only route to promotion if you aren't flight crew. The brigade is never coming back here. Will probably be made a division after Malta. I've got two friends in the Ministry's personnel office who saw the memos." The lieutenant stiffened. Schmidt decided to stop being an ass. Time to make friends. "Relax. Your request is approved. You aren't the first, but you are near the head of the line. If you've got friends hanging back waiting to see what would happen, we'll make places for them too. Just get me a list. Your personnel file won't mention your mutiny, but will list you as volunteering for combat."

"So what happens to all your junior officer friends who arrived from the ministry the past two days?"

"I promised them places, not commands. We'll just go in over-strength on the staff side. When the brigade expands, there will be enough slots to go around." Schmidt put out his hand to shake and the lieutenant, whose name he learned was Jung, shook it. In turn, Jung promised to try to at least get a tower jump in for each of the new officers before Malta. Schmidt waited until he left to call the General's new adjutant and have him inform the general that the lost junior officers were starting to come around. They wouldn't all come, but enough would. At least enough in the mind of an administrative officer like Schmidt. Malta would teach him better.

0400 hours
21 July 1940
German army transit area [tent city], Gerbini Airfield / Catania Plain, Sicily, Italy

First Lieutenant Klaus Steiner had never actually been in command of anything before. Despite his nominal (in his mind, fantasy verging on hallucinatory) rank, there had always been real adults around. For the trip from Naples to Sicily he was "the old man". He would await Strauss to tell him everything he did wrong. He was sure there was a ton more to learn. However, he had managed to arrive at the correct encampment with the correct number of warm bodies. He didn't care if there were cots. His lot was prepared to curl up on the ground like dogs, if necessary.

What he was not prepared for was 350 HJ glider pilots. He'd been worried that they would send enough. Somewhere on the chain of desks, the number must have been sharply revised upwards. Three-hundred-and-fifty young men who had been reading the propaganda accounts of the Reich's hero Steiner and his glorious fight with Soviet partisans. The senior HJ snapped to attention and turned out his guys for the officer to inspect. Klaus had not a clue, so he just mimicked what his own HJ leaders had done on inspection. He kept it fast, only found minor things to criticize, and then pulled the leader away a bit for a conference while letting everyone else get some sleep.

The HJ leader's hero worship was obvious. Once Klaus got him to show the two propaganda articles about his "battles" in Ploiesti and Hungary, it was obvious why. Klaus didn't recognize this hero officer the stories made him out to be, but saw why others would follow a fantasy version of himself. What he wanted to review was the obvious—they had girls, they had non-Germans, they had a pack of Italians whose officer seemed absent for some reason. He wanted the HJ leader to lean on his guys to avoid stupid incidents. Klaus's crew was armed and not about to take insults easily. The HJ leader was confused. In his mind, NL was Aryan like the SS. Klaus's answer was simple—this was all on direct orders of Reichsführer-SS Heydrich. Anyone who could not discipline his mouth would be given travel orders to Berlin to discuss policy at SS HQ. Klaus hoped this would work. However, right now he only wanted this over with. He wanted at least a short nap curled up against Greta before reveille. Even an hour would do. As is, he cringed at what real officers would make of his scruffy crew, half in French-blue and half in civilian clothes with arm bands.

Returning to the sleep area, he located Greta, who had staked out a place by a camp fire to sit. He put his head on her lap and was instantly asleep.

0630 hours
23 July 1940
Palestine #1, near Krakow, General Government [formerly Poland]

Gerald Ford did not regret having taken a sabbatical from Yale Law School to work for the new Hoover Relief Commission. Ford was an ardent Isolationist and the things he was seeing were fortifying his core beliefs. He was composing an essay on this that friends would see published both in New Haven and back home in Michigan. The Commission was doing much good work, but the situation in Europe was simply not something Americans should soil their hands with beyond charity. Ford had seen ghettos where the Poles mistreated the Jews. Now he was seeing a camp complex where the Jews were beastly to the Poles. Both were oppressed in turn by the Germans, but could not see past their irrational, primeval hatreds of each other.

The Nazis were, in the main, loathsome creatures. Crude, badly educated thugs and gangsters. Still better than the Bolsheviks, but then almost anything was better than godless Bolshevism. However, this Commandant Eichmann seemed a decent fellow. Very much the proper Central European bureaucrat.

His tallies of prisoners to feed and calories needed to feed them were precise and based on lucid reasoning. Men doing hard labor needed more than old people. Children and pregnant women had their own special needs. All very neat and tidy, with excellent typed English translations. After two weeks of whining, absurd attempts to extort extra food and other shameless behavior, Eichmann was a welcome respite. Ford resolved to feature him as a counter-example to the relentless anti-Nazi propaganda from the Anglophiles and Jews pushing for US intervention. Armed neutrality was the right policy for the US. Ford did not want to see his nation tricked into fighting Britain's war for the second time in a generation.

1300 hours
24 July 1940
German Army transit area [tent city], Catania plain, Sicily, Italy

Strauss had managed to reunite with both Steiner and Rommel. Steiner had been pathetically grateful to see him. Rommel had been the reverse. The general saw no reason why he needed a Lieutenant Colonel to babysit a composite company of Jews, HJ, and Italians. Rommel had tried to return the Italians to their own command and met a bureaucratic stone wall. These children had no papers, no transit orders, no clear unit designator. No one had heard of any Lieutenant Colonel Lusena, so, in Rommel's mind, these were NL recruits until someone claimed them. It doubled Steiner's strength. Find the whole combined force full German kit and get his new Italians some range training for the new weapons. Dismissed!

Chapter 25

1440 hours
24 July 1940
KG Strauss Encampment area outside Bari, Italy

The encampment area was a pile of tents in a cleared field on the outskirts of Bari. German tent encampments were sprouting like weeds around the port as men and supplies poured in. No one seemed to have coordinated their arrival with the capacity of the port to generate convoys to Libya.

Wanda left Oriana staked out like a dog, with bound hands and a rope around her neck, both held in place by an iron stake in the ground and with Hans standing guard to beat her if she tried to escape. The girl was definitely reminding Wanda of her younger self. Willful, smart, and tricky, with a nasty mouth and a facility for languages.

Once she was sure Adam had the still up and running, she could deal with Oriana. Her two guys would get the camp built. Adolph was good enough at dickering to buy lumber for the tavern/cabaret/brothel she envisioned. Gunter had left the unit funds in their joint charge. Which meant in hers.

She approached the girl warily. Even when beaten, she bit and kicked. "Girl, I'm going to have Hans free your hands." The discussion was in a pidgin of German and Italian. It lacked fine points, but communication was happening. "You will listen without your normal smart mouth or I'll beat you bloody. Nod yes or no." Oriana nodded yes. "Girl, you remind me of myself when I was your age. No way I was letting you ruin things for Steiner. He's too important of all of us. Now, you are missing the Malta adventure either way, so forget that. I'll give you three choices. First, my guys dump you on the Italian police as a stowaway. They'll probably send you home. Whatever. You are out of our hair. Second, we just turn you loose. You have five minutes to disappear and do whatever. After that, if we catch you here with us, we beat you bloody and dump you on the Italians cops. Third, I take you under my wing and teach you enough to be worth taking to Egypt and beyond. You get your great adventure, but you learn the street, learn hustling, learn people, my way. I won't peddle your ass." Wanda paused to see if the girl understood the basics of sex and exploitation. She seemed to. "You'll be safe that way, but beyond that you learn about life on the wild side and from the bottom. This will be a great adventure. It merely won't include you getting shot at by strangers in battle just yet."

"Anything those other fools can do, I could do better."

"Probably. Which is why a lot of them will die and more sent home without arms or legs. Not my problem. But they haven't got your capacity of creating self-involved mischief. Steiner doesn't need it. Boy's carrying a heavy enough cross without a little terror like you. You don't take orders."

Oriana tried smart-mouthing at Wanda. Expected Wanda's fist. Instead, she got a shrug. Wanda just turned away and left her staked out in the sun. It was deadly hot, but to Oriana that wasn't the bad part. It was boring. She was in the middle of a huge encampment. Thousands of people. And a woman was in charge. A smart-mouthed woman who did what she wanted to and got men to obey her. Oriana wanted that power. Wanda knew secrets, secrets no one Oriana had ever known knew. Damned right she wanted to be schooled by her. If the price of that was being somewhat less of a brat for a while, so be it. Somewhat less. For a while. Oriana had grown up on adventure stories like the Jack London novels her mom had given her to read. Tales of strong, willful people living on the edges of society. This Wanda promised that and more. This was the sort of schooling Oriana wanted, lusted after.

2200 hours
24 July 1940
Polish Blue Police Barracks #3, Krakow, General Government

Eichmann arrived by chauffeured auto. He had phoned ahead with his orders early in the morning. He wanted a prisoner. A young Jewess, virgin, at the start of nubility. The prisoner was to be deloused, scrubbed clean, and left in a cell clad only in a prison smock. A cell where he could have privacy for a private interrogation. He had ignored the tones of the response. Let the Slavs think what they will as long as they obeyed.

When he arrived, he asked to be directed to the changing rooms and given a locker. He changed from his SS uniform into worn clothing, old work boots, and a rubberized smock. He then had the Pole lead him to the cell. It was in a dank basement. The other cells were crammed full. Eichmann didn't care. The one cell that mattered to him had walls and a solid door. The other prisoners would hear what he did, but none would see, which was all that mattered to him.

The Pole opened the cell door. The girl was perfect. Dark hair, dark eyes. She seemed clean. She was obviously terrified, but tried to give him a tentative smile. She knew after being kidnapped off the street that something bad awaited her. She was old enough to have an outline of a vague idea of what. Perhaps if she smiled, the man would be somewhat gentle with her. Eichmann told the warder to leave the key with him and go. The Polish policeman was rigidly polite, thinking to himself that better the victim be a Jew than one of his countrywomen. Not that he could have stopped what was to happen if the German swine's taste ran to Polish convent girls. This was a sad world he now lived in, worse by far than the days of the old Russian czars.

Eichmann spent a minute studying her and visualizing what would follow. He walked up to her and placed his hand gently on her shoulder. The terrified smile brightened a little. The girl child didn't quite know what to expect. He spat full in her face and then grabbed her arm. He twisted it savagely until it dislocated and then forced it further until he heard bones breaking. It seemed to him as sweet chamber music. He tripped her, ignoring her screams, her tears, her pleading. He understood Yiddish and knew what she was saying. Instead he stomped on her thigh until that bone broke as well, until it pierced the skin.

The bitch fainted. He wasn't done yet. He'd had several buckets of water brought in before he had arrived. That was part of his instructions and the stupid Slavs knew how to obey. He threw one in the girl's face. It revived her. He took her head in his hands, pulled pliers from his pocket and started yanking out one of her teeth. She squirmed and tried to bite him. He backhanded her, then threw more water in her face to bring her around. As soon as she started moaning again, he used the pliers as a small club to smash her front teeth, upper and lower. He had to step aside quickly as blood started to fountain from the broken stumps, after which she began to uncontrollably vomit. He stepped aside to admire his handiwork. When it gone to dry heaves and shuddering, he dragged her around the cell by her hair, trying to see how much he could yank out.

The cunt then ruined the evening by fainting again. The last bucket failed to revive her so he propped her up against a wall and kicked her till he heard ribs break. Eichmann was starting to get excited. He forced her mouth open and used his tool to yank out two teeth for souvenirs. He then pushed the unconscious body to the ground, unbuttoned his trousers and pissed full force in her face, into her open mouth. Eichmann felt the tensions of his job dissolve. He had to treat that huge mass of Yids at the camp as if they were human. He had to pretend as if that pompous American fairy Ford was a real man, instead of a bearded woman. He had to treat that moron Hoess from nearby Auschwitz as if he were a colleague instead of a brainless thug promoted over his head. The camp administration service crawled with apes pretending to be Aryans.

Eichmann locked the cell and walked upstairs whistling a jaunty tune. He told the head Pole on duty to get a doctor for the whore. She was to be chained to a clinic bed and her wounds dealt with. But no pain meds. He wanted her to suffer. Be sure to tell her he'd be back for her one of these days. In the meantime, arrest another similar one and have her kept ready for his use. A happy Eichmann left to change. This was just the recreation he needed to perform his duties at peak efficiency. He laughed to himself that these fools thought he would defile his race by actually copulating with one of these animals. As if.

The Polish doctor ignored the 'no pain meds' command. He had as little choice offering his services to the Nazis as these poor policemen did. Poland was prostrate beneath the Nazi boot heel and the Stalinists were, if anything, worse to the Poles than the Nazis. His poor Poland bled from her wounds like a martyred saint.

He gave the pain meds because no one wanted to hear the howling, and besides the Jew bitch could die. That might enrage the Nazi demon. He simply left the desk officer with a syringe of a stimulant to revive the girl from her morphine when the German trash wanted to use her next. He was amazed to see that the hymen was still intact. Then again, Germans were all scum and God only knew what particular deviance this one had. However, he did have the jailors take extensive photos. The Home Army would want a full report and without photos the report might not be believed. Poland still lived and some day would rise again.

Chapter 26

0900 hours
29 July 1940
Heydrich's office, SS HQ, Berlin

Heydrich was finding Keitel's excuses for the disaster that was 1st Mountain's non-arrival in Sicily tiresome. Jodl at least had the sense to admit blame and not try to justify the chain of unforced errors. Heydrich opened a folio on his desk, and handed Keitel a note on Chancellery stationary. It was an order relieving he and Jodl of their positions. It directed them to report immediately to the Army Personnel Office for reassignment. It said the contents of their offices would be forwarded to their home addresses by courier. Keitel was shocked and indignant. Jodl seemed more resigned to his fate. He only asked that his office contents be forwarded to the officer's club at the War Ministry to hold, pending his next assignment.

Schellenberg ushered them out and then brought in the obvious next appointment, General von Manstein, who had been cooling his heels for the last hour in the SS senior officer's canteen. Von Manstein had not a clue as to why he had been summoned. Heydrich had a note for him too. Same stationary. Same signature, Herman Göring, Führer and Chancellor. Manstein was ordered to assume a temporary command of OKW and would receive instructions from Reichsführer-SS Heydrich. Von Manstein read in silence and raised a quizzical eyebrow...,

"Generals Keitel and Jodl completely screwed up the Malta operation. Let War Minister Beck substitute 1st Mountain for 3rd, then paid no attention while the Army bureaucracy slow-walked the redeployment. The attack was supposed to be first week of August. Ramcke has been pushing for another week. I'll give you a few more days on top of that. 17th, 18th or 19th. Your choice, but a firm date. What I need you to do is find a general you trust to clean house at OKW. Re-staff with people you have connections to. I can let you give each one a one-grade promotion if they switch to Waffen SS. Then find a decent planning officer to be your deputy and run OKW while you are deployed. All it's supposed to be is a planning staff for the Führer." Heydrich caught the smile on Manstein's face. They both knew whose plans would be done. "That and a theater command for your southern campaign. Personnel, logistics, administration, the usual. Operations and Intelligence, I presume, you will keep with you."

Mantsein actually started to laugh. "So, I now command Kesselring, who in turn commands me?"

"Yes, in a theoretical sense. As a practical matter, you each command your service and must cooperate."

"How do I get the people I want from the Army Personnel Office? Another Führer order?"

"Our Führer prefers to concern himself with victory parades, Party rallies, state dinners, and the like. I send a folder of these over to sign every few days and he does. Division of labor."

Von Manstein thought on this for a few minutes, shrugged, and took his leave. He had work to do. The first step was finding the Berlin-based deputy to run OKW. The second would be a quick trip to Sicily to see Kesselring and Ramcke. Time to get a revised operations order agreed to and written up.

Schellenberg walked von Manstein to the waiting limousine and returned to Heydrich's office. Heydrich reconfirmed that the operation against the existing OKW staff was to commence at once. Start at the bottom and focus on corruption. Any headquarters with access to rationed goods, especially luxuries, had leakages, had people living beyond their visible pay grades. The Army would insist on legal jurisdiction. All well and good. The field soldiers never liked the headquarters' grandees. Each arrest would be excellent propaganda.

2000 hours
29 July 1940
Von Manstein's transit lodgings, Berlin

Von Manstein found the request for a meeting by the cashiered Jodl strange, to say the least. They were not close by familial ties or service histories. Still, one does not turn down a politely worded request for a brief meeting from a general officer without cause. Von Manstein was aware that his patronage from Heydrich had ruffled feathers within the senior officer caste. Best to observe protocol.

Jodl was direct and to the point. He wanted to stay on. "I'll waive rank. I'll waive seniority. I'll help on the handover. Regardless of my past faults, I do know this headquarters. It will ease the transition at OKW to have someone from the old regime for the transition. All I'm asking is a combat command for Malta. You are never going to get all of 1st Mountain in time. So, it will be shorthanded. Give me an NL battalion. If you start tomorrow, you can probably get two by backing up Afrika Korps deployment a bit."

Von Manstein decided to be direct. "There is precedent. Von Falkenhayn in Romania and Palestine. Now explain, why you?"

"Because I have nothing to lose. OKH will park me in some third-rate garrison town as commandant. I lose rank and seniority either way. I'd rather have a chance at combat and an opportunity to redeem my sins. Yes, we fucked up. Me, Keitel, Beck, both staffs. I won't bore you with the ins and outs. No one made this particular division a priority and the usual administrative slow-walk happened. I'm willing to drop back to being a major and take a glorified militia unit into action. Better an honorable death in battle than what awaits me."

"If that's all you want...."

Jodl cut in over von Manstein. "Thought about that. A brief note and a bullet in my mouth. Paint the ceiling red. It's a coward's way out. I'll go in as a gentleman volunteer ranker if that's all you offer. I simply don't want my career to end this way. Let me prove I can be of use."

Von Manstein spent a few silent minutes thinking it through. "Okay. Provisionally, yes. I'll have to run this by the Reichsführer-SS, but I doubt he'll gainsay me. Just remember you have waived rank and seniority...."

Before von Manstein could finish, Jodl passed him a written note to that effect. Asked that his NL battalion be mortarmen. It was artillery light enough for air or glider transport.

2300 hours CET/ 2400 hours Alexandria time
29 July 1940
The private room of the upscale Alexandria Sporting Club, which catered to the RN

The party had been going on since dusk. The captains of his ships, their XO's, and a few other key players from the Eastern Fleet. It had been an open bar and a light snack buffet at a facility known for RN social occasions. No one would think twice at this group gathering at this place for a private affair. Very clubby.

The Admiral had been waiting for the right time to speak. This would not be an easy talk to give. He was trusting everyone here to keep a secret. Yes, leaking it could wreck his career, but that was dead anyway. What mattered was the fate of the Army and RAF boys on Malta. "Thank you all for coming. Now remember, officially this is an unofficial social gathering. On your honor as officers of His Majesty's Navy, I am ordering you to silence on this. No best friends or first cousin exceptions. No bringing the rest of the wardroom up to speed. Thousands of lives depend on this." He paused to survey these faces, men he knew so well, men who, in many cases, he had chosen for the positions they now hold. The faces said they were with him…but it would only take one faint heart. "Jerry will be hitting Malta in August. We think the first week, but definitely before month's end. Sourcing is top secret but quite reliable." He paused again while this registered. A few of the clever ones would think spies. A few of the brightest would think code-breakers. None would get that London was getting operational documents from someone quite highly placed in Berlin. Never full sets, but enough. Lives rode on data being accurate. "Three divisions by air and another one and a half by sea, but the sea force is bigger than the air despite all that. Over a thousand planes with more coming. The Italian Fleet plus German U-Boats and S-Boats. We have two brigades on Malta, plus some odds and sods, supposedly spread out all over the island defending every cove and airfield. Supposedly."

He paused again for them to digest this. "Now, you are all about to get a case of bad memory. Our friends in khaki you've been sharing drinks with weren't here. They are all in their hotel back in Cairo before they fly back to Malta late tomorrow." He paused again for nervous laughter. "London has this insane notion that we can hold the island. We can't. We can give the Italian Fleet a bloody nose. And we will." He paused for the cheer. His officers knew they were good and had trained their ships well. "But we cannot remain off the island for weeks on end as if it were Nelson's day. Norway and Dunkirk should have shown London what happens to ships in daylight without fighter cover. When we put to sea, you will each have a sealed envelope with a code word on the outside. The code word is 'Copenhagen'. Copenhagen for Nelson's blind eye. There will be copies of these orders in each ship's file back at Alexandria—when London looks for a scapegoat, it will be me and only me. I even typed them myself, so the clericals cannot be blamed. You will excuse the poor typing, but your admiral isn't used to this." He paused for more nervous laughter. "Short form, 'Copenhagen' means the fleet splits in two. A squadron of smaller ships—cruisers, destroyers, whatever smaller craft we have—will move at last light into the Grand Harbor. The Army and RAF squaddies will file on and we'll be off before the bombers arrive with the dawn. You will have obeyed a written order from your lawful commander. Churchill and the Sea Lords may hang me from the yard arm. I quite don't care. But those brave lads are not being left hostage to some romantic fantasy the War Cabinet dreamed up over brandies and cigars. Our ships will be packed like the London Tube at rush hour, but we are not leaving one man behind we don't have to."

He stopped here. What more was there to say than what the written order would show? He had laid out the command arrangements, signals rules, probable operational problems. He waived away attempts by his officers to make this a joint burden. The RN had never had an officers' mutiny and by God he wouldn't be the start of one. Nelson had disregarded orders. It was service tradition. The RN had never let the Army down and it wouldn't now. Not on his watch, whatever those pompous twits in London thought. But the Fleet would need these officers for the dark days that would follow. Egypt would be as a big a disaster as Malta. They would either have to make an insane sortie past Sicily to Gibraltar, or retreat through Suez before it was blocked. He had no faith in London's ability to make an intelligent or timely decision. That was for his successor. He was prepared to meet his maker and justify his actions before that throne.

2330 hours
30 July 1940
KG Strauss encampment, Bari, Italy

Gregor Vosss found the idea of himself as an officer both absurd and amusing. He'd gone in at Ypres a youth volunteer. He'd come out of the five years of war a sergeant in the Iron Division and was still one in the Freikorps when he lost his foot to a Red landmine during the Ruhr Operation in 1920. He'd often commanded a platoon, and sometimes a company, but officers were another species. They went to high school. Some even went to college and a few to university. They drank champagne instead of good German wine and beer. Even the ex-commoners who became storm officers were joining a different class, almost a different species.

In the SA, his artificial foot and cane had limited his street fighting and marching. He and the older guys protected Nazi rallies instead of breaking up Red meetings. Shrug. He'd gotten a walking stick with an iron core and bashed heads with it whenever the opportunity arose. He'd bring along Hans and a pack of street kids for extra muscle. Iron pipes and sharpened shovels were weapons he knew how to train these young men to use. The others had laughed at his "moron platoon", but they more than held their own when the Reds came calling.

At his current age, Gregor felt he could take the power and pay of an officer without forgetting where he came from. He still ate with his men. No officers' club for him. No officers' club for the unit. No officers' mess. Everyone ate the same food, slept in the same tents. Everyone, that is, except the damned Roma. Gregor didn't like foreigners. He'd served with them. At one time or another, his old units had had Yids, Wends, Poles, Danes, Czechs, Balts, Russians, even a pair of Finns for a while. Gregor didn't make allowances. You spoke German. You ate what the mess served you. You shouted for flag and Kaiser. When the Kaiser was gone, that left the flag. Then there was a Führer, which sort of replaced Kaiser, except Adolph had been one of them, a commoner. Adolph had served in the trenches, been a front pig, not some headquarters' fairy or draft dodger. Born Austrian, but he'd volunteered for the Reich.

The Roma had split into two factions. They called it clans. One had been mostly the folks from Romania with Gunter and Steiner and Rommel. They had fallen in with Wanda. Entertainers, barkeeps, working girls…Wanda had them in hand and they were no trouble to anyone. The other clan was the most useless collection of thieves, swindlers, pseudomagical hucksters, and layabouts he'd ever met. Wouldn't take orders. Wouldn't work. Lied about everything. Well, he was fixing that tonight. He'd picked out the three worst thieves. Or at least the ones who looked the shiftiest to him. Called a punishment parade. Everyone was supposed to be there who wasn't on duty at the tavern or on guard duty. He'd posted armed guards on the tents and had the bad clan herded in at gunpoint. He'd instructed his people to ignore the wheedling, threats, and occult curses these gypsy scum threw at anyone who crossed them.

With everyone assembled around two fire barrels, he'd told off the three obvious leaders of the Roma thieves. Told them the bullshit was over. First, they had denied everything. Then they hauled up their usual justifications—oppression, Christ gave them dispensation—he'd cut them off. Told them it ended now. These three thieves were going to die and the leaders were going to kill them. The leaders told him to fuck off. Called him a useless cripple. Their young men pulled knives and a few pistols. Just as he'd predicted.

Gregor raised his own pistol. Before it was fully pointed, the rifle fire began. He'd posted half a dozen sharpshooters. The armed young Roma went down. Screams, blood, chaos. His chosen NCOs knew it was coming. The circle around the condemned held. Anyone who tried to run was beaten back with clubs and shovels. Gregor shot the three leaders. Bang, bang, bang. Gut shots. A gypsy crone lunged at him with a knife, screaming curses about the evil eye and Satan. Hans took her head off with a sharpened shovel. He'd trained the boy well. Hans was slow, but not a moron. People who tried to hurt Uncle Gregor were to be put down hard. The remaining Roma went to their knees, screaming for mercy. Gregor had the number two guy of Wanda's clan along. He picked out the ones worth saving. Those were pushed aside. The rest were slaughtered. The Saved then got to prove their loyalty by digging a large, two-meter-deep hole and tossing the dead into it. Well, mostly they were dead. Some were still groaning and screaming. They got buried with the dead. The Saved shoveled the hole full and then everyone jumped up and down on the dirt to settle it. Gregor posted three guards with pistols and stools to sit on. If anyone crawled out of the dirt, finish them off.

The chain dogs had been warned there was going to be an "administrative punishment session". They still sent a patrol about the gunfire. They were shocked. Gregor was prepared. One of his Elders of Zion had been a lawyer, so there was a typed report detailing a group executed for mutiny, theft, and disregard of discipline. List of the executed to follow. By noon the next day, there was such a list with a CC on the report to Oberführer Schellenberg for the personal files of the Reichsführer-SS. Amazingly, camp administration lost all interest in the matter at that point. A chain dog sergeant just thanked him for pest control as the theft complaints had been becoming bothersome.

0800 hours
30 July 1940
KG Strauss encampment, Bari, Italy

The eight German women ranged from late forties to mid-teens. None were actively plain, but neither were they beauties. They were working girls from the slums, not glamorous young things from some high-end brothel. The leader, Gretchen, was an ex-neighbor of Wanda's who had worked in the world's oldest profession back to the Great War. The rest were workmates, as it were, of hers. All arrived minus their pimps. They all had suitcases of various sizes and pinned-on NL armbands. Gretchen gave Wanda a big hug. "How did you pull it off, dear? I send a telegram to the address your telegram mentioned. The next day we've got the Gestapo taking charge of us. Amazing how polite a fancy man can be when he's facing a brace of Gestapo thugs. We even got to keep our jewelry and clothing. So how did we wind up in the NL instead of Ravensbrück?"

"Special unit. We're Berlin's pets. They are stacking up some thirty thousand or more military lads waiting to get shipped to Africa. I've got my still up. I need more 'barmaids'."

The eight laughed at "barmaids". Wanted to know what the house cut was going to be. Wanda had already worked that out. Half and half. She'd see to having big guys as bouncers and see to the chain dogs. Lads didn't even need leave tickets to patronize this new thing of Wanda's, as the whole thing would be on base. NL was some separate game on discipline, so effectively no one this side of Berlin was exactly in charge of them. Then on to play the same game in Africa. Wanda didn't mention she hadn't told Gunter about all this. By the time he got back from Malta, there would be nothing to argue about. She'd make sure the unit treasury got its cut. Beyond that, she would pay back every penny she'd borrowed from unit funds at the traditional 20% a week interest. Wanda was quite honest with her friends. The problem was that she was Wanda.

Gretchen gave Wanda a funny look at seeing Oriana. Gretchen had seen younger turned out, but knew Wanda frowned on that for the little ones. Wanda cleared up that problem. Helper, not hooker. Oriana was sort of Wanda's apprentice. Gretchen gave the girl an appraising look, wondering if she realized how good a teacher she had taken up with.

Chapter 27

0800 hours
July 31st, 1940
Gibraltar, British Empire

Force H of the Royal Navy headed into the Western Mediterranean. Vice Admiral James Somerville flew his flag from the battlecruiser HMS Hood. The mission was to transport twelve Hawker Hurricanes fighters and two Blackburn Skua dive bombers to bolster the defenses of Malta. Currently, the isolated British outpost in the center of the Mediterranean had as its air defense a mixture of ancient Gladiators found in an old storage depot, a few Hawker Hurricanes, and roughly a dozen Fairey Swordfish. The operational Gladiators had the nicknames of "Faith", "Hope", and "Charity", and were kept flying by cannibalizing parts from non-flying spares. The new aircraft for Malta were on board the aircraft carrier HMS Argus, a ship converted from an ocean liner during the First World War. The rest of the task force was made up of HMS Ark Royal, a modern fleet carrier; the battleships HMS Valiant and HMS Resolution; cruisers HMS Arethusa and HMS Enterprise; and ten destroyers. Somerville's orders were to take Force H far enough east into the Mediterranean for the fourteen aircraft to take off and fly to Malta, and then return to Gibraltar for other missions.

As the task force headed out, Somerville wondered if this entire mission was for nothing. Since Admiral Cunningham was attacked on July 9th, more than a few had viewed the Malta situation as hopeless. The army wanted to just abandon the island all together. The Prime Minister had ordered this mission to try to hold onto the island by providing some air defense.

1300 hours
1 August 1940
"Campo di Manovra", Cagliari-Capoterra, Sardina, Italy

Major Paul-Werner Hozzel of the Luftwaffe had been on Sardinia for not quite three weeks now, and couldn't decide if he loved the countryside or hated it. On one hand, it hadn't rained once, with some truly phenomenal beaches, but over the past week it hit at least 90°F every single day, and several times 95°F. The best thing you could do in the middle of the day was hang out in the bar located next to the airfield and wait. The bar was close enough to be able to get quickly to their aircraft, but also served good meals. It could be worse. Rumors said that other Luftwaffe units were headed for Africa, and there it reached over 100°F! Here at least the company was…cordial. One of the waitresses was a raven-haired beauty and the men of the Gruppe fell over each other trying to get her attention. A combination of firm orders from himself to his men for correct behavior with the Italians, and the massively subtle hint from the woman's father, the bartender, made certain that the men's love for the waitress remained unrequited. The barkeep had a shotgun, and the first week after the Gruppe's arrival, he had hunted rabbits in the middle of the day, skinning and cleaning them next to the bar.

Today was like the ones before. Hozzel saw Lieutenant Marco Preziosa came into the bar and, from the way the Italian officer was sweeping the place, he was looking for someone; odds were him as Preziosa was the liaison officer assigned to the Gruppe. "Over here, Lieutenant."

The Italian officer was young, but earnest. Hozzel suspected that the local commander of the Regia Aeronautica had assigned Preziosa as some type of punishment to the young, humorless officer; that, or to get him out from underfoot. Colonel Nardella was the base commander and Capoterra had been some type of satellite or dispersion field with no permanent unit assigned. In other words, Colonel Nardella was an incompetent that couldn't cut it in a real unit, and had been exiled here and was now Hozzel's cross to bear. Preziosa strode up with a purpose, then paused to come to attention, "Major, I have a report of which you should be aware."

Hozzel resisted a smile—he remembered being a newly commissioned officer back nearly a decade ago. "Well, let's have it."

"British ships have been sighted in the Western Mediterranean. Warships: at least two large ships—cruisers if not battleships."

This got Hozzel's attention, as well as everyone else in the bar. Dozens of pilots stopped playing cards or reading, and someone picked the needle up from the record player; the Gruppe had been put here in Sardinia overtly in an anti-shipping role, but told to be ready to relocate on short notice. The rest of the wing was in Sicily. "Does Colonel Nardella have any other information?"

The Italian officer looked uncomfortable for a moment. Hozzel had a few guesses as to the cause; where Preziosa was energetic, Nardella was the opposite. No doubt the Italian Colonel had just handed off the report that came down from his superiors to Preziosa, and hadn't bothered to ask for more information or provide it to the Lieutenant if he had it. "Never mind, Lieutenant. Let us go and visit him." Turning to his other men in the bar—all were waiting—he called, "Hauptmann Dilley."

Bruno Dilley was from East Prussia with blond hair and in his late twenties, looking every bit the fighter pilot with the scarf he wore all the time. Pity the Gruppe flew dive bombers. "Tell Fritz to get the planes ready?" A good executive officer tried to anticipate orders.

"Exactly. Prep the Stukas, but don't load any bombs until I get back with more details."

"Yes, sir!" Hauptmann headed off to find the Gruppe's chief mechanic.

The other pilots started to chat about what they might be facing today while Hozzel and Preziosa looked for his boss.

Major Paul-Werner Hozzel had been very surprised by the meeting with Colonel Nardella. For once, the man appeared to have found a gear other than Stop or Slow. A stack of additional messages was in the Colonel's office. A follow-up on the contact report had come in from the Italian patrol plane. Multiple large ships tentatively identified as two battleships and an aircraft carrier steaming east. The Italians were putting together a major effort with several bomber wings to attack the British fleet. In addition, there was a set of orders from Generaloberst Udet in Sicily. Udet was commanding all of the bombers of Luftflotte 2 under Generalfeldmarschall Kesselring. The instruction was simple: Prepare to attack with more details to follow.

The details were not long in coming. Udet was dispatching He-111s from Sicily in addition to Hozzel's gruppe. The Bf-109s from the other Luftwaffe airfield lacked the range to reach and this wouldn't be corrected until the new E7s with drop tanks arrived, but those were months away. Because of the range they would go in without fighter cover. Hozzel wasn't thrilled with that idea, but orders were orders. Udet was attempting to coordinate the arrival of these various forces at the same time over the location of the British Fleet. The Italians, by virtue of their longer range and having the information sooner, would attack first.

1808 hours
1 August 1940
Altitude 4,100 meters, NW of Gulf of Bougie off of French Algeria
8° e 32° Stormo Bombardamento Terrestre (8th & 32nd Bomber Wings)

Colonel Vittorio Ferrante found himself in command of the Italian attack because General Stefano Cagna had been recalled to Rome. There, the general was having a meeting with Marshal Balbo. Why the Marshal was in Rome or wanted to talk to the general was above the pay grade of mere colonels. The task at hand was to attack the British. For this mission, there were 40 SM79s, each armed with 1,200 or 1,250 kilograms' worth of bombs.

1823 hours
1 August 1940
Altitude 4,000 meters, NW of Gulf of Bougie off of French Algeria
1. Gruppe StG 1

From the radio reports, the Italians had just finished their attack on the British fleet, and that had provided to Hozzel the exact location of his target and better numbers. The British had four large ships: a carrier, two battleships, a cruiser, and multiple destroyers. Two Italian aircraft had been shot down in exchange for several bomb hits, but it didn't sound like major damage. Of more importance, an Italian CANT Z.506 reconnaissance float plane was keeping an eye on the British and proving a beacon for the Gruppe to home in on. A brief check of the map and some quick calculations, "The British are in range, if just." Keying the throat mic, "Gruppe: new course...."

The other dive bombers wiggled their wings in acknowledgment.

1834 hours

The He-111s had made their attack on the British and no hits were reported. The battleships were identified as Queen Elizabeth-class and accompanied two carriers. One of the He-111s had been shot down by British fighters. The lack of fighter cover was proving expensive. Everyone was keeping their eyes open for the British fighters.

1836 hours
Hanger Deck, HMS Ark Royal

"Get the lead out! The captain wants these planes refueled and rearmed yesterday!" The Chief Petty Officer barked orders at the deck crew as they rushed to refuel and rearm the Blackburn Skuas and Rocs of 800th and 803rd squadrons. The taskforce had been hit twice in less than an hour. It would be very possible for a third attack to happen.

1841 hours
1 August 1940
Altitude 13,000
1. Gruppe StG 1

"Warships sighted!" Hozzel heard an excited voice cry out over the radio. The location followed and, with a bit of squinting, there they were, the British fleet. Another voice called out, "Fighters…." Hozzel snapped his head around to look for the threat.

1841 hours
1 August 1940
Ark Royal Combat Air Patrol

"Tally Ho! Stukas at angels thirteen! Engaging!" The British pilots threw the throttles wide on their engines and turned to engage the attackers.

HMS Ark Royal
With word that a third attack had started, Admiral Somerville ordered his fleet to begin evasive maneuvers. Dozens of anti-aircraft guns on the ships of the British fleet began to pepper the

sky. Off-center of the British fleet steamed HMS Argus. She had started life as the Conte Rosso, a passenger liner being built on the Clydebank in Scotland for Italian service at the outbreak of the Great War. In 1916, the Admiralty acquired the unfinished hull and had her converted into the world's first flush-deck aircraft carrier. She missed the war all together, spent the Twenties conducting various experiments to help the Royal Navy gain experience with carrier operations and the Thirties in reserve or training duties. The crisis of the war saw Argus being employed as a training carrier and or as a transport for aircraft. To make it easier for trainee pilots to spot her, Argus had a solid-white paint job. This now aided the German Stuka pilots and they were drawn to the carrier like moths to a flame.

The British CAP only had two fighters up currently, as the rest were re-arming and refueling. They quickly killed two Stukas but the Germans pressed their attack home and started their dives.

In singles or pairs, the German dive bombers attacked the carrier. Each carried a single 250-kilogram armor-piercing bomb. Because of the extreme range, heavier armament was not possible. Over the next seven minutes, thirteen bombs were dropped and five found their mark. The first struck the forward deck, passing through the wooden flight deck into an anchor room. The explosion sent shards flying, but no serious damage was caused. The second bomb struck nine meters behind the first, through the flight deck, wrecking one of the Hurricanes and starting a minor fire, and also through the hanger deck, but the bomb failed to explode. The third bomb was deadly, as it hit almost exactly midship and exploded in one of the boiler rooms. The shockwave from the explosion blew out the fires in the ship's boilers and outright wrecked one of them. Shrapnel also pierced the hull, causing serious flooding that would eventually doom the carrier. The fourth bomb hit the aft end of the flight deck, wrecking several of the Hurricanes parked on the hanger deck and starting a major fire. The fifth and last bomb to hit landed within three meters of the third amidship and added to the carnage in the engineering spaces. With no power the fires couldn't be fought and the flooding in the boiler room couldn't be contained.

Argus was doomed and, with her sinking, the desperately needed reinforcements for Malta were lost.

Major Hozzel didn't pay a cheap price for his victory; another

Ju-87 was lost to anti-aircraft fire and two more to the British CAP before the Ju-87s were able to break contact. Once back in Sardinia and the battle examined it was clear that the Gruppe had ignored the fleet carrier Ark Royal and swarmed what was identified as the Argus, a training carrier. What had it been doing there? Taking twenty-five percent losses to sink a training carrier was a bitter pill to swallow for Hozzel. It wouldn't be until years after the war that Hozzel would learn that Argus was the key element of the British plan and sinking her foiled the British efforts to reinforce Malta. Because of this, the German and Italian assault troops wouldn't have to face the dozen Hurricane fighters Argus had been transporting. In addition, the failure of Operation Hurry was one more nail in the coffin of the plans to make an attempt to hold Malta. The cries in London to abandon the undefendable island would grow all the louder. The only major leader not listening was Churchill.

Chapter 28

0600 hours
1 August 1940
Camp Commandant's office, outskirts of Bari, Italy

The poisoned report had sat in the incoming tray since noon yesterday, when the Legal Affairs officer from KG Strauss had dropped off the list of the deceased. Sitting beside it was the outgoing military mail envelope that undoubtedly held the CC to SS HQ in Berlin. It was addressed there and listed both this Oberführer Schellenberg and the Reichsführer-SS by name. The commandant's adjutant had made clear that neither the report or the list was to be presented to his boss. Ever. Yet he made equally clear that the staff should be able to retrieve this missive on command.

What to do? What to do! The officers were at a loss. Finally, a mere corporal, an aged veteran of decades of administrative service back to the Hapsburg Emperors, who had been recalled from retirement in Tyrol for this war, made the obvious suggestion. Send a runner, find this legal affairs officer, and solicit an opinion. Unofficially, of course. The runner returned with a middle-aged lieutenant, also a Hapsburg veteran. The attorney looked Jewish, which was absurd as the NL was part of the SS, and therefore he was probably pure Aryan. The headquarters officers hemmed and hawed, trying to ask without asking. The corporal was brighter. He chatted the man up about his WW1 service, name-dropped some people he knew who had served roughly at the same times and places with this attorney, who it turned out during the war had commanded an artillery battery and then been executive officer to a full battalion of guns. Common ground thus established, he just asked the man for a suggestion.

The attorney laughed. "Our unit is a special project of the Reichsführer. The reasons why are classified. Need to know and all that. So the simplest way to handle paper from us is to creatively file it." He stopped, looking over the file system. He saw a drawer toward the back and way to the bottom. It had no paper slip to mark its contents. He pointed, asking, "What's that drawer used for?"

"Nothing much. It's a pain to reach so we keep office supplies there."

"Perfect. Clear out the very back of the drawer, enough for half-a-dozen fat file folders. Take the report and list. Put it in an envelope. Mark the envelope with today's date and write 'office copy of Berlin report with attached list of personnel involved, KG Strauss'. Put the envelope in a file marked 'Z Records – commandant's eyes only'. And you bury it where no one will find it by accident. If we do anything else that needs a file, you make a new folder and sort them by date. No one will stumble over it by accident and you can retrieve it on command."

The officers were profoundly grateful. Asked if there was anything they could do to show their appreciation. The legal officer asked for the corporal to be transferred to his command. He had need of a good clerk. The officers thought that weird but signed the transfer order. Walking back together, the old corporal asked why.

"Because we do a lot of things outside normal administrative order and I will need help creating a proper retroactive paper trail for all the bizarre things we do. Oh, and by the way, you are now a sergeant." The new sergeant found the promotion delightful. However, he was curious at what Berlin would make of mass executions. The legal officer shrugged. "Probably nothing. We've done worse without comment. Our masters in Berlin seem to find us amusing in a street theater sort of way." The sergeant found that enlightening. The heads of the SS as guardian angels was a concept worth pondering.

The officers left behind at HQ just congratulated each other on defusing a live bomb. No one wanted to be explaining anything about this unit to their bosses in Berlin. Attracting the attention of the SS was never a pleasant concept and this Major Vosss seemed to have an executioner's mandate. They discretely passed the word to treat this unit with fire tongs.

0800 hours; 0900 Alexandria Time
1 August 1940
Bridge of the Escort HMS Thunderchild, 20 miles past the harbor entrance of Alexandria on a course for Malta

Lieutenant Commander Reginald Fraser Kirk Scott was glad to be at sea on yet another Malta run. He and the other small ship officers had been included in the unofficial meeting at the

Sporting Club, but in terms of RN social echelons it was not
their scene. Thunderchild was one of the bastard children of
the RN. A WW1-era V-Class destroyer-variant, she had survived
post-WW1 reductions in force by being stricken from the RN's
rolls. Instead, she had done two decades of service for various
colonial governors general and Asian princely states client kings.
The last owner, a Malay Sultan, had gifted her back to the RN
at war's outbreak. Thunderchild still had her original 3-inch and
4-inchguns, but had lost her torpedo tubes decades ago. The one
3-inch AAA gun was backed by six field expedient Lewis guns on
hasty makeshift mounts. Fleet didn't see her as suitable to screen
the big ships any longer. She took in supplies and personnel to
Malta. She carried mail both ways and sometimes ferried air crew
back to Egypt.

Right now, she was overloaded with some super-secret light
infantry unit commanded by two brothers named Fleming. They
called themselves commandos. Each trip to Malta seemed to be
filled with some last-minute boarding on a special unit or draft,
always on verbal orders from some high muckey-muck or other.
Scott wondered if anyone was actually keeping tabs on how many
men were on Malta or who they reported to.

Scott was not inclined to question absurd orders. His only
real battle experience had been at Jutland, or so he claimed. In
fact, his destroyer had never been engaged, but nominally it had
been part of the Grand Fleet that day. Not that Ensign Scott would
have known the difference. He'd been on temporary duty running
the engine room instead of running his gun. A matter of one
engineering officer on leave when the Fleet sailed and another
down with food poisoning from something eaten last night ashore
before departure. However, it gave him his nickname "Jutland",
which he preferred to any of his three names.

0730 hours
2 August 1940
Kesselring's HQ, Gerbini Airfield, Plain of Catania , Sicily

The meeting room was hot beyond furnace level. Not the gates
of Hell, but definitely its exurbs. Ramcke was content to remain
in the background while Kesselring, von Manstein, and Rommel
squabbled. Three hours of acrimony produced a plan that satisfied

no one but it was a plan. Kesselring was to be commander of the Malta operation, but without a separate ground forces headquarters for that function. Von Manstein designated Jodl as his observer, but not in a command function. Instead, Jodl was both a liaison officer for OKW and commander of an NL ersatz brigade of two SA/NL ad hoc heavy weapons battalions that would go to Malta by either air landing or glider. "Battalions" were being formed now with no training cycle as a mix of middle-aged WW1 veterans from the SA and mid-teenagers from HJ. The transport method of insertion would be determined later, but by whom was left open. Ramcke was to command the "first wave", but the "first wave" included Rommel's ersatz storm battalion, over which Ramcke was to have no command authority. Rommel refused to waive rank or seniority. However, despite Rommel's pleas, neither Kesselring nor von Manstein would give him command authority over anything except his battalion. Instead, that lack of authority was clarified by written orders to Ramcke and Jodl to ignore any orders from Rommel not countersigned by Kesselring. So the first wave would have two commands, ordered not to coordinate.

The operation was to be joint with the Italians, but no Italian officers were present. Kesselring reserved coordination with the Italians for himself by separate meetings he would hold later. No one could agree on how much of 1st Mountain Division would arrive in time, who would command it, or even whether it would be used as a separate formation. This too was to be decided later.

Ramcke's plan for a drop at dawn was accepted. His plan to concentrate on one airfield was not. Instead his brigade was to be split to cover all three airfields. Ramcke was directed to create three battle groups out of four battalions. No additional communications equipment was added to his brigade to coordinate the separate elements. Rommel's proposal to land collapsible bicycles for couriers was vetoed by the two senior generals. As far as Ramcke could tell, this was because Rommel had proposed it. Neither of the seniors wanted him here, but apparently neither had the authority to remove him. Heydrich's influence again.

Kesselring wanted the attack day for the 17th. Something about phases of the moon. Von Manstein wanted the 19th to maximize the time for missing units to arrive. An hour of dispute resulted in a compromise of the 18th. By now, what optimism Ramcke had about this ad hoc waiting disaster had evaporated.

The Reich Without Hitler: The Falcons of Malta

He was back to his prior original fears that he had committed career suicide in accepting this posting. He made a silent promise to himself that he simply was not going to allow himself to survive a failure. He thought of the late General Fritsch, who had chosen suicide by enemy action in Poland last year as a way to recover his lost honor. Had Ramcke been able to read Jodl's mind, he would not have been surprised to find a similar vow.

0500 hours
2 August 1940
RNAS Kalafrana, Malta

Colonels Duffy and Mason were grateful to be finally off the Short S.25 Sunderland flying boat. It had been a long, cramped, boring journey from the UK, even with a refueling stop at Gibraltar. Malta had, in many ways, cleaner, better-scented air than the London they had left. London was covered in coal-fired smog, plus the odors of a large industrial city. However, what it did not have in this summer of 1940 were the smells of active warfare. Malta had this, a sordid mix of high-explosive residues, smoke from burning buildings, and a fried meat smell of dead, roasted flesh, human as well as animal. The poor island was subject to steady bombardment from the air daily, plus nuisance raids at night. Indeed, their plane had to unload quickly, to be away before the dawn air raids.

The RNAS showed signs of both bomb damage and patchwork, hasty repairs. The colonels had read the reports and the comparisons to the heavily bombed southern ports such as Dover. Reading was one thing. Seeing was another. Still, the War Cabinet had set them a task of bucking up the defense of Malta and both colonels were determined to follow their orders.

0345 hours
3 August 1940
Grand Harbor, Malta

Jutland Scott was getting severely pissed. The loading was running late. It always seemed to. The Army had done a poor job of clearing wrecks from the harbor and a worse one of keeping the repairs up dockside in the face of large-scale daily bombings. What made matters worse was the administrative ineptitude. The wounded he was supposed to load were seldom ready when he docked despite the dockmaster's office knowing almost to the minute when he would clear the harbor mouth inbound. From six hours' out, he would time his ship perfectly and then be met by muddle and attitude. The wounded were late. How many civilian Maltese were to be taken off was never clear. They never all arrived on time. The Army always wanted allowances made for late arrivals, for pets, sometimes for livestock. He understood they were recruiting Maltese in ever larger numbers. He accepted that one of the lures of such recruitment was that the recruit's family would be evacuated, would be safe from the daily bombings. He did not accept that these people and animals could not be assembled in advance and kept close to the docks. There were always excuses. To Scott, it was a peacetime mentality. He shuddered to think of what the real evacuation would be like. He knew he couldn't ask. Officially, he didn't know his sealed orders. Officially, no one did.

1200 hours
3 August 1940
A meadow near Luqa Airfield, Malta

Colonels Duffy and Mason sat under the shade of a large, white poplar tree. They were eating good ham and cheese sandwiches while sharing a bottle of acceptable port wine. They had a fruit basket for dessert and more than ample time for a leisurely feeding. They had had a most interesting day on the island.

Their first discovery was that daytime movement was essentially impossible. Axis planes prowled the few roads, shooting up anything that moved, down to lone dispatch riders. So couriers had to go on foot or wait until dark. The garrison and inhabitants had turned into nocturnal creatures. They lazed away their days and labored through the nights.

Their second discovery was that their written orders from London were essentially worthless. The commander and Governor General, General Dobbie, had read their orders and replied by resigning his posts. This resulted in frantic signal traffic back and forth to the war cabinet, after which the colonels were re-designated as "special advisers". The powers, if any, were left undefined.

The Reich Without Hitler: The Falcons of Malta

Dobbie had dumped the two colonels on his staff. It had been a swift education. London's appreciation of the situation turned out to be so badly flawed as to be meaningless. Yes, in theory, the entire garrison was concentrated in a clump around the Grand Harbor. A map with battalion flags [8] and brigade flags [2] saw them bunched there. In theory. In practice, almost no one was in the immediate vicinity of the Grand Harbor during daylight. It was too dangerous. The towns were wrecked by bombs and gutted by fire. Any daylight activity attracted whole squadrons of bombers. So the bulk of the men were spread out in the countryside. They only came into town at night to attempt repairs, or deal with the ship or two that crept into the harbor at dusk and was out before first light.

Even then the battalion/brigade structure was essentially meaningless. Three of the eight battalions were newly formed Maltese units with a few British cadres. The other five battalions were bulked up with a Maltese platoon per company and a Maltese company per battalion. The Maltese were joining in droves to get their families off the island and away from the bombs. Some thousands more had joined semi-militarized special police units, air raid wardens service, or labor companies.

How many would fight when the Italians landed was an interesting question. No one was sure, but everyone was aware that pro-Italian sentiment existed. The Maltese Nationalist Party leader, Enrico "Nerik" Mizzi, was now imprisoned by Governor General Dobbie's order, originally inside the Fortress of Valletta with another sixty influent Maltese personalities, amongst them the Cheif Justice of Malta, His Honor Sir Arturo Mercieca, with his wife and daughter. The endless bombing had seen the prisoners first dispersed to the interior and then moved off island to Alexandria. From there, they'd been parceled out to various gaols in India and Africa. Plus, many men would opt to stay home rather than be evacuated to Egypt. The garrison officers saw resistance as futile. Not enough men, not enough heavy weapons, no air force. The colonels did not disagree and had so informed London. The answer was "no more retreats". Winston at his British lion best.

The colonels saw another problem. Every battalion was riddled with detachments. Detachments on duty to provide manpower for the RAF strikes, to provide repair crews for the airfields, especially Luqa, whose runway had to be useable by dusk. To manhandle dispersed aviation gasoline, spare parts, and bombs to Luqa at dusk each day and then disperse them again afterward. Detachments for road repairs everywhere on the island, to keep the RNAS running, to make a pretense of upkeep on the coastal defenses and the mid-island Victoria Line.

Between the detachments and the "special units", no one in command seemed at all sure of how many men were in uniform, where they were, or what they were doing. The "special units" were a prime example of Churchill's Victorian military romanticism. He kept sending out various military adventurers to form pick-up units for vague purposes. It had started with allowing Wingate to reform his Palestinian Jewish special units from the Arab Revolt to meet a transient crisis on the Sudanese border with Ethiopia. These two Fleming brothers and their "commando" chaps here were a prime example. A mix of Palestinian Jews, Spanish Civil War veterans of the Internationals, White Russians, and a bit of British cadre from the Royal Marines, RN, Army, and India Army. There were half-a-dozen such small battalions that the colonels had located so far on Malta, and no firm assurance that more weren't coming. How do you evacuate without a troop list, without any surety of fixed positions? How do you defend that way?

2050 hours
3 August 1940
Luqa Airfield, Malta

It was just past true dark when the short line of Blenheim Bombers began landing at Luqa. They had made the first leg of their trip from Egypt in loose formation. There was little danger of interception over the Mediterranean. Landing at Luqa for refueling was trickier. The airfield had to partially illuminate itself to make finding it easier and to facilitate night landing by the understrength Blenheim squadron. Hence the timing. The Axis day planes were all gone by now, as they preferred landing back in Sicily before dark. Turnaround was usually a smidgeon less than an hour. The drill was change to a fresh air crew, load the bombs, and top off fuel. Any mechanical issue was a go / no decision. A plane that needed work was scratched from the bomb run and worked over after the bombers for the night departed. It had to be off the runway by dawn at the latest or it would die under the new day's rain of bombs. The ground crews from RAF were topped off by volunteers from the Army who found airfield work less boring than sentry duty. Life in the garrison was mostly a boring mix of waiting between air raids for the next one. Helping with the bombers was sort of like hitting back.

From Malta, the Blenheims would proceed in ones and twos for the ports of Taranto and Bari. The few bombs they carried were mostly harassment. Little chance of doing the Axis real damage but, again, a good feeling to the crews of striking back for the blows England was taking. The airmen had all seen photos of the damage to Dover and the other southern ports. Thank God, London, Manchester, and the other industrial cities hadn't been hit...so far. So it was zoom over Italy, drop their few bombs, and then home to Egypt. A few planes would take a bit of flak damage and stop off at Malta for quick repairs. It was a gamble. If the plane wasn't away by dawn, it was dead. However, even then the aircrew could be saved. There was a small fleet of ships doing shuttle service from Alexandria. Stranded air crew would be back in Alexandria in a few days. Command had been clear. At this stage of the war, trained air crew was simply more valuable than the planes they flew. When in doubt, detour to Malta and save yourselves. After the Battle of Malta would be the Battle of Egypt, and air crew would be at a premium.

Chapter 29

1000 hours
5 August 1940
Reich Chancellery, Berlin

"He isn't coming," Heydrich said in a voice that showed quiet patience with something he regarded as inevitable. It was exactly as he had expected. Göring simply couldn't be bothered doing the drudgery of being boss. As long as his prerogatives were respected, he would demote himself to a titular head of state over time.

Generaloberst Franz Halder was a general of the old school, and details such as keeping appointments were the most basic skill of any military. Of course, having had to deal with Hitler and HIS strange hours and manic bursts of activity, Göring with his sloth by comparison was proving fairly tame. "I suppose you are correct."

"We send him an executive summary to sign off on and in the meantime we get the real work done." Without more time wasted, Heydrich got the meeting moving. "Now, General Guderian you led a survey of British and French tanks captured from the campaign in the west. What conclusions have you drawn?"

Guderian directed a pair of Feldwebels to place blown-up pictures of two tanks onto stands. First was the British Matilda II infantry support tank and the second was the French Char B1 bis medium tank. Taking his pointer, Guderian tapped the British vehicle and reviewed its technical details. "Twenty-five tons in weight, armor up to 78mm on the front glacis and 75mm on the turret, armed with a 40mm rapid firing gun. Maximum speed appears to be 26 km per hour and that is on paved roads. The vehicle's armor renders it immune to all but our heaviest guns. During the battle of Arras on May 21st, General Rommel of the 7th Panzer had to resort to using 88 FLAK batteries in their anti-tank role and 105mm howitzers direct-firing to defeat these tanks."

Halder was already familiar with this in broad terms from the fighting and asked the key question. "What about the new antitank gun developed by Rheinmetall-Borsig? Could that deal with the British vehicle?"

Like the well-trained staff officer he was, Guderian was prepared and had the Feldwebel hand out some charts. It showed penetration tables for Rheinmetall-Borsig's new Pak 38, a 50mm L60 gun. "Sirs, I direct you to the bottom line for the APCR ammunition, which can reliably defeat the British tanks' armor out to roughly 500 meters. The problem, of course, is that the APCR has a tungsten core and so it is expensive. As you can see, standard armor-piercing ammunition cannot defeat the British tanks' front or turret armor beyond 100 meters."

Halder and Heydrich shared unhappy looks.

Guderian moved on to the Char B1 bis, "The French tank weighs in at 31.5 metric tons; speeds similar to the Matilda at 25 km per hour, but its armor is less at a maximum of 60mm. Weapons are a 75mm hull mount howitzer and 47mm anti-armor gun in the turret. We did not have to resort to such drastic measures to destroy these vehicles, but the standard 37mm tank and antitank guns could only deal with this vehicle at point blank range or from the flank. I would also add that the French were developing an improved version of this tank, where armor would have been upgraded to 75mm maximum."

On one level, Guderian felt vindicated by this presentation, as he had pushed for a gun heavier than the 37mm one the army adopted in 1936. Still, he had to keep this presentation honest. "I will add that these two vehicles were the best protected in the late campaign that we faced. Other enemy Panzers had much lower levels of protection, closer to our own Panzers."

Heydrich commented dryly, "We are going to run into more of these British Tanks at the least, and if the French were upgrading their tank the British might consider the same. What are our options?"

Guderian turned over the presentation to General Thomas. "We are in the middle of upgrading the guns of our Mark IIIs to use the new gun developed by Rheinmetall-Borsig...."

"The one that these charts say won't work?" There was more than a bit of annoyance in Heydrich's voice at this statement.

"You fight with the weapons you have, not the ones you wish for and, while the match isn't ideal, it's not hopeless either. It can work in certain circumstances, just not all."

"Or most." Grumbled Heydrich and then, while looking down on the chart, he tapped the line for the FLAK 37. "What about the

88mm? Why can't we use this on a tank? Or, failing that, on some vehicle that can keep up with the tanks?"

Halder, as Chief of Staff, was aware in general terms of the details of the FLAK 37. "Simply, it weighs too much and is too long to fit any of our current tank turrets. The Mark IV has a 75mm, but that's a howitzer."

Heydrich forebore asking what idiot had put a low-velocity howitzer on Germany's largest tank. He had already met enough uniformed idiots with general's tabs. Still, it never hurt to appeal to ego and nationalism. Heydrich thought of a gambit. "Gentlemen, Germany has the world's best engineers. We should perhaps direct them to investigate a solution? We are all agreed that our current weapons are not adequate to deal with the worst case, and we have only imperfect knowledge as to what our "friend" Stalin is up to. We should consider our options. Especially if we are having Reichsminister Todt reorganize war production. We need to be building not just more weapons, but the right ones."

The logic was hard to argue against, Halder thought. "That is true. General Thomas, you are directed to provide a solution to this challenge."

Thomas saluted, while morbidly recalling the old adage, "be careful what you wished for." He had wished for power. He now had it, but with the power came responsibilities, often responsibilities to produce magic.

2100 hours
5 August 1940
Rommel's HQ, Gerbini Airfield, Plain of Catania, Sicily

Erwin Rommel had managed to sweep up two hundred "volunteers" from his slowly arriving 7th Panzer Division outside Bari. This gave him a nominal third company. It was still a courtesy battalion, but he would make do. At least Strauss had somehow managed to acquire a surplus of glider pilots. Rommel had traded the extras to Kesselring's staff for a battalion of 1st Mountain, so he now had a short brigade. He also had the outline of his "brigade's" place in the war plan. Ramcke was happy to give him his own airfield, Luqa, as a target. Ramcke was happy because it meant he could land three battalions at Hal Far. Why Ramcke wanted to concentrate on the far end of the island was beyond

The Reich Without Hitler: The Falcons of Malta

Rommel's ken. He saw Ramcke as an administrative officer who had been overpromoted beyond his talents. The key issue to Rommel was a glitch he noticed in the evolving plan. Ramcke kept discussing an air landing AT dawn. Kesselring's staff officers kept saying BY dawn in their plans. Rommel saw no reason to resolve the problem. Kesselring had been clear he was not in the higher command loop. He simply put his boys through a few simple night exercises without explaining why.

> 0130 hours
> 6 August 1940
> Slit trench in the far reaches of the cantonment area, Bari, Italy

It had taken several days to arrive here. It started when one of the customers had tried to beat up Dika. Dika was roughly Oriana's age and smaller in physique, but was an experienced practitioner of the world's oldest profession with several years' work history. She dove under the bed, shrieked as if Satan's legions were at her throat, and retrieved a small sharp knife she kept hidden under the mattress. The bouncers cornered the drunken lance corporal and were hard-walking him out when three of his squad mates "objected". The ensuing brawl cost the Germans' teeth and everybody bruises before the four were handed over hog-tied to the chain dogs. Oriana had been there. As Wanda taught her, she had ducked behind the bar when things got nasty. She was too small for straight-up fights with packs of drunken soldiers and hadn't the skills yet to make up for her lack of size and strength. She was being trained, and already carried a sharp dagger under her skirts.

It should have ended there. A bit of company punishment and the four guys' unit banned from the premises for a week or two for things to simmer down. The fool used one of the nightly air raids as cover to come back for revenge, sneaking into the tent area. Somehow, he found Dika's tent with Stefan. Stefan was Dika's boyfriend and protector. But not her pimp. Aunt Wanda didn't like pimps. Thought they were parasites, leeches, scum. Only now she was in a position to enforce her ideas, because she was boss whatever the two majors thought. Ha! Stefan looked after Dika, but he also worked. He tended bar. He waited tables. He was one of the bouncers. He also was a half-assed musician. Good enough for a bar that doubled as a brothel. Dika's pimp had died in the Great Purge. She chose Stefan. She didn't feel safe without a boyfriend. But Stefan wasn't allowed a stable. He could have Dika. One and only one woman at a time. Wanda's rules. Rules that saved Dika's life. When the German dove at them through the tent cloth, he sensibly went for the large man before trying to harm the small female. So, the German knifed Stefan in the ribs. Dika threw hot ersatz coffee in his eyes and rolled out of the tent shrieking. The guy chased her and the whole camp turned out to deal with him. They beat him unconscious. It made a lot of noise, but the camp was often chaotic during an air raid. Flak guns shooting. People running around dealing with fires.

Every night, there would be a few British bombers. They came in singly in no special pattern between dusk and dawn. BBC said these were attacks on the port. The only thing they'd hit in the port was empty water. Killed a lot of fish. Kitchen had been buying large quantities of bomb-killed fish cheap most mornings. In reality, however, they hit random places in town or the encampments. Sometimes someone would die. Sometimes a fire or two would start. One of the Jewish elders from Romania said that wasn't the bombs. It was the red-hot metal from the flak shells landing. Guy was smart. An engineer of some sort. Aunt Wanda believed him. So did Uncle Adolph and even Uncle Gregor, who tended to distrust everything and everyone, so probably it was true. In public before the Germans, they were Majors Wrede and Vosss. Oriana learned to stand at attention and play that game. That was for strangers. Within the family, it was Aunt and Uncle. Oriana had been adopted by Wanda the way Hans was by Gregor. Family. Family wasn't blood. It was more like a Roma clan or a gang. It was why the idiot's three squad mates had backed him without even knowing what the fight was about. Unit, clan, family—it was different words for the same thing. Oriana was learning how the world worked.

Uncle Gregor made the decision that the fool had to die. Funny. Uncle Adolph looked scary and had the visible bad temper of a street bully, but it was Uncle Gregor who was the more dangerous man. Uncle Gregor didn't stare you down. No threats. No yelling and chest-pounding. He would just reach a decision and people died. Aunt Wanda was careful to never push him too far. There was another lesson for Oriana here, and she was working hard on learning it. Life was trickier than her former brat-self had thought. The same way the brat-self had thought she understood about sex and exploitation because she knew a few older girls back home who'd turned the odd semi-pro trick. Taking money from an older guy in some taverna to suck him off, a guy you'd never see again, wasn't the same as having to take on any guy who put money on the bar and dragged you upstairs.

Dika was her friend, so Oriana asked to help. Gregor looked at her carefully. He ignored Wanda and looked at small Oriana. Asked, "girl, are you ready? This is not some game. This is a gate you only pass through in one direction." Oriana had nodded. She wanted to grow up and this was part of growing up. Uncle Gregor had the German thrown in the back of a small truck. While the air raid was still on, they drove to the far end of the encampment. Past the latrines to a slit trench out by the firing range. As close to the middle of nowhere as this sprawling encampment had. Four large guys had dragged the German off the truck and thrown him in the slit trench. Uncle Gregor took Oriana by the hand and led her to the trench. The guy's pants were off. Uncle Gregor guided her hands to where the big artery was down by the groin. Showed her how to feel for it. Said everyone did the throat, but this one could be passed off as an accident better. Made sure her hands were in position and then helped her make the cut by pressing down on her hands to force the dagger to cut true. Guy had convulsively jerked twice and bled out in what seemed to Oriana to be under a minute. Uncle Gregor had given her a little kiss on the forehead and said she was a woman now. Oriana would have to think on this. Her younger life had taught her killing was wrong. Her younger life had been wrong about so many things. You avenged your friends. Someday they would avenge you. Oriana caught herself. The thought was not in Italian. It was in simplified German. Her woman-self was multilingual, it seemed, and some thoughts worked better in different languages. Italian for childish things. German for adult.

1300 hours
6 August 1940
Vicinity of Hal Far airfield, Malta

RN Commander Ian Fleming was in charge this day while his brother stayed near the harbor to welcome a fresh draft arriving tonight under Lieutenant Commander James Money-Penny. The two brothers had sized up the lack of preparations for serious defense and decided their unit could best be employed defending this airfield and, if possible, the RNAS to the immediate southwest. However, they were prudently arranging for the third draft to bring over six dozen or so light machine guns, plus plentiful ammo. They were also laying hands on enough fishing smacks to do an evacuation when the time came. They would give the Germans a sizable bloody nose, but holding the island did not seem feasible without a much larger, better prepared garrison. Yet their friends back in Naval Intelligence who had authorized this unit had been quite certain the attack was coming this month, probably in the next two weeks.

The two brothers had also not stopped recruiting simply from being on the island. Malta Command seemed to have parceled out detachments hither and yon, losing track of many. They had been establishing ties where they could. They did not yet assert formal command control. They would wait for the actual battle for that. Once it dropped in the pot, any officer with a core command could latch onto stray pieces who would cease shirking and look for direction. Until then, it was rest during the day and then dig fighting positions after dark.

0200 hours
7 August 1940
Grand Harbor, Malta

Lieutenant Commander James Money-Penny had waited as late as he could for the missing Commander Peter Fleming. His trucks were about to leave and he was taking the ride. What on Earth his superiors wanted this draft of middle-aged adventurers for was beyond him. Money-Penny was simply happy to get a chance to actually fight. He had been denied sea duty. Too valuable at headquarters because of the multiple languages he was fluent in. Sod that. His Majesty had enough uniformed paper-pushers. Money-Penny had no wish to be another. He was physically fit and in his late-twenties' prime.

0500 hours
7 August 1940
Valetta, Malta

Peter Fleming was in Malta under the RN cover his brother

had provided, making him a provisional commander in the Royal Naval Reserve. What were the chances an old chum would spot him? A chum who knew quite well he was Grenadier Guards, not Royal Navy, an Army Captain listed for promotion to Major, not a Commander. A chum he couldn't just shake off. The chum was in charge of a roadblock and wanted the story. Which led to two other mutual friends from Oxford who insisted on being brought up to speed on Norway, his guerilla units from Home Army and the usual endless "have you seen Old Bob? Where's he posted?". If you came from a certain social set, you had connections everywhere in the Empire. It simply wasn't done to be deliberately rude over things that were not classified, or at least not classified to the right sort of people. People with Oxbridge degrees, public school neckties, titles. and the like. Besides he was learning so much about the defenses of the island. Or, more the lack thereof. The strangest part was the firm conviction that the sea landings would come first with the airborne and glider troops following to reinforce. Peter had tried repeatedly to explain that the Hun did this the other way around. Air landings to seize airfields and bridges, then the main forces. He kept hitting a brick wall. Command was certain, so the officers were certain because Command couldn't be wrong. Airborne was some silly thing like the guerrillas he had created. Just more of Winston's military romanticism. The real fight would be a landing from the sea as had been done at Gallipoli. Supposedly, the Italians had been penetrated and Command was certain the Germans, lacking a fleet of their own, would just accept the Italian plan. The idea was that the Italian attack force would sail from Naples. It would be joined by the Italian battlefleet after the transports passed the Straits at Messina. There would be a battle with Med Fleet. If that went well, the island was safe. If not, there would be landings and then an airborne reinforcement. The Army would then retreat to the Grand Harbor and the RN would carry them off to Egypt. Fleming was happy he had found his own cache of fishing smacks. Even happier that enough of his men were RN or Royal Marines who, between them, knew enough celestial navigation to find Egypt instead of Libya. Peter Fleming had seen fancy hopes implode in Norway. He felt he was staring at the same movie for a second viewing.

Chapter 30

1000 hours
8 August 1940
Italian artillery range south of Syracuse, Sicily

A pair of officers stood on rocky ground adjacent to an Italian Army firing range in southern Sicily. One wore a German general's uniform with his trousers sporting the red stripe of a General Staff officer. The other wore the brown shirt of the Sturmabteilung with the rank insignia of a SA-Sturmbannführer. The man in the SA uniform had his left arm sleeve buttoned up and pinned to the blouse because of his lost arm—a gift from an exploding French Artillery shell in the closing days of the 1914–18 war. That shell also had left his face in an expression of a sneer all of the time. The surgeons saved his eyes, but the one side of his face was a mass of scar tissue. The wound hadn't prevented him from giving good service with the Freikorps in the Twenties.

While shells whizzed down the firing range, General der Artillerie Alfred Jodl paused his observation of the regiment's firing exercise to glance at his second-in-command. "Still haven't found the proper uniform to wear, Major?"

The grizzled Great War Veteran and former street fighter snorted, "The Army said they didn't need my services in 1939, even at a training school. So, I will wear feldgrau again after the Tommies' surrender to Fatso." There was a rather overt pause before Hans Maurice continued, and in a voice that showed no contrition at all, "I am sorry..." with his face betraying no such sorrow. "Before the British surrender to the Führer and Chancellor Herman Göring."

Jodl repressed a sigh. While his second-in-command was a skilled officer and an excellent gunner, the man simply had no social graces at all and could care less about military protocol. Of course, that was a good part of why he was available for Jodl to snatch for this assignment. Under other circumstances, Major Maurice could have ended up on charges for his insubordination, but Jodl needed him to try to forge this ad hoc collection of misfit toys into a unit, the 1st Nibelungen Legion Heavy Weapons Regiment. Now there was a joke of a name. Depending on whom you cared to listen to or asked, his unit was Ersatz Brigade Jodl,

The Reich Without Hitler: The Falcons of Malta

Sturmbrigade Malta, or Luftlande NL Artillerie Regiment Berlin. The men had been combed from "volunteers" from the SA and HJ, with a staff of SS cronies of Schellenberg plus Army refugees from the purge of OKW. "Volunteers". Pressganged was closer to it. Berlin and Brandenberg SA plus greater Berlin HJ "encouraged" to serve by the Gestapo pounding on their doors. A heavy weapons unit whose SA hadn't seen a crew-served weapon since their Freikorps days. The HJs had mostly only seen them in training films. His two battalions had no cohesion to speak of and Jodl was going to have to reshuffle them again. After all but begging Manstein back in Berlin for a field command to regain his honor, Jodl wondered again if eating his pistol might turn out to be cleaner death in the end. He caught that thought and shoved it back into the dark corner of his mind. Easy enough to walk in front of a British bullet later if all went poorly.

"Very well, Major. I don't have time for our normal games today. I spoke with General Manstein and nothing has changed."

Hans Maurice gave a dry laugh at the suggestion that it was possible for anything to change with respect to the clusterfuck the General called "organization" for this operation. "So, we still have no idea when or how many Ju-52s we will have to transport our gear to Malta? Fine. What are we going to do about it, General?" That last question had honest curiosity in the tone rather than the borderline insubordination General Jodl had come to expect.

After Kesselring, von Manstein, and Rommel had worked out a plan while Ramcke had been content to keep his involvement to purely technical issues, it had been clear that there was just going to be not enough air lift for the operation. Originally, Jodl had planned on a combination of mountain artillery and heavy mortars. He had managed to get a dozen 7.5cm Mountain Artillery Model 36s and as many 10cm Heavy Mortars model 35s. The weapons were beautiful examples of the artillery art, able to be broken down into sections to allow for ease of transport. Jodl had started his units training and was in the process of obtaining a few examples of the new 7.5cm recoilless rifles model 40 from Rheinmetall that promised the firepower of the mountain gun but weighed just under 145 kg. This was all for the heavy weapons battalion, and the second battalion was to be a machine gun unit.

Originally, Jodl was going to try to get MG-34s but Major Maurice had talked him into getting MG-08/15s instead. The Great War machine guns were much heavier than the new machine guns, but they had two advantages. First of all, they hadn't had to spend time and effort fighting to get them as, despite this being the only combat operation going on, the Army was grabbing every new built gun to make up for losses from the fighting in France and the Low Countries. Of more importance, the collection of Great War veterans that had arrived with Major Maurice from the SA already knew how to use the MG-08/15.

"We are going to have to adapt and overcome, Major. Since we have no idea when or even if we can get transport for the big guns, we have to assume we will not. You know what to call a weapon that isn't where you need it, Major?"

The plastic-like scar tissue on the side of Maurice's face almost writhed at the question, "A lot of graves, General, and I planted too many good men already."

For once, Jodl and his second-in-command were in complete agreement, "Exactly, Major. Since we can't be sure that we will have enough lift for the big stuff, we downsize."

Surprised at the manner of his superior, Maurice raised an eyebrow in silent question.

"Some days back, I had a long conversation with an old comrade from my days in the Bavarian 4th Artillery. He is on occupation duty in France and he sings the praises of the French light mortars. They are 6cm weapons. They weigh 20 kg. The heavy shells weigh 2.2 kg. They nearly have the range of our 8cm mortars and far outrange the 5cm...."

Maurice cut off his general with a snort. He didn't think much of the 5cm mortars they had been sent, going so far as to avoid their use. Their range was pathetic and Maurice had repeatedly said the crews would be subject to rifle fire the moment they deployed for action.

Suppressing a glare for the interruption, Jodl focused on remembering the good points of the man. He was an expert trainer and superb battle leader. He was also available at a time when contact with Jodl was career death to most field-grade officers. "With the French providing unofficial support to Heydrich's Mediterranean campaign, I have gotten a few more train cars added, containing French weapons. They arrive later today. We should be getting plenty of these 6cm mortars and ample munitions."

Not all generals were fools, it seemed. Maurice's face lit up into a smile, or at least as much of one as his scarred face could manage "So we kick the 5cm." He had heard good things about this French 6cm, the Brandt 1935. He had also spoken to two of Rommel's officers who had used the Romanian version during their brief anti-Soviet skirmishes. If Romanian militias could get good service from these weapons, his ragtag band had a chance to attain at least minimal proficiency.

The general surprised him again. "No... we ditch all of the other artillery. It's just too large and heavy. If it can't be carried by one man, it stays and we go in with just the MG-08/15s and these French Mortars."

For once Maurice was at a loss for words, and then said slowly, "We have less than two weeks to get the men familiar with the weapons."

"I expect you to work them hard in the meantime, Major, and try to find a proper uniform before we get on a plane." But the Major had turned his attention back to the men firing, and if the General had asked if the man had heard the last part of the order, he would no doubt claim it was his partial deafness. The man fell back on that act whenever he heard an instruction he didn't care for.

Jodl was left to ponder what to do with his heavier weapons, artillery, and machine guns. He mentally decided to store them. If his regiment did well on Malta, he'd ask for more men for a second regiment. He would then bring the brigade to Libya to serve under Manstein. This Afrika Korps could always use another fire-support element.

1030 hours
8 August 1940
SS HQ, Berlin

Oberführer Schellenberg ruefully shook his head. He thanked God for bureaucracy. He had ordered all mail for Israel Levi to be forwarded to his office and wonder of wonders, the Romanian postal service had obeyed. Steiner had sent off a letter on behalf of his lady love to her parents. Her dead parents. No paper trail on this. Time for a personal emissary to Strauss. Let him handle this mess. He'd been promoted and rewarded. Time he got to earn it a bit more.

1300 hours
8 August 1940
War Minister Beck's Office, Bendler Block, Berlin

Beck and Halder were having one of their never-ending arguments. The subject, as ever, was demonic evil in the form of Reichsführer-SS Heydrich. His ongoing purge of OKW was provoking worry among the officer caste.

Disposing of the hated Keitel had been easy. He was given a command at Kirkenes in Norwegian Lapland. How much of a mess could he make of a few hundred NL border guards and garrison gendarmes? For all either general cared about the despised Keitel, he could vent his frustrations by sexual congress with the local reindeer.

The problem was the corruption investigations into the OKW personnel. A certain amount of pilferage of canteen supplies was sadly all too common in many rear area headquarters. It was, of course, illegal but was normally treated as, at worst, a menial sin if kept small and discreet. The SS was ignoring these "traditions". No one of officer rank had been arrested yet, but the rank of those arrested had been rising slowly, day by day, and would reach field-grade officers by month's end. The Army men had been turned over to the proper military authorities for trial, and the interrogations of Army personnel had been quite civilized. The same could not be said of the handling of wives, girlfriends, children, and other relatives accused of complicity. Heydrich had been using standard Gestapo tactics on those, and making a big propaganda campaign out of it.

He had put the Army on the horns of a dilemma. The Army could intervene to protect its "traditions" and expand legality to protect the relatives. Heydrich had insured that this couldn't be done quietly. Or the Army could accept that family and friends were hostages to be used against any Army officer. Beck had appealed to Göring, who had simply ignored the request. That left the threat of a coup. The LAH was by now back in Berlin. It was still only a large regiment plus a mass of new recruits to facilitate its expansion to divisional size. However, it was an armed and trained opposition. The Army had no similarly loyal force.

The argument had no good answer. The moment to dispose of all the Nazis had been lost back in June...or perhaps it had never existed. This didn't end the argument or solve the problem.

The Reich Without Hitler: The Falcons of Malta

Indeed, it seemed as if the problem had no solution.

> 2100 hours
> 9 August 1940
> Encampment area of KG Strauss, Bari, Italy

Sturmbannführer Karl Siegel was pleased to have been given this assignment. It seemed to mark yet another small step up in the hierarchy. The Sturmbannführer was what Heydrich referred to as "one of the smart ones". A lower-middle-class man in his twenties whose degree was from a provincial university, he had clawed his way up the ranks of the SS by raw intelligence and an iron, driving will for self-promotion. He was of medium height, somewhat slight build, with brown hair and eyes. Nothing like the recruiting poster Aryan gods of the LAH. He had overcome these handicaps. He had even acquired Oberführer Schellenberg as a patron.

He knew he had been sent off from Berlin with, at best, a partial story. For reasons of state, a group of Jews and other lesser beings had been passed off as Aryans. A silly girl had sent a letter home to her parents. This was not to be repeated by any of these fake Aryans, but especially the girl. But he must not frighten the girl or her "protector" Lieutenant Steiner. So he was to show the silk glove instead of the iron fist, but still get perfect results. No memo. Just a verbal order from his patron, but he'd been clearly told this was the Reichsführer-SS's private business. His written travel orders had merely directed him to this unit for a "liaison conference" with its commander, Lieutenant Colonel Strauss... who wasn't here. Even though Berlin was sure he was. What else in his briefing might not be true? His patron expected results, not excuses.

So, he was awaiting the two officers in charge, Majors Gregor and Ivan. Sentries giving first names for their superiors? This was not any German military the Sturmbannführer had ever heard of. He knew the NL was new, but this was something out of Bolshevism. Major Ivan arrived first. Tall, blond man, obvious Slavic face, but looked intelligent, perhaps aristocratic. Introduced himself as Major Ivan Gorlov. Firm handshake, good manners, his German was off, but passible. Gave his extensive service history from starting as a 15-year-old officer cadet with the original Volunteer Army in the Kuban through his evacuating from Crimea with Wrangel in 1920, leaving him a penniless, refugee Lieutenant Colonel. What could have been a tale of woe from most men was instead recounted as a juvenile adventure, something for two gentlemen to quietly laugh over. Walked the Sturmbannführer to a makeshift café that seemed to be doing a booming business. Led him inside to an office with a laboring fan and two open windows to catch what little breeze there was. A cute little girl by the name of Oriana brought real coffee and some quite good pastries. Major Ivan apologized that Major Gregor Vosss was in some sort of a staff meeting and would be slow arriving. Apologies, but the Major had difficulties—artificial foot, bad leg, cane, middle-aged. At the Sturmbannführer's expression, Major Ivan then recited his associate's war record from his service as an underage volunteer at Ypres in 1914 through the Iron Division in the Baltic to the liberation of the Ruhr from the Reds. Missed the Feldherrnhalle, but Alter Kämpfer with a Party number within the Gold Badge limit.

The Sturmbannführer took this all in without showing anything. He was well-schooled in keeping his face blank. However, when the missing Major Vosss arrived, the greeting was warmer. This was clearly a man worth knowing.

It took only a few minutes to add to the confusion. Lieutenant Colonel Strauss has chosen to accompany Steiner's assault glider company and was by now probably in Sicily. This Fräulein Greta was there, as well, officially as a cook. In practice, a quarter of Steiner's company were females from some former Zionist militia that had fought the Soviets under Rommel. The Sturmbannführer's mind was working quickly. Clearly his briefing had left major things out. So this was a test. These things were to stay out of his written report. He was being tested for his ability to maintain secrets, to adapt to the new credo that two plus two could be five when the needs of the SS dictated it should be.

The two majors heard his gently worded order and had this Oriana fetch the Fräulein's aunt and uncle. So the fake Aryan now had fake Aryan relatives. On being told what their niece had done, the uncle apologized. He had a captain's tabs and seemed a competent professional. The Sturmbannführer was surprised to hear he was a combat veteran (Honved, four years at the front) and an oil field technical specialist. And Major Ivan's boss in civilian life. Had given the half-starving White Russian refugee a job in 1922 and taught him oil field metalwork. The

The Reich Without Hitler: The Falcons of Malta

Sturmbannführer filed away the technical specialty. If Germany was to be a petroleum power, best to know experts to consult outside of the formal table of organization.

The apology was that his niece by marriage was a nice girl, but distinctly unworldly. It had been explained to her that no contact with anyone left behind was permitted. She had failed to grasp why. The rest of the Jewish elders had read between the lines when they had been 'Aryanized'. The uncle pronounced this, showing he fully realized how provisional and reversible that was. "We told everyone to treat it as if we were dead to those we left behind and as if they were dead to us. The problem was that Greta thought Steiner's authority was higher than mine. Which, alas, it was. Hence the unwanted letter. The boy meant no harm. But he's 18. He's extremely infatuated. Probably his first love..." The uncle paused to smile. What 18-year-old boy did not pray for such a willing first partner instead of the usual teen fumbles in the dark? Now add in a propaganda ministry to make him a national hero and judgment could be impaired. Ah, to be that young and clueless. "Lieutenant Colonel Strauss can control him, and Steiner never makes the same mistake twice. He's intelligent. At a crisis in Romania and again in Hungary, he instinctively did the right thing. Just inexperienced and young. My wife and I will accompany you to Sicily for this if there is time before the operation. Is there time?"

The Sturmbannführer thought fast. He had a courier plane waiting for him. Sicily was a short hop. "Why you two?"

"She's unworldly, but a good girl. She'll take it from us if spelled out clearly and simply. But she's going to be quite upset at being told her parents and siblings are dead. Which they probably are. Ruth Levi never met a bad situation that she couldn't make worse with her nasty mouth and hair-trigger temper. So we may have to beat some sense into her so Steiner never sees her tears. None of us need him distracted before a combat operation."

The Sturmbannführer was amazed. Intelligent cooperation. And this unit was a pet project of the Reichsführer-SS. "My plane is waiting at the airport. How long until you are ready?"

The uncle spoke quickly to the aunt who exited almost running. "Fifteen minutes. When we are done, my wife will need travel orders back here. I'll just go in with the attack. Keep an eye on Greta in case she backslides on the necessary happy face. I've never raised my hand to her, but I know how."

Fifteen minutes later, the aunt was back with a travel bag and a young man introduced as Peter who had insisted on accompanying the Captain to battle. Peter was near two meters tall, looked quite Slavic, and seemed well muscled enough to carry an auto on his back. The Sturmbannführer foresaw a verbal debrief with his patron before he filed any official report.

0800 hours
10 August 1940
Rommel's HQ, Gerbini Airdrome, Plain of Catania, Sicily

Greta Schwabe was in shock. She had killed her parents, her siblings, all from one thoughtless note. She had never considered that the warning not to contact anyone would have fatal consequences. She wanted to cry and wail, which is precisely what she couldn't do. The Sturmbannfeuhrer had been kind, but firm. Her Uncle Isaac had simply called her a little fool and asked if she wanted to compound things by getting them all killed. Steiner was important to the head of the SS. Why didn't matter. He was. She was important because she was part of what kept the hero functioning. If she upset him, if he lost interest, they could all be liquidated.

Her Aunt Rachel had been calmer, but equally firm. No tears. No hesitations with Steiner, with anyone. She was a woman now and had adult responsibilities. Be her good niece, not Crazy Ruth's daughter. This was a cruel world. Adapt or die. She had then let Greta spend an hour crying and berating herself before saying quietly, "Enough! You had your cry. Now you put that aside. Lock it in a room inside yourself. When the time comes, after Malta, we will mourn the dead as a family. Until then...your Klaus must not be bothered with a fretting, sad woman just before a major military operation. This is real war he's going into, girl, not some silly skirmish in Hungary like you saw. We need him. We need you to keep him happy and focused. This is a giant adult weight on you. Deal with it. We have no choices. Your uncle's skills will be useful again someday in Iraq, but for right now it's your connection to Klaus that matters. This is your task in life. Make it happen. No excuses. No 'I'm too young'. Just DO it!"

Greta was left to ponder this. Aunt Rachel left with her travel orders to return to Bari. Uncle Isaac and his companion Peter left to get kitted up. The Sturmbannführer left to confer with Strauss.

The Reich Without Hitler: The Falcons of Malta

Klaus was sleeping off some silly night exercise. Greta decided to lock more than the deaths in that room. She locked all of Greta Levi, silly little girl. She would be Greta Schwabe. Naiomi was a fighter. She would be as well. She would go to Malta with Klaus. He wouldn't turn her down. She'd make him coffee and bring him his meals while he fought his battle and was a hero again. If Lieutenant Steiner could protect her, protect her kin, then Captain Steiner could do so better and Major Steiner better still. Strauss had gone from Lieutenant to Lieutenant Colonel in two short months. Klaus from Corporal to First Lieutenant. Klaus found the whole idea that he was a hero officer absurd. Well, that status of hero officer was important to her, so she had to guide him into the role. Greta Schwabe didn't know how to be an adult woman. So she just set out to be Aunt Rachel and not be her mother. Where it went beyond Aunt Rachel, she would be a mix of this Wanda and Naiomi. She would steal from characters in movies who were strong women. She would fake being a strong adult until she learned how adults did what they did. She would not fail her kin a second time. Better to die than be the cause of their deaths.

Chapter 31

2000 hours
10 August 1940
Chancellery balcony, Berlin

Half of Berlin must have turned out for the festivities. There were delegations from every Gau in the Greater German Reich and formal embassies from every corner of the new Europa. Even the Portuguese, Turks, and Soviets sent marching bands and dignitaries. Foreign marching bands that knew enough Germanic-sounding music. The instructions for the visitors had stressed that part of joining the new Europa was some Germanization of culture.

The four who ruled were there to honor the formal announcement that the widowed Frau Hitler was officially with child. The widow was a plain-looking, nineteen-year-old, ex-part-time kitchen-helper from the dead Führer's Berghof alpine retreat. She was blonde, blue-eyed, and fresh-faced in a farmer's daughter sort of way. However, the face seemed pleasant and the eyes seemed to show a lively, shrewd intelligence. As if she knew secrets that others did not.

The story of the Führer's secret marriage had not raised major attention in the chaos of his death and the new regime's formation. Now, the announcement that there would be an heir was a major news story, generating much public joy. Their beloved Führer had wedded a simple German girl who would produce a child of the German masses. The regime had given her the Berghof as well as a company of the LAH to insure her safety in these troubled times.

The other three rulers were aware that this farce was a plot of Heydrich's, but saw no reason to break ranks to ruin it. Even if the sow carried to term it would be decades before this child could threaten anyone's hold on power. Heydrich kept a poker face at their knowing smirks. He had directed a dozen similar-looking girls be impregnated at one of the Lebensborn Houses. One of them would carry to term with a healthy male child. Indeed, if the "Frau" proved difficult he could always swap her out. He prided himself on always being prepared.

The Reich Without Hitler: The Falcons of Malta

0830 hours
11 August 1940
Heydrich's office, SS HQ, Berlin

The three exiled heads of state from the Baltic States had been surprised that they had not only been allowed to participate in the Frau Hitler festivities, but also allowed marching bands under their national colors. They were given parade places near the tag end, quite far away from the Soviets, but still it was both an honor and a sign of continued national life to their exiled kinsmen. They were still feeling their way in this government-in-exile business. Indeed, each had a competing government-in-exile in London and a shadow third version in the US. The UK and US were quite acidly hostile to the representation in Berlin. Germany ignored the London and NY versions of themselves. The Soviets actively tried to discredit all three.

Here in Berlin, the two army generals had ignored them completely. Führer Göring invited them to state dinners, although never near the main dais. Only Reichführer-SS Heydrich's office had maintained day-to-day contact. Now he wanted a meeting and they entered it with some apprehension, wondering what he would demand of them. The demand was strange. They were to set up broadcasting facilities in their native languages. Subject to Reich censorship, of course, but still they were being treated as nationalities, not unwanted guests. Heydrich had made clear Germany would not initiate a war to recover their lands. All he held out the hope for was that, if Stalin chose war, their lands would be liberated, not annexed to the Greater German Reich outright. The model he offered was Slovakia. Far less than an independent state, but not a conquered province as Poland was under the General Government. However, the strangest demand was that Beethoven's "Ode to Joy" be translated into their languages. That song was to be the new call sign of the Euro-Broadcast cartel. Europe might still be a babel of languages, but it would have one anthem. A song that was not Nazi in any way. Almost as if the glue to hold the New Europe together was older than National Socialism and far more widely shared.

2300 hours
11 August 1940
Kesselring's HQ, Gerbini Main Aerodrome, Sicily, Italy

Gunter Strauss was getting a bad feeling about this entire operation. The sort of bad feeling he kept getting for a year and change in the Baltic with the Iron Division. He'd made lieutenant there, but spent more time as an ersatz intelligence officer than as a company second-in-command. Poorly thought-out plans, too many sides, no coordination between units, no clear objectives. He kept his men alive by ceaselessly acquiring maps, making contacts with other units, actually cultivating some locals instead of acting like drunken bandits. His company always knew where it was, had a good read on how unreliable this week's allies were, knew whether the road to their rear had the bridges still up if a retreat were needed. He had found local scouts when off-road movements had to happen. No getting lost in the mud or snow for his boys.

It wasn't an exact fit. There weren't endless conflicting units fighting each other in ad hoc alliance as there were in Latvia or Estonia in those miserable months. However, the air landing forces here had four commands, two nationalities with separate languages (not like the Baltic where most everyone spoke a bit of German), and the planes were coming from different continents. Everyone had objectives, but there was no master plan to coordinate them. Just land and fight. The larger, following mountain divisions were, again, separate commands with no plan beyond flying them in and reacting to events. Lovely. His unit had the objective, Luqa, closest to where the British army was. Strauss had fought the British in 1918. It had not been a pleasant experience. Even in the face of total surprise and overwhelming German superiority in the Michael offensive, Mr. Thomas Atkins had fought hard, like the Aryan Saxon warrior he was. Tough opponents, much tougher than the Ivans Gunter had broken into war at.

He had hoped the emissary from the Reichsführer would have clarified things. No. Berlin was clueless. The man had been shocked at what Strauss had managed to uncover. However, the Sturmbannführer had the key data point. The plan wouldn't be fixed. Too late. The night of the 17th they boarded planes and the party started.

Gunter had thought that his job here was to have been to babysit Klaus. Rommel was right about that one. Steiner would stand or fall on his own. Gunter had made sure the boy had gotten two "refresher" flights with a glider. He'd master the skill or not. The key was that whoever survived getting to the ground got pointed toward the airfield. This wasn't going to be the easy victory Rommel had originally sketched out back in Romania. Gunter's duty was to the unit. He could always write a heroic epitaph for Klaus. It was war and you mastered it or didn't. Gunter had been several years younger than Klaus when he first went into the line against the Ivans in 1917. He'd mostly survived by luck. He'd learned. Learned enough to be a platoon sergeant by Michael in the spring of 1918 and a company number two in Livonia by the following year. No. Strauss would take command on the ground and take that damned airfield. That was the route to keeping the Reichsführer's patronage. Meanwhile, there were more staff idiots to chat up, share a bottle of wine with. He needed more information and better maps. Knowledge was power.

> 0930 hours
> 12 August, 1940
> Oberführer Schellenberg's office, SS HQ, Berlin

Sturmbannführer Siegel had wisely chosen to do a verbal report before committing anything to writing. Schellenberg was grateful for this. The situation had mutated beyond his dreams. Strauss's unit had doubled in size for Malta with these Italian volunteers, whoever they were. Rommel had backdoored a brigade command for himself. Also, a separate airfield to attack. An attack whose success or failure would reflect on the Reichsführer-SS, as these were his pets. Indeed, the entire operation would be seen as Heydrich's fault if it failed.

Schellenberg doubted he could improve that situation in the five days until the attack launched. Less than that until the fleet sailed. However, the Boss could be alerted to lean on Kesselring and Wolff.

The wayward letter had been resolved and there wouldn't be another. That problem was solved. The question of the bulk of KG Strauss was another story. Better to issue a formal order to this Major Vosss authorizing the field brothel he had already informally created. Indeed, it might serve as a solution to a secondary problem. Ravensbrück was starting to get overcrowded. A letter to the commandant that well-behaved inmates might as a reward be allowed to volunteer for NL service in this new "entertainment command". The whores could be whores and the others could be bar maids or whatever. The important part was they would be shipped to Africa and never brought home. If the Jews could be wished away across the water, why not socially wayward girls? He'd prepare a short memo for the Boss to initial.

2400 hours British Double Summer Time
12 August 1940
War Cabinet room, Westminster, London

The poisonous message lay on the table. The Soviet ambassador had confirmed August 18th as the attack date. Refused to name his sources. Airborne order of battle was German 7th Air Division [parachute], German First Mountain Division [air transportable], Rommel's Storm Brigade Malta [glider], NL Heavy Weapons Brigade [air transportable], Italian Folgore Parachute Brigade, Italian Libya Parachute Brigade, Italian Julia Mountain Division [air transportable]. Air landing by Commander General Jodl from OKW. By sea, Italian Friuli Division [heavily reinforced], a German Naval Infantry Brigade, the Italian San Marco Marine Regiment, and unnamed Italian commando forces. Estimate of British strength—two brigades lacking in heavy weapons and no air support.

The War Cabinet wanted to bow to the inevitable and order an evacuation. Churchill was making it an issue of confidence. Enough of the key parliamentary leaders were willing to depose him. However, Halifax was still hiding behind constitutional scruples. There simply wasn't another consensus candidate, and a general election in the midst of a war seemed imprudent. Three times the War Cabinet denied it was an issue of confidence and voted by large margins to evacuate. Three times Churchill resigned. Three times they backed down. For now....

Chapter 32

0900 hours
13 August 1940
Army Proving Grounds, Sennelager in Westphalia

In one of the barracks buildings, a collection of engineers and technocrats were assembled. The engineers were having an argument over the directive that came down from Berlin the week prior. This meeting was to, in theory, refine that directive into a useable technical specification. As such, representatives from all of the major players where here: Henschel, Porsche (Nibelungenwerke), MAN, Daimler-Benz, Krupp, and Alkett. What was surprising and annoying to these representatives was that Berlin had also invited representatives from three Italian firms: Fiat of Turin, Ansaldo of Genoa, and Breda from Milan. Breda was a heavy engineering firm mostly known for locomotives and aircraft. Officially, this was to help with industrial coordination between the two allies.

"The VK6501 specification could serve as a basis..." Began Erwin Aders, the chief designer for Henschel, but he was cut short by Todt.

"There will be no 65-ton—or, more likely, 70-ton—monsters as solutions to this particular problem. So you can consider the VK6501 specification rescinded. What else?" Todt snapped at the other engineers.

An older engineer with a receding hairline, Ferdinand Porsche, spoke up, "We should do a clean-sheet solution to this requirement. There is no way we can get a workable solution trying to redesign a vehicle as small as the PzKpfw IV or even the VK3001 project. No, we need a new design in the 45-ton range to mount a gun as heavy as the 88 and have suitable armor."

This set off protests from the MAN and Daimler-Benz engineers on the suggested size.

Into the chaos, the representative from Alkett jumped in, "Do we need this to be a Panzer?"

Intrigued by the question, Speer called for the rest to quiet down, and asked, "What do you mean?"

"The requirement, as it stands, is just to mount a Flak 37, the 88. We are producing Tank Destroyers using the refurbished

PzKpfw I chassis to mount 47mm guns in open tops. With a bigger chassis, we could mount perhaps a larger gun like the 88."

The suggestion made sense for Alkett, which as a government-owned group focused on producing vehicles rather than designing them. Such a solution would require far less engineering effort compared to a new tank. Speer saw possibilities here and looked for more information, "The PzKpfw III or IV?" These two where Germany's biggest tanks and it was obvious that something like the PzKpfw I or II wouldn't work for something like this, as the Flak 37 weighed 9 tons as towed artillery and that was nearly as large as the PzKpfw II!

"I would say the PzKpfw IV is the obvious candidate. We might need to stretch the hull a bit but it should be possible. Provide splinter protection and you have a tank destroyer able to move that gun around the battlefield."

Todt liked where this might be going, "How soon?"

"Several months for a prototype. We would need several chassis to work with...."

Very pleased at possible solution that wouldn't be a year or more down the road, Todt saw no problem in backing this particular horse, "Done, orders will be drafted for the equipment transfer and I want a prototype for testing by end of December." Then, turning back to the other engineers, "Doctor Porsche's suggestion of 45 tons as a baseline for a new vehicle sounds reasonable. How soon?"

"At least a year. Perhaps longer...for a start, we'll need a much better engine."

Speer made a note and then asked, "What are the options available? We will need to tend a request to Maybach for a power plant." The manufacturing company head quartered in southern Germany produced automobiles and engines. The later products powered every German tank other than the Czech 38(t), which was powered by engines produced by Praga.

Professor Porsche then suggested that he could also design a suitable power plant. Several of the other engineers didn't exactly snicker at him, but it was clear they didn't think much of the suggestion. This set off a near-shouting match with Porsche versus half of the other engineers. Once things settled down and there was quiet, the Fiat representative, Colonel Sergio Berlese of the Italian Army and assigned to Fiat, spoke up. "Why not a diesel engine? Maybach is only producing gasoline engines for your tanks, yes?"

"That is true," Todt replied.

Colonel Berlese ran with the opening presented and ignored the dissent on several of the German engineers' faces. "All of our modern vehicles are powered by diesel engines. They have a number of advantages over gasoline engines. If you are going to do a clean-sheet design, and need a new engine anyways, why not look into a diesel, also?"

No one in the room could think of a particular negative about the suggestion. So a tender would be put out for not only an engine of suitable power, but also using diesel; this fuel being optional. Todt said, "Since you suggested this, then Fiat can present a diesel design of suitable power."

At this suggestion, the German engineers silently decided to out-design whatever toy the Italian came up with. After all, whatever the Italians could do, certainly German engineers could do better.

The arguments among the engineers continued on all morning, but by the end plans were agreed to. A new Panzer project, the VK4501, was born as a development project, a diesel engine would be attempted, and Alkett would attempt to convert the PzKpfw IV into a gun platform to carry the deadly 88mm gun as an immediate solution.

Thomas, Speer, and Todt directed a staff minion to prepare an interim memo. They would review it and then submit it to the four who ruled. One problem down and a million more to go. Each was coming to think of himself as Sisypus. Little did they realize that Heydrich saw himself as the man at the end of the circus parade, with the rolling cart and broom cleaning up the animal droppings.

The next item for the engineers to consider at this meeting was being called the "Standardpanzer" program. Actively producing the PzKpfw III, PzKpfw IV and PzKpfw 38 (t) as Panzers, it had been decreed in Berlin, was a waste. That, and the lack of any type of parts commonality between the various chassis had also been decreed to be a problem. A previous meeting had already settled on the PzKpfw IV as the new Standard Panzer, with the other two to only be produced as assault guns, tank destroyers, and the like.

Berlese—being an artillery officer and working on a FIAT project to create an Italian Assault gun, the Semovente da 75/18— knew this was something he could talk about with some authority.

"Heer Todt, Rome has directed our various firms to coordinate our activity with Germany's."

Nods came from both Agostino Rocca, a member of the board of director of Ansaldo, and the representative for Breda.

"Fiat has been attempting to negotiate a license to produce the PzKpfw IV from Krupp, but we aren't making much progress...."

At hearing this, Todt glared at the representatives for Krupp from the vast Essen Werke. "Berlin will...facilitate negotiations. Consider it taken care of. What does Fiat have to offer in exchange?"

At that question, Berlese felt the ground drop out from under him. It was one thing to use an opening to take the arrogant German engineers down a peg, but another to offer Italian products. Rocco decided to save his countryman. "I am sure the good Colonel can suggest a number of Italian weapons, such as some of our anti-tank guns. If we are to build German products, as much of the material as possible will need to be Italian to speed manufacture, and speed is key, yes, Heer Todt?"

"Oh, speed is without a doubt key for setting up the cartels. What weapons?"

A simple technical question about artillery that Berlese had no problem addressing, "Italy produces a 75mm L46 and 90mm L53; both anti-aircraft weapons, but also able to be used on tanks."

"Excellent, now let's move on...."

The talks resumed for the required coordination. They would take time to sort out and the arguments resolved.

Chapter 33

1100 hours
14 August 1940
Woods outside Luqa airfield, Malta

Corporal Billy Lincoln cut another hunk off the hog they had butchered and roasted. He and his mates had managed to absent themselves from the formal structure of the British Army this past ten days. They had started out as a squad work detail. For one reason or another, they had been misplaced and Corporal Billy decided to stay that way. They had filtered cross country over three days, picking up other strays until he now had two dozen men under his nominal command. They had loosely attached themselves to the helpers at Luqa. At dusk they could come down, do a bit of work, and gather up whatever supplies they could before retiring to the woods before dawn. Several officers knew Billy by face. Billy made sure to know them by name. They were his alibis for the day when his own officers noted his absence and wanted to press charges. He'd not been absent from duty. He was doing a spot of work. So were his men. Luqa needed warm bodies to fill the holes in the runway, to move bombs, and fuel. His boys had done all of that. They just hadn't worked all that hard. The airfield crews were chaotic at night and scattered during the day. If an officer told him to do more than he was of a mind to, he just claimed another officer had given them an assignment that took his lot back into the scrubs.

Billy had joined up in 1915 in a pals battalion. He was underage, but no one told on him. He'd always been physically big for his age, so the lie worked. He'd survived three years in France and Flanders. After the Somme and Third Wipers, nothing would ever scare him again. Had rejoined the Territorials during the Depression for the extra three pounds a month. Been lucky again. When war broke out he was in a draft for Egypt and thus missed Dunkirk. Getting posted to Malta was ill luck, but he'd gotten on his sergeant's bad side in Egypt so a transfer had seemed the smart play. Life was like that. The officers said the Hun was coming soon. Shrug. He made sure his lot had their rifles, plus, hopefully, enough ammo and grenades. He'd been through the mill and knew the drill.

0300 hours
16 August 1940
Inside a parked DFS 230 glider, Gerbini Aerodrome, Sicily, Italy

Klaus Steiner was afraid. He regarded that as an improvement, as a week earlier he had been terrified. He knew he was a fraud, a fake hero who had no clue how to fly a glider. He had greeted Strauss's arrival as a sign of salvation, but Strauss was off on his own business. He was there, but had not taken command. That made Klaus an officer with over two hundred people to get ready for battle, with an encampment that needed day-to-day administration.

He had been saved by his sweet Greta. She had seen his distress and taken charge. Quietly. She never undermined him in public. She was just adoring and sexy around the others, fussing over him, seeing to his coffee. But, somehow, she'd gotten her Uncle Isaac here. The man was a real officer. He'd taken the position of second-in-command, waiving silly things like rank. He'd run units before and effortlessly started running this one. Even the HJ glider pilots fell in line. They'd seen his medal. They heard the crisp competence in his orders. Plus, there was Peter. Klaus didn't know the story, but this lad acted as if he were Isaac's son. Peter was two meters of muscles on a quite large frame. He would just stand beside the Captain daring anyone to be disrespectful. One large HJ tried Peter on for size. The Captain had smiled and had the men form a ring. The HJ had asked about rules. The Captain had laughed, then told Peter not to cripple the HJ. For a big man, Peter was amazingly fast. The HJ swung on him. Peter effortlessly swayed out of the way, pulled the German boy over by his extended arm and pinned him in one fluid set of moves that ended with Peter's forearm locked around the HJ's neck, very slowly squeezing. As the HJ's face started turning red and then purple, Captain Isaac just mildly said, "Enough, Peter". Instantly, the pressure was gone and Peter was over a meter away with a mild grin. He looked around, daring anyone else to try their luck. No one did.

Greta had taken Klaus off for a private chat as soon as her Uncle had taken charge. Kissed him hard, and then said, "You are making things too complicated, my love. You have three jobs. Take off properly with the glider. If you fail, nothing else matters.

Fly the glider properly. Land the glider. After is after. So you and I are going to start a study session with your manual. We are going to make a cheat sheet with the basics. Don't worry about complicated things. If anything too complicated happens in the glider, we all die. That's fate. So you will fly and I'll be on the bench behind you with the manual and the cheat sheet. Naiomi will be beside me with a flashlight so I can keep reading it to you. We're a team. You're the hero. I'm the loyal woman who worships her hero. Just like in the movies."

Klaus had interrupted, tried telling her she wasn't going to Malta. She drowned that in kisses. He then tried to say she would fly with a more experienced pilot. She found other uses for her mouth and he found he lacked the breath for arguing. When that was finished, she just repeated that she was going with him in his glider. He was her hero. They were a couple. She then found something else extremely pleasant to do, after which she dragged him off to a glider where Naiomi was waiting with the manuals and a flashlight.

In a day and a half, they would load to attack Malta. That was frightening. But no longer terrifying. What had he ever done to deserve Greta? He HAD to prove himself to be the Klaus she saw, she loved. There had to be a mistake in her genealogy. Someone this clever and loving must be at least part-Aryan. Maybe she'd been an Aryan infant adopted by Yids. It happened, or so Klaus had heard. His Greta, his princess.

0800 hours
16 August 1940
SS HQ, Berlin

Heydrich was actually amused by the dossier Schellenberg prepared for him. Whoever this Herr Ford from the Hoover Commission was, he apparently was a man of consequence. His writings on the excellent Adolph Eichmann, fair and just commandant of the Jewish camp outside Krakow, was so laudatory as to seem to have been written by the Propaganda Ministry. However, the rest of the essay was so scathing against the Nazis' regime, the Poles, Europe's Jews, and the Soviets, as to make the praise of Eichmann seem genuine. Eichmann? That faceless nothing on the cover of whatever Time magazine was? Heydrich saw that Schellenberg had already ordered an extensive workup on Eichmann. Best to be prepared. Heydrich hated unpleasant surprises.

2030 hours
16 August 1940
Fleet HQ, Alexandria, Egypt

The code-room boffins had decrypted the longer follow-on to the flash code phrase in clear. All three watch subs had confirmed it. The invasion fleet was coming out of Naples. It was beginning. Fleet had sent the warning orders on receipt of the flash. Crew leaves had been at a minimum for days. With the warning order, shore patrol did one last sweep. Now it was time to start engines and prepare for harbor sortie. The time for emergency repairs and last-minute stores' top-ups was over. If it could float, it sailed.

The preplanned orders were sent to Malta Command and RAF. RAF was asked for a maximum effort for the next night, 17th/18th. One last run at the Italian battlefleet at Taranto before it sortied to link up with the slower transports who had further to travel from Naples. Maximum effort for the obsolete Blenheims, which was all they had. Every plane that had a chance of completing the trip. No more worries on perfect airworthiness. It was down to a go/ no-go decision. England expected every man to do his duty.

2045 hours
16 August 1940
10 kilometers offshore from Naples

Gross Admiral Raeder was reduced to commanding a squadron of S boats from the deck of S-22. He was sure the hope of that obese fraud Göring was that he would refuse this poison pill and retire. As If. It was a sea command in a combat zone. He could at least die with honor.

He no longer had command authority over the German Navy. He still had friends, had people whose careers he had advanced. So he was able to use that leverage to get some of the transports assigned German crews. Whatever the cowardly Latins did, the German ships would not turn back.

There had already been skirmishes with British submarines. Three? Four? The contact reports were confused. Two small freighters, one ex-Estonian and the other ex-Danish, were burning from torpedo hits. He'd leave rescue efforts to the Italians. Their small boats had fought well. Indeed, the only possible sinking was theirs. Oil slick and surface debris, but it was so hard to tell with a sub, more so at night. The convoy was maintaining decent formation and still on track for the Straits at Messina.

2109 hours
17 August 1940
Near RAF Hal Far airfield, Malta

James Money-Penny had finished oiling and assembling his hunting rifle. He had bagged game on four continents with it. Two-legged game that shot back. He had had an interesting life since dropping out of Cambridge. University other than sports and languages simply bored him. He already had social polish. He wanted to actually DO something. So when a classmate's father had approached him with a "business proposition", he had listened carefully. A mine in the Andes. Bandits. The company was recruiting a few "consultants". Crack shots and physically fit. Good pay including ocean passage and a healthy bonus for disposing of the problem. The "disposing" had involved a two-week hunt, some difficult long-distance shots, and a close-quarters free-for-all in the dark in the midst of a mountain deluge.

The original employer had friends and associates with other problems. Borneo. China. The Hindu Kush. Albania. Lake Albert. Money-Penny had "consulted" for many firms in many wild locales. He'd lived well. Between "jobs", it had been first-class hotels, beautiful companions, and a life of luxury. Also, paid lessons in every sort of hand-to-hand or weapons combat known. James had known he couldn't do this forever. You slowed up in middle age and he was approaching 30. But he'd made contacts. There was always a market for former "consultants" running projects in rough areas. Money-Penny could be both the proper gentleman and the total rogue as the situation required. He'd also been smart. He banked a sizable portion of his "fees" against his declining years. He even had bought into the odd profitable "import/export" opportunity. He'd also been quite careful never to work against crown interests. If the local representative of the Empire warned him off, he'd just move on. However, by the mid-1930s, they were more likely to find him work. He was a known quantity. Better by far for British interests than a Yank or White

Russian.

Then along came this damned war. He'd been in Cairo "consulting" for a small group involved with some sort of Biblical antiquity out in the desert that might need movement without involving Egyptian permission. A Yank university don of all things, but a two-fisted type who carried a pistol and bullwhip. Knew how to use both. Bit crude but...but the war came. Two old university chums approached him at his hotel. Wanted him for the RN before the Army got him. James was fine with the Navy part. He was not fine with his gift for languages turning him into some office wallah. So, when Fleming had appeared with this commando thing, he'd jumped at it.

Which led to here and now. Money-Penny had seen the start of the parachute drop at last light. First reports said Italian colonials from Libya. Said near Fort Benghaisa. That was silly. The fort was barely manned. But he'd never bagged an Italian before. Or a Libyan. At least not an ITALIAN Italian. There'd been that Argie chap in that casino in Paraguay. Argument over a card game and a bint. Now, James gathered a few enlisted ranks to assist in the hunt. It was a good moon. Time to do it. He felt alive again.

2115 hours
17 August 1940
Gerbini Main Aerodrome, Sicily

Izaak Schwabe had no problem no longer being Isaac Cohen. He was willing to rename himself Jesus Germania if that would safeguard his wife, his children, his employees, and his dependents, such as Peter. The Great War had cured Izaak of both religion and nationalism. Any God who would bless those four years of brainless slaughter was a demon. No flag was worth the slaughter of millions.

Yet, here he was, an officer again. Better that then dead from a Romanian pogrom or in some Nazi work camp. You did the best you could in a nasty, fallen world. He was shepherding the company onto gliders. The first wave from Libya had landed already. The second, the Italian Folgore brigade, was in the air now. His lot was next as the first of two Germans waves. Four battalions by parachute and three by glider, first parachute and the three glider battalions as his wave. Ta Kali and Luqa first. Hal

Far second. Everything supposedly down by first light, but the loading was backing up in a cascade of little problems. Best guess was Strauss, Rommel for Luqa, and Ramcke's stray battalion at Ta Kali past midnight and Ramcke with his three para-battalions at Hal Far in daylight. Coordinating this many aircraft from two continents was a ballet in the air and the choreographer was getting a barely passing grade.

The long-absent Strauss had turned out to have been quite gainfully employed. Had given him a briefcase full of air recon photos, maps, and tentative plans for how to take Luqa dependent on where on Earth the gliders set them down. Strauss had no faith the mostly barely trained Ju-52 pilots could find Luqa in the dark. Said they'd be lucky to find Malta. He strongly suggested the first men down light fires to guide the rest.

Yet Strauss did not take formal command. He wanted to keep spending his time acquiring information. Instead, he gave Izaak clear orders to ignore Steiner if need be. Assemble the men, take the airfield, and hold hard. Clearly there was more to this Strauss than the opportunistic SA bandit he'd seen so far. The man had been through the mill and seemed to have skills. Perhaps not a Lieutenant Colonel's skills, but definitely a good number two at a company or even battalion level.

Izaak had finished his count. Every man or girl was accounted for, even his niece, the tutoring instructor for fake heroes. He boarded the last glider with Peter. The boy was a wonder. He and his two brothers (or maybe cousins, that was never clear to them) had been starving street children when Izaak found them burrowing for food in his firm's garbage. Izaak took them home. His Rachel had always joked at the strays he brought in. Laughed, but accepted them as part of the family. She's given him four daughters, but no sons. Well, now he had three boys. Peter was the oldest and such a good son he was. Had been his apprentice at work. Book-learning wasn't Peter's thing. He learned by doing and had learned roughneck oil field work, metal work, how to boss a crew with his fists, and many other things. Had insisted "father" wasn't going to war without him.

2130 hours
17 August 1940
Lascaris War Rooms Complex, Valletta, Malta

Colonel Mason was the junior of the pair. When the reports of parachutists landing on the island's southwest corner came in, both colonels were shocked at the lack of response. Command staff was firm that parachutists were a mere nuisance. Fleming's commando battalion was phoned up to handle it. The colonels thought otherwise, but lacked any authority. However, they did have their tabs of rank. Mason was junior and off he went. A colonel could give orders to majors and captains, could organize some sort of a response out of the stray detachments at the airfields and RNAS. Parachutists in the dark would lack heavy weapons. They would probably lack unit cohesion. Besides the reports said colonials. Libyans. Glorified colonial police, not white men, or even the professionals of the India Army. Strange, but then the Italians were scarcely a first-rate foe.

There remained the matter of transport. Leaving the inner chambers of the bunker, he encountered "Commander" Fleming. "Commander". The man was a Grenadier Guards officer. A Captain. Posted to Major. Which is not the same as "Major". Still less, Lieutenant Colonel, which is what "Commander" translates as between services. Mason addressed the man by his proper rank, took him away from his chums, and off they went, with the Colonel as passenger on the back of the Captain/Commander's motorcycle. Where the man had purloined a motorcycle on Malta, much less an apparently mint-condition Vincent Rapide, was unknowable, but to Mason it just marked Fleming as the sort of enterprising junior needed for a night's work.

2200 hours
17 August 1940
Luqa Airfield, Malta

Corporal Billy Lincoln kept working on the Blenheim while the Colonel barked orders telling everyone to drop what they were doing and form up. He was an officer, but he wasn't HIS officer. Besides, any fool knew the planes needed to have their work done NOW! One of the pilot officers had enough rank and the screaming session was fit to wake the dead. In the end, the stalemate was resolved by the Colonel, whoever the bloody hell he was, giving in. Get the Blenheims off first and then everyone away to fight some gang of armed Italians and Africans. Billy quietly passed the word to his lot that they were going nowhere.

This many bombers and for sure one or two would need Luqa as a rescue field because they wouldn't be in any shape for the long flight back to Egypt. That meant hands would be needed to light the fire barrels along the runway, to manhandle bombs, and fuel away before the usual morning air raid. Officers! Never thought anything through.

Chapter 34

2230 hours
17 August 1940
Harbor, Bari, Italy

Major Ivan Gorlov made sure he was the last to board of his 300-person "advance party" of KG Strauss. He and a short platoon of NCOs he trusted had to herd the contingent onto the former SS Andrea Sgarallino, which for duration was Naval Auxiliary F123. Pushed the people along as if they were a herd of cattle being driven to market. Which, in a sense, they were. Cattle with duffle bags or packs for their worldly belongings and carrying personal weapons. Only he and the NCOs carried ammo. Safer that way. No crew-served weapons or unit supplies this trip. They would be overcrowded enough on this voyage.

The KG was more a moveable refugee camp than a military unit. Steiner had taken the most motivated to Malta. Gregor had kept the most useful back to keep the "business" running. When Command had required him to prepare the "advance party" to fill out a gap in 7th Panzer Division's movement caused by a delayed arrival of some subunits, the only guidance from above had been a body count. The three majors had found the least useful bodies. What good this detachment would be in Libya was beyond him. However, he'd seen stupider things in three years of civil war across southern Russia and the Ukraine.

Gregor gave him simple written orders. Find an encampment as near to the port of Tobruk as possible. The transferred Austrian clerical NCO had proven to be a godsend. A bottle of Wanda's firewater and some complementary passes to use the girls had gotten him near-total access to the camp's official archives, so the three majors had the full deployment plans for the Afrika Korps. Tobruk was to be the key supply port, so it was where to set up.

The idea of a reinforcement convoy sailing with the Italian battlefleet had seemed absurd. The surface logic was that it worked last time. The British went at the battleships and ignored the transports. Major Ivan was not sure if this was logic or luck. Didn't matter. Orders were orders. No way to dodge them at this level. There'd already been one British bomber over the harbor. It had killed a bunch of fish and shot water high in the sky from its bombs. The ship captain had shared a laugh with him. Said the safest place to be when the British bombed was what they were aiming at, as they always missed.

At least Major Ivan knew how to swim. Most of his "troops" didn't and most of the rest didn't especially well. He wasn't sure he could swim to Africa from a sinking ship, but at least it was a chance. He'd survived worse odds multiple times in his life. Fate would catch him when it would. In the meantime, Isaac was counting on him. Isaac. The man had saved him from starvation and taught him a trade. Weird even for a Jew. But a true friend and one worth having.

2300 hours
17 August 1940
Gerbini Main Aerodrome, Sicily, Italy

Erwin Rommel was fuming. Three planes aborted on takeoff from mechanicals out of the two waves, and one was his. His brigade was in the air without him. That was no place for a storm officer to be. What was more galling was that fixing his plane was not a priority and his rank didn't make it one. The priority was getting Ramcke's wave off and then recovering the prior wave of Italians. Ramcke and Jodl had made QUITE clear that they had written orders to ignore him unless any request were countersigned by Kesselring. Who was quite too busy running his air fleet to deal with a mere ground commander, whatever that man's rank. So Rommel waited. And fumed.

2350 hours
17 August 1940
Lascaris War Rooms Complex, Valletta, Malta

Colonel Duffy was able to get a better response when a German wave of invaders arrived. The first reports had them centered on Ta Kali, but scattered groups were all over the island... or so first reports said. There were even glider troops attacking the golf course. Duffy wasn't about to let the dither deter him. He simply marched out of the bunker, rounded up a company each from Royal West Kents and Royal Irish Fusileers, and led them off on the road to Ta Kali via Mosta. He planned to bypass the golf course and recapture the air field. Yes, the golf course was in the suburbs of Valletta and, thus, in theory, serious. It was also a battalion encampment. Even with most of their men out on detachments, a battalion should be able to deal with a few platoons of strays. If they couldn't, the defense of the island was hopeless.

Duffy saw holding air fields to interdict further reinforcement by the Axis as key. He'd sent Mason to deal with Hal Far. There were no reports yet of problems at Luqa, so the current priority was Ta Kali. His short battalion should be able to retake it. Or at least make a good start on trying. Both companies were understrength from detachments and especially deficient in crew-served weapons. He got incoherent accounts of where the missing machine guns were and was not inclined to wait.

Chapter 35

2400 hours
17 August 1940
KG Strauss encampment, Bari, Italy

Oriana had never been religious. Her family had been free thinkers and most of their social circle were atheists of various Marxist stripes. Religion was a sham. All the adults in her old world agreed on that. Yet, Uncle Gregor had called a prayer meeting. He never actually said it was compulsory. Uncle Gregor didn't have to raise his voice that way. If he said everyone was showing up who wasn't on duty, no one would stand up and defy him...except Aunt Wanda. Wanda was Wanda.

It was a fairly brief meeting. Uncle Gregor made a short speech about how Lieutenant Colonel Strauss and Lieutenant Steiner's company was going into battle tonight. Major Ivan's group was sailing tonight, which was battle of a different sort. Uncle Gregor said everyone should bow their heads and then some Magyar lay deacon led them in a few simple prayers. The Magyar was from some Protestant sect Oriana had never heard of. The prayers were in German. Many of those assembled were Jews, Roma, or Catholics, and just muttered a different prayer. Oriana saw the point. The words didn't matter. It was the family coming together in a time of troubles. Some of theirs would be dead before the day was out. Family, clan, unit. There were ceremonies and everyone took part. To not do so was to not be part of the collective whole. That was bad. Uncle Gregor was someone worth learning from. He never explained, but what he did always seemed to have a good reason. So Oriana followed the German words of the prayers as best she could. She wanted to belong.

Wanda had skipped the stupid prayer session. Just like Gregor to hold church parade. He was a traditionalist that way. Wanda hadn't seen the inside of a church since her folks turned her out at 12. Religion was for old farts like her Dad and Mom. Church, Kaiser, all that old-timey drivel. Yet when the girls started mumbling prayers between customers, Wanda had gotten caught up with it all. Her guys were going off to a fight. A fight where she couldn't be there to do her part. Damn it to hell, but Gregor was right. She called for a moment's silence and recited a Hail Mary, the only prayer she could remember. Many of those assembled, staff and customers both, followed along and the rest bowed their heads. She then gave everyone a round on the house and led a toast to the souls of Steiner's kids who were bound for death or glory. Maybe real war was different than street brawls with the damned Reds or the cops. Maybe this gang of theirs was turning into some sort of a freikorps. The brat Oriana had been right to take part. Wanda would never admit it to anyone, but sometimes she was wrong.

0010 hours
18 August 1940
In flight to Malta

Peter Schwabe knew he must have been something before he became Peter Cohen. He had dim memories of Papa Isaac finding him in the garbage bin and taking him home to Mama Rachel. He had dimmer memories of several women called mother or auntie. They were bad memories. No food, often crude shelter, and always the strong hand that beat him. That beat his younger brothers, Paul and Luke. Brothers? Cousins? Whatever they had been then, they were brothers now. They had a mother, Rachel, and a father, Isaac, and four dear sisters. They were a family.

So there was no way Papa was going into battle without him. Peter cradled his weapon, an MG-34 that he'd had a few days of range practice on. It was an easy weapon, more so for someone of his size and strength. The family needed Papa to survive until Iraq so his skills could earn them a place in the new oilfields. Luke knew the theory, the science. Paul had the eye and the hands to do the fine machining. Peter could ramrod the crews to do the installations. But only Papa knew it all. They were valuable to these Nazi overlords as a team, as a company, but Papa was the key. And Papa had chased off to war to deal with silly Greta. His cousin who would now become his sister. That meant Peter was responsible for her, and for this new man of hers, Steiner. Peter was never afraid of a fight. He'd been fighting all his life. In the gutter you fought to survive. Papa and Mama had taken him out of the gutter. Now he fought to stay out, to be one of those with a bit of power and prosperity. Mama fed him MEAT. Meat every day. The same food she and the girls ate. Real food and as much as his huge body needed. Nothing he ever did could repay them for making him part of the family, but Peter would die trying before failing them in anything. He would keep Papa alive and they would return to Mama's cooking. To MEAT. Important people ate meat, and Peter would kill to keep them all at that level.

0100 hours
18 August 1940
Scrub between initial drop zone and Hal Far aerodrome, Malta

First Lieutenant Enrico Cirillo was getting tired of this game. His patrol had been trying to push out to make contact with the Germans, who were supposed to be landing at Hal Far. Instead, he was reduced to playing Red Indians with a small British forward outpost. His 4th Company of the Black Devils Parachute Battalion were all well-trained professional soldiers. However, this British sniper was damned good. So far he'd lost a dozen men to bag two British enlisted. All this to advance under two kilometers. There was no sign of the Germans. Something was wrong.

0125 hours
18 August 1940
Luqa Aerodome

It had been one hell of a second-round faceoff between the Army colonel and the senior RAF colonel/command pilot. Flyboys called them Group Captains and Billy had known this one from prior missions. A red-headed Ulsterman with a hair-trigger temper. The Ulsterman insisted on keeping his men. Many of the extra Army lads had been dragged off by the colonel, sent marching behind some Naval officer on a motorcycle. The Navy officer, for some reason, was in Army uniform but with Navy rank badges. Things were getting weird with these special units, in Billy's opinion.

The Group Captain had recognized Billy and insisted his lot were now seconded to the RAF. Colonel argued uniforms. Army uniform meant these were his. Group Captain was a smaller man, but louder. Cocked his balled fist and threatened to settle it man to man. The colonel was not up to fisticuffs with a man easily ten years his junior and just threatened to put Billy and his lads on report. Billy stayed stubborn and kept repeating that he didn't know the colonel, but had been detailed by his officer. Wanted a written order from his officer to leave. Billy was bluffing on his officer, but the phones were out again. Something about German glider troops out by the golf course. When Billy hung tough, nearly half the remaining Army lads claimed they were with him. Colonel took the rest and marched them off.

Good thing Billy's lads had been held back. Less than five minutes after the idiot colonel had left on the road to Hal Far, the first distress call came in. Bomber with engine trouble. Dumping its bombs and turning back. Billy got his lads organized and the runway barrels lit up to guide the Blenheim back. Odds said it wouldn't be the last. They had pushed every plane they could in the air and a lot were being kept going on spot repairs and prayers.

0130 hours
18 August 1940
Command bridge, HMS Kent, at sea en route to Malta from Alexandria

Admiral Cunningham had chosen to fly his flag from a cruiser instead of a battleship for this operation. When the time came, he would command the evacuation from this ship while leaving the main battlefleet safely out to sea. He was holding two signals from submarines on forward patrol off Taranto. Each had sent the code words "Lady Hamilton". The Italian fleet was coming out. If things went well, one of the submarines would hit an Italian ship. More likely they would fire blindly and dive to safety. Either way, the game was afoot.

Chapter 36

0140 hrs
18 August 1940
Somewhere in the air near or over Malta

Klaus Steiner could not afford to show the naked terror he felt. He could not disgrace himself before Greta, or even Naiomi. Their running coaching had gotten him this far, but now he was alone at the controls in moonlit-black night somewhere around Malta. The Tante Ju had just cast him loose. He needed to find his airfield. He was not certain he could even find dry land. Moonlight is better than no light, but Klaus had no experience of finding things from the air at night. There were occasional brief flashes of what might be gunfire far below. Or maybe he was wishing there was, as he needed a clue, a beacon, something to guide him.

He was a hero officer. He had to DO something. Fate had blessed him with excellent eyesight. At the extreme of his vision he could vaguely make out a small fire. It seemed to be moving but water doesn't burn so it had to be on land. He steered for the fire, doing small adjustments as it seemed to move across his vision slowly from left to right while sinking lower or falling. Klaus was out of ideas. He was following something and it was descending. Doing something was better than sitting like a gibbering monkey or crying like a lost child.

Strauss was seated directly behind his HJ pilot. The pilot was lost, frozen in indecision. Strauss had seen units lost on night marches. He had never done so thousands of meters in the air. Suddenly his pilot was maneuvering. Steiner was doing something and Strauss's pilot was following the hero. Following the small formation lights on his glider. Strauss could see the glider swarm start to do the same. Hopefully the others he couldn't see were doing so as well. Steiner. The idiot kid seemed to have a clue after swearing he was a fake glider pilot. Strauss chuckled at the vagaries of war. His good-luck find from Berlin to the rescue again. Strauss could almost start believing in religion again. Almost. Maybe.

Billy Lincoln looked up from the end of the runway. The injured

Blenheim with the burning engine had reached the runway and was rolling toward the other end, but something was landing right behind it. Weird plane with wings FAR too large for its frame. No engine noise. Just a sort of whoosh or swoosh sound. Billy knew this was supposed to mean something, but he was blanking on whatever day's lecture this had been. Billy was a hands-on working man. He tended to nod off while some toff droned on in a lecture hall.

Billy squinted in the bad light and suddenly he remembered his recognition drills from weeks ago. "German glider! Find your guns, boys!" Billy scrambled away into the darkness. His lads had their arms stacked off in the scrub near where they bedded down. Why lug the extra weight back and forth each day? Shit. "To me lads!" He heard footsteps as dozens joined him. He'd lost his night vision from the airfield lighting and so stumbled a bit. It was only a mile to get the gun stash, but it was taking too long. Looking back, he could see dozens of gliders landing in and adjacent to Luqa, hitting all of the four runways.

Klaus brought his glider to safe halt twenty meters from the injured bomber. There was a gang of Brits putting out the fire and seeing to the crew. Klaus ignored them. He'd run an airport before. Step one was securing the buildings. To his left was a building. He could see a few uniformed figures. He screamed "Hands up!" in badly pronounced English. Rommel had made everyone practice this. His voice broke and he stuttered on both words so what came out was closer to "Huh nens ooooop!" One man turned toward them with something in his hand. Before Klaus could react, someone behind him fired her MP-38. Greta? Could be Naiomi. A brief burb. The man went down, dropping a tea mug. The other three raised their hands quickly. Naiomi's girls swarmed past him to complete the conquest of the cook shack.

Gunter Strauss's glider was not in the first few dozen to land, so the conquest was complete by the time his pilot reached the runway and rolled up to the end. Steiner had rounded up fifty or so British prisoners, near half of them officers. Split between British Army and RAF. Gliders were being manhandled off the side to leave runway space for new arrivals and more kept landing minute by minute. Steiner even had outposts out. Not well-positioned, but covering the two roads and the ends of the runways. Strauss spent ten minutes hearing Steiner's report and making changes in where the sentries went. He had an intact airfield, complete with fuel and a dozen British Vickers machine guns.

He also had a problem. Five of the gliders were missing. Two of them had his communications section, a detachment from 7th Panzer. But he had an airfield. He seemed to have a working British radio. He'd jotted down the correct frequencies. Without the code books he was reduced to sending in clear. Just announcing that he'd seized Luqa invited British response. Then a thought came to him. Steiner was a national hero. Everyone had read the damned propaganda stories. Klaus and Greta were the German Romeo and Juliet of the summer of 1940. To Germans, but probably not to British. So he had Joey get the radio running. Joey turned out to know those machines as well. The man had golden fingers. Got the clearest voice among the girls to send a message in German, Yiddish, Magyar, and Romanian. "Klaus and Greta invite you to where they first met to have latkes for breakfast." She was to keep repeating it every five minutes. The two lovers had met at an airport. The four languages should show which unit it was. Latkes should be easy to read as L for Luqa. Breakfast was the dawn meal. It might work.

Strauss then put Captain Schwabe in charge under Klaus while he set off with a captured bicycle to do a quick recon up the roads. Time to learn the terrain. A counterattack had to be coming soon.

0200 hours
18 August 1940
Near Hal Far, Malta

Commander Ian Fleming looked again at the documents. They seemed absurd but the words were still there. They were Soldbücher, paybooks, recovered from German soldiers killed in a glider crash nearby. They clearly said Seventh Panzer Division. He had two waves of Italian parachutists to his west. Money-Penny was off on some mad adventure of his own. The man had almost no concept of orders or chain of command, but came well-spoken of as a fighting man. Now here was proof not just of Germans, but of airdropped or air-transported panzers. Panzers. A division of panzers. The phones were out and his brother elsewhere, someplace with his motorcycle. Nothing for it but to send two couriers with this information by bicycle. One through Luqa and the other the long way around via the coast. Time to get his men in order to defend the airfield. The Italians were undoubtedly waiting for first light to attack.

0210 hours
18 August 1940
Ta Kali airfield, Malta

Colonel Duffy's column had straggled badly on the fairly short march to Ta Kali, so he had only a short company by the time he arrived. That had proven enough to chase the few dozen Germans away. They seemed disorganized and confused. He'd captured half a dozen. The paybooks showed 1st Mountain Division, 7th Panzer Division, and school troops from the Jäger school. Also two Tatars from something called the NL who claimed they had enlisted in Romania. He'd sent a runner back to HQ with this data and detailed a squad to escort the prisoners back. He made sure the corporal in charge knew HQ was expecting six live, healthy captives. That the number would be in his written report. Otherwise, he feared the squad might arrange an "accident". He detailed a captain to locate his missing men and set about wrecking what he could of the airport facilities. If whole divisions were coming by air there was no way he could hold for that long, so best to leave nothing useful for Jerry. There wasn't much fuel here, but it was enough to douse the buildings. They burned well. What he needed was explosives to wreck the runways. They already had enough unrepaired bomb craters. He sent off another runner requesting dynamite and some engineer officer to supervise. Told the runner to confirm the part about six prisoners. Men hated prisoner guard duty. Without higher control, it was often temping to just "dispose" of them.

He pulled off the field into the surrounding scrub to await the probable dawn counterattack. He could hear noise from the scattered Germans.

0215 hours
18 August 1940
Road from Luqa to Hal Far

Colonel Mason had stopped the Hal Far courier to read the dispatch. Airborne panzers? Absurd, but Commander Ian Fleming did not seem a complete hysteric, so maybe...His column had managed only a plodding pace. So slow that he'd sent the other Fleming brother on ahead aboard his motorcycle. The rider behind him had a BREN gun. Would be useful to get it into action faster.

This mob of pressganged men had also started melting away. He'd been reduced to staying at the back with a few officers to push the laggards along. None of these men felt any loyalty to this scratch unit. It was less poor morale than lack of cohesion. This is why units are supposed to train together. Sadly, it was also inevitable that their parent units hadn't sent their best men to work details. So it was odds and sods he was pushing, constantly checking the roadside for those trying to abandon the march. He detailed a lieutenant to push ahead with the most willing, compliant men while he kept forcing the shirkers to at least pretend to march.

0220 hours
18 August 1940
Scrub, one mile east-northeast of Luqa

Billy Lincoln had taken a few minutes to convert his makeshift platoon into sections. There was no way he had enough men to retake the airfield. So the obvious move was to work his way to the Luqa to Grand Harbor Road and block it. Billy doubted his men could stop a determined push, but at the least they could slow one down. His biggest problem was ammo. He didn't have enough despite his best hoarding of what could be found. He'd enough for one serious action, but no more. His second biggest concern was cohesion. The lads were willing to fight, but not used to working as a group. If he had to maneuver them, they'd likely fall apart.

The moonlight was enough to navigate the scrub. He detailed off the youngest guy he had and sent him off at a faster pace. He scribbled a fast note explaining what happened. The runner was to push up the road till he found an officer and report.

0230 hours
18 August 1940
Road from Luqa to Grand Harbor

The moonlight made bicycling easy. Gunter thought he could smell smoke when the breeze shifted toward the north. He thought he heard shooting somewhere far ahead of him. He was a kilometer beyond the outpost he'd placed. The road was starting to slope uphill toward the island's center. He stopped to listen and take it in. His combat senses still worked. He'd known there was a reason to stop before he comprehended why. There was noise to his right off the road. People moving. More than a dozen. Probably less than a hundred. British reinforcements would come by road, so these must be some of the Luqa garrison that Steiner had chased off. The intel that the airfields were unguarded was off, but not by a lot. There hadn't been a serious defense.

Strauss quietly backed himself and his bike a hundred meters up the road. He went down to one knee and stayed quiet, waiting. It didn't take long. He saw the first Brits reach the road. He backed away slowly until line of sight was broken. Then, turning his bike, he retraced his steps back to his outpost. Alerting the squad he placed there, he went back to the airfield to see about getting a machine gun forward. A Vickers gun was heavy, but if positioned well he could block the road.

0245 hours
18 August 1940
Cook shack, Luqa

Greta had sensibly left Naiomi's girls to go set up to fight. Instead, she'd grabbed a few of the Italian volunteers as helpers. Naiomi's girls were veterans. The Italians were untrained children, even if of roughly the same ages. She had boiled up water to make mugs of tea for as many of the arriving troops as she could locate. The officers kept moving them and she hadn't runners to wander about finding the outposts. She'd see to them when they were relieved. Tea first and then she'd try to find some sort of hot snack to cook up. Even in the middle of the night the shack quickly got quite hot. Abysmal ventilation. Two of the captured officers had left luggage behind. She used the big steamer trunk and the three suitcases to prop open the door. They were quite heavy but her helpers had pushed them into position. Heavy was good. It meant they would stay in place. By afternoon this shack would truly be a furnace.

The Reich Without Hitler: The Falcons of Malta

Joey had found a tractor that could be used to get the gliders off the runways. He'd shown a few people how to do this and then started looking over the British bomber with the defective engine. Maybe he could fix it. A bomber had to be worth something to someone and, besides, he'd never worked on this engine before. It wasn't exactly an auto engine, but he thought he could figure it out.

0300 hours
18 August 1940
Road from Luqa to Hal Far

Colonel Mason had not seen front-line service since the Somme in 1916. He'd been staff ever since. He lacked Gunter's ingrained combat reflexes, so he let himself be surprised by the small mob of people coming up behind him from the fall of Luqa. Didn't hear them pounding down the road, panting, until they were upon him. He refused to believe the first four, but the fifth was an officer. Not from a good military family and only a lieutenant, but still...German gliders following in a crippled Blenheim on emergency approach. Mason had wanted to berate the lieutenant, but was enough of an honest man to see where his own actions had stripped the base of many of its defenders. When the final man arrived, gasping from exhaustion, he had twenty-nine more men. Men, some without weapons, in no discernable formation. They would be useless until he marched them to Hal Far and got them kitted up again. Yet, something had to be done about Luqa. Hopefully the courier would have the sense to detour. Hopefully. One could not count on it. So he gave the lieutenant his own Webley pistol. Gifted him with a dozen armed stragglers from the earlier column and clear orders. Go back up the road. Make contact. Note how close to Luqa you are. Send back a runner. If necessary, fall back up the road, but stay in front of the Germans. He then gave the boy a fairy tale about how this revolver had seen him through three years of combat in the First War. Let the lad think it was a lucky talisman. Mason was sadly aware that mass warfare meant shopkeeper's sons as junior officers. They weren't brought up with the right habits for command, so one had to make it sound like some Hollywood movie.

0310 hours
18 August 1940
Riding at anchor in the protected harbor of Syracuse, Sicily

Admiral Raeder had used this port visit for supplies to catch up on signals traffic. His juniors had tried and failed to get the Old Man to take a nap. He could nap at sea. For now he needed to confirm last known positions for the British and Italian battle squadrons. His torpedo boat squadron had been relieved from convoy protection duty by a flotilla of Italian small ships out of Messina. The German S-boats were supposed to rejoin them. Raeder had other plans. He was going out to attack Cunningham.

0315 hours
18 August 1940
Luqa, Malta

The Italian Captain had been lost. He had been scattered on drop. Found himself alone in some upland far from where he was supposed to be. He had started walking downhill. Over the next two hours he had picked up other strays in one and twos. None from his company. His rump unit had also acquired four British prisoners. They had been lost as well. He spoke a bit of English and gathered they were fleeing a German attack on the airfield at Luqa. He now seemed to have found the airfield, mostly because they had a runway marked with fire barrels. It was clearly occupied. Issue was by whom. He saw a mix of uniforms—Nazi HJs, Luftwaffe blue, and old WW1 French blue. He heard a mix of language—German, Italian, and Yiddish, of all things. At least he thought it was Yiddish. Yiddish with the Nazis?

Not seeing a better way to resolve the situation he took a small element forward to make contact. No one paid any attention to him until he reached the airport buildings. Some officer in a French blue uniform asked him in German who he was. When he replied in Italian, two youngsters in Luftwaffe blue answered. What was this?

Klaus was surprised to find an Italian officer amid the chaos. Two of his new recruits acted as translators. The man was lost.

Klaus gave a fast explanation of the unit structure and helped the man orient himself. He needed to be at Hal Far. After he called the rest of his men in, Greta got them strong, sweet tea and a snack while Joey dug up a map for them. Klaus and Joey offered to radio to higher Italian authority but all the captain wanted was to drop off the four prisoners and be on his way. Klaus detailed the two Italian "translators" to walk the paras beyond the picket on the Hal Far road. He made a note to tell higher command that 28 Italians led by a captain had passed through and to give them credit for the four prisoners captured.

0320 hours
18 August 1940
Road to the Grand Harbor from Luqa

Corporal Billy's runner was a new recruit barely beyond basic training. He'd been in lockup on petty charges again when his sister had arranged for him to enlist instead of appearing before the magistrate. His older sister had finished school and had an office job. Knew people. The right sort of people, one of whom knew a retired officer who knew a recruiting sergeant.

The runner was a city boy whose idea of the great outdoors was an urban park. This whole running around in the woods by moonlight spooked him badly. So he'd been grateful to be sent off as a runner. Only he lacked the stamina to run the whole way back. It was four or five miles and he'd run out of breath at half a mile. He smoked too much and, besides, city boys don't do distance running. So he was walking, holding his side and gasping, his total focus on each labored breath when he blundered into the Jerries.

The mountain troops were walking away from their wrecked glider. They could see the fight down-slope toward the town. It looked fairly one-sided. Without an officer, they saw no reason to blunder into a fight they had no way to win. If the harbor was behind them then, the small map they have been given showed an airfield was ahead of them. An airfield where there should be more German troops. Kampfgruppe Strauss. Some weird NL unit. Then the Brit prisoner had blundered into them. They could claim their attention had been focused behind them. Which was a laugh. It was mutual surprise. But now they had a British captive.

Their first thought was cut his throat, but there had been a long lecture by their officers on how to treat prisoners. A lecture that included mention of firing squads. So best to bind his hands and bring him along. He was too exhausted to move fast. That was fine with them. They were in no hurry.

0325 hours
18 August 1940
Scrub west of Hal Far

First Lieutenant Enrico Cirillo had had enough of this British sniper. There were no Germans and seemed to be no Brits besides this damned marksman and whoever was helping him. He motioned his men back and began carefully fading away back to the drop zone to report. Time to radio higher HQ for where the missing Germans were.

0330 hours
18 August 1940
Road from Hal Far to Luqa

The young lieutenant clutched the Webley revolver staring down his mutinous men. He wasn't quite sure of the weapon, having only used one briefly during his officer-training course. He had certainly never expected to have to use it on fellow Englishmen.

Grammar school and a year at a minor university had led the Army to deem him "officer material". Not a real officer, of course. Those came from military families and the gentry. But good enough for a quartermaster such as himself, a glorified shift manager of a warehouse. Only, on Malta, he'd been detailed to help out at Luqa. It was still mostly record-keeping but they let him get his hands dirty helping on the planes. The real mechanics were skilled tradesmen in civilian life and NCOs in the service. They humored him on being a higher rank...sometimes...when they felt like it.

Only now here he was leading this group into combat. They had no faith in him and no desire for combat. They had waited till the colonel was out of sight and just sat down on the side of the road. Two were smoking cigarettes and the rest were quietly chatting. He had ordered them to fall in. One laughed at him and two others just told him to sod off. He had waved the pistol about, not quite pointing it at anyone. He ordered. He shouted. He pleaded. One stuck a rifle barrel in his gut and dared him to try to aim his pistol. They could watch the damned road from here.

The lieutenant was still trying to think of a way out of the stalemate, a way to fulfill his orders, when he heard a shot. Before he could react, he felt a blazing pain in his shoulder, after which he fell over, still barely clutching the pistol. One his lads fired back... and got his head blown off for his trouble. The rest dropped their rifles and rabbited down the road.

The Italian paratroop captain took the pistol from the English officer's weak, shaking hands. He swiftly took the man's wallet, paybook, and letters. He had retained the two Italian lads from the German unit as runners. He gave them all the papers from the officer and the two dead men. His men got the lieutenant on his feet. Had one of the lads take him on each side, holding him upright, ignoring his screams and whimpers. Sent them back to Luqa with him and the documents. Told them to give the papers to the German officer, then trot back to catch up. He had conscripted them for duration. The English who got away would run until they caught up with another unit. Best to proceed cautiously. He sent his best sergeant with a quick-formed squad into the scrub to the right of the road. Told him to advance cautiously until they made contact. He would follow behind slowly on the road. This was just to be advance to contact, so don't take foolish chances before morning. The Germans had an airfield. Reinforcements would land and he could join up with a real unit. A slow advance would minimize casualties and get his guys used to working together.

He started south up the road humming a jaunty tune to himself. He was redeeming his honor as an officer. This business of parachutes at night meant getting separated, which could look to others like shirking, or worse. But now he'd won a skirmish and done something positive.

Chapter 37

0345 hours
18 August 1940
Gerbini airfield, Sicily

Alfred Jodl was going crazy trying to manage the two German waves. Kesselring had his staff elsewhere, preparing to direct the "air battle" to come after dawn. He had left no one above the rank of colonel to manage the transports. In theory, this was all covered by an elaborate operations order. This order's choreography had been collapsing with the first German wave of Rommel's brigade, one of Ramcke's battalions, and a stray battalion of 1st Mountain that seemed to belong to no one. It had imploded trying to get Ramcke off. Planes returned in one and twos, were turned around as best the exhausted ground crews could manage, and were reloaded with bits and pieces of Ramcke's other three battalions. Ramcke had gone ahead early in the process, in the only glider in this wave. That left no ground force officer above the rank of major other than himself and Rommel. The two majors were Jodl's from his weapons battalions. Jodl had seen Manstein's orders excluding Rommel. Having met the man, he did not question the logic. Rommel was an egotistical wild card even without his Blue Max or accolades from the French campaign. However, Jodl himself, in theory, had no command authority.

No authority, but he was a senior general. He was the personal representative of the head of OKW and by, implication, of Reichsführer Heydrich. Most important, he was here. So he kept getting juniors from both services running to him for decisions. Jodl had tried referring matters to Kesselring's HQ. That entity did nothing beyond acknowledge receipt of message. Jodl had called himself. Kesselring's junior adjutant, a major, had been icily polite about refusing to wake his boss. Jodl was a general. This was a ground force matter. Deal with it and stop bothering the Air Force. The Luftwaffe major had been almost rude about it. Or as rude as a well-trained adjutant would allow himself to be with a general, even one in disgrace. The core of the major's answer was that nothing that happened with the idiot airborne forces could matter compared to the pending air battle against the British fleet. Or so this major, and by implication his superior, asserted. Tunnel vision. Each service thought only of itself. Jodl resolved to give von Manstein an earful later. That was later.

Now was chaos. Bad light. Thunderous noise from the planes. Constant decisions. No information. Kesselring had kept all coordination with the Italians in his own hands. There was considerable signal traffic from the Italians. However, the Germans around Jodl lacked code books to make sense of it. They had been reduced to calling random Italian HQ's trying to get information. Perhaps they would eventually find the right people. In the meantime, there was no signal traffic from any German at all except one weird message about breakfast. Breakfast? It was in clear and in three other languages as well. His staff presumed the other three said the same, but lacked translators. It had to be a code. Ramcke's code books did not include this message. First Mountain's didn't either. That left the son of the devil, Rommel. Who would want his plane fixed. Jodl had delayed approaching the ogre as long as he dared, longer than he rationally judged prudent. Time to talk to Rommel. Jodl started across the airfield....

0350 hours
18 August 1940
Road from Luqa to Hal Far

This time Colonel Mason was sufficiently aware to actually hear the fleeing men 20 meters before they reached him. Their labored breathing sounded like a pack of railroad yard engines pushing cars up a steep incline. He mentally deleted their claims of hundreds of Germans on their heels. He screamed at them for abandoning their weapons. He could see his own pack of shirkers starting to edge away towards Hal Far. No longer lagging to avoid combat up the road, they were now prepared to flee to avoid combat here.

He was saved from the dilemma by the reappearance of the bike messenger. The man had turned back after being fired on by Axis pickets near Luqa. Said he heard German, Italian, and something else that seemed sort of like German being spoken. Failed to find his way around the pickets between the dark and the scrub. Had been working his way back towards the Hal Far road when he witnessed the Italian attack. He was sure it was Italians. More than twenty. Less than a hundred. Very few rounds fired before most of the Brits had run like whipped dogs. Italians had a group off in the scrub and were slowly following up the road. Be along within half an hour.

That did it. This lot wouldn't hold for two minutes. He sent the bike messenger ahead to request reinforcements. He got his lot in motion. Marching away from the pursuing Italians towards Hal Far where no one knew what awaited them. Amazingly, they were no longer hanging back. Hiking with spirit, they were. Damned cowards. This lot had no fight left in them. Too long on fatigues and thus out of proper command. He would have to use them from fixed positions and have Fleming's lot be whatever maneuver element was needed. The colonel laughed to himself. He was now depending on a thrown-together band of adventurers over storied regiments of Britain's army. Sad day, this was.

0400 hours
18 August 1940
Hal Far

The German planes had been coming in hiccups. One, two, three, sometimes as many as four, they had reached the island, swerved to avoid the fire of the massed Lewis guns around Hal Far and deposited their troops seemingly at helter-skelter over the southwestern third of the island. They dropped on the British, on the Italians, into the uplands. Some dumped their loads over Luqa, which was lit by fires. None thought to land and the tower did not have the proper radio frequencies to contact them. A few sorry paratroopers were dumped in the ocean to drown.

Ian Fleming could make no sense of it. Surely airborne troops should land in massed waves for mutual support, not small penny packets scattered seemingly at random. The supposedly disorganized Italians manage two tight, coordinated landings and the Germans, masters of Teutonic precision, seemed to be pretending to be drunken Poles. His unit had killed well over a hundred and captured twice that many. He had worried that his thrown-together unit wouldn't fight well. However, enough of his men had seen battle before—Spain, Russia, against the Arabs in Palestine. A core of veterans is what makes most units work. More important, he now had some three dozen of their excellent MG-34s with plentiful ammunition. When dawn came and the Italians attacked, he would need all the firepower he could muster. It had seemed an easy weapon to master. Indeed, his men had already bagged some Jerries with them. If the Italian attack was with the competence their two airborne landings had shown, he doubted he could hold Hal Far for as much as a day.

Gerhard Ramcke watched his glider pilot frantically maneuver trying to avoid the machine-gun fire coming seemingly from every direction. As a general, he had rated a trained pilot instead of an HJ "volunteer". The pilot was good, but the situation was hopeless. With all the evasive maneuvers, the glider was still hit twice. The pilot barely kept control as it fell earthward. As is, he clipped a stone wall and flipped the plane. Ramcke was knocked unconscious. When he came to, armed men were extracting him from the wreckage. He seemed to be the only survivor. The men were Italian, a language he knew less than twenty words in. Fortunately, their captain knew enough German. He was on the road from Luqa to Hal Far, although much closer to Luqa. The Italian officer pointed him toward Luqa, which he alleged to be under the command of an NL unit. Strauss. That ragtag freikorps had taken an air field. His professionals seem not to have. He was sure this would reflect poorly on him.

The general had a splitting headache, pain in his spine, and a slightly sprained ankle. No matter. He was a German officer. He shook the Italian's hand, saluted, and started off toward Luqa. He did not allow himself to limp or wince until he was out of sight of the Italians. It just wasn't done to show physical difficulties.

0405 hours
18 August 1940
Gerbini airfield, Sicily, Italy

Erwin Rommel tore the signal copy from Jodl's hands. The code was idiot-simple. The problem was that he was confronted with an idiot named Jodl. "The message is simple. Strauss has taken Luqa. He wants reinforcements by dawn to hold it and advance on the Grand Harbor. This is the moment of decision. Do you want your reputation restored or not?"

Jodl neither respected nor trusted Rommel. But if the message said what Rommel claimed, he instantly grasped the opportunity. "What do you propose? I can have your plane worked on at once."

"To hell with that. There's a plane being readied over there." Rommel pointed thirty meters away to a Ju-52 about to start loading. "It's mine now. I'm flying to Luqa. Give me a code book to communicate with you. Strauss must have lost his. This is an emergency code we prepared." It was nothing of the sort, but Rommel was not about to waste minutes explaining. Lies were so much faster. He saw a plane starting its taxi. He pointed to one of Jodl's staff lieutenants and told him to flag that one down. "That one follows mine. It circles while I land. If the message is wrong, it reports my death. If the message is right, it radios you confirming. What's your wife's name? That's the code. Something simple. A name. That confirms that the messages from Luqa aren't with a gun at the code clerk's head. Now I'll need your two weapons battalions first and then mountain troops. Also ammunition. You will, of course, assume command here, coordinating the flow of men and material, plus coordinating with Kesselring, Rome, and Berlin. It's what an officer of your rank does. Manage and issue orders. I'll assume command of the main attack. If I can find Ramcke, he can command the ersatz division that will clear the rest of the island while I take the harbor. This could be bigger than my exploits in Italy in '17. You and I will be the twin heroes who deliver Malta to Berlin, to Führer Göring. Are you in?"

Jodl thought frantically. He could say no. By all prior orders, he should say no. Yet, if Rommel were right, the battle would be lost and his fingerprints would be on the defeat. Or he could risk two planes. Small change as higher command counts costs. He'd allowed Beck, Keitel, and proper procedures to wreck his career. Here was vindication in one giant roll of the dice. Besides, if it failed, von Manstein might thank him for killing off Rommel before the North African campaign. The thought gave Jodl a shot of joy, which covered his fear at throwing away what remains of his career on the ravings of a madman who trusted his intuition, not proper staff logic. Jodl laughed at himself and put out his hand to seal the devil's bargain.

0410 hours
18 August 1940
Skies over Hal Far

The Ju-52 pilot had originally washed out of multiengine training. Then the Malta operation was laid on. Standards were revised down. He had been recalled from his new posting and told he had retroactively passed. Barely. He could take off and land without destroying the aircraft. He could maintain level flight in good weather if nothing went wrong. Lacking any real concept of night flying, he had just trailed two more experienced pilots to Malta. There was enough moonlight, so that worked...until the first plane he was following exploded in a blaze of light as the sky lit up with machine-gun tracers.

The other plane dived violently away, leaving him exposed to every gun. Belatedly, he dived away in the opposite direction. He could feel the plane shuddering from hits. He could hear screams and curses behind him as his paras took damage. He knew he had to do something. He just kept diving lower and further from the deadly hail of machinegun rounds. The Tante Ju's controls were getting mushy. He decided to just get out of the sky and went looking for someplace to land.

Suddenly, in the distance, he could see lights. As he approached, they proved to be burning barrels lighting a runway. He saw gliders and a large multiengine plane. He did not see machinegun fire. He tried radioing the field. No luck. So he lined up on the runway and brought his plane down. It was not his best landing, but it would have to do.

Klaus was delighted to see a German plane land. He hadn't a clue as to what to do next. Fortunately, Captain Isaak took charge. The wounded were given what comfort they could. The dead were carefully set aside. The most of the rest were put on the Grand Harbor road backing up the Vickers gun. The big deal was the radio operator. He had a code book. Gunter hustled him up to the radio shack to notify Sicily. Joey started looking the plane over to see what he could fix. He had somehow recruited three Maltese helpers out of the prisoners. No one asked what he had promised them. Some things were better left to silence.

0415 hours
18 August 1940
Gerbini airfield, Sicily

The radio room was sending Jodl's reports of the fall of Luqa to Rome and Berlin. It was being presented as confirmed fact, per Rommel's "special code". The senior radio officer noted an omission. No one had sent a message to the planes in transit telling them to divert to Luqa instead of doing airdrops. So he had the message sent. This was the sort of chaos one got when Army officers interfered with Air Force operations. They understood nothing. His understanding of the situation was confirmed by a message from one of his planes, down at Luqa with battle damage. He had a message sent back asking for an update. Was the plane fixable if he sent a team of mechanics and parts? The message in reply said the head mechanic at Luqa was still inspecting the Ju, but, in the meantime, had repaired a Blenheim that could be flown off if a flight crew could be provided. The radio officer detailed a captain to chase down a reserve flight crew. Asked after the "head mechanic", as Gerbini was unaware such a cadre had been sent. Was told it was an NL officer, an American Volksdeutsche. Also that there had been linkup with an Italian contingent and that there were prisoners to be sent back with the returning planes. A message was passed to the Italians on their man and his successes. Berlin and Rome were copied on everything. Alas, no one thought to tell Jodl any of this.

0420 hours
18 August 1940
Luqa airfield, Malta

Klaus was trying to bring order out of the chaos on the airfield. Two more planes had just landed and half a dozen were stacked up waiting their turn. Strauss had taken off with the first group of paras to personally place them on the road to the Grand Harbor. Captain Isaak was doing something technical with Joey that seemed to involve inspecting the planes before they flew back to Sicily.

In the midst of this chaotic activity, Klaus was vaguely aware of two Italians returning with a wounded British officer. He noticed, but the Ramcke medical section that had landed from one of the stream of arriving planes took charge of the man, and it thus passed from his mental activities...until he saw the same two Italians plus four more hauling off a Vickers machine gun. They had it on some cart that had been lying around the airfield. Had probably dumped the parts the cart had been holding.

Klaus went running over screaming "STOP" at the top of his lungs. None of the six spoke much German, but one of the recently landed German paras turned out to know a bit of Italian. He was from someplace called Tyrol. The Italians were claiming they had met up with their officer, Lieutenant Colonel Lusena, a kilometer or so south on the road to Hal Far. The officer wanted a machine gun for a second engagement with a British unit retreating before him. Klaus knew he couldn't give orders to a lieutenant colonel, but he wanted his lieutenant colonel to approve this. Except Strauss was, as usual, absent. The Tyrolian offered to go with these kids and get authorization for the machine gun. Klaus decided that sounded military and said yes. The Tyrolian whistled up a few of his buddies to help with the ammo load and off the combined force went, pushing and dragging the cart.

General Ramcke was near enough to the airfield to see the lights in the distance when he saw the cart and joint squad approaching. He took a report from the senior German, a corporal. Action to the south and an Italian lieutenant colonel requesting heavy weapons support. Ramcke had only seen a captain, but wasn't sure there hadn't been a higher officer present. His head hurt and he was less than sure he was fully functional. So he sent his men on their way, but told them to send back a runner with a more complete report once they met this officer. The sight of Italian lads in Luftwaffe blue was confusing enough.

Chapter 38

0430 hours
18 August 1940
Road from Luqa to the Grand Harbor

Corporal Billy had been through the mill. He had posted a three-man group watching his backtrail "just in case". They heard the Germans before they saw them. Disciplined troops would have let the Germans keep walking unaware into the kill zone. Three stray rankers keyed up by combat nerves who were complete virgins at actual shooting war...The first one to panic fired at the noise. The other two fired because the first one did. The German noise vanished. The Germans never actually appeared. Instead a man came running up the road yelling, "Fuck! Don't shoot me!" Billy gave a good look, saw it was his runner, and slapped down two fools aiming rifles. The idiot runner arrived with his hands tied and a story that made no sense. Had probably been paying no attention while trotting back to HQ. Recruits! They needed two or three battles before they were worth their cost in rations as anything except brute labor.

The noise and firing were followed by a machine gun shooting at them from the front. The noise confused Billy's guys. It sounded just like a British Vickers. Billy's lads were puzzled by that and held their fire. Billy was wiser to front-line soldiers seizing enemy weapons when opportunity arose. He'd spend two days working a Spandau 08 a bit southwest of Arras in '18. So he ordered his guys to return fire and then started pulling them out before Fritz finished surrounding them. He freed his runner's hands, knocked him half-silly for getting caught, and led his guys back into the scrub to the south. If he couldn't block this road, he'd try for Hal Far. There were probably still British fighting there. Billy was not about to spend the rest of the war in a German prisoner camp if he could help it. King and country meant something to him. Besides, compared to the real battles he'd been in, this was kids playing slapping games after the pub closed.

Gunter nearly took the head off the idiot who had opened up with the Vickers. He kept screaming to cease fire until his idiots did. All they were doing was wasting ammo and exposing their positions by the muzzle flashes. It took nearly two minutes to calm his guys and another before the British stopped firing. A lot of noise but no one seemed to have been hit. Five minutes on German voices called out, "Don't shoot! First Mountain!" He yelled back to come forward slowly with weapons pointed to the sky. They told him of the mess down toward the ports. They said the British blocking group had cleared out southward. They neglected to mention losing a prisoner.

Gunter sent the mountaineers to the rear for tea and food. He went forward with three paras. Confirmed that the British were gone. They had probably burned a fair bit of ammo themselves, and so probably wouldn't be back. He left the paras posted forward as an outpost. He left an airborne sergeant in charge of the road block with the Vickers and started back to see what trouble Steiner had gotten into in his absence.

0440 hours
18 August 1940
Luqa airfield, Malta

General Ramcke let the medics give him a quick inspection but wouldn't allow any more treatment than wrapping his ankle. Some NL officer named Joe found him a walking stick that had previously done service as a metallic shaft of some sort. American Volksdeutsche, or so he claimed. His German was pathetic and quite low class for an officer, even a technical specialist.

The command situation was absurd. The base was under the command of one of Rommel's units, over which he had no direct authority. More so as the man was apparently en route. Yet Sicily had no contact with any of his men. Jodl tried to appoint him base commander, but admitted that Berlin had yet to sign off on this. This SA officer Strauss seemed totally willing to take Ramcke's orders pending Rommel's arrival. However, there seemed little to do for the moment. Strauss had the airfield properly picketed with a good outpost on the road to the Harbor. The Italian lieutenant colonel and captain were pushing down the road toward Hal Far. The main Italian force was down and readying for a dawn attack. It seemed to Ramcke that his best possibility was to wait to confer with Rommel and for some of his boys to make contact.

Ramcke was surprised that Rommel's NL had brought a cook

staff. A perky young thing in an NL French blue uniform brought him coffee and some oatmeal. She couldn't cook. The coffee was vile and the oatmeal worse. But hot food and caffeine were fuel. He noticed with approval that as each of his planes unloaded, this Fräulein Greta had hot drink and a snack for the men. Unusual that this unit introduced people by first names instead of rank and family name. Must be some NL thing borrowed from the SA's Roehm days, or even the Bolsheviks. Commendable planning. Possibly Strauss's unit was not the joke he had supposed. Perhaps Strauss had some military training beyond being a street fighter for the SA. In the meantime, Ramcke got the prisoners and wounded off to Sicily on departing flights.

0450 hours
18 August 1940
Ta Kali, Malta

The runner from HQ had confirmed receipt of the POWs. The newly arrived engineer officer had reported that the Germans at the golf course had been mostly driven up-slope toward Luqa. No word on what had happened at Luqa. Hal Far had been in British hands some hours back but the message was by bicycle courier. With the phones still out, the current situation was uncertain, but it did not look promising.

Colonel Duffy's men were taking harassing fire from Germans in the surrounding scrubland. They were also getting British and Maltese from outlying detachments filtering back. There had been multiple unfortunate incidents with this, some of them fatal. Most of these chaps didn't know the current password. Duffy had been reduced to telling his men not to fire on the English language. He hoped the Germans didn't figure this out, as enough of them knew a few words of English. The fire was annoying rather than serious. There were clearly more than a few Germans out there. He was mostly surrounded and a company of reinforcements didn't change that. His men would be sitting ducks when the bombers returned with daylight. So he hurried the engineer in his demolitions work. It would be daylight in barely an hour. The sound of the explosions cratering the runways boomed out. Would be heard miles away. No helping it.

0455 hours

The Reich Without Hitler: The Falcons of Malta

18 August 1940
Luqa, Malta

Ramcke took the report from the sergeant courier who had reached Luqa. He was part of the force that had been landed at Ta Kali. They had been completely scattered on drop. A combat command had formed under a captain. The captain reported he had assembled the equivalent of two weak companies, but this included men from Rommel and First Mountain. They had been driven off the airfield by a British force he estimated at brigade strength. He'd sent this patrol looking for a higher HQ at Luqa or Hal Far to report to, as the radios were lost on drop. The report included paybooks taken off British dead from two different British regular battalions. Captain wanted reinforcements and a working radio set with crew. Ramcke told the sergeant to get his men a meal from the cook while Sicily was radioed for new communications equipment and staff. Sicily answered that loading could not be changed that quickly, so figure three hours for communications troops to arrive. Right now they would be getting a machine gun battalion first.

0500 hours
18 August 1940
Road from Luqa to Hal Far

Colonel Mason heard the motorcycle a good mile before it arrived. Fleming again, this time with some naval officer named Money-Penny sporting a distinctly not-Ordnance Board rifle. Looked like some fancy civilian rig for a professional hunter. In this case, more probably soldier of fortune. Man looked like he knew how to use it. Oxbridge accent, but a street tough's demeanor. Told Mason to get on the motorcycle and go to the rear to confer with the senior Fleming brother. Mason tried to explain that this band of men wasn't worth warm spit. Money-Penny gave an evil smile and said he'd commanded worse in several nasty places. Mason was dubious, but this thug might be just what was needed. These men were immune to the normal notions of discipline and command.

Chapter 39

0505 hours
18 August 1940
Scrub uplands northeast of Hal Far

Captain Schmidt had survived his first parachute landing. The battalion he dropped with had not. Lieutenant Jung's platoon had come through intact and Schmidt had dropped with them. By blind luck they had landed to the rear of the Hal Far cauldron of fire. Using Jung's platoon as a nucleus, Schmidt had assembled a force of some two hundred men out of the three battalions dropped on Hal Far, plus two gliders' worth of mountain troops. What he did not have was a radio. He had three of his officer friends from the Air Ministry out scouring the scrub looking for one. They kept sending back men they had located in twos and threes. They had even found a medical section with its supplies. Apparently, every radio equipment drop had hit the ground around the airfield, which was solidly held by a British force of battalion strength. Or maybe more, as it seemed to have a brigade's worth of machine guns. So he was in the scrub northeast and up-slope from the airfield. He left Jung running the company. He sent two of the ministry lieutenants north by northwest to try to find Rommel's troops up at Luqa. He expected the British to attack with daylight. Jung assured him these troops could manage a fighting retreat ahead of that attack. So far, combat didn't seem too frightening. Just odd shots from the British. He would learn better during the coming day.

0510 hours
18 August 1940
Bridge of HMS Kent, north-northeast of Malta and closing on the Italian battlefleet

It would be daylight shortly. A flying boat was sending the position of the main Italian squadron. They would be in range a few minutes after dawn. Alexandria had relayed reports from his subs. They were claiming an Italian cruiser, supposedly the Pola. That would be nice, but Admiral Cunningham wasn't counting on it. He was relying on the skill of his ship commanders and the high training levels of his crews.

The messages from Malta were confusing. Two divisions of Axis airborne were down. There also seemed to have been airborne tanks. Was this even possible? Yet, somehow, no airfields were lost. Malta command was saying they could not justify an evacuation under these circumstances. Justify? Cunningham's fleet might just survive a day of air attack. It wouldn't survive two. This meant reversing course by dawn on the 19th and retiring out of air range of Sicily. The plan had been for an evacuation the night of the 18th/19th. Now somehow this must be reworked to the 19th/20th. Was anyone on the British side using cold logic instead of imperial nostalgia? The Admiral despaired of his poor nation in this new modern world. He seriously questioned if its ruling class was up to the challenge.

0515 hours
18 August 1940
Road from Luqa to Hal Far

Money-Penny had started off by moving his new unit several hundred meters down the road towards Hal Far. He told them he was looking for better terrain to set up a defense. Actually, he wanted to get a sense of the fifteen men with which he'd been left. He'd picked the least useless-looking and had sent the rest to the rear at double-time after relieving them of all their ammo and the few grenades they had. Fifteen men. No spirit. No sense of unit. Not quite whipped dogs, but definitely skittish virgins. Late teens to early twenties. None of them carried themselves like veterans or even seriously tough guys from civilian life. Pathetic.

He told them to halt where the stonewall flanking the road on the right sported another extending perpendicular to make a field boundary. When he ordered them to fall in behind the new wall, they balked. No real serious backtalk. Just mute refusal. He chose one at random. After years of leading gangs of stray toughs that his employers had recruited before calling in experts like himself, he felt he had a sense for the least useful man. Or the most recalcitrant, which was often not the same thing. "You. Move now." Money-Penny hadn't a command voice in an army sense. What he had was a dead-level monotone of a professional tough guy. The lance corporal hung his head. Muttered no. Refused to move. Money-Penny didn't ask a second time. Just walked up and looked the man up and down. The man was shivering but still shaking his head no. Looked to be about twenty. Medium height and build, with slumping shoulders and a terrified expression.

Money-Penny shrugged and smashed the man's kneecap with a quick kick. The lad went down screaming. The others were in shock. Screams of "NO!" and "You can't do that!" and "You're not our officer!" Money-Penny ignored them. He kicked the man in the head. Once. Twice. The boy stopped rolling in pain. Money-Penny pulled out his pistol. He gut-shot the prostrate man. "Anyone who helps him dies." He now had his men's attention. Their undivided attention. "Anyone got the balls to try and take me?" Dead silence. Only four were shooting murderous glances. Good. He had a few men with some spine left. "Now, here's the score. I'm not a regular. That game's over until you're off the island. I am a professional at these types of situations. Call it a soldier of fortune. Call it a professional killer. I go places and kill people. Get paid quite nicely for it. Now the Italians pushing up this road may kill you. I definitely will. I've already bagged over twenty with this rifle just overnight. Stick with me and some of you may live. I've even got a fishing boat to get us off this flyspeck of an isle when it all goes to shit in a day or three. Or, hand me your rifle and go sit with your mate there. Half an hour and the Eye-ties will be along. You surrender and it's off to the cages for you. You'll be doing labor service in Italy and chasing dark-eyed girls." They mostly eyed him with naked terror now. "Serious offer. I have no use for total cowards. Better you just go into the bag. But this is a one-time offer. Try to run later and I'll kill you. I'm a crack shot. None of you lot has the field craft to run far enough fast enough."

Monypenny had guessed right. Three handed over their ammo, stuck their rifles in the ground, and slunk over to the screaming lance corporal. He had regained consciousness and was howling his life out, driven near insane by the pain and terror of imminent death. Money-Penny led the others back to still another wall a 130 meters further south. Had them set up a thin line facing north. He himself was ten meters behind them on a small grassy rise maybe a couple meters above the field. Not a great position, but it would do. Dawn was coming. Time for some serious killing.

0530 hours
18 August 1940

The Reich Without Hitler: The Falcons of Malta

Hal Far airfield, Malta

Colonel Mason got a rude shock on meeting the other Fleming brother. Ian was junior in age, junior in rank as the two services reckoned such things, and a most difficult person. He blandly denied he was under Army command. He and his unit were RN. So was his brother, Peter. Peter had been Grenadier Guards, but he was now Royal Navy Commando. Ian produced a letter on War Cabinet stationary signed by one Winston S. Churchill confirming all of this. When the acid discussion—carried on in the quiet tones befitting two members of the Empire's ruling order, but full of ever-so-polite bile on both sides—was done, Mason was de facto commander of an odds and sods company whose core was the cowardly lot he had taken from Luqa. Men who would break at the drop of a hat. Fleming the Older had offered a few of his veterans as cadre. Mason rejected this out of hand. He was not having even abysmal British troops commanded by Jews, White Russians, or Spanish Reds.

The position was bad and likely to get worse. They had a probable Italo-Libyan parachute division to their southwest. Only Money-Penny's tiny outpost covered a move south from Luqa. There were the remains of a German parachute brigade to their northeast. The bombers would be back with the dawn, mere minutes away. Another courier had been sent to HQ requesting reinforcements, but both Flemings doubted any would come.

Mason had not been a company officer since the second day on the Somme, when he had been breveted captain as senior survivor of his battalion officers. The year 1916 was two ice ages in the past in terms of military art. Mason smiled sourly. Some lessons you NEVER forget. He could do this job in his sleep. He'd done it for eight days on the Somme in what had later been diagnosed as shell shock. His dreams would never stop repeating going over the top that morning, the carefully dressed lines being shredded by German machine gun fire. A battalion went out of the trenches. A short company reached the German first trench an hour later. When he was relieved eight days later, he took twenty-nine men out of the line with him, not more than half of them from his original battalion and only two from his original company. "Thin red line of heroes when the drums begin to roll". Kipling had that one dead right. You put on the King's uniform and you left a will with the family solicitor. His estranged wife would get the insurance. The rest for his two sons, if either survived this war. One had gone for prisoner in Norway. Red Cross had his name. The other was a fighter pilot back in the Home Counties. That left his mistress. She had the cottage he'd bought her, plus an insurance policy his solicitor held that was not mentioned in his will or estate papers. Making the fan dance work for the tax man was part of what the solicitor did to earn his fees. His family had left their blood for King and Country back to Cromwell's time. He was ready to make the next deposit in the account if needs must.

Chapter 40

0535 hours
18 August 1940
Briefing salon, Chancellery Berlin

The OKW colonel's report was concise, if somewhat lacking in detail.

Lieutenant Colonel Strauss's NL KG had taken Luqa. There were prisoners and a captured British bomber that the Luftwaffe was going to fly back to Sicily as a trophy. General Ramcke was at Luqa. He reported that the drop on Ta Kali had been partially unsuccessful. The battlegroup there had been chased off the airfield by a British brigade and was awaiting reinforcements to counterattack. Those were being flown in. Ramcke anticipated taking the field by evening. He had a preliminary report from the remains of his main drop at Hal Far. Total disaster. A British brigade overloaded with heavy weapons was in control. The surviving Germans were reforming and could at least harass the British. However, an Italian battlegroup was driving south from Luqa and making progress. Ramcke was blaming Kesselring for doing a night drop instead of the dawn he had asked for. The pilots simply lacked the air navigation skills for a night drop and people had landed all over the island. The only force to land properly had been Lieutenant Colonel Strauss's glider company. Strauss gave the credit to the navigation skills of Lieutenant Steiner, the prior hero of Romania and Hungary. Ramcke saw this as validating the NL. He also complemented them on the foresight to have brought along a technical section, which was assisting in airplane repair on the transports, and a cook staff that was seeing to the aircrew and arriving reinforcements. Being met with a hot beverage and something to eat in the midst of battlefield chaos was a huge morale boost.

General Jodl's report had Rommel about to land at Luqa. Jodl asserted he had taken command at Gerbini because General Kesselring's HQ was ignoring the ground forces. Jodl said he was only doing staff work, but someone had to so he would continue unless ordered not to. He also confirmed Rommel was in the air and due to land within minutes. Rommel planned to make a direct attack on the Grand Harbor with whatever forces he could assemble. Jodl was not sure this was wise, but felt at worst it would distract the British until the other two airfields could be seized.

Führer Göring blustered a bit defending his pet service. The other three accepted the loss of time. Beck was mostly enraged at the NL being given credit for a simple administrative measure, the cook staff. Halder was mostly relieved that this had not been a complete disaster. Given one airfield, the plan would work. Heydrich used the time to pass a note to Schellenberg to get Siegel back to Sicily. He wanted a direct eyes-and-ears report from someone with a brain. This was an amazing propaganda coup for Germany, the NL, and himself. However, it couldn't be faked the way Soviet partisans had been in Romania. The core story must be sort of true to make it work.

0555 hours – almost dawn
18 August 1940
Luqa airfield – Malta

Rommel was amazed at what he saw. An organized airspace with a tower calling down circling planes one by one. A technical section working on planes to ready them for return to Sicily. Strauss had the defenses of Luqa well in hand. Ramcke was present and had tenuous connections with his two main remnants at Ta Kali and Hal Far.

Of greater importance, Strauss had pushed a recon element forward to the downslope toward the harbor. He was getting a slow stream of survivors from the platoons driven off the golf course. The British response had been disorganized. Scratch platoons of administrative types. Enough men, but no real cohesion.

Rommel was especially impressed with the technical section Strauss had formed up. Some ex-Honved Captain and a Volksdeutsche technical officer. An American recruited in Italy. Strauss seemed, as ever, adept at gathering up useful strays. Gerbini had been chaos. Luqa was orderly and efficient. Kudos to Strauss. Rommel gave field promotions out sparingly, but felt they were deserved in this case. Strauss to Colonel, Schwabe to Major, and this technician Bats to Captain. Strange name, Bats. Must be some American change from something like Baur.

Ramcke gave a good report. Rommel appointed him commander at Luqa on his authority and Jodl's. Also gave him command of the reinforcements and instructed him that the priority was to reinforce his own attack on the Harbor. The other airfields were secondary. Ramcke protested, but was overruled. Rommel was a superior rank and a storm officer. Ramcke was recently a Colonel and an administrator.

This new Captain Bats brought gifts. Turned out there were three Italian air-transported tankettes being readied for service. The Italians had sent them over as cargo in SM82s, one per plane. Surely these would be of use to a panzer general. There was also an Italian mountain mortar platoon awaiting orders. Rommel gratefully commandeered them. Tanks. He would be leading tanks on Malta.

The command conference was interrupted twice. First, by Steiner racing past, screaming, "Follow me!" A small mob of mixed uniforms led by a young giant with an MG-34 ran after him. Apparently, another British probe. Rommel ignored this. The hero seemed to have things in hand and Strauss seemed unperturbed. He was coming to trust this Strauss. Rommel put little faith in service records and formal schooling. Combat showed you who was worth what. Strauss delivered.

The second interruption came at the end. Six young lads requesting the honor of accompanying his advance. The one doing the speaking said he had cleared this with his lieutenant colonel. The six seemed educated. Said they were volunteer Arditi. Italian storm troops. Rommel remembered them from 1917. Worthy opponents. No rank badges, so Fahnenjunker—officer cadets. Such were usually brave, and besides he would need translators for his Italian tankette crews and gunners.

Before dawn was an hour gone, he was on the road to the harbor leading a scratch unit of German paras, Italian tankettes, Italian mountain mortars, and stray volunteers. The road led to victory. His battle intuition told him so.

Klaus led his reaction force into the scrub north of the airfield followed by Peter. Sixth British attack and the fourth from the north. Thankfully, the British seemed unable to coordinate these things. A few minutes' shooting and they vanished back into the scrub, as the five before them had. They left behind two wounded. Klaus had them sent to the rear. They would be dealt with by the med staff and be in Sicily by dark. As he started to pull his reaction force off, four Italian lads approached him. In a mishmash of German and Yiddish, they seemed to be saying that their officer, Lusena, had ordered them to do a patrol to see if more prisoners could be obtained. Klaus shrugged. He was a first lieutenant. Higher officers were demi-gods.

Gerhard Ramcke was grateful to see Rommel gone, even at the price of having lost to Rommel the combat reserve he had been assembling for the drive on Ta Kali. Rommel had settled that—Strauss was now under his command. Also this Italian Lieutenant Colonel Lusena. As for Rommel's priority...Gerhard laughed to himself. Manstein, Kesselring, and Jodl had all made clear that Rommel had no command authority over him. So, absent new orders, the priorities remained the airfields. Ramcke radioed such to Jodl. If the plan were changed, let some superior send a message.

0600 hours
18 August 1940
Ta Kali airfield, Malta

Colonel Duffy was not surprised to be greeted with air attacks at first light. He was taken aback that all that had arrived were Italian biplanes doing strafing. CR42s, if he still recollected his recognition drills. Good pilots, but not enough of them to do more than chase his lads off the airfield grass. Duffy had already thinned out his forces. He'd sent half back to the harbor in small groups keeping to cover off the road. He himself kept the other company, with all the automatic weapons spread out in the brush adjacent to the airfield, waiting to dispute possession with the Germans to his west and south.

Chapter 41

0602 hours
18 August 1940
Mediterranean north-northeast of Malta

HMS Eagle had turned into the wind at the first light of dawn to launch its strike. Flanked by its two distinctly un-battleworthy escort vessels, she was sending all 18 of her Fairey Swordfish strike aircraft off to have a go at the Italian fleet. The little, string-bag biplane bombers were a joke in contested airspace, but they were the only strike planes the Eagle had. For this mission, the Eagle also carried 18 fighters, a sad mix of obsolete Sea Gladiators and obsolescent Fairey Fulmars. Many of the fighter pilots had never taken off from a carrier before. Assembling this many had severely taxed the Empire's slender resources in the eastern Mediterranean.

Seventeen Swordfish took off armed with torpedoes. The eighteenth was flown by an argumentative flight lieutenant who had fought command all the way back to Alexandria for the right to try this attack loaded with a bomb instead. His logic was flawless. The string-bag was helpless in the face of modern fighters and there would be swarms of these. The attack profile for torpedo use magnified this. Straight-level flight at fifteen-hundred meters followed by a still straight approach descending to around six meters. Then the torpedo must be dropped in a narrow window at least a three hundred meters from the target but no one more than twelve-hundred meters away.

The pilot accepted that he wasn't coming back. Rule Britannia. He did not accept dying for nothing. Skimming the waves, he might be able to close on a target and fling his bomb into the side, or at least into the command bridge. He was Anglo-Irish. He knew the customs for facing death. The Irish War had been bloodstained out where his people had lands since before the IRA finally chased them out after the peace. You wrote your last letters and then they killed you. Most of his clan were dead of the late war. So it was one note for his gran in Belfast, another for his sister in Canada, and a final one for his brother off serving in India. He soared off into the air, the final plane on a mission of the damned.

0605 hours
18 August 1940
Hal Far

Ian Fleming had expected his position to implode with the dawn. He anticipated a full-out assault from the Italian division to his west, a pinning attack by the German brigade to his northeast, and massive bombing raids disrupting his ability to shift forces around his perimeter. Even with the men Mason brought, plus a steady trickle of small groups seeking a still-British outpost on the now contested island, his initial small battalion could at best be called a large battalion now. Fortunately, he had arranged for those 72 extra machine guns and then captured more from the Germans, so he had well more than a battalion's firepower even if less than a battalion's reliable manpower. Mason's men were suspect and the fugitives likely would be near-useless. Fleming thanked his God that, so far, the air attacks had been quite limited, one- and two-plane strafing missions. The Italians were feeling out his line like the competent professionals they were. The skirmishes showed a purposeful battle plan. The Italian commander was searching for his flanks. The Italians were, in Fleming's opinion, being needlessly conservative, but it was still orthodox. The Germans seemed inert, doing little more than show a forward defense. Fleming needed his southern anchor to hold firmly, so this meant his northern flank was weak. The southern flank was the connection to the fishing boats, to escape, to Egypt. So, it was clearly time to send a pair of runners to Money-Penny to start backpedaling fast. Time to send a final courier 'round the island to GHQ. Message would be simple: Hal Far would be lost today. Write off Fleming's unit. What could would escape to Egypt. Fleming would wreck the facility as best he could, but expected a sauve qui peut at the end. Fleming chuckled at the over-dramatic French term. He actually doubted his commandoes would implode, but felt GHQ needed the added emphasis. About Mason's luckless contingent, the less said the better, and the other odds and sods of mostly Maltese were already leaking shirkers.

0610 hours
18 August 1940
Scrub northwest of Hal Far

The Reich Without Hitler: The Falcons of Malta

First Lieutenant Enrico Cirillo thanked God for the chemical miracle of the new German stay-awake pills. His heart was pounding and he knew his judgment was a trifle suspect, but he was awake and fully functional. His men had managed a bit over an hour's nap. He had had his time taken with a new briefing. The original war plan said Hal Far was undefended. Italian air reconnaissance had shown a small infantry battalion there. The Germans had ignored this in the run-up to the Malta operation. Those Germans were arrogant swine whether under a Kaiser or Führer.

Yesterday's action made clear that far more than a battalion was there. No battalion had that many machine guns. Now Berlin was admitting a large brigade was there. A brigade that had smashed the German brigade that had tried landing earlier in the darkness. Berlin claimed there was a coherent German airborne remnant to the northeast. Berlin also claimed they had taken Luqa. Italian command in Sicily was suspect on both matters.

So, for now, the Italian parachute division was sending patrols to feel out the British positions. All they had pinpointed was one battalion facing them. So it was needful to find the other battalions before fully committing the division to action. Cirillo's platoon had a different mission. They had looped far north, kilometers beyond the probable end of the British line, before cutting east through the scrub toward the Hal Far-Luqa road. Sicily claimed there was a makeshift unit of Italian and German strays pushing south on this road, supposedly under the command of a Colonel Lusena. There was no Colonel Lusena. Cirillo was to ascertain if the entire attack column was similarly fanciful. Beyond that, he was to try to make contact with the Germans Sicily claimed were in the hills northeast of the airstrip and east of the road.

The Lieutenant was more concerned about the aircraft overhead. He had been given recognition panels and flares to show he was friendly. So far neither had worked. He had been strafed several times and bombed once in the few minutes since dawn. Thankfully, the planes had hit no one, but dodging them was already slowing him down. The only thing that seemed to work was throwing everyone flat whenever the sound of a plane's engine was heard. Strange way to fight a war.

0615 hours

18 August 1940
Northeast of Hal Far

Colonel Mason had been de facto demoted to captain in that
he only had command of a makeshift company. He had spent the
remaining time of darkness organizing the company into a set
of squad strong points. He pulled out the best twenty men for
himself as an attack force. Three five-man Lewis gun sections, plus
himself with a Bren gun and four runners. He was mentally back
to 1916 in Picardy. You never gave the Hun time to get his feet
under him. Once Jerry did, it was one counterattack after another.
That was their way. Saddle orders and quick reaction times. The
trick was keeping them on their heels once they took a pounding.
So you pushed and pushed until clearly repulsed. It was a first
lieutenant's work, but it was a job he sadly knew all too well.

He started pushing a few minutes before daybreak. Two
sections as base of fire. One as maneuver. He would alternate
between the three, changing the maneuver element to maintain
the base of fire while continuing the advance. It had all been
easier than he remembered. These Fritzs hadn't the steel in
their spines their fathers had back in the real war. They never
quite broke, but he was driving them in small five- and ten-meter
bounds uphill into the scrub. His losses weren't bad by Big Push
standards. They were even starting to take prisoners. Strapping
young lads, but not as much fight in them as he'd expected. A
small part of his brain worried it was too easy, but he would deal
with the inevitable surprise when it happened.

Captain Schmidt was getting his first taste of real ground
combat. Once contact had been established with General Ramcke
at Luqa, Lieutenant Jung had announced that the force would
retreat there to regroup. No more suicidal stands to redeem a
plan gone to crap like Rotterdam in May. Obviously, a rear guard
of walking wounded would have to stay behind to delay the
British. Jung had looked him clearly in the eye and waited for
a reply. Waited to see if Schmidt, a jumped-up office boy from
the Ministry, was a man or not. Schmidt stared the Lieutenant
down and said that, of course, as senior commander he would be
in charge of the rear guard. Six of his friends from the Ministry
volunteered to stay as well. As if a few more machine pistols
would matter. What mattered was showing that insubordinate

swine Jung what sort of men they were. He made Jung's mutinous plan his own, sending him back with a written report to that effect.

And so far he was fairly proud of himself. The British attack, which he estimated to be at company strength, was only slowly pushing him back. While he and his played Red Indians in the bush taking potshots and then moving a few meters uphill, he was drawing the British onto him and away from the retreating brigade column.

Lieutenant Jung had put himself with his own rear guard at the tail of the retreating column. He expected nothing from Schmidt but cataclysmic failure. The swine had at least proven to be a man. Captain Schmidt was holding his two platoons together and maintaining a coherent front. Most of the British had refused to attack. Must be second-raters. They could clearly see their combat element was advancing, but stuck by their original line and didn't even provide covering fire. Once he linked with Ramcke, he would acquire some heavy weapons, ammo, and a few radios. He'd come back and take this damned airfield. But that was for later. Now was for saving his men. He'd known the plan was designed by idiots, but even he couldn't believe the bits-and-pieces arrival of the brigade. You dropped all at once. What was higher command thinking? Even Ramcke, who was no parachutist, knew THAT much.

Commander Ian Fleming came running when he heard the firing to his rear. He found Mason gone and no one in command of his company. Typical damned-fool Army officer. Goes off on his own with no concept of the higher plan and no communications. He sent a runner to bring up six of his English-speaking cadre, Palestinians and Internationals from Spain. He arranged a command structure for the company Mason had left behind. This had all turned absurd. He would let himself get pushed off the airfield and make a run for the fishing boats at dusk.

Chapter 42

0700 hours
18 August 1940
Sea north-northeast of Malta over the British Mediterranean
Fleet

General Ernst Udet was circling a thousand meters or so above the developing air-sea battle. At three thousand meters, the first mixed wave of German bombers was trying to hit Cunningham's fleet. A squadron each of Ju-88s, Do-17s and He-111s were dropping bombs in near-perfect formations. The ships below were wildly zigzagging. No doubt, the frantic maneuvers were burning the British fleet's fuel reserves. However, there appeared to be no hits on the warships. Probably some near-misses had caused damage from overpressures rupturing side plates. Indeed, one cruiser seemed to be trailing an oil slick. Pathetic.

Udet had ignored Führer Göring's assurances that his transfer was for operational reasons. He knew it was Milch and Richthofen sabotaging him over dive-bombing. They were administrators. They saw dive-bombing as a more expensive frill. However, Udet was a better pilot than any of his rivals. Richthofen had been with the Condor Legion in Spain. He had seen with his own eyes what dive-bombing could do. Seen it and then ignored it when it came to what features the Luftwaffe's planes needed. He, Udet, would show them all. He would dive-bomb the battleship beneath him. Let them deny his theory when only he scored a hit, only he did the enemy serious damage.

Preoccupied in his internal monologue, Udet had neglected to notice that the other bombers were done and exiting the combat zone. So, his diving Ju-88 attracted every anti-aircraft weapon in the British fleet. Udet could feel the plane taking hits. A lesser pilot would have lost control. Udet had been among the best in the old World War One Flying Circus. Not quite as good as Wener Vosss himself, but definitely in the same class. He had refined his skills during the interwar years doing stunt flying for movies and public exhibitions. He held the dying plane on proper vector down to under five hundred meters. By then, even his excellent reflexes couldn't compensate for the damage to the control surfaces. But it didn't matter. The battleship couldn't dodge in time, especially when the plane had become an unstable projectile. Udet's last thought was regret that he'd just missed the command bridge. Instead, he plowed right into a turret.

Admiral Cunningham on Kent watched with horror as the last German bomber crashed into the B turret on Malaya. The huge explosion that followed could have been the bombs or ammunition for the guns. Thank God, it wasn't a magazine. The turret flipped over in the air, landing off the port side of the ship. Cunningham didn't need lookouts' reports to see the fires raging.

The damage to the Malaya decided him. He had the radio room send a message to Malta Command. The Navy would come into the Grand Harbor this night. The fleet would then retire permanently out of air range. Two days of this and there would be no Mediterranean Fleet. The days of fleets operating without fighter cover were fast drawing to a close.

Over the Italian battlefleet west-northwest of the British
0715 hours
18 August 1940

The flight lieutenant was skimming the waves heading for what he knew was an Italian man-of-war and hoped was a battleship. He was pretty sure he was the last remaining Swordfish. He had seen over 12 brought down by the cloud of German and Italian fighters flying cover over the Axis squadron of steel-fighting platforms. It was just as he feared. The Swordfish at altitude was simply a target-shooting exercise even for Italian biplanes, much less the lethal twin engine Me-110s. The lieutenant had been assured that the 110 was obsolete. Perhaps it was against a Spitfire or even a Hurricane, but against the Swordfish it was a sword of destruction.

He was alive because, at wave height, he was not where the enemy was looking. Besides, his plane was hard to pick up against the background of water. So climbing to diving altitude was out of the question. His original solution would have to suffice. He would release his bomb when he was almost on top of his target and use inertia and gravity to fling it at the enemy. He was within 200 meters when the anti-aircraft gunners on the target finally caught sight of him. The frantic fire spoiled the final approach so that he was somewhat climbing while executing a part left turn as he released the bomb. Inertia and gravity fought each other. The bomb missed the side of the ship, hitting the command bridge instead. The explosion flipped his plane into the sea.

He had no idea how he made it out of the sinking Swordfish. The last thing he remembered was losing control as his bomb went off. He looked around the sea for his two crewmates. No luck, but he could see a raft about 20 meters distant. He was no great athlete but he'd always been a decent swimmer. It took a few minutes to arrive at the raft. The lieutenant was surprised to find it occupied by an Italian. The man was wounded, but helped him onto the raft and shared some decent red wine with him. Hopefully someone would pick them up, but for now both of their war was done.

0730 hours
18 August 1940
Palazzo Marina, Roma

Crown Prince and Lieutenant General of the Realm Umberto got off the phone call from Berlin and felt an almost physical relief that the ordeal was over. His senior naval commanders had let him down yet again. They had totally failed to educate their Berlin-based German counterparts on the Italian style of surface battle. The process was to keep the battle at long ranges by slowly retiring in the face of the British. The British had better-armored ships, while the Italians had the speed advantage. This tactic lured the British fleet ever further into waters dominated by Axis airpower. It also maximized Italian training in the accuracy of their main batteries. It minimized losses of expensive battleships and heavy cruisers. Italy had overspent itself to acquire such a large battlefleet. Italy lacked the money and industrial base to reconstruct it from scratch in the midst of a world war. Italy was a first-rank power more by courtesy than by actual financial and manufacturing strength.

Berlin saw none of this. They saw Italian cowardice. Berlin felt they had made clear that losses were the price of the imperial gains Heydrich had offered back at the initial conference a month and a half ago. Italy's senior admirals were to have cleared up this "confusion"...only they hadn't. Berlin was livid, more so as they had "proof". Italy's admirals had also failed to coordinate among themselves. The slow retreat of the battle force out of

Taranto had panicked the invasion convoy, which had sailed from Naples. No one on the Italian side had properly coordinated the two naval commands. The convoy commander had ordered his ships to put about into Sicilian ports to await the conclusion of the fleet engagement. This, to the Germans, was proof of panic and invalidated the argument that this was all a carefully worked-out operational scheme.

To compound the problem, a fraction of the convoy refused the order. Some were German-crewed ships seized from neutrals. Some were German ships interned in Italian waters since 1939. A fair number were Italian merchant ships, torpedo boats, and coastal escorts shamed by the withdrawal order. When the German admiral Raeder sent off his refusal to retire on Sicily, his order for the German Navy to show the Italians, "how to die like men instead of running like rabbits", enough Italian ship commanders had shown they were lions. Umberto had been personally humiliated. As soon as Malta fell, he was purging the Navy. Seniority be damned. There had to be some good men hidden among the dead wood of a defective service.

0800 hours
18 August 1940
Ta Kali

Colonel Duffy almost refused to believe his ears. The runner from HQ was claiming that a German tank force had come over the uplands from Luqa and was advancing on the golf course. Tanks? Tanks from Luqa? So Luqa had fallen. That Duffy could accept. Airborne tanks were more difficult to swallow. However, there was precious little more to do at Ta Kali anyway. His engineer officer had cratered the landing strips and demolished every building. So, dropping off two sections with Bren guns as a cover force, he started the rest of his men back toward the golf course and a tank battle. Hopefully, HQ had some anti-tank weapons, because Duffy did not beyond some sticks of dynamite. The lieutenant he left in command of the two sections had orders not to do anything silly. Keep sniping at the Germans, but scoot away once a clear push was underway. No sense losing good men for nothing.

0815 hours

18 August 1940
Luqa

General Ramcke's attempt to bring order out of a chaotic arrival of reinforcements, German and Italian, was interrupted by two messengers. One brought notice of Lieutenant's Jung's retreat from Hal Far with the shot-up remains of three battalions. The column was perhaps an hour out. It needed ammo, food, and command direction of what to do next. The other report was from two of the Italian volunteers who had been to Ta Kali were returning with a written report from the officer commanding the rump battalion there. The British had wrecked the field, but were contesting any advance by the Germans to actually take possession. Despite being outnumbered over two to one by British regulars, the Ta Kali force was making slow progress, but desperately needed reinforcements and ammo resupply. Ramcke sent the Italian lads back with a German NCO to get a better report. If the airfield was useless, why reinforce that action? Better to rebuild Jung's force and then lead it himself against Hal Far. Surely Strauss could run the airfield here at Luqa on his own. Yet, Ramcke was dutiful enough to get a message back to Sicily requesting confirmation that he was not chained to commanding the airfield.

The Luftwaffe had control of Luqa's radio tower. Once the original radio operator from the first damaged Junkers had been led to the radio room with his code books, the ground combat forces officers in charge had left that function to the Luftwaffe flying arm. In turn, the air service had dispatched a proper communications section from Sicily with the first few hours. The radio section duly logged in Ramcke's message and then put it aside to deal with more pressing matters involving keeping the air transport bridge working. Running an air bridge was a serious administrative enterprise, more so as two nationalities were involved. If the ground forces needed rapid communications, why had they not sent their own equipment with personnel to man it? It was obvious that the airfield's equipment was for an airfield, and thus should be used to support air operations. Air power was the way of the future, after all.

Chapter 43

0830 hours
18 August 1940
Conference room, Reich Chancellery

The Chancellery conference room reeked of tobacco. With Hitler dead, the old rule banning smoking from state functions was gone. The walls were covered with maps of the eastern basin of the Mediterranean, of Sicily, of Malta, of the Ionian Sea. Marked on these maps were unit locations, combat summaries, and other pertinent military data. A large staff of Army and Air Force officers hovered, making updates as new data came in. There was a constant stream of such data. However, it was all Air Force technical matters. Sorties launched and returned. Status updates on aircraft down-timed for maintenance. Sectors being patrolled over the developing air-sea battle. Little information was coming from the Navy or the Italians, and nothing from the ground forces beyond Jodl's previous missive. This left the four rulers waiting, marking time. The battle was clearly happening, but until news arrived they could do little beyond badgering aides for more reports.

A smartly uniformed girl brought a message envelope to Schellenberg, who was standing behind his boss, Heydrich. The uniform was that of the League of German Girls, known by its abbreviation, BDM. None of the important people looked twice at her. Important messages were brought by uniformed officers, not teenage girls playing make-believe in uniforms of, what were to all intents and purposes, Nazi Girl Scouts. The other three rulers just hid their irritation that Heydrich would allow an important meeting to be interrupted by petty office business.

Schellenberg asked his boss to leave the table for a moment. Again, smirks and sighs all around. Heydrich left the table with a poker face, but Schellenberg did not keep his position by not being able to read his boss's mood. "It's important". Heydrich walked over, read the message, and shot a look to his subordinate. "How?"

Schellenberg kept his face passive and his voice down. "Strauss again. There is a block of some kind getting messages out from the island. He's bribed a group of pilots to hand-carry messages to Sicily. He pays them when our replies are received. I've already sent off a fast reply to keep the message traffic coming or prepare for a visit to the Gestapo, but somehow Strauss has acquired funds to bribe people. He said the message-routing is via SS HQ because no one is stupid enough to go slow on information to THAT address. Anyway, it's chaos in Sicily and thus on Malta. Jodl has usurped authority to keep the reinforcements flowing, but is getting pushback from flying officers and base commanders on whether he has authority over Luftwaffe assets. Strauss says Jodl needs a message from here fast making this happen. We are winning, but could still lose."

Heydrich nodded and asked Führer Göring to join him for a coffee to discuss an administrative situation. The two army generals had no problem letting Göring, who they did not regard as a professional equal, exit to deal with "a Party organizational matter". Indeed, they preferred to deal with the military message traffic themselves, without the two Nazi amateurs.

Göring heard Heydrich out. Thanked him for not airing Luftwaffe dirty laundry among the Army men. Göring called over one of his aides, a Luftwaffe general, who exited quickly to contact Jodl and resolve the matters. He returned to the table muttering about Kesselring. A Führer did not enjoy being made to look the fool in front of senior people, and by his own service no less.

Heydrich waited till Göring was again occupied with the generals and the message flow. He wanted an update on Sturmbannführer Siegel. Was he in Sicily yet? When he arrived there, Heydrich expected hourly reports. He also wanted Siegel wired arrest authority over non-cooperative officers, even those of higher rank than his own. Schellenberg nodded. Siegel was one of the "smart ones". He had enough sense not to abuse such a broad grant of power. Schellenberg had actually sent him with such a written authority in several versions, so that if the Boss activated it there was paper to wave under some colonel or general's nose. Always wise to plan ahead.

Within twenty minutes, updates starting arriving from Jodl. The two Army generals were obviously curious at what had changed but were too caste-proud to ask. Beck just fumed. Halder, the more sensible of the pair, sent an aide out to message Jodl directly for a private update. Jodl might be Heydrich's creature now, but he was still a member of the senior officer corps. Halder doubted Jodl would refuse the courtesy of an answer. If the Army was to preserve its prerogatives, the key was learning this new world of Heydrich's rather than just standing aloof while sneering. The Army had tried that in the Thirties, and ended up firmly under Hitler's thumb.

0845 hours
18 August 1940
Road from Luqa to Hal Far

Lieutenant Cirillo's patrol had made quite poor time arriving here. The air attacks on them had been ceaseless. The recognition panels were useless. The flares were ignored unless fired directly at the pilots in the manner of anti-aircraft rounds. Machinegun fire seemed to work. Indeed, he was fairly sure his men had shot down one plane. His report would list it as a British Gladiator fighter. It simply wouldn't do to take credit for knocking an Italian plane out of the sky. Pilots! They must be picked for their movie-star good looks, as none had the brains of a good army mule.

The advancing Italo-German force had been grateful for his reinforcements. Cirillo quickly discovered why. The same damned British marksman was here. There was no way the British could have two this good.

As to Lieutenant Colonel Lusena, the supposed Arditi confirmed that he was their commander. They hadn't seen him since leaving Luqa, but had no reason to believe he was not around. Cirillo thought Arditi uniformed in Luftwaffe blue and carrying German arms was odd. He noted all this in his report. Indeed, he made two copies of the report. One messenger was sent north up the road to Luqa, while the other would retrace his steps to battalion HQ back at the jump-off point. The main point in the report was the abysmal behavior of the air force. What made it more galling is that the force coming down from Luqa had had no such difficulties.

Money-Penny noticed the reinforcements arriving. He was down to six men. He'd done all he could, but it was time to backpedal quickly. He sent two of his six ahead to alert the brothers Fleming that a reinforced company was advancing down the road from the north on them. Money-Penny moved his remaining men uphill away from the road. He would move in the fringe of upland woods and stop at intervals to snipe at his pursuers.

0900 hours
18 August 1940
Scrub northeast of Hal Far, supposedly heading to Luqa

The strong, wet, south wind came up just after dawn. Lieutenant Jung had never seen such a weather event. The wind was wet off the ocean, yet full of sand and grit, probably blown in from the vast dunes of the Sahara. It left a blood-red dew on the leaves in the scrub forest they were marching through. Jung vaguely recalled details on all of this from his pre-drop planning briefings. The words hadn't really registered. He was a veteran of Norway and Holland. He had focused on the combat aspects of the plan. Aspects that were suspect enough to keep his full attention. A dawn-drop after an over-water approach with half-trained men flown by poorly trained aircrew.

And yet the reality had been worse than his forebodings. The undefended airfield had a brigade of British plentifully supplied with machine guns. The German air force had failed to produce a coordinated drop. Instead, it had been two-plus hours of hiccups. He cursed Ramcke for accepting this death ride of a mission. Then he shrugged. No one had seen Ramcke since Sicily. A runner had him at Luqa, but that was absurd. Odds were the bastard was dead and it was some other general at Luqa. Luqa had been designated as an NL landing zone. How that militia had taken an airfield was a mystery in itself. The entire service hadn't existed two months earlier. This NL unit had been boasting of battles in Romania and Hungary. Battles? Jung mentally laughed at the thought. Battles were fought against Nordics, like the British and Dutch he had fought at Rotterdam. Slavs and Magyars were barely fully human.

Still the wind, the vegetation, the plantings in the fields...it was all alien. It wasn't proper German weather or proper German forests or proper German farms. Norway and Holland had looked like home, like Germany. Jung could see adding those to the Reich. This Malta felt alien. Leave it to the worthless Italians. It seemed strange to be allied to Italy. His uncle had fought the Italians at Caporetto. They belonged on the other side.

Jung had led his column off with the walking wounded aided by what few support troops he had. The best men brought up the rear—the only fully formed company left after the debacle of the night. The middle was a mass of ersatz squads formed out of bits and pieces of shattered platoons. This seemed sensible. The threat was from the British to their rear. While the terrain was unfamiliar, Malta was a small island and Luqa and Half Far were reasonably close together. A half-dozen kilometers should see the unit to Luqa.

Yet, now he heard firing up ahead. A runner breathlessly announced that the van had been smashed by a carefully set-up British ambush. Jung had to hurry his ready company forward past the milling chaos of the rest of the column. He trotted, wildly wondering what else could go wrong on this bloody abortion of a mission.

Corporal Billy Lincoln had halted his march with the dawn. Daylight brought air attacks. Old Malta hands knew the system. Find a field with trees or a farmhouse by daylight. Everyone would nap with perhaps a light meal in the early afternoon for those that were awake. You did your big meal an hour or two before dusk so that you could form up and move out as soon as the last planes followed the setting sun west toward Sicily.

The night march had been agonizingly slow. Many of the newbies who had latched onto Billy's makeshift unit had no outdoor skills at all. Away from roads, they kept finding roots to trip over, rocks to stumble on. Plus, there was a constant churning of personnel since the firefight on the Luqa-to-Grand Harbor road earlier. Native Maltese and lads who had acquired sweethearts on the island would drift off, looking to fend for themselves. New lost lambs from stray work details would hear the column moving and join. In addition, enough newbies to the island had various versions of the Malta trots, falling out to void themselves before stumbling on to regain the unit. When lost, they ignored elementary march discipline and called out through the dark scrublands.

Malta's landscape was nothing an Englishman would be accustomed to at home. However, the Empire took a Brit to many a strange land and clime. Billy's core guys had been on Malta for months. They had grown familiar with the smells, the sights, the sounds of this small but important part of Britain's patrimony. Even the south wind, the cloying humidity it brought, the nasty grit that fouled weapons, requiring endless cleaning and oiling, were familiar. The grit got in your food, in your nose, in your eyes. Best to wear a damp cloth across your nose and mouth during the daytime. Of course, a damp cloth meant contact with the water, which gave you the trots even if you brewed it up first. Old hands drank only tea, and rolling boiled that.

The daytime halt had been centered on a farmhouse. An old stone building with a shed provided shelter for most of the men. The rest slumped along the stone walls of the garden, nominally on sentry. It was nominal because it had become obvious during the night that the Germans couldn't move through these woods without making enough noise to be clearly heard. Their training must not have included familiarization on similar settings in Sicily or Italy's boot. Officers! The German ones seemed to Billy as dense as the British ones he had worked around back to Haig's days.

His lads clearly heard the approaching German column. Despite instructions from Billy to get him before doing anything, two fools had panicked. Newbies he'd picked up that night. Not from his regiment, the Manchesters. Manchester Regiment had standards. One fool ran screaming. The other blazed away at the noise. Half the other fools then fired because they thought they'd missed the order. Billy ran around banging heads to get them to stop. Still, they hadn't done badly. There were six Germans down about 70 meters in front of them, and a bunch more backpedaling fast. Billy considered sending two men forward to see if they could retrieve paybooks or letters. While he was considering, the return-fire grew brisk enough that he decided to leave well enough alone. He hadn't wished for a serious fight, but it seemed he was in one. Best to organize his mob into something resembling sections with one of his guys running each and some idea of a fire plan. He also had to pick a rally point and make sure the section leaders knew where it was. His "unit" didn't have enough ammo for more than an hour's serious fighting. Best to know how to get out of this without being driven back on Luqa. Hal Far was still the only place to go. It was Hal Far or the white flag. Billy wasn't ready to sit out the war quite yet.

James Money-Penny reflected on that south wind as he moved his lads along. He had seen it at its source in the mighty Sahara one time, chasing relics in the deep desert. Nominally he'd been in Libya, but no colonial power really ruled those wastes. They garrisoned the oasis villages and patrolled. He had eaten grit from this wind to the south of the dunes, in the vast plains called the Sahel, a time or two helping out mine owners or mercantile interests. However, he had mostly seen the seasonal wind from the north. Albania, Spain, Egypt, Palestine, and now here. He recognized the vegetation, the settlement pattern, a thousand little things. He laughed to himself. He was more at home in the reaches of the Empire than he was the few times he had set foot back in the Home Counties. He was an Englander and would be to the day he died, yet England no longer felt like home.

Money-Penny was starting to get into this whole commando business. He had been proud of avoiding the army, because he had little use for mass warfare, or indeed mass-anything. He enjoyed the fighting, the killing, the whole active part of warfare. He just preferred doing it in small groups the old-time way, before mass armies, before trenches, before a war of dueling artillery brigades. His father had died of that in France in the last war, as had a baker's dozen of male relatives. Killed in action, missing presumed dead, died of wounds. All had vanished into the meat grinder that was Haig's army group in France and Flanders. Here on Malta, Money-Penny was still fighting a war of heroes and adventure that went back to the classics, such as the tales of brave Ulysses.

Malta was lost to the Empire. All that more fighting here could do was give the Huns and Eyeties a bloody nose before the next Dunkirk, which would be dusk today as far as James was concerned. It would be a feat worthy of heroes keeping Hal Far in business through the day. One forlorn commando battalion against what appeared to be three airborne divisions.

After Malta would be Egypt, and after that, Palestine. Money-Penny had his doubts on whether the Empire could hold either. He knew too well how unprepared the Army was and how few planes the Air Force had. A man with his connections learned things outside official channels. The shrewder financers and operators were liquidating their holdings, sending younger brothers or sons abroad to safety. The big fish would mostly get out. They always did.

James knew enough of the smaller fish—local hardboys of various stripes. Once he hit Alex, he was going recruiting. For the next fight, he would have his own gang of proper villains. He could pay in the best coin of all. He had contacts that could get families out, out with their meager household goods roughly intact. He knew officials to approve permits, ship-owners who sailed the Red Sea and outward. He had a mate who owed him huge favors. Ran a gem mine in the wilds of the interior of Ceylon. A mine that always had need of labor that could be close-mouthed. The mine was the man's retirement project. Much of its production never made it onto the company books or the tax rolls. Cash sales out via tramp freighters and no one in officialdom the wiser. Food was never a problem up there. It was mountain jungle and near anything grew.

Money-Penny heard the firefight. Could tell by the sounds it was British Lee-Enfields versus German MP-38s. It wasn't his fight. He could easily avoid it. But, damn, he was still an Englishman. King, country, flag. He could smell the cordite over the traditional island forest smells. It was like catnip to him. Got his blood up. Made him feel alive. "Okay, lads, step lively. We've got some new mates to rescue. Follow behind me and don't start shooting until I do. We're about to fuck over some Huns!" With a jaunty wave and a mordant laugh, he led his squad toward the fun. He was whistling "Land of Hope and Glory".

0920 hours
18 August 1940
Paralleling the Luqa-Hal Far road about 50 meters to the east.

Lieutenant Cirillo noticed that the annoying British sharpshooter seemed to have vanished a few minutes back. Perhaps he had flapped his arms, like the wings of a large bird, and flown home to Britain. Britain, Egypt, Hell, the Grand Harbor of Malta, Cirillo just wanted the man gone from his small piece of this island.

The Lieutenant smiled at the thought. He was already thinking of this island as "Italy". It certainly felt home-like. He was from Naples and, while Malta was not Campania, it was enough like the Mezzogiorno to be familiar. The same basic flora and fauna. The trees, the songbirds, the houses, all looked familiar to a young man who had taken his motorcycle through Apulia and Calabria during his teens. It was all of a common Mediterranean style.

Even the local dialect was near enough to the dialects of the Italian South. Maltese was a bit more Arabic and the popular slang had acquired a bunch of British loan words, but he had been able to communicate with the few locals he had met. Dedicated Italian patriots, or so they claimed. No doubt, their former British uniforms were safely buried against another turn of the wheel. He doubted there had been any noticeable number of real patriots here. Per his briefings, the British had arrested those on the outbreak of hostilities.

His briefing officers had stressed that Berlin had promised Malta to Italy. Cirillo was glad of this. His unit had missed the debacle that had been the brief Alpine campaign, but he'd heard the details from friends. Italy's divisions foiled by a few French reservists in antiquated entrenchments. The French claimed it was an extension of the Maginot line, but while some small pieces were modernized, it was still unconnected blockhouses rather than the massive installations on the real Maginot line in Lorraine. The port of Genoa bombarded by the British and French. British air raids on Italian industry. A complete balls-up of a war, with Italy being spared from total humiliation only by the French collapse under the German onslaught.

Yet, these German supermen had looked inept here in Malta. They hadn't managed a coherent airdrop, in contrast to the Italians who managed two from different continents. True, the NL, whatever that was, had taken an airfield. As far as the lieutenant knew, NL was some makeshift militia cobbled together in late June. How could such a make-believe service have taken an airfield with one glider battalion?

Italy would have Hal Far before today was out. Have Hal Far in spite of German failure there. Cirillo had been raised on the ideas of German technical superiority. The German results in France would seem to validate this, but personal observation here on Malta left him skeptical. Whatever. Italy was allied to Germany and this was beyond his power to change. It was unnatural to him to be allied to, what seemed to most Italians he knew to be, a larger version of the ancient Austrian enemy, but Cirillo was content to let Il Duce make such decisions. The lieutenant believed in Italy's leader and Fascism.

Indeed, he believed enough to have chosen to be a combat officer and help realize the creation of the new Roman Empire. Cirillo was trained as an accountant with the proper university degree and professional credentials. Had he allowed nature to take its course, he would have done service in the Finance Corps or some similar rear-area entity. None of that for him. He was a combat officer in a new elite corps. He was part of a young Fascist Italy that would restore Italy, just as the old Roman legions had won an empire back in the glory days. Il Duce had given Italy an empire in East Africa. Now Italy must link to that empire via Egypt and Sudan. To take Egypt, Malta was needed. So here marched Cirillo with his brave assault troops. He commanded good Libyan professionals, sturdy auxiliaries of Il Duce's legions. Caesar's legions had had their Gallic cavalry, Balearic slingers, Numidian light horse. Italy would have Libyans, Eritreans, Somalis, Albanians, and now Maltese.

He realized what he was hearing after his ears had registered it. He had already motioned his men down. Firing at a distance of under a kilometer to his left front, Germans against British from the differing sounds of the weapons. British weapons, but not the special rifle of that damned marksman. That one had a distinctive sound all its own. The Germans were probably the parachute unit he was tasked with locating. The location meant they were running away from Hal Far. Superman, what a laugh. Cirillo motioned his men up. Time to make contact with his "allies". Make contact carefully, as meetups in the midst of battle could go disastrously wrong. Silently, his men fell in behind him like the well-trained formation they were. The unit began to stalk forward toward this new battle, prepared to bring further glory to Italy. The thought of such a victory brought joy to the lieutenant's heart. He was living his dream of being a virile Italian combat hero, worthy of his corps being the new Arditi.

Chapter 44

0930 hours
18 August 1940
Road from Luqa to the Grand Harbor

Rommel could see the golf course a few hundred meters in front of him. It showed signs of prior fighting. The British troops he had driven back were trying to regroup and dig in there. They hadn't been especially well-led, but there had been a lot of them. Probably at least a brigade, even if many were administrative troops hastily organized into combat units.

The problem was that counting rallied survivors of the drops, Rommel had under a battalion of men. His unit was bits of pieces of German, Italian, and whatever the hell the NL had fielded. Squads and platoons, often remnant pieces of such units, grouped around his three Italian tankettes and a good Italian mountain mortar battery. His promised air support attacked him as often as they did the British. He had no radios to communicate with the planes, so was reduced to sending runners back to Luqa to communicate that way. It seemed to be partially working. The idiot pilots had figured out that anyone fighting alongside the tankettes was a friendly. So that left Rommel's men bunched up around the vehicles, which limited his attack frontage and did nothing to drive this brigade away. He could see the puffs of flak guns firing from the Harbor. It was a handful of kilometers. There had to be a way. Maybe if he stopped attacking over the 12th green and tried to slide around the sand trap on the 14th hole.

0940 hours
18 August 1940
Northeast of Hal Far

It was over. Captain Schmidt, former adjutant to General Ramcke and current battlegroup commander, was nearly out of unwounded men capable of a further delaying action. He was also almost out of ammunition. He was quite proud of himself. He may have been an administrative officer, but he had led men in combat and accomplished his mission. Jung could take his high-handed attitude and shove it up his posterior. He and his lads from the

Ministry had acquitted themselves well. A few were dead and all the rest wounded except himself. Schmidt tied a handkerchief to a branch and stuck it up waving it at the English.

He got answers in English, which he didn't speak. He called out in German that his unit wished to surrender. When this failed to elicit a response, he tried French. His French was poor but passable. He had used it shopping in Belgium before the war when on holiday. Had come home with some nice table linens for his mother. The answer in French was weirdly accented, but he understood. He got slowly to his feet and, waving the stick with the white cloth, advanced slowly. A British officer came forward to meet him. A middle-aged colonel of all things, a full field officer. Schmidt revised upward how many British were at Hal Far. If they could spare a colonel to command a medium-sized pursuit force, then the garrison must be a full division. No wonder the attack had failed. The intelligence was hopelessly off.

Colonel Mason was winded, but exhilarated. He hadn't had this much fun in ages. These Germans were nothing like the iron Huns of his nightmares from wartime service. The rot of the Twenties must have ruined Germany's younger generation the way it had in Britain. French had never been Mason's best language. He spoke much better Arabic, Hindi, and Urdu. However, the memories of having to speak French were linked to other recollections from the war years. Besides, it was all formalities. The young captain handed over his sidearm, saluted, and followed simple orders. The problem was, of course, the wounded. It would take the unwounded Brits and Germans working together several trips to get all the injured to the field hospitals. A most pleasant morning's work.

Commander Ian Fleming caught up with Mason just as the column of POWs was starting its march to captivity. He was fully out of breath from running down Mason. He would have loved to have berated the fool. The colonel had abandoned his command without orders and potentially had opened the rear of the Hal Far position to counterattack. Yet, it all seemed to have worked out. There were a lot fewer Germans than Fleming had expected. He made a mental note to try questioning the prisoners on where the missing men were. He also smelled smoke. The fighting had started numerous small fires in the scrub and underbrush. This would bear watching, lest it burn out of control and come back at him on the airfield. Fleming was aware of all the loose ends, but simply lacked the time to tidy things up. The Italians were hammering him hard to the west. Absentmindedly, he did notice there was large scale gunfire coming from the north to northwest of here. Gunfire he hadn't heard back at Hal Far. Might this be where the missing Germans were? If so, who was fighting them? Had Malta Command sent a relief force?

0945 hours
18 August 1940
North-northwest of the surrender in the prior scene

Lieutenant Jung had gotten his column back into fighting order, which had not been easy. Elite paras so spooked they had been on the verge of rout. This operation was clearly showing him there were limits to even the best selected and trained men. He foresaw training in post-drop chaos as a pressing need. Forcing the men to form ad hoc units and perform. Running them through exercises until they were exhausted and doing so in the dark on unfamiliar terrain. He certainly wished the men he was commanding had such training. There were moments when he wished he had been through such a course.

This was one of them. Having started a movement around the British right to roll back their ambush, his attack had triggered a second British force with a most annoying marksman. The man was dropping his men as if they were clay pigeons at a trap shoot. The survivors of the flanking platoon had gone to ground and Jung had no way to extract them.

Now he had organized another platoon to flank the British left. He had followed it with a second squad of mobile walking wounded with orders to swing wide and find Luqa. Reinforcements were needed. Damn! He'd wanted to bring in his men as a marching column, to salvage their pride. Now he would need that idiot NL militia to bail them out. Shit! Jung was finding higher unit command a burden he hadn't anticipated.

Billy was grateful to this new officer Money-Penny for bailing out his men. Man said he was RN but was dressed in a soldier's kit. Whatever. He was a King's officer and clearly knew what he was doing. He'd bumped Billy to sergeant and refused to take no for an answer. Billy chuckled to himself at the thought of what his RSM would make of that. Billy's guess was that the papers would show he had always been a corporal this day unless he was busted back to private for going sort of AWOL. Didn't matter. The same machinegun round hit sergeant or rookie squaddie. The officer could shoot like God's gift. He had an eye for terrain and a command voice. He also had a clear idea of where the now combined unit was and how to get off this God-cursed isle. Billy thought him a man worth following. Got a laugh out of the officer handing him his sergeant's stripes torn off the uniform of a dead German. Billy remembered this sort of graveyard humor from the real war.

Lieutenant Cirillo had found the missing Germans. Sort of. He could hear their main column. He could see the smoke and hear sounds of firing. However, there was the same annoying British marksman between his platoon and the Germans. Or most of the Germans. Two had crawled into his lines wounded. Aryan superman, bah! He sent the less badly wounded of the two Germans to do a long crawl around the battle space and make contact with his officer, some Lieutenant Jung. A brigade and the highest officer was a lieutenant? Didn't make sense. Cirillo was not sending his men into a firefight where the supposed friendlies had no way of knowing he was friendly. That was a formula for taking unnecessary casualties. He would keep his men in position and await a German courier with suggestions for a combined battleplan.

Chapter 45

1000 hours
18 August 1940
Luqa airfield, Malta

Lieutenant Klaus Steiner was savoring the aroma of his latest cup of coffee. Before joining the NL, he had never had real coffee. His parents had strained to maintain lower-middle-class respectability. Even with them both working, coffee was a luxury. They allotted themselves one cup each in the morning before work. Klaus and his siblings knew better than to touch the magic beans themselves. HJ had only served ersatz coffee and herbal tea. Only now, Klaus was an officer. An officer with a recognized mistress who had his coffee hot and waiting between rounds of combat. Klaus decided he could allow himself to become accustomed to this new state of affairs.

He had mastered the basics of being a combat officer. He didn't see himself as a hero, but men followed him into battle and, so far, the results had been satisfactory. Had they not been, Colonel Strauss or Greta's Uncle Isaak would have quick to point out his defects. Strauss had done so on arrival. Klaus had his outposts in the wrong places. Strauss did not have a tantrum or belittle him. He just told him what the correct answer was, why Klaus's was suboptimal, and how to fix it.

Klaus was sure there had to be manuals for combat the way there were for glider-piloting. When they reached Libya, he was putting in a request for these books. With his Greta as a study partner, there was nothing he couldn't learn. The thought of the study sessions for glider piloting brought a bemused look to his face. Klaus had been, at best, an indifferent student before joining the NL. Then again, his teachers had not used Greta's reward system for chapters learned. German teachers did not use sex to motivate students. Sex worked much better on teenage males than screaming or swats from middle-aged annoyed teachers.

Klaus asked Greta for another cup. When she brought it, he handed her his new hat. Joey had taken the two hats off a pair of "Canadian" prisoners. Joey had laughed when they said Canadian. Told them they were American in what the prisoners called a Brooklyn accent. They both had these funny hats on. Light cloth circles with a reinforced bill to keep the sun out of your eyes. Joey had called them "baseball caps". Klaus had no idea what a baseball was, but the cap was light and kept the bright Mediterranean sun away. Joey had kept one and given Klaus the other. It was simply more comfortable than his steel helmet. Now he wanted Greta to stitch on his lucky original officer's insignia, the one that made him a Ukrainian nationalist major. It had been lucky for him in Romania and he'd kept it in his pocket ever since. Turned out Greta wasn't much use with a sewing needle, but one of Naiomi's girls did a fast job to hold it in place. Klaus made himself two promises. After this battle was over, he would get Major Ivan to explain this dead ghost army so he could make up some convincing connection to it. One of his uncles had served in the East in the Kaiser's War. Klaus was clueless on where in the East or even where Ukraine was. The uncle had been a corporal in a field bakery, but it could be the start in creating a legend for himself. He remembered that from his school literature class. Heroes had legends and he was now an official hero of the new Reich. The second promise was to find out what a baseball was.

Klaus smirked and went back to savoring his coffee. Decided to down another stay-awake pill before the next round of combat. Falling asleep in battle did not seem a wise notion. He idly wondered what soldiers had done before these new modern miracle pills.

1020 hours
18 August 1940
Luqa

General Gerhard Ramcke found the "German" of this newly promoted Captain Bats hard to follow. He had been forced to get newly promoted Colonel Strauss to translate. Indeed, half the back and forth seemed to be in some American dialect of English. Still, once past the language barrier, the idea was brilliant. Bats had repaired a British Bristol bomber captured during Steiner's initial successful assault on Luqa. The Luftwaffe had sent over a crew to fly the prize back to Sicily. Bats's minions had even repainted the plane in German gray with proper markings to avoid confusion by Axis fighters or air defense. Bats and the pilot proposed a test flight over Malta before risking the plane and its precious crew over open water back to Sicily. It had occurred to Bats that this would provide a lovely opportunity for General Ramcke to actually see where his missing men were, what the British were up to, and, in general, to do a reconnaissance.

Put that way, Ramcke was intrigued. The lack of radios had been a major annoyance. The island was small, but he was reduced to messengers in the manner of a 17th-century commander. Messengers without decent maps who took forever and kept getting lost. He hopped on the plane and marveled at how small Malta seemed once they were airborne. He would write a letter of commendation for this Bats fellow. Strauss had made a major find in recruiting him.

1030 hours
18 August 1940
Luqa

Gunter Strauss made a mental note to find Joey a German tutor when this battle was over. New York street-German just wouldn't cut it when trying to communicate with higher officers. He'd ask Wanda to find some girl she knew from the old neighborhood who'd find spending a Captain's pay to be a step up in life. Wanda always knew desperate people eager for a sweet deal. Strauss smiled. Wanda was a pain in the ass, but he was stuck with her, so why not milk the connection?

His reverie was interrupted by the two walking-wounded messengers from Jung. Strauss surprised them by swearing at them. He saw their distress and explained. The senior officer, General Ramcke, had just left the runway on an aerial tour of the island. As number two, he, Strauss, could not abandon the installation. So he would have to send his second-in-command, Lieutenant Steiner. Steiner was a good lad, but still learning the trade. However, he was an official hero.

Steiner came running when summoned. Strauss outlined the problem. Trapped German force. Large British force. The two guides needed medical attention, so Steiner would have to find his own way. Put scouts out in front and use sound and smell to guide. Shooting is loud. Gunpowder has unique odors, plus it usually causes brush fires. Make sure of who you are shooting at before engaging, as there was always danger of friendly fire. Steiner seemed to be taking it all in. Strauss spoke in clipped phrases hoping the bullet points would stick in Steiner's young mind. This was the sort of learning experience that could kill him.

Klaus had come running when his colonel called. He gulped twice when told he was leading an independent attack deep into the brush away from the airfield. He was also proud he was being trusted with this task. His Greta needed him to be a hero, a protector to her. He must prove worthy of her love. Gathering what men he could find along with Peter and his MG 34, he exited back in the direction Jung's men had pointed, screaming, "Follow me!" over his shoulder as he trotted by the various groups huddled on the runway. His guys knew who he was and he presumed the rest would ignore him.

The mountain infantry captain had been chatting up Greta as she saw to tea and snacks for his newly arrived company. He half-knew it would go nowhere. She kept making clear she had a boyfriend who was her unit commander. That didn't bother him. A friendly Aryan girl to chat up was worth the time. Might be his last chance to flirt with a girl. He'd flown here for combat, not a vacation. Her German was a bit off. She had explained she was racial German from someplace called Transylvania. She spoke Romanian and Magyar in her hometown. The captain was proud of how Germany's scattered blood were being ingathered by the Nazis. Whatever the NL was, it seemed more patriotic than the girls back home, obsessed with movie stars and good times.

Greta had been content to let the officer flirt with her. She saw it as a chance to practice her German, which she knew was still rudimentary. She was amazed German had so many dialects. This officer's Bavarian accent was difficult for her but practice makes perfect. She had a family to protect. Klaus waved at her as he jogged by. She blew him a kiss. Klaus kept shouting "Follow me!" Meant another battle or skirmish or whatever soldiers call these things. She hoped he'd be careful, but didn't call that out to him. She needed him to keep being brave, to keep being a hero.

The captain caught that Klaus was the boyfriend. He saw the insignia on Klaus's cap. Its meaning was unknown to him. Did this new NL have weird ranks like the SS and SA did? "Follow me" shouldn't apply to him, as he'd been told to await orders by a general. Except the general wasn't here. So he asked the girl what the badge on her man's cap meant.

Greta was concentrating on getting the words right. He asked what the insignia was. "That's a major's insignia. It's special to him and he wears it in battle." She thought those were the right words. She hoped she had answered the question properly. She never really understood quite where Klaus had gotten the insignia from. He'd had it when she first met him.

The captain took it in. A major was calling for men. He thanked the gracious Fräulein for her reply. He didn't correct her grammar as she was a superior officer's woman. Better obey the major and let him sort it out with the general later. Gulping down his tea and pocketing two extra snacks for later, he yelled to his two lieutenants to get the men in a column. They were following the major to battle. He asked the Fräulein for her man's name and was told Klaus Steiner. This triggered a memory of the newspaper story. Klaus and Greta. Hero from Romania and Hungary. Heroes get followed. One got promoted that way.

Klaus never looked back to see the hundred and twenty mountain troops following behind his few dozen fighters from his original company. He was more concerned with finding his way. He had no map, no skills in reading terrain, and no clue.

Chapter 46

1040 hours
18 August 1940
Chancellery conference room, Berlin

By now, the assembled dignitaries had grown used to the parade of pert, young, BDM girls bearing messages from the island. Halder was fuming that Jodl had not replied to his request. Jodl had failed to reply because the communications staff at Gerbini had never given him the message. This would not be cleared up until the post-battle "lessons learned" study. It became retrospectively apparent that only messages to or from SS HQ made it past the roadblock. A dozen Luftwaffe officers would find themselves transferred from communications work to being weather officers in Lapland over this.

So, a message that needed a conference between Heydrich and Göring over "an administrative matter" caused little notice to the rest of the room. They only paid attention when Göring started shrieking at his Luftwaffe aides to get him Kesselring on direct line, NOW! Göring's face was red. His eyes were bulging. His screams and bellows included a cloud of spittle. His hands were making motions as if he were strangling someone. All that was missing was actual smoke coming out of his ears.

The "administrative matter" had started some hours earlier. Jodl had sidelined the Luftwaffe technical team that had wanted to proceed to Luqa. Jodl simply didn't see them as a priority. NL's technical staff was fixing planes. At a moment when the battle hung in the balance, when every man sent had to be weighed against multiple priorities, including the need for more ammunition, Jodl saw no reason why the technical people couldn't wait quietly for an opportune moment. They were not quiet about it, but they did wait. The technical chief was a major. Jodl was a senior general.

Joey was a genius mechanic and Isaac Cohen was also fairly good, if from a different level and set of qualifications. Isaac knew theory and science, which he had a lifetime's experience applying to metal work. However, he did not per se know planes or autos, which were in many ways similar. Joey had none of the science or math. He had practical experience, intuitive brilliance, and had taken paid lessons in mechanical engineering, metallurgy, and automotive mechanics. Together they could troubleshoot almost anything.

What they could not do was manufacture parts. One of the courses of study Joey had paid for lessons in was mechanical drawing. So whenever he needed a part he would send back a drawing showing what the part looked like and where it went in the plane to aid the parts manager in figuring out what he meant. He also included dimensions. Sadly, Joey's eye was trained in inches not millimeters.

He would sometimes get his part. More often, he would get back a written complaint at not using the proper requisition form signed by a Luftwaffe officer and referencing the exact part ID number in the Ju-52 maintenance manual.

Joey had plenty of Luftwaffe officers passing through, so signatures were not a problem. He didn't have forms or the manual. Sicily refused pointblank to provide either, claiming he had no authorization. Joey was reduced to sending back the defective part. Sometimes, this produced a new part. Mostly, it didn't. He now had 14 planes sitting on Luqa's runways. He could steal parts from them. He did. That just meant more work and that the grounded planes were more broken. Joey was politely asking higher authority to get him his manual and forms. The airlift needed every plane.

Schellenberg had tried giving the order himself. The maintenance warehouse chief would only accept an order through Luftwaffe channels. Hence, the appeal to Göring, whose patience with his idiots was at an end. So, he waited, fuming, while Berlin got a phone line to Kesselring's HQ, after which he was left standing there because Kesselring's HQ could not physically find their boss. The deputy chief of staff who was available could not even make a proper excuse. Kesselring and six other senior people had left to go somewhere for a conference about something with someone. Kesselring did not consider those details as something his HQ needed to know. "He's never gone for more than an hour when this happens." This was not taken as a satisfactory response by the Führer and Reichsmarschall.

1045 hours
18 August 1940
Woods east of the Luqa-Hal Far road, Malta

Money-Penny saw little purpose in waiting to be ground down by superior forces for dirt he would freely give away before midnight anyway. Once he was sure there was a lull in the fighting he had organized the men into a marching column, sending them out under Billy Lincoln looping beyond his left toward the island interior to be sure of passing around the German right flank. Billy's orders were to get everyone to Hal Far and report to Commander Peter Fleming. Money-Penny gave Lincoln a written order which confirmed his promotion and the attachment of his force to Fleming's commando battalion.

Money-Penny had remained behind with half adozen men. He was the only one doing the shooting. He had taken nearly all of the ammo from the departing column whose orders were to avoid contact. He was shooting with standard Enfield rifles, which he left partially visible at various places along the former perimeter. He had his gun being carried by a private. His gun made a distinctive sound. He wanted the Germans to think there were still many British here. He figured to give it another half hour or so and then fade away.

1050 hours
18 August 1940
Luqa, Malta

General Ramcke had returned to the ground with a MUCH better picture of the fighting, even if the bomber had sensibly stayed away from the caldron of machinegun fire around Hal Far. He had found his missing brigade. He had been amused to see Rommel make war on a golf course. He decided that what he needed was a Fieseler Fi 156 Storch single-engine reconnaissance plane. While in the air, he had radioed Sicily requesting one... and been peremptorily refused by Kesselring's HQ. They wouldn't even let anyone important come and explain. It wasn't in the plan and everyone of rank was too busy to deal with a mere division commander.

Ramcke tried one last tack. Before landing, he radioed Jodl, who promised to make an appeal to Berlin via Heydrich.

1100 hours
18 August 1940

The Reich Without Hitler: The Falcons of Malta

East of Luqa-Hal Far road

By all rights, Klaus should have gotten deeply lost. Sound carries. By now, he knew the sound of a British rifle. He followed the sound. He was at the head of his column when some Brit dropped the man next to him. Klaus went to ground shouting for his people to do likewise. He spread them out in a line and got Peter with his machine gun into action. This gave time for the Bavarian captain to arrive at the head of his mountain troops. Klaus told him there were Italians to the right, probably within a few hundred meters. Klaus wanted the mountain troops to swing left. The captain thought this sensible and set about doing so. This was the biggest firefight of Klaus's young life and he wanted to get things right.

Money-Penny heard the machinegun come into action. This was getting serious. He sent off his force of six and stayed behind for two minutes to cover the retreat. Then it was time to scoot for home. He'd delayed these Germans long enough.

Lieutenant Lars Jung had heard nothing from the messengers he'd sent out, therefore he was gathering his people to start working up on the British position. His Anglo-Saxon foe was sensibly keeping his fire to a minimum, waiting for Jung to have to expose his men during the assault. All of a sudden, he was taking machinegun fire. German machinegun fire. It could have been a captured German gun being turned on him, but why wait this long? A machinegun could have truly massacred his men in the initial contact. Shit. He had found his relief column. Now to get them to stop shooting at him.

1100 hours
18 August 1940
Chancellery conference room, Berlin

Ramcke's message reached Göring while he was still enraged at the failure to find Kesselring. His Air Force had refused a plane to his general on Sicily. Had refused to even discuss the matter. Göring was, on some levels, aware that it was his example that had created the Air Force's attitude of antagonism towards other services. Aware, but not about to let it stop his temper from going volcanic. He fired the assistant chief of staff in Sicily over the phone. Instructed him to return to Berlin to face a general court martial for dereliction of duty. The next most senior officer then had to take the call. In the meantime, one of the lieutenants at Kesselring's HQ had thought to ask the motor pool where the general's vehicle was. The general was in conference...at a luxury restaurant.

On being told of this, Göring had asked to speak to the lieutenant. Told the man he was now a major. Told him that ANYTHING Generals Jodl and Ramcke asked for was to be seen to at once. He was still shrieking twenty minutes later when Kesselring reappeared at his HQ just in time to get dismissed. The lunch guests were also dismissed. All were to join the dismissed assistant chief of staff on a plane to Berlin. Heydrich chimed in that he had a courier plane en route, so perhaps they could all take this flight back to Berlin. It was due at Gerbini in the next two hours. Heydrich looked over to Schellenberg for confirmation and the subordinate nodded.

Schellenberg had used the time to summon Göring's personal physician and General Richthofen. The sight of the two of them forced Göring to get control of his temper. He had allowed himself to become a spoiled, pampered man-child, but deep inside him lay the core of the iron-man pilot of WW1, and the man who did not waver at the Feldherrnhalle. He visibly fought to bring his temper back under control, calming his breathing as he did so. The new Führer allowed himself to be given a sedative and sent off for a "brief rest". He first promoted Richthofen to Air Marshal and left him to "sort out the administrative mess Kesselring had allowed". Richthofen was Göring's man and would rescue the dignity of the Luftwaffe.

Richthofen waited until his Führer had retired from the room and then asked the senior-most officer who had not yet been dismissed to come to the phone. It was a lieutenant colonel who had been number two in the operations section. Richthofen never had to raise his voice. He simply issued firm commands. The lieutenant colonel was in charge pending the arrival of Colonel General Alfred Keller, the hero of Budapest and formerly Kesselring's number two in the Western campaign. All parts requests from Malta were to be honored with Berlin carbon-copied to his direct attention for each request with a time stamp for when the request was received and when the part reached

The Reich Without Hitler: The Falcons of Malta

Malta. Find someone who could do the translation between British and German measurements until the NL technical section could be retrained, which would probably not be before the Egyptian campaign. Please tell the offending warehouse manager that he, Richthofen, would expect a full report by dusk today on why this situation had been handled so poorly. Three Storches were to be prepped for Sicily and Berlin notified when they left and on their arrival in Malta. Everyone at HQ was to remember that Ramcke was a Luftwaffe general and divisional commander. The air invasion was a Luftwaffe operation. Find a way to work with the Luftwaffe ground forces, or their successors would. Second Air Fleet had embarrassed their Führer and service head. Atonement would have to be made. Expect a teletype confirming all this, but do not wait for the teletype to implement these orders. He then sweetly asked the lieutenant colonel if he had any questions. The man could not wait to assure his superior that all was now in order and terminate the call.

Beck and Halder were nodding approvingly at all this. This is how proper German officers dealt with a screw-up by subordinates. Heydrich kept a bland face, but was cursing himself for not leaving Siegel at Gerbini to be his eyes and ears. He was also inwardly preening that his NL had done so well. Schellenberg was praying he had guessed right on when Siegel's plane would land.

1120 hours
18 August 1940
Malta

Klaus had gotten Peter to stop firing the machinegun so as not to injure the mountain troops. Lacking any means of communication with them, he was sensibly awaiting them making the flank attack. He saw this as one more issue he would need Strauss to train him on. One more manual to master with Greta.

Jung had given it a good five minutes. No more fire from German weapons. So, the issue was how to communicate with his "rescuers". He had an idea. He started singing the "Westerwaldlied" at the top of his lungs, while motioning others to join him. It was the most popular marching and drinking song in the German military, a part of the hazing rituals by which veteran troops welcome in the newbies. The paras of 7th Air Division had devised their own off-color variant, which every recruit had to master while drunk to have his airborne wings accepted by his new mates. The airborne troops had just finished the last verses when the flank attack began...with clearly German weapons.

The mountain captain had moved quickly, positioning his men for a flank assault on the British. They were making a lot of noise. Singing of all things. He wondered what the song was as he gave the order to advance. Pity the wind was blowing the wrong way to make out words. His men charged forward to the last words of the "Westerwalied" and the first ones of the "Horst Wessel". Oh, shit! He was attacking Germans. Naturally, his men were firing as they advanced, so it took a few minutes to bring the chaos under control. He was running up and down his line doing so when the English sniper drilled him with a carefully placed round behind his ear. His skull exploded and the attack went to ground.

Money-Penny was proud of his last shot. Bagged an officer. Pity he couldn't cut a trophy, but needs must. He quickly climbed out of the tree he had fired from and started off after his men.

Jung was still sorting out the mess with the mountain troop's number two, a first lieutenant, when some new officer in a strange cap came forward. A kid with a funny hat and a giant beside him with an MG-34. This was his rescuer? The mountain lieutenant immediately came to attention and saluted the "major". Jung could make no sense of the insignia so it must be an NL thing. He saluted as well. The "major" had clear, sensible orders. Gather his men together and return to Luqa. The "major" would supply a half-dozen of his men as guides. General Ramcke should be back from his air reconnaissance by now and wanted his men at the airfield for reorganization. Jung was surprised that Ramcke was still in charge, as Luqa was Rommel's, but more than willing to find a higher commander to take responsibility. This jump from platoon command to brigade had been taxing for him. Let someone paid for this much responsibility do some of the work!

The "major" politely asked for six of his paratroops as guides to lead his command on toward Hal Far. While this was happening, an Italian party arrived.

Lieutenant Cirillo had taken the singing as proof the fighting was over and had led his men to make rendezvous. He had fulfilled his last order. These were the missing Germans. He would report to his command that Major Steiner was leading an assault force to the left of the Italian push down the Luqa-Hal Far road. He half-wished he'd had his entire company along. Then he could have sent a platoon back with his report and gone into action with the Italian column. Having just a platoon, he started his return to his own lines. A most successful day's work. He would be sure to mention this NL Major Steiner in his report.

Chapter 47

1200 hours
18 August 1940
Sea north of Malta

Admiral Andrew Cunningham was sick of this. His fleet was scattered yet again. First, from dodging yet another mass air attack. Then from dodging volleys of torpedoes from what the lookouts reported as dozens of submarines. The sighting reports on the subs undoubtedly included many duplications. There simply hadn't been time to cross-check them. However many there were, the torpedo tracks were real. Real and far more dangerous than the bombs. The RN was being proven right with regards to the air power zealots. Hitting ships trying to evade the bombs was hard, more so for pilots untrained to the task. The submarine packs were simply volley-firing at ninety-degree angles, so that it was impossible to evade everything. By now every major ship had been hit at least once. The Battleship Malaya had eaten three fish as well as losing a turret to the crashed bomber. He'd detached it with two escorts to head back to Alex. On the way, it could take the wreck of the aircraft carrier Eagle under tow.

From preliminary reports, the damage control parties on Eagle would generate more posthumous Victoria Crosses than Rorke's Drift had. One lad had sealed a key bulkhead from the inside and drowned himself. Another had walked through live steam to turn off a key valve before falling over with the skin sloughing off his parboiled body in flashed-fried flakes. It was the lower decks of the RN at their finest. Britain had every reason to be proud. As proud as they should be of the 18 brave pilots who had died to a man defending their carrier. Died without doing much more than show bravery, as their obsolete fighters were blasted out of the sky by clouds of better planes. At least two pilots had died ramming bombers. There was no way to tell which two, so the deserved citations couldn't be written. But Eagle was a wreck that, even under tow, would be lucky to make Alex. Even then, it would only be fast patches and then on to Singapore for a full rebuild.

The truly sad part is that all these sacrifices were for precisely nothing. The Italian battle fleet had danced in front of him, drawing him on without letting him close. His gunners had given as good as they received, but no better. The Italian ships had proven to be well-schooled in gunnery. The one saving grace had been the erratic fall of their shots. Probably second-rate powder as mere poor aim wouldn't manifest that way. It would be frightening to think what the poor Eyeties could do if they could ever get their act together on procurement.

He would give this silly buggers' game another hour and then break it off. All that mattered now was saving as many men as possible on Malta.

1300 hours
18 August 1940
The burning ruins of the airfield control tower, Hal Far, Malta

Colonel Garth Mason had finally evacuated the flaming wreck of the building. He had lost more than half his assault force of the morning during the day's fighting. He'd been gifted with five new machine-gun sections. They were mostly ex-Internationals from the Spanish Civil War. MI-6 had gotten some hundreds of these out of France when that nation fell. Passed them off as Empire nationals and transited them through Spain. Transparent, but MI-6 had enough Spanish generals on the payroll. Hell, Franco had been flown to Morocco at the start of the coup by an MI-6 pilot on a British plane. So International veterans and Jews could be ferried across Spain as long as the proper palms were greased and the travelers made no commotion on the journey.

These Internationals were mostly middle-aged, but all veterans, and their hatred of Fascism made them excellent volunteers for this sort of forlorn hope. His original company had been shirkers, likely to run when fired on. They had run from Luqa and run again whenever faced with combat along the way to Hal Far. These men had the reverse problem. Unless kept under a commander's watchful eye, they would stay on their machine guns far too long. As if they didn't care much about personal survival as long as they could kill more Fascists and Nazis. The Palestinian Jews were even more determined, to the point of near suicidal.

Fleming's total force was barely over a thousand men, counting every British and Maltese detachment who had run to Hal Far for succor. On paper, that would make them a large battalion, if short on unit cohesion, but between the extra machine guns the Fleming brothers had brought from Egypt, the ones captured from the German paras, and the ones assigned to Hal Far as AAA, the battalion boasted a bit over one-hundred-and-fifty machine guns of various types—Lewis guns, Bren guns, Vickers, MG-34s, and even one American M-2 heavy gifted to the Empire by the Americans. It was no longer light infantry. It was a weapons battalion. A quite over-gunned one, and he was being allowed to fight it as one. Interlocking machine gun positions, with a second line behind to withdraw through when hard-pressed. As long as he didn't press the issue of who was ultimately in charge, the Flemings were allowing him de facto field command.

Once Money-Penny had arrived, Mason had a second weapon—a marksman platoon centered on Money-Penny and his "magic rifle". The younger Fleming had rounded up a baker's dozen with sniper-training. Money-Penny had his own specialized weapon, but the rest had Lee-Enfields, which, in competent hands, was a good sniper weapon at these ranges. The marksmen could support the forward machine gun outposts. More important, they could cover the withdrawal of each as the Italians worked their way to grenade range.

Mason had been surprised at the professionalism of these Italians, especially the colonials. He'd been told these were armed police. Not hardly. These were excellently trained and led light infantry. To Mason's eye, the Italians were a tad conservative in their approach. They were taking their time to minimize their losses, when a good hard push could have collapsed the British line several times. Then again, in the space of half a day over half of Hal Far had been lost. Luqa was already gone. It made a certain sense for the Italians to minimize their casualties. They would have the wrecked airfield by dusk at the latest.

Chapter 48

1220 hours local time/1320 hrs CET
18 August 1940
Villa of a Portuguese naval officer, suburbs of Lisbon, Portugal

The assistant Italian naval attaché was an aging lieutenant commander. He was nominally past retirement age, but had been kept on with the outbreak of war. The diplomatic posting to Lisbon suited him quite nicely. He had never personally approved of the German alliance with Italy instead of its more traditional Western orientation. His own wartime service had been against the Austrians in the Adriatic. Austria, the traditional German-speaking enemy, was the birthplace of the dead dictator Hitler, so to him, Nazi Germany was just a super-large Austria reincarnated.

Besides, on a personal level, not fighting the British avoided unpleasantness. His wife was British. So was his aunt. He'd had a year of university in England. Between relatives and his university chums, he had many English friends. He spoke excellent English. Those connections had led to today's appointment for tennis and lunch at the home of a Portuguese naval officer. The officer was some years his junior, but a relative by marriage to his aunt. This was not the first such social engagement. What had been strange was the insistence that it be this day and time. It was on short notice and the Portuguese had been almost pleading in his wording.

The lieutenant commander was not surprised to find an English officer waiting at the villa. He knew the man, a cousin by marriage to his aunt's sister's husband. Despite the war, the two had been cordial to each other when circumstances caused them to be at the same state function or sporting event. What was surprising were two other Englishmen. Englishmen who shook hands, but did not identify themselves. Who insisted this was a friendly meeting, but that no formal notes be taken. The Italian chuckled to himself. He didn't need names. The English class system let him place them well enough. The older was an aristocrat. The accent was Home Counties with a clear Oxbridge veneer. The younger was one level down, provincial squire, possibly Anglo-Irish, but definitely from the class who ran the empire under those like the older aristocrat, who was from the ruling class. They had a message for "the right people in Rome". Churchill's days as prime minister were probably numbered. Possibly months, but probably not years. The fall of Malta wouldn't finish him, but the fall of Egypt probably would. A "more sensible" government could be expected in London by New Year's at the latest. These two gentlemen were one of several groups tasked to begin preliminary discussion of terms.

The Italian mentioned that, without paperwork, he would have to pay for his travel himself. The junior Englishman understood and slid a pair of hundred pound notes across the table to cover "airfare". The Italian smiled and took his leave without his tennis game. He would, of course, brief his superiors before getting a courier flight to Rome. The no-paperwork would be honored, but that did not mean no discussion. If the Lisbon embassy moved fast, they could set Portugal up as the contact point for the peace conference instead of Switzerland. Damn, but this German entanglement might work yet.

1330 hours
18 August 1940
The original Battlegroup Schmidt/Jung positions northeast of Hal Far

Klaus was back where Jung had been that morning. Before him lay what appeared to his quite untrained eye to be an interlocking set of British light machine-gun positions. Klaus had not a clue of how one attacked such a thing and was more than aware that his men had no training to do anything more than the silly skirmishes he had been in all day. So he arranged a firing line centered on Peter with his MG-34. He told the mountain lieutenant to swing wide until he was past the British line and then hit it end on at its south end. If there was no open end, find out how far away the sea was and send a runner back to Klaus for further orders.
The mountain lieutenant understood easily. Flank attack against what he accurately judged to be a British outpost line. He was happy that this hero Storm Major was being careful of casualties in not ordering a frontal assault.

1340 hours

The Reich Without Hitler: The Falcons of Malta

18 August 1940
British positions southwest of Klaus's lines

Peter Fleming came running when he saw the shirkers leaking from Mason's old line. This force had been worthless since it arrived. Too many of the men responded to renewed German machinegun and rifle fire by abandoning the few experienced veterans his brother had used as cadre. The Internationals and Palestinians were fighting their MG-34s. The rest were fading away as fast as they could first crawl beyond the German fire and then trot off toward the beach. Fleming led his own reaction platoon at double time. His twenty men were the last reserve. Once the Germans attacked, the position would be lost. He sent runners to his brother, Mason, and Money-Penny, alerting them that this could be sauve qui peut. He wished he had a bugler with him. This seemed like something out of the Afghan Wars. What a sad, fucked-up way to die. Units trained together for a reason. You fought for men you knew. Odds-and-sods companies like this rarely performed.

1345 hours
18 August 1940
Klaus's lines

Peter Schwabe/Cohen's machinegun fire was hammering the British line. The rest of the group made odd shots, but mostly they just kept feeding him ammo from the boxes they had carried. The six airborne soldiers were firing with deliberate aim, calling out targets for Peter one by one. The British were down to three machine guns. To two. To one. The airborne sergeant in charge asked permission to lead his men forward against the last one, with Peter and the rest providing covering fire. Klaus was about to say yes, mostly because he presumed the sergeant knew what he was doing, when a runner arrived from Colonel Strauss. Strauss had not told Klaus to go after the British. Klaus had been sent to retrieve Jung's unit. He had accomplished that mission. Return at once. The airborne sergeant wanted to argue. The colonel couldn't possibly know the real situation. Klaus realized he had exceeded orders. Strauss knew best. He sent the airborne sergeant and his men to fetch up the mountain troops. Everyone was going back to Luqa as ordered. Klaus had tried to be a hero. He was happy to go back to just being Klaus.

1420 hours
18 August 1940
Formerly Mason's position, now Peter Fleming's, on the east side of the Hal Far cauldron

Former Guards Captain Peter Fleming pinched himself. The line had been gone. He and his brother had lost the battle. Yet the German fire had tapered off and then ended. They seemed to have disappeared. He had sent a section forward as recon. There was no one there. The section had heard noises to the north, but the noises were fading away. What on Earth had happened? God must love the British lion.

Chapter 49

1440 hours
18 August 1940
Hal Far

Captain Alois Schmidt had been spending his time as a prisoner helping in the hospital tents. The British had thoughtfully set these up overlooking a beach. There were no armed units around and big Red Cross flags. The nearest "military" facility were the prisoner cages. They were two hundred meters away and also marked with a big Red Cross flag. It wasn't quite the normal marking for a prisoner encampment, but so far it seemed to be working. The few Italian planes that had buzzed them had wagged their wings and flown off.

Schmidt had been amazed to have been sent for by the British commander. He had met the man earlier in the day. Some officer in the naval ground forces. Schmidt had said "Marine" and the officer had corrected him. Apparently, the British had a separate Marine Corps, which was something else again. The runner was a middle-aged German International with a working-class accent. Sounded Lower Saxon, probably Hamburg or one of the other northern ports. The man guided him to the Naval officer and the Army colonel to which he had originally surrendered. The runner served as translator, so Schmidt avoided having to use his limited French. Took five minutes of hemming and hawing before they got to the point. The British expected to lose the airfield before dusk. When this happened, they wanted Schmidt to go forward under a white flag and arrange a safe handover of the hospital tents. They expected Schmidt to guarantee fair treatment for the Empire wounded. Alois was on firm ground answering. There had been direct orders on this from Führer Göring. All the rules of war were to be observed, even on Jews, colored, or whatever. The International seemed dubious on this. Schmidt just told the man not to be a fool. If he surrendered, claim he had emigrated before 1933. There were German colonies of expats in much of the world. He was in British uniform. Just give a false name and claim to be from Canada. There were no SS on Malta. No Gestapo. In British uniform he'd be treated as a military prisoner, more so as, given the location, the prisoners would probably be taken to Sicily and remain in Italian custody. The airborne division operational plan did not include formal prisoner-of-war arrangements. The instruction was proper treatment and then dump the job on the Italians.

1520 hours
18 August 1940
Hal Far

Money-Penny's marksmen were covering the withdrawal from the last defenders of the wrecked airport buildings. The Italians were still being careful in their advance, but by this time they had a few howitzers and what seemed like two batteries of mortars as support. The British had no guns of any sort for counterbattery. Most of the men would get off in time to the next set of positions 50 meters or so behind the two burning hangers. This meant abandoning two more of the Vickers heavy machine guns. The lone American M-2 had been lost half an hour ago. The damned Vickers HMGs were good weapons, but too heavy for quick redeployment. And yet again, he had the same problem. The crews simply refused to abandon the weapons. Even with his own excellent cover fire, there was simply no way to avoid having the Italians work their way within grenade range. Pity. These were good men. Men who would be needed for Egypt. But when a man decides to die in battle, there was damned little an officer could do about it but help them slaughter as large an honor guard as possible for the march to Hell. The Italians rolled over both guns roughly at once. Grenades, then a brief action with trench knives, rifle butts, and pistols. In a few minutes, the same guns would be turned around and firing on him. Sod this whole stupid battle. It was long past time to be off to the boats.

1600 hours
18 August 1940
Seas north of Malta

Admiral Raeder was leading his S-boat squadron out to battle. Six Italian small craft were accompanying him. The seas were slightly choppy with a steady wind from the south. He knew he was leading a death ride, but it was the salvation of his reputation. It was also the final sortie for honor denied the Navy in 1918 by the Red November criminals. It was not exactly suicide, so his stern Lutheranism was not offended. His men accepted his order in good cheer. No shirkers or cowards here. He had kept the Navy pure, even in wartime. As he passed the Italian battlefleet, they radioed him luck and provided a smokescreen. Raeder had thought little of Hitler's Italian alliance. He had been wrong. These were worthy allies fighting bravely. He would not have fought their battle-line in the manner they were, but Raeder recognized the professionalism of their ship-handling and gunnery. He sent one final message for retransmission to Berlin stating what he proposed to accomplish. There was no need to add personal details. Those who knew him would understand and the rest were vermin who didn't matter. However, he did get one last blow in. Instead of ending the message "Heil Göring", he signed off "Hoch Der Kaiser".

1610 hours
18 August 1940
Conference room, Chancellery, Berlin

The latest message from Malta came via the Italians, and had actually gone to the War Ministry instead of to SS HQ. One section referenced Lieutenant Cirillo's report of his meeting with the NL Major Steiner. The two army generals, Halder and Beck, passed over this detail, focusing on the bigger picture of an emerging victory. Halder even was gentleman enough to congratulate Heydrich on the success of his plan and of his creation, the NL. Heydrich made the usual pro forma replies, then told Schellenberg to follow-up with a congratulatory message to his senior officers on Malta. Schellenberg took that as a cue to get the story of how Lieutenant Steiner was now a Major.

1630 hours
18 August 1940
Golf Course by the Grand Harbor

The last tankette was burning on the fifth green. The air stank with the roasted pork smell of fried human, as the crew had been trapped inside. In another few seconds, the ammo would start to cook off. Rommel had joined the rest of his depleted spearhead in the half-bunker formed by the sand trap behind the green. It was two meters below the flat surface of the grass around the burning tank. The lip of the trap provided cover against the British fire.

The fighting had not gone well. He was gaining ground against a superior force, but losing men faster than that office boy Ramcke was pushing reinforcements forward. If Rommel fully lost the initiative, he could be pushed all the way back off the golf course…again. It had already happened twice. The holdup this time seemed to be a platoon strongpoint in the rough off the fifth fairway. It was centered on a Boys antitank rifle and two Vickers machineguns. Rommel needed to put fire on the position sufficiently in order to lead a storm group in to take it out with grenades. He needed the mortar battery to his rear to shift fires. The problem was that it meant a 150-meter dash across the green and the sixth fairway. A dash over space that British snipers clearly had zeroed in.

"Let me, sir!" The Italian boy offering had passible German. These young cadets had proven clueless, but fearless. Rommel had also expended them fairly rapidly. He had only two left and the other's poor German made communication difficult. Rommel wrote quick instructions for whoever commanded the mortars. They had originally been Italians from some mountain unit, but Ramcke's haphazard reinforcements had not respected unit integrity or even common nationality. The guns were still Italian 45mm mortars, but who was manning them was an open question. The Germans and Italians had worked well together despite the intermixing of units and the usual battlefield chaos. Rommel had come out of 1917 with contempt for the Italians as soldiers. Other than the Arditi, they had seemed useless. This new Fascist generation were worthy comrades in arms.

Turning to the lad, Rommel scribbled out the new fire coordinates. He then explained them to the young man. Rommel had a terrain eye for battlefields. He could visualize how the target would appear from where the mortars were and gave visual cues to pass along to the platoon commander. He patted the lad on the shoulder and off the youngster ran. The kid must have been an athlete as a school boy. He ran low to the ground, zig-zagging to throw off the British marksmen. That got him fifty meters before the bullet hit his shoulder…and down he fell. Rommel shrugged. Men are lost in war. He had just started briefing the last remaining cadet when the first one raised to a crouch and lurched forward again. Made it twenty more meters before he took a round to his leg and again went down.

The bullet to the shoulder had hurt. Then the arm went numb. The one in his leg felt like heaven's fire was coursing through it. He wanted to scream, to cry. This war was supposed to be an adventure. Instead he'd seen friends die. Now he could feel the life ebbing from his young body. He couldn't let it be for nothing. One arm still worked. He extended it forward, used his fingers like claws to get a purchase and then used the remaining still-working leg to push off. He'd moved a bit. Time to repeat it. Centimeter by centimeter he was moving. The bullets kept coming. One eventually took his ear off. What need did a corpse have of ears? A few more meters. Another broke his jaw. What need had the dead of speech?

Rommel watched in awe. Meter by meter the near-dead young man slithered. Bullet by bullet he took hits, stopped for some tens of seconds and then started his slow progress again. By all rights, the hero should be in shock, should have bled out, should be dead. But he still moved and, somehow, he was still on-line to reach the mortars. He was ever closer to that position. He couldn't see it that low to the ground, but some iron will keep him pointing true.

If the pain before had been heaven's fire, what he felt now was orders of magnitude worse. His jaw was mostly gone. Meant he couldn't disgrace himself by screaming like a child. He would die a man. Another centimeter. Just once more. He thought he could hear voices now. Must be the ear on the ground. Maybe angels? The thought made him try to laugh, which cost him pain and blood. So what? The pain would end soon. Suddenly there were hands on his body. He tried to shout "Viva L'Italia!" but all that came out was a new spray of blood. With his last dying strength, he handed whoever it was the note from Rommel. Mission accomplished. Now he could die.

Rommel had been transfixed by this bloody progress. He still didn't see how anything human could have done what he'd witnessed. But somehow it had worked. The mortars had shifted fire. Rommel sprinted out of the sand trap, his storm party behind him. Time to redeem what the hero's sacrifice had paid for. The timing was perfect. The storm party reached the British just as the mortars ceased fire. Rommel's grenade was the first of a dozen that landed on top of the defenders. The machine-pistol fire and trench knives then finished them off. Rommel called forward his main party. Time to flush out the snipers and try to finally reach the clubhouse.

Chapter 50

1650 hours
18 August 1940
Seas north of Malta

The initial S-Boat squadron attack had come from near due west, out of the setting sun. That had limited British spotting, as had the smoke. However, the largest British problem was that, by pure chance, Raeder had timed his attack just after Cunningham had given the Copenhagen execute order. This required the British fleet split in two with the remaining battle line and a few escorts headed back to Egypt while Cunningham with bulk of the cruisers led the rest to the Grand Harbor on Malta. The Copenhagen order file had many contingencies, but not a fleet as scattered as this one was by prior torpedo attacks and air strikes. The S-boats and their smaller Italian compatriots charged into chaos for their death ride. Mostly they died, but they added a few more hits and a truckload of chaos.

Any concept that Raeder was commanding a squadron collapsed during this. The torpedo boats fought as individual ships and the former Grand Admiral was reduced to doing the job of a twenty-something lieutenant. As if he cared. He would die as a warrior even if deprived of command. As the High Seas Fleet should have died in 1918 but for the mutinies of the Red traitors.

Fifteen minutes of furious action found Raeder's S-Boot, S-22, badly damaged—no more radio, the guns on deck either shot away or out of ammo, all torpedoes fired, with the exception of one torpedo reload, where some stray round had destroyed the torpedo's engine, leaving them only with a warhead. He had fought gloriously, but he was still alive. That was unacceptable. Miraculously, the engines still worked, the hull still held together, and the pumps were—barely—keeping up with the water. So, S-22 was seaworthy enough for a last sortie, for Raeder to find an honorable death. Admiral Raeder ordered his remaining crew to pull the forward half of the remaining torpedo and tie it to the bow railing with the torpedo fuse protruding over the bow. Then he ordered all crew off board, but was refused. This was a handpicked crew. They knew what they volunteered for. The German fleet, not just their admiral, must recover its honor. The story of the Navy's demotion by Göring rankled. Their service was still living with the shame of the 1918 mutinies, of the failures in the Great War. Malta must be the start of the Navy's resurrection, not a victory of the Army and Air Force alone.

The Admiral was adamant that they follow his order and abandon ship. The lieutenant who, before the Admiral's arrival had actually commanded S-22, seconded this. He announced that he and the ensign would stay with one senior boatswain. The rest tearfully went over the side to the waiting life raft. As S-22 roared off, they saluted their comrades. S-22 bored in on the British cruiser HMAS Sydney, weaving between the geysers from its secondary four-inch dual-purpose guns. The British captain tried to turn bow on, to comb the torpedo he expected to be launched. The boatswain had anticipated this and twisted past the turning bow to ram the cruiser near the stern.

Sydney rocked from an explosion as the dead torpedo hit just in front of the propeller shafts. Damage to the propellers and rudder left the cruiser turning in slow circles. That and the developing fires on board distracted the crew sufficiently that the cruiser was finished off by S-19 a few minutes later. The remains of S-22's crew, adrift in the raft, saw it all. When S-19 looped back to rescue them, they had tears in their eyes from the patriotic sacrifice they had witnessed.

1700 hours
18 August 1940
Remains of base command center, Hal Far

Captain Alois Schmidt advanced slowly under a white flag. He had waved it from cover for almost ten minutes before the Italians noticed it sufficiently to cease firing. He had then slowly stood up, hoping his Italian allies would notice his Luftwaffe para uniform. Step by step across the now mostly-silent battlefield he walked, waiting for a proper officer to come forward. Eventually, he reached the Italian lines, where a young second lieutenant greeted him in passable schoolboy German. Schmidt shook hands and asked that senior officers be summoned.

Finding those in turn consumed precious minutes. Finally, a Lieutenant Colonel Goffredo Tonini arrived, with several Libyan askaris in attendance. Schmidt didn't speak Italian, but had passable French. Tonini spoke some French, more than sufficiently for military matters. Communication happened, but there was a problem on concepts.

Alois had been sent forward by the British to accomplish two things. The first was relatively simple. The front, such as it still remained of one, was approaching the field hospital. The hospital had wounded from all three armies. The British could not evacuate these men. They wished a truce to have the hospital change hands. To preserve continuity of care the doctors of both nationalities, British and Maltese, and British orderlies would remain and surrender. Most of the orderlies were German prisoners as were over half the wounded. The British wished a truce to cover this transaction. The truce would cover the airfield, the RNAS station, adjacent beaches, and a five-kilometer circle around the original Hal Far control tower. Tonini had no problem with this. His problem was with the second linked proposal. The British had some thousand Axis prisoners. Less than a hundred were Italian and somewhat more than two hundred of the Germans were working in the field hospital. The British were offering the other eight hundred or so prisoners back in return for a longer truce. A truce that would give them time to flee out to sea.

The British commanders had prepped Schmidt with a concept from an earlier age of warfare, the honors of war. A defeated but still fighting garrison was offered the opportunity to retreat with their weapons under terms rather than engage in a bloody last stand. Tonini was failing to see where such quaint notions fit into modern warfare. Schmidt wanted higher command contacted. Tonini felt that his superiors would think he had lost his mind even considering such an absurd request. Tonini and Schmidt both worried that the problem might be in translation. Fortunately, a German-speaking reserve lieutenant was found. This Lieutenant Vincenzo Pentangeli had learned German and English while living with relatives in the Bronx some years back, but had returned home to do his patriotic duty.

A combat officer would have been defeated in Schmidt's position. A captain does not push a lieutenant colonel on matters of basic military etiquette. Schmidt's combat experience was a few hours on Malta. His skills were as an administrative weasel in the bureaucracy of the Air Ministry. Accordingly, he asked Tonini if a different approach could work. Accept the truce to gain the hospital. Then, everyone takes their time logging in every person in the hospital. Make an administrative slow walk out of assembling lists of people, checking against their military ID to be sure the lists were accurate, verifying that every patient's file was attached to a proper record of his personal handover. If this didn't take enough time, the British could start sending over prisoners in lots of fifty. Each of them would need to be ID'd, logged in, given a medical check.

Tonini was a skilled combat officer. He knew military red tape. Like all combat officers, he detested such administrative busywork, but he was aware of just how slow this could all be if everyone involved was moving at a peacetime pace. If the paperwork covering three separate militaries was done with meticulous care, it could consume days not hours. Besides, he had been fighting this British force all day. They had too many machine guns. His men were elite professionals, the product of years of training. To waste them on attritional butcher's work was a crime. Schmidt's subterfuge would suffice to cover Tonini's report to higher authority. Italy needed a victory on Malta and taking Hal Far was that victory. He sent Schmidt back to get a British officer to sign the "truce". Schmidt returned with a naval officer named Money-Penny. Money-Penny spoke excellent Italian. He also had a pint of good, aged scotch for the three officers to toast the battle. Tonini felt this Money-Penny was a proper British gentleman and would honor the understanding. Money-Penny went further, saying he would return the Italian prisoners first as a gesture of good faith. Tonini was finding himself liking this more civilized approach to warfare. He would prepare a memo in his after-action report, justifying what he had done and claiming it as precedent for the future. Right now he wanted a picture of the British officer saluting the raising of the Italian flag over the wreckage of the building. Money-Penny was most happy to oblige.

Near-dusk
18 August 1940
Seas north of Malta

The naval battle was over. The English battlefleet had left. Its two squadrons had stopped taking air strikes maybe thirty minutes ago. These late-day attacks had done little damage, but had confirmed that the British were no longer operating as a single unit. Air units tended to be abysmal on ship recognition. All that the contradictory reports agreed on were that fewer ships were tracking east-southeast than south-southeast. Then again, based on prior air reports, the combined Axis bomber forces had sunk the British Mediterranean Fleet three times over today. Five times over in battleships and seven times over in carriers.

The Italian battle fleet was retiring on Naples, towing its cripples behind them. Naples had far better repair facilities than Taranto. The fleet had need of them.

The admiral in charge was unwilling to spare any of his escorting destroyers for cleanup, so what was slowly plodding through the wreckage of the sea battle were the few surviving torpedo boats and some minor Italian coastal escort vessels. They had been fishing survivors out of the water for three-quarters of an hour. British, Italian, German...none of that mattered at this point. It was men, often hurt or wounded, to be saved from the sea. The MAS boat was not really suited for deep-water service but the sea was fairly calm and the need great. The crew was using their searchlight in the fading daylight when they spotted the life raft. They eased the MAS slowly up, and were surprised to discover two aircrew. The Italian was wounded. The Britisher was not. Both seemed more inebriated than exhausted by their ordeal afloat. Then again, the three large empty Chianti demijohns with their characteristic basketwork covering in the raft made it apparent how they had passed their time. The Englishmen helped them transfer the Italian over. He saw the Italian boat crew eyeing him strangely. He asked. One of the crew had once lived in Liverpool and had a bit of English. Turned out he was the only British aircrew recovered so far. The Swordfish pilot sadly shook his head. Said a small prayer softly for his squadron mates whose young lives had been wasted by old fools. He spent the rest of the night helping fish sailors out of the dark waters. It was, to him, a fitting end to a squalid, futile day.

Dusk
18 August 1940
RNAS, Malta
Second Lieutenant Vincenzo Pentangeli took charge of the last fifty German airborne prisoners from the British naval officer Money-Penny. The Brit was a proper gentleman and everything in the agreement was followed to the letter. The Italians had all the prisoners and the British had not done any last-minute

demolitions. Even the arms and equipment they had left behind had been undamaged. Pentangeli had volunteered to return to the colors for this British war. The disgrace of Italy's Alpine campaign had wounded his nationalist pride, his and many other good Italian patriots. He had been lucky in his posting. He'd had parachute training, mostly because it had seemed an exciting, virile thing to do while serving his original two years. Through family connections, he had secured a placement with the Libyan airborne unit. Probably his two languages, German and English, had helped with this, but mostly it was the usual matter of knowing the right people to call on his behalf.

The British officer shook his hand and joked that they would meet again in Egypt or Palestine. Vincenzo was not privy to high-level secret war plans, but geography made those two places obvious. He saluted as the Britisher and his last dozen men pushed their sailboat away from the ruined dock and raised the sail. This sort of war seemed a grand adventure, not the endless horror show that his father and uncles told of along the Isonzo in the last war. He was going to see the pyramids and the Nile as a conqueror, not a tourist. Fascism had truly restored Italy to its Roman glory.

Money-Penny helped Sergeant Billy to raise the sail. The 18th-century formalities had worked. Most of Fleming's men were undoubtedly already boarding the armed merchant ship that was three kilometers out to sea. Money-Penny had been told they would wait for him. He didn't believe it. He was the last by more than an hour, and the ship's captain would want every minute of darkness in the short summer night to get further east toward Alex. No matter. He knew his navigation. He'd kept the most seaworthy fishing boat for himself and filled it with water jugs. He'd make Alex on his own. Malta had been a defeat however London would spin it. Egypt was likely to be the same. The British lion was in for a rough season.

As he tacked beyond the harbor mouth, the wind swung from its normal southern orientation to the west. Right where he needed it for the run to Alex. Stranger still, the west wind was blowing hot. He laughed to himself at it. A demon wind for a season in Hell. He took it as an omen that his luck was in, even if his nation's was not. He would serve his own interests well in his nation's hour of darkness. He'd recruit his villains and be the demon lord of the British retreat. The wind must have approved because it gained in strength, surging his boat over the darkening seas.

Chapter 51

2030 hours
18 August 1940
Grand Harbor, Malta

It had been just after dusk when the lead ship entered the Grand Harbor. Cunningham on Kent had been third ship in. The unseasonable west wind was blowing smoke from the day's airstrikes across the harbor. Of more importance, the squadron was short two cruisers and three destroyers from a combination of battle losses and the need for tow ships. Additionally, an armed merchant vessel had been diverted south to pick up the commandos. The Flemings had at last found a working radio and established contact with both Cunningham and Army command. The reduced squadron size was the barest minimum needed for the evacuation, and that only if everything ran smoothly.

Smoothly? The Army had done nothing to properly prepare. Their engineers were supposed to have cleared the harbor of wrecks, to have the docks in some semblance of working order. Neither had been done. The troops were supposed to be concentrated to begin immediate embarkation. They weren't. There was supposed to be a firm count of how many men were coming. Instead, there turned out to be approximations of ration strength and no idea where precisely the missing men were. The Army staff people had excuses. Fighting at the golf course, at Ta Kali, elsewhere on the island. The phone network totally nonfunctional. Axis air superiority. Excuses. Excuses wouldn't make the night any longer. Cunningham argued. He pleaded. Nothing seemed to make them take the situation fully seriously. Malta was a tiny island. Communication by runner was certainly possible. Possible, but not done to the extent needed. It was a rule-book, peacetime, staff-centered mentality that it seemed nothing could penetrate. The loading started, both on the remaining docks and by small boat to ships anchored in the harbor. It was going too slowly and the lines of waiting men were getting longer, not shorter.

2050 hours
18 August 1940

The Reich Without Hitler: The Falcons of Malta

Club House of Malta Golf Course

The British were pulling off and Rommel was not inclined
to pursue. His mixed national, mixed service force was a wreck.
He was almost out of ammunition. His people were exhausted.
They needed a night for rest and to reorganize into coherent
formations. As is, he was amazed the British were conceding the
golf course. One good push would have driven him back again,
given their superior numbers.

He was out of officer cadets, but had found two Italian
lieutenants who spoke enough German to act as liaisons. Rommel
shook his head at the feats those cadets had performed. If Italy
had had heroes like this at Caporetto, they would never have lost
that battle. In the meantime, he found another German walking-
wounded to take yet another written message to Luqa, to Ramcke.
The office boy general wasn't sending forward men and supplies
fast enough. Where were these going instead of to support
himself, the obvious main thrust?

2130 hours
18 August 1940
HMS Kent, Grand Harbor, Malta

The Governor General and his senior staff were, by now, on
board Cunningham's flagship. Cunningham was not impressed at
how many "important people" and flunkies there were. All these
badges of rank and no one could still answer the key questions.
How many men were coming? When would they all be here?
He would have loved to have just sailed away, but refused to let
the brave rank-and-file pay for the sins of their leaders. Those
poor men must be saved somehow. For now, he was reduced to
sending naval officers ashore to try to get answers, to get some
sense of urgency. Dawn was a few minutes before 0600. His ships
must be well clear by then. Could not these pompous fools see
this?

2220 hours
18 August 1940
Luqa, Malta

"He asked about the insignia, not Klaus's rank. My German

is poor, but I know the difference between those two words. Insignia. The piece of cloth we sewed on Klaus's new cap." Greta was defensive, but definite. Something had gone wrong and Berlin was upset with her...again. She was trying so hard to be a strong, adult woman. What had she done wrong now? An officer asked her a question and she gave a civil, accurate reply. This military nomenclature was tricky to a teenaged civilian.

Strauss had quizzed her carefully in Yiddish. He had called over her Uncle to be sure he grasped the fine points. Berlin wanted answers on why the Italians were praising MAJOR Steiner. Wanted to know when and why he had been promoted. Only he hadn't been. The Italian lieutenant was unreachable. The mountain lieutenant had been located. His unit had been forwarded on to Ta Kali but now had radios. The mountain officer had confirmed that his dead captain had named Steiner as a major. The same dead captain Greta had spoken to.

Strauss decided to use Ploiesti as his guide. The key was not lying to Schellenberg and Heydrich. They would get the raw truth, as unfortunate as it was. Better to take whatever punishment they thought he deserved than risk getting caught in lies with people that highly placed.

2400 hours
18 August 1940
HMS Thunderchild, Grand Harbor, Malta

Jutland Scott was not surprised at the chaotic sloth of the loading process. It was everything he had seen on his prior Malta runs, redoubled, vulnerable, and in spades. The Army couldn't organize a mess party in a whore house. Indeed, he had seen Army types bringing tarts in pieces of British uniform on, claiming they were ATS or WRENs. As if. Those ladies had full uniforms and proper British accents. They were also boarding with dogs, cats, officer's luggage, and, in one case, an attempt to take a favorite horse. Trying to enforce a British-only policy provoked near-riots and the Army officers supported their men. Some even encouraged these acts of disobedience. This was going to end badly. His ship was swarming with embarked men to the point where most below-deck corridors were impassible. The other ships in harbor looked as bad and the lines waiting to board looked worse than they had at sunset. Surely Cunningham wasn't a complete idiot. Yet, Scott's two requests to get under way had been rudely rebuffed. The original order had the squadron leaving port as a unit. Little ships like Thunderchild were slower than the fleet cruisers and destroyers. There was no way they could keep up on a high-speed dash for Alex. Insane. What did an original plan matter when the facts changed?

0300 hours
19 August 1940
Luqa, Malta

General Ramcke had actually been sent an intact battalion. It was a machine-gun unit from Jodl's brigade under a one-armed commander, a Major Maurice. The one that was supposed to be the first reinforcements from Sicily, only somehow it hadn't been. The man was an Army and Freikorps veteran in an SA uniform. Maurice was not from his branch. Maurice had been artillery. Ramcke had been Navy and then infantry before transfer to the Air Force. However, both had been Freikorps and thus had past friends in common. Friends from twenty years ago, but still a basis for some bond of common good feeling and mutual understanding beyond the usual respect of officers for others of their caste.

A separate machine-gun battalion was unusual, but when Jodl had reorganized his two battalions with weapons that could actually be transported to Malta, he had created one battalion each of mortars and machine guns to simplify administration. The whole unit was a hasty kludge down to the last-minute change in weapons.

With Hal Far secured by the Italians and Ta Kali mostly secured by the battlegroup that had dropped there, aided by the reinforcements Ramcke had sent, the logical place for Maurice's machine-gunners was to reinforce Rommel. This galled Ramcke. Everything about Rommel was annoying. Hence this discussion on whether Maurice thought he could manage to take his unit north to Ta Kali and form the core of a second drive on the harbor. Maurice was willing, but dubious. His unit was barely trained. They could fire their weapons and had good morale. They would fight. Whether they could handle maneuvering down secondary roads that in many cases were scarcely better than game trails in the dark was a challenge Maurice felt was simply beyond his men in their current state of training. Oh, well, best to go by a commander's view of the limitations of his men, more so when the man seemed a competent professional. Nothing for it but to send them down the road to Rommel.

0530 hours
19 August 1940
Air over Luqa

The Ju- 88 squadron had taken off in the dark. It was badly understrength after yesterday's actions against the British fleet. The squadron had lost no planes but many came home with sufficient damage to sideline them for today. So, it was a squadron in name, but seven planes in practice. They had found Malta by homing in on the Luqa tower radio. The Luftwaffe signals people had cranked up the wattage on one transmitter as a navigation aide. The Luqa staff were using American big band music on the frequency. The music was officially forbidden, but remained popular. Their excuse was that the British had left the records behind when possession changed hands.

The planes were armed with anti-personnel bombs. Some Army general near the ports had gotten a working radio and was demanding dawn air strikes. Luqa control directed the Ju 88s to a holding pattern east of their airport, so as not to interfere with the transport airlift that had been going on all night. Pre-flight briefing said all three airfields were now in friendly hands, but only Luqa was functional. One of the Ju 88s had a green pilot. He drifted east on the racetrack pattern. Attracted AAA from the port area. He got back out of range quickly, but claimed he saw multiple British ships firing from the harbor.

0540 hours
19 August 1940
Grand Harbor, Malta

Cunningham was sick to his stomach. AAA fire meant gun crews. Meant these idiots still hadn't called in everyone. The lines at the piers were starting to shrink, but who hadn't been given the order to regroup to the docks? A few rearguards would have had to be left, but if AAA, what else had been omitted? The Army staff people had looked puzzled when he screamed at them. Started buck-passing right in front of him. Convoluted arguments on procedures, personalities, lines of authority. Cunningham would cheerfully have hanged the lot of them...but those poor, brave men waiting for embarkation. How could he let the RN fail them?

Scott's patience was at an end. His ship was packed. He could hear the bomber. He could see the ack-ack guns firing. He ordered Thunderchild's engines started. His executive officer screamed at him that this was against orders, that they must await the signal. Scott shouted him down. There was a duty to the ship, to the crew, to the embarked men. Lines were cast off and Thunderchild backed into the harbor. He had the radio shop notify flagship of his decision and turned Thunderchild for the harbor mouth and Alex.

Cunningham was frozen. Scott was doing the right thing. He knew it. Knew it and simply could not give the order. He silently prayed that the other captains would see the little escort leave and follow his example. But the Admiral could not give the order. The RN simply couldn't let those poor brave lads down. Night-flying was uncommon. Surely he had a bit more time, could save a few more. Surely, hopefully. What a sad, sick way for this all to end.

0550 hours
19 August 1940
Club House, Golf Course, Malta

Major Maurice arrived to meet his new commander just in time to see said General Rommel throwing a fit over the radio. He'd just been told his dawn air strike was diverting to hit British ships in the harbor. Rommel was not accepting that anything had a higher priority. Sicily was quoting Generals Keller and Jodl, reminding Rommel just how small a fish he really was. Maurice let it play out, then offered to contact Jodl himself. Rommel became attentive. Maurice said he was a direct report to Jodl and would ask for priority on sending the mortar battalion from Jodl's brigade. Good French 60mm mortars with eager crews who were good enough to replace air support. A few messages back and forth accomplished this. The mortars could be up to the lines by early afternoon. Rommel was somewhat mollified by all this and welcomed Maurice aboard.

Dawn
19 August 1940
Grand Harbor, Malta

The man on the dock seemed a Colonel Blimp out of a David Low cartoon. He was somewhat short, quite rotund, and well past military retirement age. His brigadier's uniform was out of Edwardian India and seemed tailored for a man a few centimeters taller and perhaps fifty pounds lighter, which the officer might well have been when on active service in the distant past. His slouching frame was more suitable to an armchair than any form of public exercise. He was attended by an equally aged Sikh batman also in India Army uniform, and a somewhat younger Chinese servant carrying his ample luggage on a cart. The Indian had the officer's shotgun case and an umbrella.

Admiral Cunningham stared at him, wondering where this caricature had materialized from. It was a fitting punctuation point to an absurd situation. Then again, this was a retired officer and could not be rightly blamed for the fiasco the serving commanders had made of this entire operation. Cunningham was cursing them all and Churchill with them when he heard the ack-ack start again.

The Ju 88 was most unsuitable as a dive bomber. However, General Udet, now deceased, had insisted on this characteristic. So, the seven planes dived onto the largest target they could find, which in this case was HMS Kent. They had general-purpose bombs, not armor piercing. All they should have done was kill people on the packed decks. However, the ship was both extremely overcrowded and at dock. Docked meant it was a stationary target. Packed with men meant the hatches were open for ventilation. One bomb went down a hatch leading to a magazine two decks below. Three bombers went into the harbor from AAA. The other four barely made emergency landings at Luqa. One was a total write-off and the other three were dead until Luftwaffe ground crews with proper parts inventories could arrive.

HMS Kent blew up with a spectacular roar. Humans, live and dead, whole and in pieces, were flung into the air and all over the harbor. A turret sailed clear off to impact a harbor warehouse... actually the bombed-out remains of one. The ship's back broke and it settled quickly on the bottom.

The retired brigadier still had a command voice. As the remaining men stood stunned, he shouted out orders to cast off lines from the ships still docked. NCOs knew an officer's command. They also knew the key military adage—do something. They gathered work parties. Lines were cast off and the fleet prepared to depart. Under the general's orders survivors were fished out of the harbor, fires put out, and the dead gathered for burial. He was still barking firm, sensible orders twenty minutes later when Colonel Kevin Duffy came upon him. Duffy's men had been ignored in the chaos. He had marched his men to the port on his own authority.

The brigadier coolly looked him over and asked what regiment he was from. Duffy himself was Welsh Guards. His men weren't, but Duffy understood the question. The general was asking for Duffy's personal status. Guards officers were important people. Territorials were not. "Guards. Good. I'll organize this lot. Need you to get a white flag to Fritz. Time to pack it in. I'm not active service. The German will want someone current to give the surrender."

"Surrender?"

"Fleet's leaving. Stayed too long as is. This farce is over. No need to get good men killed for nothing. But insist on dealing with someone of rank. Wouldn't do to have a British colony surrendered to a lieutenant or captain. Between the Germans and Eyeties there must be a general officer. Ask for medical supplies. We have burn cases here. Now, off you go, my good man. Don't worry about responsibility. It's mine. I'll write a nice note for your personnel file confirming responsibility once we are all safely in prison camp."

Duffy looked the old fool over, shrugged, and trotted off to do as he was told. First sensible order he'd been given since he was sent to this stupid island. Besides, a man like this probably knew half a dozen MPs and an undersecretary to send letters to as well. The notes would help Duffy's career. There was always an after to any war, and the same damned people ran things, victory or defeat.

Chapter 52

0700 hours
19 August 1940
Conference room, Chancellery, Berlin

As ever, his three fellow members of the junta saw nothing in Heydrich excusing himself to leave the room to deal with yet another "administrative matter". In the nearly two months of the regime's existence, they had all grown quite used to Heydrich doing all the scut work of government and Party. They saw themselves as sensibly focusing on the big-picture demands of governance.

Heydrich had had a long night. Malta and the entire southern strategy were his creation. If they failed, he would get 300% of the blame. That they were succeeding—and in no small measure doing so because of his creation, the NL—was in turn cementing his position as de facto head of government. However, the stress was showing, even on a brilliant workaholic such as himself. Schellenberg saw himself as providing a useful diversion with these semi-comic reports of Strauss's antics.

Schellenberg had just finished briefing him on Major Steiner's promotion. "So, it was all a mistake of the fake Aryan mistress, this Schwabe person?" Heydrich shared a small chuckle with his aide. "This Ukrainian insignia, get drawings. It is now the official NL badge of the rank of major. Also, get drawings of the cap. It is now official NL officer's headgear. Steiner's unit is to be raised to a battalion for Egypt. Have Eichmann send a thousand of these Betar from Nowa Huta. Have someone track down two dozen German-Jewish language teachers to educate Strauss's command in proper German. They don't have to be able to have literary discussions. They damned well will be taught enough fluency to avoid mistakes such as this in the future." Heydrich stopped for a minute in thought. "Have three more of these caps made. Highest-quality materials. One for each of us and one for Führer Göring. The Führer loves fancy uniforms. Time to make him a field marshal in the NL with a velvet cap of rank. Also, find out what does 'baseball cap' mean." Heydrich was getting into the joyous spirit of this. Victory felt divine. "Schellenberg, you will go to Malta yourself. I want this done right. Steiner's unit is now official.

It is the Malta battalion." He thought of Strauss, this useful tool that had presented himself. He'd never met the man, but knew him as a type: ruthless, opportunistic, ambitious, and capable. "Have Strauss find some more formal name of the type military men favor—eagles or lions or something. Have some sort of formal uniform pin made for the veterans of this operation. The propaganda ministry can have a field day with it. Our regime's Romeo has won the Iron Cross First Class with his Juliet by his side. He will now conquer the pyramids and subjugate King Tut."

0815 hours
19 August 1940
The ruins of the golf course clubhouse, Malta

Colonel Duffy had been pleasantly surprised by this General Rommel. The German had agreed to a proper handover ceremony, had accepted a long-retired brigadier as senior commander for signatory purposes, had agreed to a Maltese Red Cross presence to guarantee an accurate list of POWs. He had even arranged for transport of the British wounded by air to Sicily. Rommel hadn't been able to do much about medical supplies. The Germans were short of those themselves, but he'd sent doctors and orderlies through the lines to assist in treatment. Everything had been quite proper, a touch Edwardian, but that fit the aged brigadier. The man seriously couldn't be THAT old, but then why the uniform-styling? Duffy laughed. He'd have a long time in the prisoner camp to learn the man's full biography. There would be jack all else to do.

Right now, there was a bit of symbolism to see to. A British work party had rebuilt the clubhouse flag pole. A second party had located an intact Union Jack. It had been run up the flag pole. Then, with the propaganda cameras rolling, it had been run down and the Italian flag run up while everyone saluted both banners. The senior officers then shook hands. Rommel and the brigadier reenacted the signing of the surrender document. The brigadier lamented that he lacked a sword to hand over, but was allowed to do an on-camera turnover of his prized custom hunting shotgun. He then gave a five-minute speech on the glories of the Empire and the special characteristics of the weapon, down to what sorts of small game it was best suited for. A speech in grammatically perfect German delivered to the waiting microphones. Meanwhile, a senior sergeant was filmed properly folding the Union Jack, which the British leader then ceremoniously handed to Rommel as a trophy of war. All that was missing was a feast and a round of toasts to make this something out of the time of George II. Duffy wearily shook his head trying to repress the thought that Churchill would have fit the 18th century much better than the 20th.

Chapter 53

1400 hours
19 August 1940
Conference room, Chancellery, Berlin

Führer Herman Göring rarely concerned himself with actual governance. He had Heydrich for that. However, when he chose to exert himself, he was quite competent. This day of victory was one of those rare moments. "Gentlemen." He paused to look his three colleagues in the eye one by one. "Our strategy worked. We have a victory, on our own and without Adolph the deceased. We have our dead heroes: my dearest fallen comrade General Udet and Admiral Raeder. Udet died as he should have, a great pilot performing an impossible feat to damage an enemy battleship. We have live heroes, such as Rommel and this Major Steiner."

War Minister Beck started to cut in, to object at belittling the Army. Göring plowed in over him, cutting him off and drowning him out. "Yes, War Minister, I am sure the Army has other heroes from the mountain division, the one you so belatedly supplied. I'm sending Jodl to Sicily on an inspection tour. He can find you a dozen heroes to decorate. Colonel General Keller will do the same for the Air Force. Every service will have its decorations day with promotions and a remembrance service for the fallen. Thankfully, there aren't too many casualties. Our colleague Heydrich's plan worked in that aspect, as well. The public will be suitably impressed. We will also make sure our brave Latin allies get their proper share of the credit. Perhaps even a little more than their share, as our public must be educated to take Italians seriously as warriors."

Göring paused for dramatic effect, letting the three beaming faces show their joy in victory and relief that this half-assed attack had actually worked. "Now, that's the public face. Privately, the Army sabotaged the mission. The Navy behaved like dunces. 'Hoch Der Kaiser'. What a sick, sad joke. The man was a fossilized relic and we are better off without him. My own service, the Air Force, made such a hash of things that I had to relieve the main commander and half his staff. Kesselring is lucky he works for us and not Stalin. In the Soviet state, he'd have been put up against a wall. We need a thorough after-action report and a very definite lessons-learned commission. We've never done a multi-service operation this complex before and it showed. The only service to totally cover itself with glory and professional attainment was the NL, a company of untrained militia. General Ramcke warned us before this operation that the plan was a disaster waiting to happen. Thank God we had him there."

Beck and Halder frowned at this. It seemed no one had told them of the parachute force's reservations. They would have loved to have protested, but were aware that they had shown no interest in any of this. Beyond stalling 1st Mountain Division's deployment, they had ignored the entire Malta operation. "We have only a month before serious fighting begins in Egypt. Backbiting among ourselves is not the road to victory." With this, Göring shook each of their hands and exited. Heydrich asked if there was any other business. The two generals preferred to take their leave and discuss the matter between themselves at the War Ministry. Heydrich had no problem being excluded. The Gestapo had the building bugged. He'd have a transcript within hours.

1350 hours
20 August 20, 1940
Carinhall, country residence of Hermann Göring, North East of Berlin

Chancellor, Party Chairman, Head of the Air Force, and Führer. Herman Göring may have hated his actual job of nominal ruler of Europe, but he quite loved the benefits. He was an art lover. The spoliation of Europe's Jews, stripping them of their wealth and possessions, yielded treasure troves of art and antiquities to loot. He obviously had first choice. Precisely whether these masterpieces should be seen as his personal property or part of the swank of his official residences could be left for history to sort out.

He also loved the dress-up and ceremonial parts of the combined offices he held. He had a love of wearing elaborate uniforms and costumes at parties, state dinners, and public spectacles. Göring would change his clothes several times over the various stages of the production, guided by both his own exquisite taste and suggestions from his actress wife and her confidant, the actress Olga.

This particular afternoon, Göring was looking over

The Reich Without Hitler: The Falcons of Malta

photographs of art work confiscated in France. The Rosenberg Taskforce since the armistice with France had been busy looting the wealth of Jews in Western Europe, in particular their private artwork collections. Helping Göring make selections for the art wing here at Carinhall was his wife Emmy and the Russian actress, Olga Chekhova, who had become part of his inner circle. Rumor had extended that to a semi-permanent, full nighttime threesome, but those who knew didn't tell and those who gossiped didn't know for sure.

Standing nearby was a small collection of military officers and Reich bureaucrats to provide briefings to Göring on the state of the Reich and the war effort. Führer Göring had restricted his work hours to afternoon, but often avoided working even then. The men had been waiting for over an hour and Göring showed no signs of breaking away from the photo albums of looted artwork. This was a source of amusement and concern for the Russian actress. Her NKVD handlers had been pressuring for more intelligence, but Göring was such a dilettante with respect to his official duties it was at times impossible to get anything real. She could report all the decisions he avoided. She could, after the fact, report his criticisms of decisions made by others, usually the Reichsführer-SS Heydrich. Her handler kept asking her for suggestions on how to penetrate THAT ministry, but Olga was clueless. Heydrich was polite to her, but distant. He always had this little knowing smile. Quite annoying. Deciding it was time to nudge Göring, she spoke up, "Oh, dear, Hermann, these poor gentlemen have been waiting forever for you. The albums will wait." Her subtext was that if he dealt with whatever silly things they wanted, they would go away, ending "work time" for the day.

The officers and bureaucrats sent Olga silent thanks, as many days he avoided dealing with them at all. Hitler's manic micromanagement seemed less awful in retrospect. Sensing an opening, Göring's secretary used the break to try to get his boss on track for the day. "Mein Führer, a report has arrived covering award requests for the Malta operation. It's from General Rommel." The vast majority of military reports Göring didn't care about, but he had shown an interest toward award citations and that could, at times, provide an opening to get Göring interested in larger events.

Göring looked up from the album. Malta had been a his regime's first victory and Rommel had played a key role in the island's conquest. Turning to his wife, "Emmy, why don't you keep looking. I will be back soon." As was normal, Göring moved only across the room to a nearby couch and table.

Emmy and Olga resumed looking through the photo albums, but Olga kept her ears open for anything useful to report.

The Heer briefer, a General, read off Rommel's report and the award citations. Three of the awards were for a group of Officer Cadets, Italians. Rommel wanted the Blue Max reinstated, with these three as the first recipients. Hearing these were awards for Italians, Göring was interested and asked for more details. The briefer provided what information he could. Rommel had borrowed a group of six of these Fahnenjunker from an elite Italian Arditi unit that had taken the main airfield with Rommel's own storm battalion, using them to command teams of Italian parachutists. The air drops had been a disaster, with the men scattered all over the island and more than a few into the water. As such, the parachutist's organization was wrecked and Rommel used these cadets to improvise some. The descriptions of the individual actions, even in abbreviated form, sounded like someone out of the Greek classics, as if Achilles had returned to earth to once more make war.

As the descriptions of the various award citations continued, Emmy spoke up from her table, "These men sound very brave. Why can't they get your award, darling? You could present it and remind people that you won it for your daring in the skies of the Western Front. One generation passing the torch of glory to the next." She too loved the ceremonial and was acting a part for the audience of official flunkies and leeches.

Without even thinking about it, Göring's hand strayed to the gold-and-blue award that hung from around his neck; the Pour le Mérite, known informally as the Blue Max, was the highest award for valor that the old Kingdom of Prussia could bestow to regular soldiers. The Blue Max was awarded for extraordinary achievement in battle and, as such, more than a few of its winners received the award posthumously. Göring had received his Blue Max after his 20th air-to-air kill in spring of 1918; that and his being successor to Manfred von Richthofen, the Red Baron, as commander of the famed "Flying Circus", Jagdgeschwader 1, had helped Göring's post-war political career. As such, Göring was understandably proud and attached to his Blue Max, wearing it just about any time he was in uniform.

The Reich Without Hitler: The Falcons of Malta

"The Blue Max was an award of the Prussian Monarchy, and when the Kaiser was deposed in 1918, the award died with it." As Göring explained, there was a bit of remorse in his voice. While Göring wasn't born of the Second Reich's nobility, his father had been an army officer and diplomat. He strived to act the part and had adopted many of their positions. Then a thought occurred to Göring. Hitler had resurrected many of the awards of the Prussian Monarchy or created new ones based on them. The Iron Cross and Knights Cross being the key examples. Why shouldn't he do the same? After all, Herman Göring was now Chancellor and Führer of Germany. Turning to his secretary, "I want a proclamation drawn up restoring the Blue Max and the first to receive it will be the brave men who conquered Malta."

Among the nearby soldiers and bureaucrats was an SS Officer. Officially, he was just another adjutant and briefer, but his real function was to keep an eye on the Führer. Back in Berlin, Heydrich had made clear that he wanted to be kept informed of the doings of Germany's new Führer, especially any time he made a decision. All actions, no matter how trivial, were to be reported.

Göring, feeling he had accomplished something with his decree, returned to help Emmy and Olga view looted art work. The assembled soldiers and bureaucrats restrained sighs and returned to their waiting. They didn't have long to wait. Within a few minutes, the Führer announced that the work day was done and dismissed them all.

1600 hours
20 August 1940
HQ Sicherheitsdienst in Prinz-Albrecht-Palais, Berlin

"The Führer made several critical decisions this afternoon during his daily briefings Reichsführer-SS."

Heydrich knew when Schellenberg was being sarcastic, even if the man's voice was utterly respectful.

"Oh? What did our Führer decide on this afternoon?" Any time Göring decided something, it was of critical interest to Heydrich. After all, it would be up to him to clean up whatever mess has just been created.

"The Führer has decreed that the Pour le Mérite is to be restored as a battle award for Germany ." Schellenberg gave the bare-bones version of events that the SS Adjutant at Carinhall had provided, along with copies of the award citation that Rommel had written. Through Strauss and Siegel's reports, he and Heydrich already knew who these Italian children really were.

Heyrich folded his hands and thought about what Göring had done and it occurred to him that this was something that could prove very useful. "Make sure that the draft of a decree for the Blue Max to be restored is not as an award of the German Reich, but of a National Socialist Europa. The title is French, after all, even if it was an award of the Prussian Kings and German Kaisers. With the first award being given to our brave and gallant allies, it will be perfect to help knit together the new Europe. Men fight for many reasons, but glory and pride are chief among them, especially the young. For such men, military awards are proof of their valor."

"Of course, Reichsführer-SS; I will see to it. One question. Should Strauss's pet Hitlerjugend Major Steiner receive one of these?"

Pausing to think, Heydrich considered quickly the implications, "No, not at this time. We want the focus to be on our allies, I think. The boy has received enough attention for now. Keep the thought in the back of your mind, though, for down the road. If nothing else, whenever the boy's luck runs out, we will make sure he receives a hero's death story and then the award. Or, if his luck holds, he can get it eventually."

With that out of the way, Schellenberg made a brief note and they moved onto the next time, a report on setting up the aircraft production cartels in France and the Netherlands.

Chapter 54

1900 hours
21 August 1940
Luqa Airfield, Malta

General Gerhard Ramcke felt he had aged ten years in the past several days. It had been over one hundred hours since he had had a change of uniform, or indeed more than ten minutes' unbroken rest. Sleep was a distant dream. Since his arrival on this God-cursed island, he had been a total professional failure. He never truly took charge of his "division". He never had a handle on the situation. That bastard Rommel had just marched off with a ragtag battlegroup to the sound of the guns, while he, Ramcke, like a rear-area swine, had never left this idiot airfield. Endless hours converting chaos into some semblance of order, only for chaos to reassert itself. As fast as he had cobbled units together to meet some emergency request from real combat officers, he had had to repeat the process for the next crisis. Personnel and supply work. Work that hadn't ended with the formal British surrender. The only people firmly under his command had been a few hundred multinational youngsters under this Strauss, a jumped-up street brawler who seemed a bit of a gangster even by SA standards. Now three superior officers had arrived by air. Probably to relieve him for incompetence.

The two generals, Keller and Jodl, had waived off his attempt at a briefing. Ramcke rigidly kept his temper, although the discourtesy rankled. However poorly he had done, he was owed the chance to make his report before he was sacked. Instead, it was a brief handshake and then that bastard Strauss had guided them to a captured British auto, had sent them off to see the hero of the hour, General Rommel. They had only paused to pin an Iron Cross First Class on newly promoted Major Steiner, the more junior hero.

That left Ramcke with his mouth half-open, his guts filled with rage, facing the third visitor, his acquaintance from Berlin, Oberführer Schellenberg, immaculately dressed as always. A headquarters pig to the last. Schellenberg had firmly guided Ramcke back to Greta's kitchen shack and told the young lady she was to leave. At least he would not be relieved in front of the worst cook he'd ever met. Perky young thing, but she could make even boiling water an adventure. Again, Ramcke tried to make his report. And was rudely told to be silent.

Instead, Schellenberg had ordered Strauss to guard the door. This was to be a private meeting, apparently. Ramcke felt grateful for that mercy. Schellenberg ordered Ramcke to seat himself, then poured them both some of Greta's abysmal coffee. It was captured British stock, so at least it was real coffee, not ersatz. Ramcke was then ordered to drink. This went on in silence for a few minutes. Schellenberg then handed Ramcke an envelope and ordered him to read the paper inside. The paper was Chancellery stationary and said:

"The bearer of this letter, Oberführer Schellenberg, is our personal emissary and speaks with our voice. On your honor as a German officer, obey the verbal orders you are about to be given."

Signed – Herman Göring – Führer, Chancellor, Reichsmarschall

Reinhardt Heydrich – Reichsführer-SS and Deputy Party Chairman

Ramcke read, sagged, and waited to hear his doom.

"Take off your rank insignia."

Ramcke used every bit of his training and breeding to neither curse or cry. To be relieved was bad enough, but this was past all dishonor. He then almost bugged his eyes out when Schellenberg took the old insignia—without stars, of the lowest grade of general, rank Ramcke had been so proud to have been promoted to just a few weeks ago—and handed him back new one star ones, of the next highest grade. Promotion? For this debacle? Ramcke's control snapped. "What? Why? How...?"

Schellenberg patted him lightly on the shoulder as one would a junior who had just had a great shock. "The real rulers know the difference between propaganda and reality. The headlines will give Germany heroes, new Siegfrieds. In this case, Rommel and Steiner. A general who should never have been promoted over brigade command and a clueless boy with the devil's own luck. You won this battle. Yes, the British were not especially inclined to fight and most of them got away. But the initial air drop was the precise disaster you foretold and the follow-on worse than anything our planners could have imagined. We'll do better next time. First big air-sea adventure, so it was all new to everyone. You got the key points right in advance back in Berlin and kept it from imploding despite next to no help from your superiors."

Berlin saw his actions as successful? Was proud of him? Ramcke was blinking and trying to organize his thoughts. "How could you possibly know what I was doing? We weren't broadcasting it. Not enough code books, code clerks, anything...." Ramcke suddenly started adding up bits and pieces he had dismissed as trivia. "Strauss! He was sending back written reports on the returning transports while his mechanic was checking planes. That Joe fellow. The American Volksdeutsche..." Ramcke caught his breath, as he had just repeated as true something he never believed for an instant.

Schellenberg held up a hand to silence Ramcke. "A small matter first. We are now doing something my superior, the Reichsführer-SS, requires. It will seem a silly litany, but he is your superior officer as you were informed in Berlin. I am going to say something. You will then repeat it back to me. Nod if you understand." Ramcke nodded. "Two plus two is five."

Ramcke lost it. "What idiocy is this? I am not a child to do my sums and, in any case, you know very well it's four."

"In the normal world, yes. Sometimes, in the affairs of state, facts are what the Nation and the Party needs. So, we have a litany. We tell each other two plus two is five and then we learn the lies that are needed. Nod if you understand...." Ramcke slowly nodded. "You will give a proper report AFTER you have had a day's sleep, a clean uniform, and a proper meal. When you can be functional and objective, which is NOT now. However, certain 'facts' will be stated as I am about to give them to you. These are matters of state security. Nod comprehension." Ramcke nodded more decisively. In an absurd way, this was starting to make some sense.

"Joe is Volksdeutsche if Strauss says he is. Strauss is a direct report to the Reichsführer-SS through me. Anyone he says is an Aryan is Aryan, even obvious Yids, even darkies. There are reasons for this. We may explain them when you get your next star...." Schellenberg paused for this to register. Ramcke was now totally in shock, but extremely attentive. Still higher rank was possible? "...or perhaps not. That's the Reichsführer's decision. Oh, you are also now a direct report to him. He's effectively Deputy Chancellor and operational head of government as you were informed in Berlin and as the paper you just read confirmed." Schellenberg paused while Ramcke absorbed this, remembering the twin meetings with Göring and Heydrich that had been the start of his

"Maltese adventure".

"There will be a new liaison officer for your staff to handle such reports within the week. Now, the Italian youths with Strauss are actually an elite Arditi battalion commanded by a Lieutenant Colonel Umberto Lusena. You will praise them lavishly. No, you are not losing your mind. They are untrained children and Lusena was never on the island, has no idea he had a battalion to fail to command. He and Steiner are your two heroes. We'll forward you the fantasies about both that go into your final report. Strauss will not be mentioned unless it is unavoidable, and then he will be mentioned as minimally as possible. Rommel's actions will not be criticized in your report. Instead, you will give your new liaison an eyes' only letter in ten days with your actual critique of his conduct. Ten days and no sooner. We need you calm and objective instead of ready to strangle him. We know he's 'difficult'. Rommel will never see this. Indeed no one except myself and the Reichsführer ever will. Rommel is a weapon to be wielded, but we must better know more about his defects. In a perfect universe, he'd command a storm brigade. He would be given more and more impossible missions, which he would execute and each time we would invent new higher grades of the Blue Max for him until the final time when he failed and the award was posthumous. You, on the other hand, have a future as a real commander of men. Modern war is a chaotic shambles. We need officers who can ride the chaos waves to victory. You did. You will be expected to do so again. In the meantime, you are now Commandant of the German garrison of Malta. There will be an Italian as your superior, but the German forces are yours until they can be evacuated back to Sicily. For right now, get some sleep, man."

Ramcke finally allowed exhaustion to hit him, Schellenberg summoned Strauss to carry the rapidly fading Ramcke to a bed and post a guard to see that the General got at least 24 hours' undisturbed sleep.

Chapter 55

2100 hours
21 August 1940
Palazzo del Viminale, Rome

SS General Wolff was amused at the reactions of Italy's co-rulers to this latest diktat from Berlin. "Yes, I'm aware these were untrained children who ran off on an adventure based on absurd rumor. Yes the 'lieutenant colonel' is actually a captain and has never heard of his unit. Yes, you disbanded the Arditi after the Great War, and have none. Why does any of this matter?"

Deputy Prime Minister and Air Marshal Balbo was trying to make this Alice in Wonderland tale into the real world of men and nations. "But we had real units on Malta. Many were heroic. Why this farce? His own older brother was there, Major Guido Lusena, a wounded and decorated veteran of the Spanish Civil War, commanding a battalion of the "Folgore" brigade. These were actual elite, trained soldiers. Did brilliant work."

"By all means, provide me with details and the European newspapers will trumpet their exploits. However, Major Steiner 'captured' the key airfield we reinforced through. He had roughly one hundred Italians with him. He thought they were real. They did, in fact, help him take the airfield...."

"Take? The British mostly ran away..."

"Yes, they did. And then tried to retake it a few times."

"More like stray British blundered into the perimeter the following day."

"Steiner tells the story his way. He's an 18-year-old HJ who keeps getting promoted, mostly by accident. He also has the devil's own luck. He's singing the praises of your people and of this officer who, as far as he understands it, was involved, even though he somehow never met him...."

"He wasn't there! He was scheduled to start initial training for the parachutist corps later this month in Tarquinia!"

"Steiner thought he was there. The children invented him as a commander and kept reporting his actions. Steiner had no reason to disbelieve them, as the whole action was chaotic and, besides, he's untrained himself. Brave, loyal, decent. The perfect hero for this age of mass communications. Our propaganda corps have adopted him as a talisman. Thus, every newspaper in Germany says your captain colonel was there. I have an Iron Cross 2nd class to award him. Besides, there's worse."

"What could be worse?"

"Rommel took six of your untrained children with him. They spoke German or a bit of German. He thinks they were officer cadets. He used them to command various stray Italian parachutists he pressganged during the battle. Yes, in fact, they were translators and runners, but he lists them in his report as officer cadets. Indeed, he has recommended them for promotion and decorations. Apparently, they were near-suicidally brave. Three of the decorations were the Blue Max, two posthumous."

"He what? They what?" How...?"

"Yes. Rommel put them up for an award that had ceased to exist in 1918 because Rommel held it and felt these were Fahnenjunkers, officer cadets, worthy of equal praise to his own exalted, heroic self."

"Can a mere general reinstate an award?'

"No. The four rulers of Germany can. And did. The first three new recipients of the revived award are to be Italians. Awards presented personally by the four rulers of Germany in a ceremony to be broadcast throughout Germany and to be carried by our new Europa broadcasting cartel to the other major capitals of Europe. Indeed, you two are invited to be part of the ceremony."

"Us? To Berlin? How can a band of children and one willful officer make this much chaos?"

"Does it matter? Heroes. Heroes anointed by a Blue Max holder who was one of the heroic victors of Caporetto." Wolff ignored the Italian reaction to that bitter defeat. "A man who beat you Italians like a drum in 1917. Think what it means for him to sound this positive about Italian military prowess. He is singing the praises of Italy's new generation to every reporter who will listen. He's a national hero to us, so a great many are listening. He's asked for this Arditi battalion to be attached to his 7th Panzer Division for the Egyptian campaign. Berlin wants the live heroes for a big propaganda presentation and a tour of German cities. They are the face of the glorious alliance. Now you can refuse, but after your French disaster, doesn't your regime need heroes?"

"And what of our real heroes?"

"Send us a dozen and we'll honor them as well. We are selling the alliance and your new regime to our public, to the wider

The Reich Without Hitler: The Falcons of Malta

European publics, too. To publics who do not see Italians as capable of heroic military behavior. Who remember Caporetto and your Alpine disgrace, not what your men endured on the Isonzo. Leave reality to the general staff reports. You wanted a new Roman Empire and glory. Why are you turning the glory down?"

The Prince had heard enough. He tried to work with Balbo in a collegial manner, but sometimes he would assert royal prerogative. "Just do it. I'm making the promotions and sending the men. I'm Lieutenant General of the Realm and supreme commander. Italy needs this. The Arditi battalion was part of the Militia. A special unit you created. That gets around some Army staff officer spoiling the party with snide rumors. Let this Rommel have a large battalion. Start with this lieutenant colonel and fill in good veterans of Spain. Perhaps some of our Hungarian 'guests' as well. Why are we arguing about something that reflects well on Italy, on our regime?"

Balbo stopped arguing and accepted that reality seemed not to matter so much in this brave new world. Balbo had not just been a military man. He had been a major founder of fascism, a politician, a government minister. He understood the importance of propaganda, of skillful public relations. A populist mass state needed mass media to educate and guide public opinion. He was successfully doing this back to when Riefenstahl was flat-backing her way to success in Berlin films. The reestablishment of Arditi units as part of the Militia fit seamlessly into his own plans. Not the human material he would have started with, but the concept was right. Arditi were clearly Italian storm units with a glorious history that flawlessly linked to the early glory days of fascism. Even children running off to be heroes was an old story. His own friend, Undersecretary Lieutenant Colonel Ettore Muti had tried to join illegally the Army at 14 and succeeded at 15. Command discovered the deception only when they tried to award him the Gold Medal for his heroism in battle as an Ardito, one of the 23 survivors from an 800-man strong battalion. A story of Italy's glory that could be retold in reintroducing the Arditi. However, one reality was going to be iron-hard. This battalion would be the best unit the Militia could produce, not a propaganda caricature. He would make sure the officers knew that he would be personally following their campaign and expected their names to shine.

Chapter 56

1900 hrs
22 August 1940
Hal Far, Malta

Some Italian fighter aircraft had been moved to Hal Far to provide forward air defense.

The airfield cantina was full—someone managed to liberate a few cases of beer and wine and the off-duty pilots were in the process of re-moistening their throats after the afternoon patrol. Of course, there was also a small collection of Bialetti Moka pot coffee machines of different sizes with a large one bubbling and hissing away on an electric hot plate behind the bar.

The door opened and a few Italian officers came in—a first lieutenant and some second lieutenants of the Libyan airborne unit, a bit scruffy-looking and still with guns on their back. They made their way to the bar, ordering an espresso each. Unusual for ground-force personnel to be in an air force club, but things were still pretty fluid this soon after the island's liberation from British colonialism. Then the senior officer of the three turned around and asked casually: "That aeroplane outside, the CR42 with the three patches on her tail—she is carrying the designator 278-6. May I ask if the pilot is here?"

A brash young man with pilot insignia, still wearing his silk scarf, asked back: "Why?"

The first lieutenant lifted his hands like he wanted to hug somebody, smiling widely: "I want to congratulate, to say thank you..." He paused, still beaming, and only someone looking very closely would see that the smile was as fake as a three-lire coin.

The pilot grinned and answered, "Well, that one is mine."

The first lieutenant stretched out his hand like for a handshake, took the pilot's hand with both of his hands and... pulled hard. As the pilot came off balance, the airborne infantry officer gave him a very hard jab into the solar plexus. The young man went down onto the ground, wheezing and gasping. The three parachute officers proceed to stomp him half to death. Their quiet rage kept the rest of the room momentarily at bay.

"Cretino, Imbecille, Stronzo..." the officer continued jumping up and down, screaming at the prostrate pilot, going on in more and more incomprehensible Italian for over a minute. One of the second lieutenants finally pulled out a piece of fabric, unfolded it, and spread it over the still-wheezing pilot like a shroud—it was clearly a well-shot-up and bloodied recognition panel.

"Those bullet holes are yours...blind Idiota, you murdered three of my men."

The other second lieutenant took his heaving superior by arm and gently led him out of the cantina while he was still shouting in Italian. The remaining second lieutenant took out a flare pistol and fired it into the roof of the building.

"Green, you fools! The recognition color was green. Do this again on the next campaign and we come back with machine guns and castrating knives." He gave a sardonic grin, daring the air crew to try to fight him. None did. Smiling, he spat on the unmoving pilot, kicked him twice more in the head and left while the pilots started to extinguish the fire just starting in the cantina ceiling.

Chapter 57

2100 hours
23 August 1940
Administrative HQ, Mediterranean Fleet, Alexandria

Jutland Scott was at rigid attention. The senior officer he had reported to on arrival had relieved him of command. Now he was being given his next posting by an officer who was making clear that he would rather be unclogging sewers than demeaning himself by this conversation. "No one wants your excuses. You disobeyed orders and ran away while a brave admiral died doing his duty. Nothing else matters. Nothing! Do you see this pile in front of me? These are requests for transfer by every man in your ship's company from your executive officer down to the two recruits you took at dock on Malta." The officer pulled three pieces of paper from the pile. On them were paw prints. "Even your ship's dog and both cats asked off to avoid your yellow stench. I'm amazed the ship's rats haven't done the same. You will never get another posting as anything, much less a command. You are a disgrace to the uniform and, once we have time for such bother, I'm sure a general court martial will agree. Pending formal charges, you are confined to quarters. Your meals will be brought to you. You may leave only when ordered to or to use the loo down the corridor. ARE WE CLEAR?"

2400 hours
23 August 1940
Transit barracks, Alexandria

They had escorted him to an attic in an old Victorian-era building about two blocks from the docks. There was no lock on the door. If he wanted to add desertion to his resume, the powers that be would do nothing to stop him. Instead, they had thoughtfully prepared the room. A small pile of good writing paper, half a dozen envelopes, a length of good rope, and a loaded revolver. The chair for the desk was left under an exposed overhead beam in case he was too stupid to put the pieces together. He was expected to spare the service and his family the humiliation of the trial. A trial whose conclusion was obvious. Dead, Cunningham was now a sainted hero instead of a sentimentalist who had frozen when faced with an impossible decision. It wasn't politic to punish the Army for the bungle, so they would hang him out to dry. He'd be stripped of rank, pension, personal honor...or he could make the expected final apology and it would all be buried. His death would appease the acolytes of the martyred Admiral.

He mentally shrugged. He knew he'd done the right thing. He knew to his bones that right or wrong often didn't matter against the needs of service and Empire. He took the chair away from the beam and threw the rope in the corner. He would end his life as an officer and a gentleman, not swinging from a rafter like a cuckolded husband or an embezzler about to be exposed. He set down to write a last letter to his aunt explaining the truth. When he was done, he addressed the envelope, but didn't bother to seal it. They would insist on reading it anyway. He then wrote a second note, labeled "last will and testament". He had some property beyond accrued pay. He directed that the postage on the letter be taken out of the accrued pay and that the balance, along with his savings account and the remainder of his worldly possessions, go to the Chinese couple who'd been his house servants at his last Malay posting. They would be pleased to get the cottage, as they were still living in it. He had kept it, expecting it to be his retirement home. No need for that now, but he could still be buried in his garden.

He felt proud at getting in the catty comment on the postage. It was a petty way to strike back, but it made him somewhat happy in this fucked situation. He took the pistol, put the barrel in his mouth, and thought of England.

Chapter 58

1000 hours
24 August 1940
Luqa, Malta

The unit was almost packed up to begin loading the Ju-52s. As official heroes, the Malta battalion of the NL rated air transport. Most of the other men on Malta would make do with sea voyages of varying lengths. To Sicily, to Naples, to Bari, to Libya. The guys had been doing some policing up on the island. They were chasing after trophies—British unit insignia, pistols, unit flags, which they were using to pay off air crew and to sell to newly arrived men. Also, of course, to "liberate" anything with alcohol. Men! Never think anything through. She had Naiomi and a crew gathering up useful things—coffee, tea, chocolate, sugar, canned meats. She had passed off this weight and volume as "necessary kitchen supplies". The men had been too busy to question her. They'd thank her in Africa. Real coffee and tea instead of ersatz. Enough meat. Her sort-of cousin Peter had grinned at the meat and put a gang he'd assembled to work retrieving it, using "borrowed" British vehicles to empty abandoned British supply dumps. It was too much weight to come by air, but Peter had organized a group to guard it all until it could be sent by sea. Waste not, want not. Peter was a large man and liked to eat.

Greta banged her shin on the pile of luggage propping open her cook-house door as she dragged the last carton of coffee out. She'd been beating her legs for days on these, but hadn't moved them because they kept the door of the stifling-hot cook shack open, even in the face of the prop wash from the endless stream of transports. She wondered what was in them and decided to satisfy her curiosity. She opened the first heavy cloth bag and stared at a sea of gold pieces. Gold!

"Naiomi!" Naimoi came running. "Get your girls and form a guard around this building. Send someone to find Klaus, the Colonel, and my Uncle." Naimoi looked askance at Greta, wondering yet again whether the girl was up to her role. Up to it or not, she was the officer's woman and spoke with his voice.

Five minutes later, Klaus, Gunter, Isaac, Joey, and Peter were all there wanting to know what was the matter. Greta felt show was better than tell. She reached into the bag and started pouring gold pieces onto the dirt floor. Gunter Strauss stopped her quickly. He was strong enough to lift the reinforced-leather heavy cloth carry bag off the two below it. They also proved to be full to the brim with British gold sovereigns. That left the metal-on-reinforced-metal steamer trunk. It was locked. Joey knew how to deal with locks. He opened it without breaking the actual lock. That dexterity was a matter of professional pride to him. He was the master of mechanisms, not the reverse.

Inside this very near-unbreakable piece of luggage were five objects. Joey picked one up, removing the protective wrappings. It appeared to be a life-sized sculpture of a large falcon. The falcon appeared to be gold, judging by weight and the visible part on the base. The rest of the bird was not really visible. Instead it was encrusted with what appeared to be precious gems. Diamonds, rubies, emeralds, sapphires. A fortune in its own right and possibly an art object of some antiquity, worth still more on that account. Carefully removing the protective packing material from the other four, he discovered four more falcons. Different poses, but all large, lifelike, and covered in jewels.

Strauss shot her a look. Greta was less unworldly than she had been two months earlier. She understood the implied question. She recounted the story of the two captured British officers, their luggage, and using it to keep the shack's door open. Gunter didn't know whether to laugh or cry. All this time, the treasures had sat unguarded. Anyone could have walked off with part or all of it. What a war! Screw the weight. This was coming by plane and with him personally. He told Isaac and Joey to make it right. They would juggle loading to balance the weight. If a few more men had to come by sea, so be it. Just make sure the stay-behinds were from the silly Italian kids.

Strauss laughed to himself. Heydrich wanted a proper name for this unit. Not lions or tigers or eagles or hawks. Falcons. It was the Falcons of Malta battalion. He and Peter started lugging the four bags to the flight line. Today they were flying with personal luggage.

Afterword

This particular AH stems from my abiding interest in WW2. The more I read, the more I pondered "what ifs". I am also a military board-gamer, both player and, in the past, designer and publisher. These games are a way to explore "what ifs", and many of the operational "counter factuals", as they are now called, are an enjoyable exploration. However, on a macroscale, once you get past Stalingrad and Tunisia, there is simply no way for Germany to win. At best, they can force a draw that leaves some ember named Germany alive. Once you get past Kursk and Italy switching sides, there is no way for Germany to get any result besides being wiped out. The side with the vastly larger numbers of men and weapons, vastly larger economies could and did bludgeon its way to victory by force of attrition. Yes, Hitler's mistakes helped make it happen faster. Yes, the defects of the Nazi governance did so as well. Had Hitler and his cronies been a mixture of Napoleon, Bismarck, and Henry Ford, by late 1943 they would still lose. It just takes another year and maybe ten million more dead, including Berlin and Munich being the first cities to be nuked instead of Hiroshima and Nagasaki.

After decades of study, I came up with two turning points that could not have been largely preordained. The first was the period from late 1932 into 1935. The most likely end result for the Weimar chaos was not Hitler as Führer. It was a soft military coup backed actively by the Nationalists and the Catholic Center Party, and with the passive support of the Social Democrats and a tame rump of the Nazis under the Strasser brothers and perhaps Göring. The rest of the Nazis and the Communists get put down hard. The street chaos ends. Instead, a bizarre series of plots centered around von Papen and utilizing President Hindenburg as a sock puppet, make Adolph Hitler Chancellor in a mostly Nationalist and technocrat cabinet. The old elites thought they had bought a populist front for a different version of the soft coup. Hitler outmaneuvers them. He has to purge the Nazi Party in 1934. The Army and the elites insisted. They still had the power to remove him then. He's forced to kill Rhoem, defang the SA, and disown his Party's radical wing with their vision of a second, populist revolution. In return for that, the elites let him set up a personalist dictatorship and, step by step, destroy their bases of power. Writing an alternate of this would be fascinating, but, alas, I lack the language skills needed for the requisite detail.

The Reich Without Hitler: The Falcons of Malta

So, I wrote the second meta-turning point, the Fall of France. No one expected this. The French army was rated the best in Europe by all contemporary observers. In retrospect, this was an over-statement. However, the postwar meme set of the French as worthless surrender monkeys is even more off-base. The Nazis were absurdly lucky. By platoons and companies, the French fought quite well, as the large German casualties show. The French failure was at the higher levels of command: supreme, the main army group, and a few armies. A handful of generals chosen for political reasons were simply unable to grasp the tempo of modern war. Petain's generals of 1918 would have held. Weygand's from the second-half of the 1940 campaign likewise would have not imploded. Gamelin, Georges, Billotte, and Huntziger were in the wrong places just long enough to magnify the institutional defects of the French army (an overcomplex chain of command; a doctrine that relied too much on prepared actions with massive artillery support; bottomless quarrels on how to use and oppose armored vehicles; a communications system orders of magnitude worse than WW1, despite all the tech advances in radio and telephone) into losing their nation in sixty days.

This was a world-changing moment. No one in Berlin or the other capitals had ever considered that France could be destroyed in a single two-month campaign. The obvious question was what would come next? Most of the world expected the British to take a speedy exit. Save the Empire by accepting the new status quo in Europe. Churchill refused and managed to carry his cabinet colleagues with him. Many had reservations, but no organized challenge to his rule appeared. Hitler then proceeded to waste the next year. He makes a halfhearted try at an absurd invasion plan. Sea Lion was unworkable, but halfhearted wasn't going to do it. While he sits, the British, Soviets, and Americans are frantically arming. He is not. He then invades the Soviet Union, and doesn't even give that a full mobilized effort. He wins huge victories but fails before Moscow. He compounds his error by declaring war on the US right after Pearl Harbor. The US was already a de facto belligerent (Arsenal of Democracy; an undeclared shooting war in the West Atlantic) but adding them to his formal enemies finishes digging Germany's grave.

This wasted year was a meta-turning point worth exploring. Yet, Hitler was Hitler. He was not the man to seize the moment. He was a dilettante who detested organized bureaucracy and refused to ever stick to a previous decision. No priority was ever safe from the next man to get his ear. He also tolerated in Bormann, Himmler, and Goebbels a set of scheming empire-builders of little talent. The obvious thing is to imagine a Reich without Hitler. Disposing of Hitler was easy. He had been getting "treatments" from a set of quack doctors for years for his digestion and other ills, real and imaginary. These "medical geniuses" would inject him with varying cocktails centered on vitamins, amphetamines, and strychnine, mixed with various naturopathic remedies plus whatever else excited their fancy. Hitler had lived in the demimonde of Munich for years and had a soft spot for quack doctors and pseudoscience. The miracle was that none of these practitioners managed to kill him in OTL. Having him given a hot shot on the plane back from Paris passed my smell test.

Hitler's death is the only major deliberate change from our history. Specialists in Soviet and Baltic history will find some minor changes in how the occupation of the Baltic States worked. To me, that was a minor fudge that saved multiple chapters, making that mass evacuation work around the actual stricter Soviet control mechanisms. I also moved up the date of the mass promotions after the Fall of France. Again, that's minor, but avoids me having to write that scene and puts the senior officers at the rank most readers know them at. Extreme gearheads will find a very minor change in Book 2 as regards
airships, the result of an order not being followed.

Beyond that, we should be dealing with the real world up to the moment Adolph dies. I had a dedicated group of history assistants. See the credits page. Much of what is good here and in the volumes to follow comes from them. Any mistakes are, of course, my responsibility.

The coup sparked by Hitler's death is, to my mind, a quite possible response to that opportunity. It's the old elites getting the chance they passed on in January of 1933 and again in July of 1934. It's sort of what they tried with the July 1944 Bomb Plot. How Göring and Heydrich deal with this and the war is the core of this series of books at the macro-level. I'm not young, and I have the war plotted out into Central Asia, so it remains to be seen if they all ever get written. But what I plan to offer is a road not taken to a truly different WW2. It will be both recognizable and totally alien. I hope you enjoy.

WW2 was not just a macro-level struggle of nations and

The Reich Without Hitler: The Falcons of Malta

armies, with supreme leaders moving little flags around a map.
It was also the defining experience of the lives of hundreds of
millions of people in the Atlantic world (and several times that
when the companion war in Asia involving Japan and China is
included). The second track of this series is to follow individuals.
I invented the NL as a convenient prop from my macro-level
changes, but also because a brand-new service with no rules
allowed a make-it-up-as-you-go-along band such as Kampfgruppe
Strauss. Centered on our Romeo and Juliet, Klaus and Greta, we
see the war from a quite low-level point of view. Two clueless
kids who grow up on campaign. The Klaus we meet is a clueless,
rear-rank HJ with a breaking voice. Greta is a teenage girl whose
summer adventure was staying at her aunt's house hundreds of
kilometers from home. This book shows them starting to grow
and learn. There's more to come, as there is for Gunter, Isaac,
Joey, Peter, and the rest of the merry band. World war is not just
voyages and battles. For many, it was the great adventure of their
lives.

Two other matters bear note. Neither is a change from history,
per se, but both turn on my views of that history. The first is on
who is a Soviet agent and how many there were. Seventy-seven
years after the fact, there is simply no firm agreed list even on
the most notable ones, such as Alger Hiss. I take a somewhat
expansive view of how vast the net was. Your mileage may vary.

The second is, of course, "the Jewish Question". One cannot
deal with the Nazis without arriving here. The Nazis didn't like the
Jews. Neither did most of Germany. Neither did most of Europe.
When Hitler offered to send away his Jews, no one wanted any
more. This book starts in June of 1940. Our history shows no
Final Solution at this point. The Nazis had alternately oppressed
the Jews and tried to expel them, but mass murder was mostly
in the future. As the book recites, there had been pogroms the
first few months in Poland. Pogroms against Jews and separately
against Catholic Poles. Some tens of thousands of each were
killed and then it died down. It started again against the Jews with
Barbarossa and the Einsatzgruppen. That's 1941, and it's only
on land conquered from the Soviets. This spreads to occupied
Poland in 1942, and more generally to the rest of Europe in stages,
thereafter. I choose to take Germany down a different path. The
Final Solution was technocratically stupid, even if one were an
exterminationist anti-Semite. I see the change as part of a series

of changes designed to maximize the transient advantage the Fall of France gave to Germany. My readers are welcome to think I am letting the Germans off the hook by this. Maybe I am. However, the Germans had made expulsion the core of their policy before. The war, as I am taking it, will provide places to transplant Jews, to regions that, unlike Madagascar or Tasmania, do not depend on other powers cooperating.

Finally, the next volume of this series, the Reich without Hitler, will obviously take the war and our merry band to Egypt. That book, Deaths on the Nile, should be out later in 2018. See The Reich Without Hitler on Facebook or TheReichWithoutHitler@ groups.io for updates on future volumes and some additional worldbuilding background.

Dramatis Personae

Historic (all death dates are OTL).

Balbo, Italo (1896-–1940): WW1 veteran. One of the founders of Italian Fascism. One of the creators of the Italian air force as a major service. Governor General of Libya, 1933. Did not support either the anti-Jewish laws or the Nazi alliance. Killed by Italian AAA while trying to land at Tobruk, 1940. Highest rank: Marshal.

Beck, Ludwig (1880–1945): served as a staff officer, Western Front WW1. Backed the Nazis in the early 30s but never joined the Party. Fired as head of Army General Staff 1938 over his opposition to Hitler's military adventurism. Part of many anti-Nazi plots, including 1944 Bomb Plot where he was slated to be chief of state. Executed when the coup failed. Beck was smart and capable, but incredibly narrow-minded. As with many in his generation and class, he regarded the Nazis as gutter-trash. Was enraged when Hitler did not let himself be "guided" by the better sort of experts such as himself. Widely revered among the old Army officer corps, which is why I make him part of the junta. Beck's name would swing the old Reichswehr officers to the new regime. He never understood how his kind lost control of Hitler and will be equally mystified over losing control of Heydrich. Highest rank: Colonel General.

Beria, Lavrentiy (1899–1953): Old Bolshevik with a slightly checkered political past during the Civil War years. From Georgia, but not exactly Georgian (similar to Stalin in that respect). Number 2 at NKVD in 1938, then in charge a few months after. Effectively Stalin's Number 2 in WW2. Stalin told FDR at Yalta that Beria was "his Himmler". Compared to Himmler, Beria was smarter and far more competent. Might have been the most competent of Stalin's henchmen. Highest rank: Marshal and Deputy Prime Minister.

Bormann, Martin (1900–1945): Served in late 1918, but never saw action. In Freikorps. Did a prison stretch for an assassination. Joins the Nazis in 1927. Founded the Nazi Socialist Motor Corps when driving or fixing autos were relatively rare skill sets. Rose in the Party bureaucracy based on financial and administrative competence, plus a natural skill at currying favor. Became Number 2 to Hitler's Number 2, Hess. Assumed Hess's job, but not his title, when the idiot flew off to Scotland chasing a madcap peace plan. Used his control over access to Hitler and to the after-meeting memos to attain vast power. Mostly used this power to sabotage every other power-holder. Also sabotaged the war economy and manpower mobilization currying favor with the Gauleiters. Last seen leaving the Bunker in one of the escape parties. Supposedly killed. Body supposedly found some decades later. Rumored to have been a Soviet agent. Rumored to have survived into the 1960s with a lavish dacha in the Moscow suburbs. Highest Rank: Führer's Secretary and Party Minister

Chekhova, Olga (1897–1980): Actress. Related to Chekhov by marriage. White Russian "refugee". Probably Soviet agent. Star in Berlin cinema. Probable mistress of Goebbels. Friendly socially with Hitler. Postwar she worked in East Germany then moved to Munich.

Ciano (Count), Gian (1903–1944): From a wealthy family. Bomber pilot in Ethiopian War. Mussolini's son-in-law. Cultivated a playboy's lifestyle. May have been lover/customer of Duchess of Windsor while in diplomatic service in Shanghai. Turned on Mussolini, 1943. Executed by Mussolini (at request of Nazis), 1944. Highest rank: Foreign Minister.

Cirillo, Enrico (1909 - ?): He's a real officer from the Libyan paratroop order of battle. The limited data we found for him gives him an accounting degree in 1926, parachute training in 1938 and the Bronze Medal for Military Valor in August 1941 for gallantry in the desert war. Retires in 1959 as a lieutenant colonel for medical reasons. Still alive in Rome as far as our researches show.

Cunningham, Andrew (1883–1963): WW1 veteran. Commander Mediterranean Fleet, 1939. Beat his fleet half to death covering the British force on Crete and then in the evacuation when resistance collapsed. Refused to leave the Army to its fate. First Sea Lord, October 1943. Oversaw naval demobilization and then retired, 1946. Highest Rank: Admiral of the Fleet (5 stars).

De Laitre de Tassigny, Jean (1889–1952): WW1 veteran. Youngest divisional commander, Battle of France, highly successful. Vichy until Germans overrun the "Free Zone". Heads Free French 1st Army ETO 1944–1945. Moderately successful. Allowed his troops to loot and rape in several German cities at war's last days. Probably guilty of a massacre of French SS prisoners. Brilliant command in Indochina cut short by his untimely death. A protégé of Weygand. In this series, uses nom de guerre of François Kellerman, a general of the Napoleonic Era. Highest Rank: Marshal of France.

Dietl, Eduard (1890–1944): WW1 veteran. Freikorps veteran. Early Nazi. Hero of Narvik in 1940 campaign. In OTL, led 20th Mountain Army in the Arctic against the Soviets. Died in an air crash, 1944. Capable divisional commander. His army command was unsuccessful—whether that was due to his faults or being given small resources to accomplish huge things across amazingly poor terrain can be debated. Highest rank: Colonel General.

Dietrich, Sepp (1892–1966): WW1 veteran. Joins Nazis, 1928. Protégé of Hitler. Head of his SS bodyguards, LAH. Key role in Blood Purge. Inept commander of LAH (which grows from a regiment to brigade to division), France, Greece, Russia. Learned on the job. Good commander at corps/army level, Normandy and Ardennes. Often blamed for failures of his army in Ardennes, although the main problem was poor higher plan and abysmal road net. Highest Rank: SS Colonel General.

Doenitz, Karl (1891–1980): WW1 veteran. Created Nazi U-boat service after Versailles limits were put aside by Hitler. Created the wolf pack tactics. Head of Navy after Raeder. A Hitler groupie more than a Nazi. Fanatic anti-Communist and anti-Semite (with the usual caveat of protecting a few part-Jews who were senior naval officers). Hitler makes him head of state after his suicide. Acquiesces in the final surrender. Convicted at Nürnberg, in part for using the same U-boat tactics USN did in the Pacific. As rigid a martinet as Raeder. Highest Rank: President of the Republic and Gross Admiral.

Eichmann, Otto Adolf (1906–1962): Oil salesman who joins Austrian Nazis and SS in 1932. Joins German SD in 1934. Made head of 'Jewish Department' [probably because he spoke Yiddish]. Works at various emigration schemes, including helping terrorizing Austrian Jews into fleeing in 1938 after reunion with Germany. Helps create ghettos in Poland. When Final Solution is implemented in 1942, he becomes a transportation bureaucrat, especially for the liquidation of Hungary's Jews in 1944. Goes back to Austria at war's end. Emigrates to Argentina 1950. Kidnapped from there by Israelis in 1960. Tried in Jerusalem and executed 1962. Originally post-trial opinion pegged him as a mere clerk, a faceless minion. Recent findings of his papers from Argentina show him as far more hardcore.

Eicke, Theodor (1892–1943): WW1 veteran. Failed policeman who became a security guard at I.G. Farben. Joined Nazis and SA, 1928. Joined SS, 1930. Forced to flee to Italy, 1932, over bomb plot. Insane asylum, 1933, over internal Nazi politics (he fell afoul of a Gauleiter). Himmler pulled him out of mental hospital to be replacement commandant of Dachau. Converts the camp from sloppy SA model to the SS strict regime we all know. In Blood Purge, personally liquidates Roehm. Head of Camp Administration, thereafter. Forms corps of camp guards. Recruits a division out of them when the war starts. Heads the division. Inept commander, frequent massacres of prisoners and civilians. KIA, 1943. Fanatic anti-Semite and anti-Bolshevik. Not a stable personality, but not the lunatic portrayed postwar. Highest rank: Obergruppenführer and Commandant of Camps.

Fallaci, Oriana (1929–2006): From a family of political resisters. Served in the partisans, WW2. Famous journalist, first of the left but turned anti-Islamist late in life.

Fleming, Ian (1908–1964): Eton. Left Sandhurst after one year, due to VD. Failed foreign service exam. Worked in journalism and finance. Made a naval intelligence officer, 1939, purely due to family connections. Was involved with spies, commandos, Enigma. Postwar journalist who wrote a series of spy novels about a man named James Bond. Highest Rank: Commander.

Fleming, Peter (1907–1971): Successful British adventurer, journalist, and travel writer. In WW2 was reserve officer, Grenadier Guards. Served in Norway, Greece, China, Far East/South Asia. Involved with commandos, guerillas (included preparations for guerillas in UK in the event of German invasion), spies and various classified intelligence operations. Literary executor for his brother. Highest Rank: Major.

Ford, Gerald (1913–2006): 40th President of the US. In OTL, was in Yale Law School in 1940 where he helped found what became the America First Committee. The trip to Europe and work on the Hoover Relief Agency is quite fictional, but fit his views and those of his associates.

Goebbels, Joseph (1897-1945): No war service from physical disability (short leg /club foot). Short and fairly ugly. Compulsive womanizer. University graduate and failed author/journalist. Successful as professional Nazi Party official and propagandist. Good public speaker. Bureaucratic empire builder and fanatic Hitler loyalist. Commits suicide with Hitler in the Bunker 1945. Highest rank: Propaganda Minister and Berlin Gauleiter.

Göring, Hermann – (1893–1946): WW1 ace pilot with legendary Flying Circus. Early Nazi. Hero at Feldheernhalle when

The Reich Without Hitler: The Falcons of Malta

Adolph ducked and covered. Wounded there. Became a morphine addict while a fugitive. First wife was a Swedish aristocrat, the second a Berlin film star. In many ways was the "respectable" face of the Nazis during their rise to power. Founded Luftwaffe. Good bureaucratic empire builder, but disliked doing the actual work. Libertine, art collector, probably bisexual. Loved speeches, dressing up, and the accoutrements of wealth and power. Highest Rank: Reichsmarschall and Deputy Führer. Nickname: Fat Herman.

Guderian, Heinz (1888–1954): WW1 veteran. Freikorps. Iron Division. Reichswehr. Helped found the panzer troops. A favorite of Hitler until late 1941. Sacked for retreating against orders. Held staff positions of high title, but little power 1943–1945. Sacked before the end after a fight with Hitler. Helped organize the Bundeswehr post-WW2. Intelligent, but did not follow orders or play well with others, both characteristics he shared with Rommel. Highest Rank: Colonel General.

Halder, Franz (1884–1972): Staff and then General Staff officer, WW1. Head of OKH 1938–1942. Half-hearted involvement in the early anti-Hitler plots, but bowed out before the 1944 Bomb Plot. Arrested anyway, but not executed. Worked postwar as historian for US Army. Capable. One of the few higher Army officers to take any interest in the Mediterranean Theater. Highest Rank: Colonel General.

Hausser, Paul (1880–1972): WW1 veteran, general staff on Eastern Front. Retired Reichswehr, 1932, with rank of Lieutenant General. Joined Stalhelm, and from there SA, and then Waffen SS. Helped create Waffen SS. Rose from division command in France, 1940, to corps, then army and finally army group. Best operational commander the Waffen SS produced. Worked for US Army historical division under Halder postwar. Highest Rank: SS Colonel General. Nickname: Uncle Paul.

Hess, Rudolph (1894–1987): Hitler's Secretary and Deputy Führer. In OTL, flies to Scotland, 1941, as part of an insane peace plan. Bisexual or homosexual, accounts vary. May have been Hitler's lover, but then the same is alleged about Speer. Supposedly Bormann was the biological father of Hess's children. Nickname: Fräulein Anna.

Heydrich, Reinhard (1904–1942): Junior naval officer expelled for "dishonorable conduct" (broke an engagement with one girl to court and marry another). This left him in 1931 with a Nazi bride-to-be and no job. Her connections got him a job interview with Himmler. Rose rapidly in the SS from a combination of raw intelligence and extreme competence. Founded the intelligence arm of the Nazi Party, the SD, in 1931. Head of the Gestapo in 1934 and all of Party and state security agencies by 1936. Consolidates this in a meta-agency, RSHA, in 1939. Accused several times of having Jewish blood, a taint he never quite shook. In OTL, wounded in 1942 by Czech assassins in the pay of the British (they would say they were resistance fighters and Free Czechs, but assassin is descriptive; saying the Nazis were evil does not make using killers in civilian clothes into a wartime attack instead of an assassination). Died in hospital, quite possibly on orders of Himmler to his doctors, who were sent by Himmler to take charge of the case. Himmler was believed to be terrified of him. Virtually all the higher Nazis were afraid of him as well, as he had blackmail files on them all. Ruthless, amoral...and the only competent bureaucrat among the higher Nazis. Hence my use of him in this series. Highest rank: Obergruppenführer and General of Police. Nickname: The Blond Beast

Himmler, Heinrich (1900–1945): Did officer training in WW1, but no active service. Involved with SA and Nazi Party. Failed chicken farmer who became a fulltime Party official. Lapsed Catholic who dived headfirst into occult, Nordic magic, and similar outre circles. Founded SS. Good bureaucratic empire-builder but poor administrator. Threw up after watching a mass execution. Betrayed Hitler in 1945 in absurd scheme to have the West make him head of a German government. Committed suicide when captured by the British. Highest rank: Reichsführer

Hindenburg (von), Paul (1847–1934): Half of the governing duo in WW1 with Ludendorff after major victories in the East. President of the German Republic, 1925–1934. A reactionary even by the standards of his social class and age, he was mostly a figurehead in the key years of the early 1930s. Highest Rank: Field Marshal.

Hopkins, Harry (1890–1946): Social worker. Active in various relief projects during the New Deal. One of the voices to the left of FDR within the administration, but not as extreme as Henry Wallace or Eleanor Roosevelt. By 1940, de facto number 2 to FDR, replacing Farley. Headed Lend Lease. Also, FDR's frequent emissary to Stalin. Pro-Soviet, but uncertain whether he was a sympathizer or an active agent.

Horthy, Miklos (1868–1957): Austro-Hungarian admiral, WW1.

The Reich Without Hitler: The Falcons of Malta

With French help, formed "National Army" in 1919 to oppose
Red regime in Budapest. Led two-year "White Terror" after Reds
expelled by Romanian invasion. Although a reactionary, Horthy
himself was never a radical right fanatic. Instead, he had an uneasy
alliance with them, which ended in him reigning in their pogroms.
He became regent of the Hungarian Kingdom, whose "king" was
barred by the Allies from returning. The radicals formed an ever-
shifting grouping of small splinter oppositional parties divided
mostly on personalities. Horthy had some sympathy for Fascist
Italy, but none for Nazi Germany. He bowed to the inevitable
after 1940, but was at best a halfhearted ally. When the war
turned against Hitler, he tried (and failed) to change sides twice.
A prisoner of the Nazis, he was sheltered by the Americans from
extradition and execution postwar. Highest Rank: Vice-Admiral and
Regent.

 Kaltenbruner, Ernst (1903–1946): Austrian. Law degree.
Childhood friend of Eichmann. Joined Nazis in 1930, SS in 1931.
Party leader by 1934. Headed security services in Austria after
reunification with Germany. Succeeded Heydrich as head of
RSHA. Convicted at Nürnberg and executed. Highest Rank:
Obergruppenführer.

 Keitel, Wilhelm (1882–1946): WW1 veteran. Artillery officer.
Helped organize Freikorps postwar. Staff officer in Reichswehr. Ran
OKW from beginning to end. Sentenced and hanged at Nürnberg.
Total toady to Hitler and a cypher in terms of the actual war.
Highest Rank: Field Marshal. Nickname: Lickspittle.

 Keller, Alfred (1882–1974): Kesslering's number 2 in the 1940
Western Campaign. In this series, he is the hero of first Budapest
and then Malta. Highest Rank: Colonel General, so far.

 Kesselring, Albert (1885–1960): Artillery officer, WW1 (both
fronts). General staff, 1917. Involuntary transfer to Air Force,
1933 (Air Force and Waffen SS both stole officers from the Army).
Commanded air fleets in Poland, the West, Blitz, Barbarossa, and
Mediterranean. Commanded army group in Italian campaign,
1943–1945. Successful with both service forces. VERY fond of
luxury accommodations and food. Optimist, good people person
to equals and superiors, but often high-handed with subordinates.
Art lover. Highest Rank: Field Marshal.

 Kluge (von), Günther (1882–1944): WW1 veteran, staff officer.
Reichswehr. Very well-regarded among senior officer corps.
Competent army and army group commander. Corrupt and a

weasel. Toadied to Hitler while tolerating anti-Hitler plots by his staff. Avoided committing to Bomb Plot, but compromised by his ties to major plotters. Committed suicide when recalled to Berlin. Highest Rank: Field Marshal.

Lusena, Umberto (1904–1944): Of Jewish descent. Father was a general. Umberto was a legionnaire with D'Annunizo. Trained paratrooper. Fought the Germans in 1943 with Royal Army and afterward with partisans. Captured, tortured, and executed.

Manstein (von), Erich (1887–1973): From old Prussian military family. WW1 veteran. General staff. Was the author of the Ardennes campaign concept in 1940, which he pushed through outside official channels. Probably best operational field commander in WW2, especially at the army group level. A military technocrat willing to overlook the regime's crimes and be complicit in them. Highest rank: Field Marshal.

Messe, Giovanni (1883–1968): Helped create Arditi in WW1. Commanded motorized brigade in Ethiopian War. Corps commander in Greek War and Eastern Front. Took over the Italo-German Panzer Army command from Rommel in Tunisia. Served Royalist Italy after the side-switch in 1943. Highest rank: Field Marshal and Senator. Nickname: The Italian Rommel (quite deserved).

Müller, Gestapo (1900–1945?): Given name was actually Heinrich, but there were two Heinrich Müllers who were SS generals. WW1 service as spotter pilot. Bavarian political policeman until the Nazi takeover in 1933. Turned his coat and became a protégé of Heydrich's. Does not join the Nazi Party itself until 1939. Careerist and not especially brilliant, but hard working. Probable Soviet agent. Alleged to have died during the breakout from the Bunker. Also alleged to have retired to Moscow. Complete weasel. Highest Rank: Gruppenführer.

Nebe, Arthur (1894-1945): WW1 veteran. Career policeman who opportunistically joined the Nazi Party and SS in the early 30s. Headed the Kripo/Criminal Police. Involved with prewar euthanizing of "unfit" citizens. Headed Einsatzgruppe B in Belarus and Smolensk. Succeeds Heydrich as head of Interpol on Heydrich's death in 1942. Associated with the 1944 Bomb Plot against Hitler. Went into hiding after its failure. Betrayed by a mistress, he was arrested and executed in early 1945. He was competent, but a total weasel. Highest rank: Gruppenführer and Lieutenant General of Police.

The Reich Without Hitler: The Falcons of Malta

Paulus (von), Fredrich (1890–1957): WW1 veteran. Served with Freikorps and then Reichswehr. Staff officer until he assumed command of Sixth Army for Stalingrad Campaign. Not a decisive leader or good field commander, but the blame for Stalingrad rests with Hitler's obsessions. Captured by Soviets and served as a stooge for them in their Free Germany front. Given a sinecure in new East German military. Related to the Romanian aristocracy. Highest Rank: Field Marshal.

Philby, Harold 'Kim' (1912–1988): One of the famous Cambridge spies. Journalist, MI-6, War Office, Special Operation Executive. Philby used his class and educational contacts to work through most major organs of British power during and after WW2. Penetrated OSS and CIA. Exposed numerous times by Soviet defectors, Philby was able to avoid arrest because no one believed someone of his class would betray Britain. British allowed him to flee to Moscow in 1963 when this pretense became untenable. Highest Ranks: OBE and Order of Lenin.

Raeder, Erich (1876–1960): Naval officer. Rabid, narrow-minded reactionary/right-winger, but not a Nazi per se. Fanatically indoctrinated Navy in Nazi ideology, Hitler worship, and strict Lutheranism, all to avoid another set of naval mutinies as had happened in 1918. Raeder was obsessed with avoiding another such taint on the Navy's honor. Extreme believer in capital ships. Fired as head of Navy January, 1943, over failures of capital ships in the Arctic convoy battles. Resigns in May from active service. Rallies to Hitler during Bomb Plot. Highest Rank: Gross Admiral (first one since Tirpitz).

Ramcke, Herman-Bernhard (Gerhard) (1889–1968): WW1 veteran. Freikorps and Whites in Baltic postwar. Reichswehr. Transferred to Air Force and assigned to 7th Air Division (the airborne force). Hero of Crete, 1941. Led an airborne (motorized) Brigade with Rommel, 1942–43. Formed and commanded 2nd Parachute Division, 1943. Commanded Fortress Brest in Brittany, France, 1944. POW with Americans when the port fell. Saved from French war-crimes prosecution 1951 by Americans. Unrepentant admirer of Third Reich, postwar. Highest Rank: General (3 star).

Richthofen (von), Wolfram: Cousin of Red Baron. WW1 veteran flyer. Engineering degree postwar, then Reichswehr. Transferred to Luftwaffe. Commanded Condor Legion in Spain. Specialist in close air support. Extremely competent, but did not suffer fools well. Highest Rank: Field Marshal.

Riefenstahl, Leni (1902–2003): Actress and film director. Hitler groupie, but apparently not an actual Party member. Propagandist for them. Her film, Triumph of the Will, on one of the Nürnberg Rallies, is deemed a classic.

Rommel, Erwin (1891–1944): WW1 hero with mountain jägers (spetsnaz-level special commandos). Won Blue Max for his actions at Caporetto. Finished the war as a staff officer. Deemed not suitable for general staff training and higher command in the Reichswehr. Wrote a well-regarded book on infantry tactics, which led to him being requested as commander of Hitler's army escort battalion. Hitler then bumped him to one-star general in US terminology, and gave him a panzer division as a patronage appointment. Performed brilliantly in the French campaign, but repeatedly violated orders and acted more like an advanced guard commander than a divisional general. Readers should remember that the Desert Fox legend is in the future. Rommel was still, at this point, a brash storm officer promoted over his head. He still was in OTL for his first few North African battles. It took until 1942 for him to learn how to be a higher commander. Implicated in the Bomb Plot, he was ordered to commit suicide, which he did to safeguard his wife and son. Highest rank: Field Marshal.

Schellenberg, Walter (1910–1952): Joined the SS out of university in 1929. Protégé of Heydrich and Himmler. Amoral weasel, but extremely competent. Encouraged and abetted Himmler's late war schemes to overthrow Hitler and do a separate peace with the West. The schemes were absurd. The desire for self-protection and self-promotion were characteristic of the man. Was prosecution witness at Nürnberg. Given short sentence, which was commuted for ill health. May have had connections to British MI-6 from mid-war period.

Speer, Albert (1905–1981): Trained architect. Joined the Nazis 1931. Protégé of Hitler. Rumored to also be his lover. Armaments Minister from 1942. Guilty of war crimes in connection with slave labor, etc. Turned on the Nazis at Nürnberg Trials to save himself. It worked. Did long prison term, but saved his life. Complete weasel. Competence level is still debated.

Steiner, Felix (1896–1966): Yes, THAT Steiner. The one from the endlessly parodied Downfall scene. WW1 veteran. Freikorps in same geographic region as Iron Division. Reichswehr. Retired as Major, 1933. Joins Nazis, the SA, and finally the SS in 1935. Meteoric rise from battalion to divisional command (5th SS Viking

Division). Excelled at division and corps level. Army command in last months of war. Good with foreign and Volksdeutsche troops and officers, which was unusual in the SS. Second best panzer general in Waffen SS after Hausser. Highest Rank: Obergruppenführer.

Thomas, Georg (1890–1946): WW1 veteran. Administrator and logistics planner Reichswehr and Wehrmacht. Coup-plotter with ties to Beck's circle, but not active in 1944. Arrested and imprisoned, but avoided execution. Highest Rank: General.

Todt, Fritz (1891–1942): WW1 veteran. Trained engineer. Gold badge Nazi Party Member. Built the autobahns and West Wall fortifications. His Todt Organization, OT, was a de facto labor service for Wehrmacht. Highest Rank: Armaments Minister and Major General.

Udet, Ernst (1896–1941): WW1 ace fighter pilot. Interwar was stunt flyer, including Hollywood. Joined Nazis in 1933 when his old unit mate Göring recruited him. Playboy who never coped well with bureaucratic life. In OTL, a suicide. Dive-bombing fanatic. Highest Rank: Colonel General.

Umberto II (1904–1983): Crown Prince under Victor Emmanuel III. De facto head of state from 1944. Briefly King in 1946.

Victor Emmanuel III (1869-1947): King of Italy 1900–1946. Allowed Mussolini to take power. Mismanaged removing Mussolini in 1943 and Italy's switching sides the same year. Dethroned, 1946.

Wolff, Karl (1900–1984): WW1. Freikorps. Banker and public relations man. Joined Nazis and SS, 1931. Protégé of Himmler's. Head of SS in occupied Italy. Helped arrange a surrender of Axis forces in Italy, April 1945, without Hitler's permission. Turned state's evidence at Nürnberg, but nonetheless did two small sentences for war crimes. Returned to the public relations business. Appeared to have had ties to CIA and US protection. Highest Rank: Obergruppenführer.

Fictional

Battaglia, Giuseppe (1915–?): Also goes by "Joey Bats" and "Brooklyn". Italo-American mechanical wizard. Not exactly Cosa Nostra, but ran in those circles. Highest Rank: Captain, so far.

Cohen, Isaac (1896–?): Greta's uncle by marriage. Artillery officer WW1, Honved. Metallurgist specializing in oil field pipes and machines. Fluent German, Magyar, Romanian, English. Knows some French and Italian. Also known as Isaak Schwabe. Highest Rank: Major, so far.

Cohen, Peter (probably born 1922– ?): de facto adoptive son of Isaac and Rachel. Physically huge and extremely strong, even for his size and physique. A born survivor, extremely loyal to his adoptive family, including his brothers/cousins and de facto household members, such as Greta Levi and Ivan Gorlov.

Cohen, Rachel (1898–?): Crazy Ruth's older and wiser sister. Greta's aunt. Also known as Rachel Schwabe.

Dika: underage sex worker from Romania. Roma.

Duffy, Kevin (1894–?): Staff officer sent to Malta. Welsh Guards. Highest rank: Colonel.

Jung, Lars (1919–?): Veteran of Norway and Rotterdam. Highest Rank: First Lieutenant, so far.

Gorlov, Ivan (1902–?): Officer cadet with the Whites in 1917. Evacuated from Crimea in 1920 as a lieutenant colonel. Massive combat experience in between. Washes up in Romania as a starving refugee in 1922, where he is taken in by Isaac Cohen and taught the family business.

Gretchen (1895–?): Prostitute and friend of Wanda.

Levi, Greta (1922–?): Also known at various times as Cohen or Schwabe. Less socially awkward than her boyfriend, Klaus, but, if anything, even more politically clueless. She's intelligent in a teen, space-cadet way, but a faster learner.

Levi, Ruth (1902–1940): Greta's mother. Also known as "Crazy Ruth". Belligerent, argumentative, seen by her sister and daughter as a how-not-to manual for adult behavior.

Lincoln, Billy (1900–?): WW1 veteran, one of the pal's battalions. Old sweat, working-class. Highest Rank: Sergeant.

Mason, Garth (1896–?): Staff officer sent to Malta. Coldstream Guards. Highest rank: Colonel.

Maurice, Hans (1894–?): WW1, artillery. Freikorps. SA. Highest Rank: Major, so far.

Money-Penny, James (1913–?): Harrow. One year of Cambridge. Soldier of fortune/gun for hire. Speaks over twenty languages. Excellent physical health, amazing reflexes, high intelligence, and no visible scruples. Highest Rank: Lieutenant Commander, so far.

Naiomi [no last name given but is Saxon] (1915–?): Romanian Betar lieutenant. Veteran of Rommel's brief Soviet campaign. Befriends Greta.

The Reich Without Hitler: The Falcons of Malta

Pentangeli, Vincenzo (1909–?): Italian reserve second lieutenant. Good connections to secure posting. Trained paratrooper. Fluent in English and German.

Schmidt, Alois (1919–?): Ramcke's aide. A hero of Malta. Highest Rank: Captain, so far.

Siegel, Karl (1910–?): University graduate, law. SS. Protégé of Schullenberg. "One of the smart ones". Highest Rank: Sturmbannführer.

Scott, Reginald (1900–1940): WW1 veteran and commander of HMS Thunderchild. Not the sharpest knife in the drawer, but a decent officer. Nickname Jutland. Highest Rank: Lieutenant Commander.

Strauss, Gunter (1902–?): WW1 veteran. Iron Division and other Freikorps, postwar. Early member Nazi Party and SA. Feldheernhalle veteran. Spent most of the rest of the 20s in New York, but maintained Party membership. Active in SA 1930–1934. Sidelined after Blood Purge but got postal job from patronage. Very tall, extremely muscular, bright. His ideals burned out after 1934 and he's in it for himself. Highest Rank: Colonel, so far.

Steiner, Klaus (1922–?): Socially awkward, young man who fate will make a hero. Short (his growth spurt is possibly late from restricted nutrition), squeaky voice, stutters. The classic "good kid". Highest Rank: Major, so far.

Stephan (1920–?): ex-pimp and worker at Wanda's bar/brothel. Dika's "boyfriend", Roma.

Voss, Gregor (1900–?): Underage volunteer, WW1. Iron Division and Freikorps, postwar. Early Nazi and SA. Worked at the post office with Gunter and Adolph. Artificial foot and bad leg. A reactionary, nationalist hard-ass, but never took to Nazi ideology. He was Nazi instead of Nationalist because he's a populist who dislikes the old ruling elites. His adoptive "nephew" Hans is a 25-year-old with the mind of a 12-year-old. Gregor never married.

Wanda [last name never mentioned in text, but was Duch] (1914–?): Her father was a Pole from Lodz who chose to serve Kaiser instead of Czar. Marries his Polish girlfriend at the end of the war, legitimizing the daughter he had by her, Wanda. Wanda is Polish by blood and German by rearing. Thinks of herself as German, but is proud of being known as "the Polack". Thrown out of her parent's house at 12 as incorrigible (boys, drinking, wild living). Has her oldest son, Adam, at 13. Always been in the fringes of the criminal life, but a hard worker and inveterate entrepreneur. Longtime bootlegger. Never was a sex worker and never did strongarm. Was friends with people who did both and worse. Hates most establishment figures and the Communists (a set of puritan zealots, in her opinion). Never a Nazi, but in the culture of the ex-Freikorps street fighters. Six children, the last two by Adolph Wrede. Through him friends with Gunter Strauss. Never pretty and the years have not been kind. Medium height, massive muscles (did heavy labor much of her life), sharp wit, acid tongue. VERY loyal to her friends.

Wrede, Adolph (1898–?): WW1 veteran. Freikorps, but not Iron Division. Early Nazi and SA. Postal worker. A hard man whose one soft spot is his common law wife and their children.

Glossary

AH – alternate history

Air Marshal – term used for Air Force Field Marshals

Arditi – Italian shock troops from WW1. Similar to German storm troops, but more elite in the manner of the mountain jägers Rommel served in. Many of these veterans helped form the Fascist Party postwar. In our ATL, Italy will bring them back.

Arrow Cross – Hungarian far-right political movement. The Hungarian right and far-right post-1918 was a maze of feuding small parties set beside the dominant ruling Horthyites. Arrow Cross were not as crazy as Romanian Iron Guard or Croatian Ustache, but even the local Hungarian Nazis thought they were insane. OTL, the Nazis force them into power when Horthy tries to dump the Nazi alliance to save Hungary, 1943–1944.

ATL – alternate time line. This book is an AH set in an ATL

BDM – League of German Girls. Nazi Girl Scouts.

Betar – paramilitary youth movement of Revisionist Zionists (short form, modern Likud). Strong in Poland, Baltic States, Romania.

Blood Purge – liquidation of the SA leadership and, to a lesser extent, of the radical wing of the Nazi Party in 1934. Used as a cover for more generalized score-settling by Göring, Himmler, et al.

Bomb Plot – the closest of the many anti-Hitler plots to come to actually killing him. Its failure put the radicals firmly in charge and contributed to the huge German losses of people and physical capital in those last ten hellish months. July 20, 1944.

Blue Max – Technically, Pour le Mérite. The highest award for bravery under Prussian Kings and German Kaisers. Dropped with the Weimar Republic. In this series, reinstated 1940 by Rommel then confirmed by Göring.

Castle Hill – government quarter of Budapest.

Chancellery Guard – fictional security force created by Heydrich and Nebe. Nebe is first head.

Chain Dogs – German military police. The name comes from a metal gorget they wore as a means of branch identification. Deserved reputation as "hardcore".

Counterfactuals – new term for AHs by professionals trying to remove the amateur and fiction taint from such speculations.

Fascist Grand Council – a mixed body of Italian state and

Fascist Party officials that ran Italy under Mussolini. This was the body that voted Mussolini out in 1943.

Fascist Militia – in theory, a separate Party Militia in the manner of the SS. In practice, a reserve force for the Italian Army that also had public order duties.

Feldherrnhalle – a building in downtown Munich. Site of the ending of Hitler's Beer Hall Putsch in 1923. Having marched with Hitler on that day made one an "old fighter" in the Nazi Party comparable to being in Napoleon's Old Guard.

Gau – Nazi Party divided Germany (and later many surrounding annexed areas) into Gaus as the step below national organization. The head was the Gauleiter. In OTL, many of these ran their Gaus as semi-independent fiefs, backed by Bormann, who controlled access to Hitler.

General Government – the Nazi colonial regime imposed on Poland after the 1939 conquest. The Nazis sliced off portions of their sector of prewar Poland and formally made them part of Germany (essentially, the 1914 borders with some "improvements"). The rump was labeled the General Government and run from Krakow, not Warsaw.

Gestapo – state security police. Founded by Göring from the pre-Nazi Prussian political police. Had a deserved reputation for violence, even by Nazi standards.

GRU – Soviet military intelligence. From Lenin's time semi-immune to Cheka/NKVD. The two were bitter rivals (worse than FBI/CIA in US or MI-5/MI-6 in UK). GRU always had vastly fewer resources, but usually accomplished more, in part because they were willing to provide accurate information even when it was not what the bosses in Moscow wanted to hear. They were also less likely to rely on ideological sympathizers for agents, preferring the more normal intelligence methods of blackmail, cash, etc.

Hauptumsiedlungslager für Juden Rakowitz / Palestine #1 Jewish Relocation Center – fictional camp/ghetto adjacent to the old site of Krakow airport and adjacent "new city" suburb of Nowa Huta. Nazis clear the Poles out to make this happen. Think of it as a Jewish-run and guarded ghetto. Eichmann is nominally in charge with a tiny SS staff, but otherwise the Jews administer the camp themselves while being fed by the Hoover Relief Agency. Initially a place to ship the Jews of the Baltic States, it will over time have added the Jews of Poland, Slovakia, Romania, Greater Germany, and the Benelux, plus many of the Hungarian Jews. It is vast and keeps growing. It's also thrown together and eclectic in the manner of many modern refugee camps, such as Goma in 1994. Rakowitz #1 is a tiny administrative facility run by Eichmann with a small SS and BDM staff. Palestine #2 and after are the ever-growing numbers of residential camps with attached light industrial workshops.

Heer – the German Army

HJ – Hitler Youth. Nazi Boy Scouts, but with more emphasis on physical fitness and basic military skills.

Honved – the national guard of the Kingdom of Hungary under the Hapsburgs and then Horthy. It was technically a separate military service, not part of the Army.

Hoover Relief Agency – Fictional organization used for this series. It is a copy of an actual historic relief agency that Hoover headed in WW1, which fed Belgians and French behind German lines and later expanded to postwar relief, including saving Lenin's regime from self-induced famine. German policy allowed the Jews and, to a lesser extent, the Poles to starve to assure adequate food for Germans. Churchill historically vetoed proposals for relief aid through the blockade in the manner of Hoover's WW1 work. In OTL, Churchill would finally relent to save the starving Greeks in 1943. Here, we have Heydrich making a diplomatic push that FDR chooses to answer. FDR, running for a third term in 1940, was a major breach of US customs. His victory was quite uncertain down to election day. So, this would pander to US citizen Poles and Jews, who would raise the money and gratefully vote for him. The British were, in fact, in no position to risk firing on US ships going to neutral ports. This is something the Cabinet would have sacked Churchill over.

Iron Division – a post-WW1 Freikorps that operated in the Baltic states nominally on behalf of Germany, the Whites, and, at times, the Latvian Government. It was one of a grouping of similar such collections of embittered veterans and freebooters. Sometimes combat-effective, but other times acted like a bandit gang out of the Thirty Years' War.

Iron Guard – Romanian far-right movement. Also called the Legion of the Archangel Michael and the Green Shirts. Extreme nationalists, populists, anti-capitalists, anti-Communists, anti-Semites. Used by and made use of the ruling Romanian royalists and military reactionaries. Fanatic Orthodox Christians. They were ultra-violent, emphasized action over ideas, and prone to spontaneous outbreaks against Jews and the ruling Romanian classes. Think chaotic evil with a strong emphasis on chaotic. Even other right-wingers such as the local Nazis thought they were unstable and violent. In OTL, Gestapo found their pogroms to be revolting overkill.

Kreis – county or district. The next level down from Gau. The leader was a Kreisleiter.

Kripo – the national criminal police under the Himmler/Heydrich reorganizations of the 30s. In US terms, the FBI minus the counterintelligence function.

LAH – Hitler's life guards. Originally personal bodyguards, they expanded to headquarters guards, and then a hit squad for the Blood Purge. The original members were chosen for size and physique. This changed when the unit went to war in 1939. Over time, it just became an elite SS mechanized unit. Had a bad record of prisoner murders, but never got the rep for it that the 3rd SS Death's Head division did. This is the unit that perpetrated the 1944 Malmedy Massacre of US prisoners in the Bulge.

Livret militaire – French military identity papers

Luftwaffe – the German Air Force

Movement – the Nazi Party, speaking broadly to cover all its attached organizations. The Party/state overlap is confusing for many Anglophones, in part because it tended to chaotic/overlapping authority. One could be a believer in the Movement even while despising the formal Party for its petty tyrannies and bureaucratic absurdities.

Nibelungen Legion – new Party Militia fictionally created in this series.

NKVD – Soviets went through multiple rounds of re-namings and reorganizations of their security forces back to Lenin's original Cheka. For this period, the main designation is NKVD. I avoided burdening readers with the variant sister organizations and plan to continue to do so. They will all be NKVD. For current readers, think KGB/FSB.

Nürnberg Rallies – annual Nazi national gatherings (1923–1938). In Nürnberg from 1927. Largest reached a bit under a million participants. Elaborately staged and filmed for propaganda purposes and to inspire awe among its participants.

OKH – Army High Command

OTL – our time line. History as we know it.

OKW – Armed Forces High Command. In 1940, still a

small planning staff serving as an adjunct to Hitler's personal headquarters. In OTL, becomes a parallel OKH, handling all theaters of war other than the Eastern Front and the Replacement Army.

Polish Blue Police – Polish police under the General Government. Completely penetrated by Home Army.

Polish Home Army – the Germans overran Poland in 1939, but the Poles set up a parallel state to preserve their authority for their supposed liberation by the West. The military branch, the Home Army, was dominant, but not out of civilian control, both within Poland and from the exile government in London.

Race Laws – the Nürnberg Race Laws were a series of laws designed to remove the Jews (and other undesirable by Nazi criteria minorities) from German social and economic life. The specific subpart that will come up in this series are the rules on "race-mixing". Sex between Aryans and non-Aryans was banned, with punishments including possible use of the death penalty. Needless to say, the rules were more likely to be applied when the Aryan was female. From 1938, there were a parallel, but less extreme, set in Italy. Italy will repudiate it in this series over time and in OTL never enforced their Race Laws with German rigidity and enthusiasm.

Ravensbrück – Concentration Camp some 80 kilometers north of Berlin, founded to house female inmates. A hellhole late in the war in OTL. Most of the camps imploded in the period from late 1944 to war's end from a mix of lack of resources, fantastic overcrowding as inmates from camps about to be overrun were death-marched to new camps deeper in the interior, and the guard forces being increasingly from the ever-diminishing portion of the German people who were still fanatic regime supporters. At this point, the inmates were mostly German women with Poles as a secondary population. The Germans were mostly a mix of prostitutes, Jehovah's Witnesses, and rebellious young girls down to tween ages (what we would today call minors in need of supervision rather than actual juvenile criminals). The Poles were a mix of religious orders and politicals. The Jehovah's Witnesses were political oppositional, but completely non-violent about it, thus tending to get the best treatment when confined as they were easy prisoners to deal with.

Red November – the revolts against the Kaiser and war that overthrew the monarchy and led to the German surrender.

Supposedly a conspiracy of Marxists, Jews and traitors that stabbed in the back a still victorious Germany army and people [this is the rightwing and nationalist myth, started originally by Luddendorf]. The professional naval officers felt special shame for this as the trigger is the mutiny of the High Seas Fleet. The naval officers had planned a suicide death sortie. Their crews were not of similar mind and a series of acts of disobedience culminated in the November 3rd, 1918 mutiny of the fleet under Communist leadership. These red sailors were a major feature of the immediate postwar chaos in Berlin and northern Germany. The officer corps regarded this as a matter of personal dishonor to their caste and institution. Hence they created a new navy dedicated to creating a new mythos of an ultra-loyal, ultra-nationalist Fleet. Raeder was extreme but hardly unique in these views.

Reichstag – German parliament of the Weimar and Nazi eras.

Reichswehr – the interwar German army of the Weimar years.

Reichsführer – fancy rank invented for Himmler as supreme leader of SS and police.

Reichsmarschall – fancy rank Göring invented and got Hitler to give him so he would still outrank Army and Air Force Field Marshals.

RSHA – a composite organization of all police and security forces of both the German state and Nazi Party.

Royal Carabinieri – Italian paramilitary service. In US terms, they had both police and military functions. Extremely loyal to the Crown.

SA – Original Nazi Party militia. Somewhat open question of whether they are part of the Nazi Party or allied to it. Leadership liquidated by 1934 Blood Purge. Vestigial after that, but still had hundreds of thousands of members in 1940. Blood Purge also settled their subordination to Nazi Party. Had a deserved reputation for disorderly, violent behavior. Also tended to be populist/second revolution types.

Second Revolution – from the beginning, the Nazis always had a radical wing that took seriously the socialist part of the Party name of National Socialist. Pressure for a second, populist revolution was one of the causes of the 1934 Blood Purge. In OTL, this was then suppressed until after the 1944 Bomb Plot. Comes back to the forefront in the short year between that and final defeat.

SD – Nazi Party intelligence service. Founded by Heydrich.
SS – A split-off from the SA. Always subordinate to Hitler and the Party. Often higher social class/better educated than the SA. After the Blood Purge, the main defenders of the regime.
SS House – Prinz-Albrecht-Strasse 8 was Himmler and Heydrich's HQ. With several adjacent buildings, they formed a complex in which SS, SD, Gestapo, RSHA, etc. were based.
Wehrmacht – the Nazi Army
Stalhelm – the street militia of the Weimar Era Nationalist Party. Like the SA, also an illegal reserve for Reichswehr.
Tante Ju – nickname for Junkers Ju 52/3m transport plane.
Volksdeutsche – Germans by race or culture, but not citizens of the German Reich. It was Nazi policy to ingather these large populations of "Germans" to the Reich. The problem was defining who was such a "German". Of most interest in this series is the Class 5 "Germanizable Elements". This was a quite flexible term, although OTL's Nazis did not in fact use much flexibility before 1944 (by which time the war was lost). Here, Heydrich takes a somewhat more expansive path.